William Bedford has had fe... *Catholic Herald, Independent,* ... *Queen.* His short stories have ... *Telegraph, London Magazine* and ... *Books,* and several have been broadcast on Radio 4. He is the author of four previous novels: *Happiland,* which was shortlisted for the 1990 *Guardian* Fiction Prize, *All Shook Up, Catwalking* and *The Lost Mariner,* as well as collections of poetry and two novels for children: *The Golden Gallopers* and *Nightworld.*

He published a third children's novel, *The Joy Riders,* in 1998, and is now working on an 1882 murder trial involving a fishing apprentice which *The Times* described as 'the worst murder of the nineteenth century'.

Also by William Bedford

THE LOST MARINER

THE FREEDOM TREE

WILLIAM BEDFORD

An *Abacus* Book

First published in Great Britain in 1997
by Little, Brown and Company
Published by Abacus in 1998

A CIP catalogue record for this book
is available from the British Library.

ISBN 0 349 10904 4

Typeset in Plantin by M Rules
Printed and bound in Great Britain by
Clays Ltd, St Ives plc

Abacus
A Division of
Little, Brown and Company (UK)
Brettenham House
Lancaster Place
London WC2E 7EN

For Fiona, Rachael and Thomas

But freedom's clapping hands enjoyed the sight

JOHN CLARE,
'To a Fallen Elm'

One

My nightworld began when I signed on the trawler *Happy Jack*, running from the grief and anger of mourning my mother and father. I was twenty-two years old, and the young don't mourn that deeply if everything else in life is going well. I was in some kind of furious despair, not knowing how my father had died, not understanding why my mother had followed him to her grave so hopelessly, without even trying to fight. That wasn't like her. I sought the fleets because I knew they were a living death, floating helltowns of drink and violence, and I was yearning for oblivion. But I also sought them because I was angry. My father had drowned on the fleets, and I wanted to know how he had met his death.

I was born in 1852 in Staithes, a fishing village off the north Yorkshire moors. My father worked on the inshore vessels, lining for cod or using driftnets for herring when they were in season. He was a quiet, self-contained man, wary of the sea and never one to look for trouble. He could bait a line faster than any fisherman I've ever known, and would talk about his childhood in Whitby, his early years running the cobbled streets and helping the old women mend the nets, his early trips to sea. His parents died when he was a child, and he went on the smacks straight away, fishing from the age of eleven. He had never known a different life.

'You ent going to find an easier way,' he used to tell me when we sat outside our cottage baiting the lines on summer evenings. 'Not in this life anyway, no matter what folk tell you. It's all rumour and gossip.'

A lot of the fishermen were leaving the sea in those years, going to the ironstone mines on the moors. When my father was a boy, there were eighty boats working out of Staithes. By the time I was born, there were fewer than fifty. A lot of the families had gone down to Whitby where the crowds of summer visitors meant you could sell your fish more easily and there was a chance of work on the quays. Some of the younger fishermen had gone on the trawlers, working the fleets out of Grimsby and Yarmouth. There was easy money on the fleets, they told us when they visited with their friends. But my father wouldn't move. He wouldn't listen.

'There will always be fish on this coast,' he used to say calmly when my mother was frantic with worry about how we were going to make a living.

'That doesn't mean folk will buy them,' she shouted at him.

'There'll always be farms,' my father insisted steadily.

'Then you take the basket round!'

But my father wouldn't leave Staithes. 'You keep to what you know, Matthew,' he told me solemnly. 'The fishing is what you know about. Only don't go on the trawlers. That ent a way of catching fish. That's unnatural. You'll be lost forever if you let that way of life tempt you.'

He would talk so, and my mother would lose her temper. She had blazing red hair and green eyes. She came from Sheffield, walking across the moors with her father when she was a girl and settling in Staithes as soon as she met my father. They used to smile at each other in the middle of their arguments, as if they were remembering days long gone past, and then my father would get his melodion from the shelf in the parlour and play hymns. The melodion had delicate green mermaids carved on the ends, and he played with his eyes closed, lost in some dream I never knew about. He had a big voice, and sang the hymns in our tiny parlour, the fishing lines over the range hung with herbs and drying fish, the wind cold outside along the deserted shores.

'You don't go on the trawlers, Matthew, whatever else you do.'

That was all he said to me about the life of the fleets.

We used to walk the shores, when he had a day to spare, and he showed me the crabs in the rockpools, how to search out the shellfish for bait from the shores. I knew how to crack the shell of a cockle by the time I was five, and could bait a line beautifully when I was seven.

It was in my seventh year that my grandfather came to live with us. A clenched, angry old man with cropped white hair and a stack of canvases under his arm. He had been a signwriter all his life, and painted ships and birds in his free moments. He had a voice like the shingle on the beach, tugged by the tides, rasping and tumbling. When he had an attack of coughing he spat thick green phlegm into the fire. The phlegm needed a lot of medicine.

'The terns scratch their signatures on the sky to tell you who painted the clouds,' he used to tell me solemnly when he was staring out at the moors on summer evenings.

'I don't know what you mean, Grandad.'

'They write their story.'

'They don't do that!'

'Oh aye.'

One winter morning bright as steel, we went out together into the frozen fields, the moors yellowed by bright sunlight. We walked through tall grass stiff with frost, the broken fragments kicked up by our heavy boots like flying rainbows, the breath of sheep smoking in the air.

'I painted murals before you were born,' he told me. 'Oils and watercolours on pub walls, summat unusual for folks to look at.'

'Did you always do that, Grandad?' I asked him.

'There wasn't much call recent years. Not so much money about.'

We ate our sandwiches on a low stone wall, and I watched the brilliant erratic scrawl of the terns, wheeling across the canvas of the sky, my grandfather's voice like warm charcoal inside my mind, his paints stacked tidily in our kitchen like a barn full of corn.

He was truly ill towards the end and, in the early months of 1863, the cough racked his body night and day, and we could get no sleep in the tiny cottage. My mother fetched medicines from Whitby, medicines we couldn't afford to pay for, but they did no good. She gave him laudanum, in Godfrey's Cordial, and he slept most of the time, his body wracked periodically by bouts of pain. You could hear the phlegm ruttling in his lungs. He died in the February of that year, and my mother wept for hours, walking the shores on her own, refusing to take my hand. My father watched helplessly.

In the summer of 1863, we were so much in debt for the medicines that my father had to break his word. He had to go on the trawlers. He left us one fine clear morning, his fishing gear in a shoulder bag on his shoulder, his food wrapped in a greased cloth. He caught a lift on a drifter making for Lowestoft, and they dropped him off in Grimsby.

We heard the story when the drifter came back. He found work on a trawler in Henry Mundol's fleet and went straight to the Dogger Bank. Henry Mundol was the biggest fleet owner in the Humber Estuary. His fleets trawled the northern seas winter and summer and he controlled the markets where the fish was sold. They said in Whitby he was a cruel man, forcing his men to work in all weathers, searching the towns for fresh boys to go as apprentices. The boys signed indentures they couldn't read and hundreds of them went to prison every year for trying to escape. They were children really, lured from the workhouses and orphanages by stories of easy money. When they disappeared, there were plenty more to follow them.

My father drowned in a storm and there was no chance of saving him. That was all we heard. There was no message from Henry Mundol, no letter saying how he had been lost. A man from the herring drifter came to see us in the October, as the herring fleets were making for home and Lerwick. He was stiff with awkwardness. He left money for my mother on the kitchen table, hidden under a saucer. The melodion had gone with my father.

I shan't forget that morning as long as I live.

I walked with my mother along the deserted shores. We were the only people out, it was so rough and cold. For some reason, my mother couldn't bear to be in the cottage. I was eleven years old, and I didn't understand what was happening to us. She packed some lunch, and we walked for miles, never mentioning my father, hardly talking at all. I had no sense that when we got home the empty house would be waiting for us, and the reality that my father would never come back. I walked with my mother, alone on the northern shores, and danced with the glistening wonder of the sea, collecting shells from the pools of water, skimming them across the turbulent waves.

It was on that morning my mother told me about Lindisfarne.

'I went there with your grandfather,' she said. 'I was only fourteen. He was a signwriter, you know that, always looking for work, travelling the North Yorkshire moors, painting pub signs and houses. He was a lovely man, kind and quiet with children. He painted a picture of me once, with lovely, long red hair down to my waist, standing on the shore at Lindisfarne. I had lovely hair. It caught fire one night when I was going down the cellar to fetch coal. The flame from the candle must have blown in a draught. He wrapped his arms round my head to stop the flames. You could see the scars on his arms to the day he died. He painted the picture so that I would remember, but he never let me grow it out again.'

I asked her why they had gone to Lindisfarne, but she didn't really tell me. I think she didn't know. It was not long after her own mother died. Her father was feeling restless, needed to be on the road.

'He called it Holy Island,' she said quietly.

'Why?'

'Because there were holy men lived there a long time ago.'

'What are holy men?'

'I don't really know. Men who are very good, I suppose.'

She said they went there and spent the day walking round the Island. It was very flat and there was nothing much to see. The ruins of the monastery didn't interest her very much. The men and women in the village brought them drinks and hot potatoes. She remembered everything they saw, the birds and the sea, the deep blue of the sky, the long day's walking. It was late when they returned, and the sea was rising all around them. Her father said they would be perfectly safe. She held his hand and believed everything he told her. They reached the mainland as the little ripples of waves ran across the causeway. The sand was ribbed by the pull of the tides, and was full of lugworms.

She never talked about Lindisfarne again.

After that I had to help with the work, we were so poor.

We had the apothecary's bills to pay, and there was nobody to catch the fish. We mended nets for other fishing families, and collected cockles on the shores. I never knew a childhood after we buried my father. I spent my life cleaning and baiting other fishermen's lines, or walking twenty miles up and down the coast looking for shellfish for bait or to sell round the isolated farms. When the other families were too busy, we carried their dried fish to Whitby and sold it for them on the quays, taking a shilling for the work.

The last good memory I have of my mother is sitting in the sunlight with her in front of our cottage, the sea wild and blue, the summer air warm. We were shelling peas. She talked about my father. There were tears in her faded blue eyes. She told me about the time they met, dancing on the quays at Whitby, him playing his melodion, all the girls after him. She must have talked for two or three hours, going over her past life. Her voice sounded young again, not tired.

In the November of 1866, she went out selling dried fish to the farms on the moors, and got caught in a storm. She was drenched. The pneumonia killed her within two days. She didn't fight: she didn't want to live. The cottage seemed like the grave when she stopped breathing. I sat in the darkness for hours, listening to the sea, the wind sighing down the chimney. There was no wood for burning. I thought she must be cold, and I wrapped her in all the blankets we possessed, but she remained frozen. Nothing would warm her now.

I was fourteen.

That was when I went on the boats. I worked the liners. I travelled up and down the coast, listening to the old fishermen, learning the fishing. I spent eight years on the liners, working from Lowestoft and Yarmouth and doing the summer trip to Iceland every year. I loved the summer trip: the endless nights, the shimmering brilliant sunlight.

I tried not to think about my drowned father, my mother breathing like an old woman, her breath hard and rasping like the wind frozen in winter, her death agony rattling in our tiny cottage. I never went back to Staithes. I drank myself into oblivion whenever we were in port, and spent my money recklessly, working for more until I was too exhausted to think. I never went near Grimsby or the Humber ports.

Then this summer, 1874, I visited Lindisfarne.

I was working the lines on a dawn tide, hauling cod and haddock over the side for gutting, and suddenly I knew I had to visit Holy Island, I had to walk where my mother had walked. I left the vessel in Scarborough and travelled up to Seahouses. I walked across the causeway, the tide rippling in brilliant morning sunlight around my feet, so urgent was I to get across to the Island.

It was a strange haunted place. The sand was white. The shores were immense and deserted. Huge skies tumbled to the horizon that shone like glowing gold. Over my head, enormous herring gulls wheeled and screamed. I stood and breathed the cold air. I shouted my mother's name, but she was not there. I was alone. I went down on to my knees and wept. My whole body shook with grief.

When I looked up, there was a figure at the tideline, plunging into the icy waves. I wiped my eyes and tried to see. It was a man, wearing a long black garment. He waded out into the sea, the waves thundering around his feet, soaking his body. I stood up, trying to see, taking a step towards the tideline. But the man was down on his knees. He was holding his hands up and staring into the merciless sunlight. I couldn't move or speak.

Then I saw the otters ambling along the tideline, sniffing at the air and playing in the white sand, tumbling over and over. As the man turned and waded out of the sea, the otters rolled towards him, and when he reached them they blew on his hands and dried his feet with their fur. The man was laughing, not seeing me, not bothering. I felt the air leave my lungs.

I knew I was going insane.

I was losing my mind.

Then I was running. I was twenty-two. I don't know if I'd hidden from it, but I suddenly couldn't bear my life any longer. I was fleeing from Lindisfarne, or maybe I was fleeing from myself. I had been on the run for years. My father drowned when I was a boy, and then my mother grieved herself into a grave. Their voices went on calling in my dreams. The more time passed the more I missed them. I had to drive myself into oblivion to forget them. I had to escape the dreams I kept having about my father's drowning. I had to flee my mother's tortured face. I knew I had to go on the fleets. The fleets were murderous, but I needed that murder. There was oblivion on the trawlers where you could work for eighteen hours a day and if that didn't stop the pain, drink yourself into darkness with the alcohol the traders brought to the ships. I was yearning for the living death of the fleets, or maybe I was simply yearning for death. It had to be the fleets, and it had to be with one of Henry Mundol's vessels, the man who owned half of the fishing fleets, the man who hadn't written to tell us when my father drowned. It had to be with Henry Mundol, the man who lived in the shadowlands of my mind.

Two

So I travelled to Whitby and by chance walked straight on to *Happy Jack*, one of Henry Mundol's smacks. I asked around the quays for a vessel needing hands, and was directed to the skipper. I found him drinking in a beerhouse not far from the harbour. He was slumped against the counter, staring blearily into a glass of ale. His name was Ben Lowther. 'So you want to try the trawlers?' he scowled when I explained what I wanted.

'They say there's good money to be earned,' I answered, trying to sound cheerful.

'Is that so?'

'So I heard.'

He drained his glass and held it out to the barmaid. 'What's your name?'

'Matthew Lidgard.'

'You think you can handle the work?'

'I've been on liners all my life.'

He scoffed. 'Liners! That's not work. That's pleasure.'

'I can learn.'

He stared at me with contempt, his eyes doubtful, unsure. 'You don't make mistakes on one of Henry

Mundol's smacks,' he said coldly. 'He ent a forgiving kind of man.' He drained his second glass of ale, and watched me with his baleful expression. Before I could reply, a thin wiry man joined us at the bar. 'You think he'll do?' Lowther asked him brusquely.

The man ordered a beer and didn't look at me. He stared straight ahead, not interested, lost in his own thoughts. When he spoke, his voice was hard and matter-of-fact. 'Can you handle a smack?' he asked bluntly.

'I've taken the tiller these last four years.'

'Big mizzeners?'

'Yes.'

The big mizzeners were ketches, two-masted vessels with the mizzen forward of the tiller so that the crew could cast their long-lines from the stern. Most of the liners working Iceland were ketches.

'Are you on *Happy Jack*?' I asked as nobody seemed likely to introduce us.

'Second hand,' the man said briefly. 'Howard Martin.' He did not offer his hand.

'What about your vessel?' I asked him.

'She's a ketch,' he said.

Lowther watched us during this conversation, his eyes sullen and derisory. 'You finished?' he said when Howard went back to his drink. The second hand didn't even answer, just drained his glass and listened. 'You indentured, Lidgard?' the skipper went on.

'Worked them out when I was twenty. I'm twenty-two this year. I've been on the fishing since I was fourteen.'

'I didn't ask for your life story,' he grumbled. 'We sail this afternoon. Whitby Ground. Then the Dogger. Mundol's are working with Coffee Smith's and Fenners. Henry Mundol wants us there for the rest of the summer.'

I nodded. August was the dead time of the summer

fleeting season, and the smacks would all be trawling together to cut costs. The summer season would be over by the end of September.

'Eight weeks,' I said thoughtfully.

'You want to think again?'

'No.'

'All that money,' he sneered. 'If you can earn it.'

He got himself another ale and turned his back on me. I went to my lodgings to get my gear, and signed on *Happy Jack* that afternoon. As we tacked out of the long winding harbour, the cliffs and ruined abbey towering above us, the quays screaming with seagulls, I helped get the bowsprit run out and hoist the jib and staysail ready for the open seas. A close-hauled fishing smack passed us as we left the harbour, angling trimly up into the wind's eye like a witch. The abbey glowered above us on the cliffs, and I thought about St Hilda, flailing the grass for snakes and hurling them down to the sea. The sun burned down on the ruins, and there was fog drifting beyond the banks. I felt the sweat on my face and watched as Howard Martin guided the vessel away from the crowded quays. Ben Lowther was already down below, and I could hear him singing. It would be a fine berth, with a drunkard for a skipper.

'She's a handy vessel,' I said to Howard as he kept his eye on the mainsail.

'She can whisper in a breeze,' he nodded. 'Twelve knots and no straining. But she's a bugger in a calm, heavy as a pregnant cow, and clumsy. You won't want the tiller then, Matthew.'

I had a good look round. In the calm of the harbour *Happy Jack*'s dark red sails had hung from the spars as stiffly as barn doors, and it had taken three men to hoist the peak halyard, but feeling the breeze, she lifted off the surface of the sea and was racing for open waters. As I saw her take the wind, I felt sure and confident, certain we would have a good trip with Howard Martin at the helm. The skipper could stay drunk.

I spent the sailing time to the grounds talking to the crew. They were a cold, unfriendly bunch. There were three of them to work the trawl: a couple of eighteen-year-olds, Peter Watts and Arthur Gatrill, and a married man from Yarmouth, Frank Dawber, who smoked a foul-smelling pipe and spat black tobacco regularly over the bulwarks. Frank was the only one to shake my hand. The galley boy, Allen Hannah, looked after the food. He seemed too nervous to spend time talking. There were a couple of iceroom boys to help stack the gutted catch: Dougie Pope and Simon Long. They didn't look old enough to be out alone at night. I guessed they were both runaways. It's hard to find a fishing smack without a handful of orphan children working the sails.

I told the older men I hadn't worked a trawl before.

'Why'd Lowther take you on then?' Gatrill asked suspiciously.

'Maybe you should ask him.'

We were sitting by the mainmast, mending nets. *Happy Jack* carried two sets of nets and they had to be kept repaired and ready for use. They were expensive to replace.

'You just watch what we do,' Frank Dawber told me. 'It isn't difficult. You get the trawl net over the side. Then the beam, which keeps the mouth of the trawl open. Watch yourself when the beam goes. It's forty feet long and heavy, and you can get caught up in the trawling ropes. Second hand takes the tiller. Skipper might watch, if he's in the mood. He's more interested in the catch.'

'Doesn't he take the tiller?'

I noticed Gatrill glancing over his shoulder towards the companion and then grinning at Watts. We could hear

Lowther singing down below in his cabin. The men eyed each other briefly and got on with their work.

'He sets the course for the grounds,' Dawber said. 'Howard takes the tiller mostly.'

'Fair enough,' I said with a grin. 'As long as we catch fish.'

I took a needle and started to help with the nets. I didn't know what was wrong, but they were a miserable lot. They probably weren't catching fish. That usually explains a fisherman's misery. Or they didn't like strangers. Henry Mundol sent spies to watch his skippers, and they weren't popular. They would have some lovely stories to tell about Ben Lowther. He hadn't the sobriety to be handling an expensive sailing smack. I was glad Howard Martin looked such a likely hand. One experienced seaman was all you really needed on a trawler. The rest was hard labour.

We worked at repairing the nets for hours, and rested between huge meals of fried fish and plum duff. The tea was hot enough to take the skin off the back of your mouth. When we weren't working, we smoked our pipes and got as much rest as we could before the trawling began.

The skipper didn't come on deck until we reached the Whitby Ground and were ready for shooting the trawl. 'Let's get fishing, Howard,' he grunted, rubbing the sleep or drink from his eyes. I said nothing, but I was surprised he didn't bother to cast the lead-line. Most skippers would have cast a lead-weight armed with tallow over the side to tell them more or less where they were before they started fishing, but I assumed Lowther knew what he was about. He sounded full of confidence.

The tide was favourable, so the wind was spilled from the sails until the smack was barely moving, then the net was paid over the bulwarks into the sea and allowed to stream away to windward. Lowther watched as we sweated.

I could hear Gatrill breathing heavily, Peter Watts cursing the effort. Frank Dawber worked with his eyes clenched shut, struggling to keep going. I wondered whether he was ill, fighting to keep his berth.

'Let go the beam,' Lowther yelled when the net was overboard.

With a grunt, we unlashed the heavy beam which held the trawl net and levered it over the bulwarks until it dropped into the sea, floating on the surface and held tight by the trawl ropes.

'Stream the gear,' Lowther ordered, and we stepped back quickly to watch the ropes run out until they reached the wooden beam.

'That's it,' Lowther said finally. 'Let her go.'

As *Happy Jack* took the wind and got moving again, the ropes were slowly paid out, and the beam sank beneath the surface of the sea.

'Watch yourself, Matthew,' Frank Dawber warned me.

The ropes were straining and twanging. As the beam came square to *Happy Jack*, Dawber and Watts secured the ropes with two turns round the towpost ready for hauling the net on board again. When the skipper had the length of net out that he wanted, the ropes were made fast so that they took the whole strain of the trawl. When the trawl was all square and forty fathoms called, 'Wear away,' Lowther shouted, and we were towing.

Lowther drank corn brandy right through this operation, which took half an hour. The minute the gear was down on the bottom, he went below and started singing again. He had a raucous, tuneless voice. I collapsed against the fish hatch amidships and took the hot tea the galley boy brought round. I closed my eyes and let the sweat dry on my face. The trawl would be down five or six hours, and until we had our first catch, there would be nothing to do.

Finishing the tea, I went down below to grab what sleep I could in the dog-hole of a cabin. The cabin was about eight feet long and barely five feet high, which wasn't much standing room for a six-footer like me. I dropped my seaboots to the floor and lay down. It wasn't easy trying to rest. The hatch was fastened to keep water out and the cabin stank of stale tobacco and corn brandy. The bedding in the bunk was filthy. I closed my eyes, and thanked God the coke stove wasn't lit. In this heat, that would have been hell. I went to sleep immediately. In my dreams, a man's voice cried desperately for help.

I was dragged out of sleep when the smack lurched violently into the wind, and for seconds we seemed to be climbing out of the water. In a daze, I scrambled out of the bunk and pulled my seaboots on, and stumbled out into the corridor outside the galley. I reached the companion ladders and climbed, almost falling as the smack lurched again, this time to starboard. As I got on deck, I fell awkwardly and went sprawling for'ard, losing my balance. I tried to stand, and slipped against the side of the fish hatch, falling backwards with a thudding crash into the mainmast. The pain shot through my head. I tried to stand again and then slithered down to the deck. There was blood running down my left cheek as I slumped against the mainmast. In a daze, I saw Lowther staggering drunkenly across the deck, a bottle of corn brandy in his hand.

'Mind the tiller,' he was yelling.

The tiller was swinging loose. Against the bulwarks, a man lay sprawled on his back, struggling to get to his feet. It was Peter Watts. Lowther took a run at him and kicked him savagely in the ribs. I was on my feet by then, blood pouring down my face. I saw Howard Martin scramble from the companion and grab the tiller, pushing the skipper out of his way. The smack seemed to be jerking backwards and forwards, as if she was caught on some obstruction and fighting against the tide. I thought she might turn right over if there was a sudden heavy water. As I tried to hoist myself to my feet, there was a shrieking tearing sound, and I knew the ropes had parted from the trawl net. *Happy Jack* broke away with another sickening lurch, and then she was floating free.

'The trawl!' Lowther yelled, choking with rage.

Happy Jack took another wild lurch to starboard as Martin righted her, and then the rest of the crew were on deck and I was collapsing again beside the mainmast, my eyes full of blood. Through the blood, I could see Lowther's face, distorted with rage, wet with sweat and spittle. He was staring wildly around the deck, his face red with drink and fury. He seemed to notice me for the first time, and started moving towards me.

'Jonah,' he seemed to be shouting. 'Jonah.' It was seconds before I realised he was shouting at me. 'Damned miserable Jonah.'

I never really learned what happened, but it wasn't too hard to work out. We were on a steady course. Howard Martin had gone down to the galley to get a brew of tea. Lowther must have come back on deck while I was asleep. From what Peter Watts said, the skipper stumbled out of the companion blind drunk and fell straight into the tiller, knocking Peter Watts sideways and turning the smack into the wind. The trawl ropes twisted and then parted under the strain.

You couldn't replace a trawl net and keep the cost secret.

Not from an owner like Henry Mundol.

Nobody said a word. They seemed frightened, terrified to talk. If Lowther had stayed sober, he might not have lost us the trawl, but that wasn't a thought you mentioned. He went below and stayed there, drinking himself into a stupor. Everybody was relieved.

We worked the smack under Howard Martin's orders after that.

Days went past. Lowther continued drinking in his cabin. We caught two poor hauls on the way to the Dogger and then dropped the gear for the fourth time on Southernmost Rough. The fishing wasn't good: a ruck of underweight cod and haddock, squirming among clumps of grassy seaweed, seaslugs, starfish and duffs. I kept my watch, wondering what would happen if Lowther decided to take the tiller, but Howard Martin had been at the helm for most of the two days since we lost the trawl, only fetching Lowther from his cabin when we hauled the net. He refused to take charge of the fishing.

The nightmare began when I was on night watch, standing at the tiller alone beneath the feverish clouds. The spare trawl was down and we were towing at two knots under full sail. I could hear the canvas straining, the creak of oak beams and tackle. The sky was full of strange dread, yellow and lowering over the sluggish sea, flickering with pale moonlight. *Happy Jack* floundered in the airless heat, the muddy feverish waters. There is almost no tide on the Dogger to help a becalmed smack, and the terrible heat seemed to suck the wind out of our sails. I hadn't slept easily for three days and my eyes were gritty with fatigue.

'All clear, Matthew?' Howard Martin asked, clambering up from the companion and standing beside me at the tiller. His voice was hard as mahogany, harsh and grating in the sultry silence. When the rest of the crew were talking in muttered whispers, Howard never kept his voice down, as if he didn't care what any man thought.

'All clear.'

'That's a rare sky,' he said with a puzzled frown, glancing round at the threatening horizon.

We were tacking along the edge of Southernmost Rough.

Great banks of cloud scudded heavily across the moon, the dull yellow light glowing behind the clouds making them look like enormous bruises, lumbering towards the north, reflecting sluggishly in the heavy waters. It was a dangerous sky.

'You think there's going to be a storm?' I asked, keeping my hand steady on the tiller.

He shrugged, not bothering to answer. He wasn't the kind of man to waste time on speculation. I don't think he had looked me in the eye since I'd come on board. He couldn't be bothered. He didn't want friends. He had been with Ben Lowther on *Happy Jack* for years. He was the only man on board who wasn't scared of him.

I could hear the skipper, in his cabin aft, singing and pouring brandy down his throat, but I had been with *Happy Jack* long enough to know better than to criticise the skipper to his second hand.

'You just keep your eyes sharp, Matthew,' he said. 'We'll worry about storms when they come.'

He went back down to the galley and I stayed at the tiller.

My head still throbbed from the cut, and I hadn't shaved since the accident. My hair felt matted with sweat and dried blood. I held the tiller, and my hands were wet with sweat, a clammy, unpleasant fever. I had a bottle of water on the tiller post but it was lukewarm and dirty from the barrel. Tea was all that refreshed you in this heat.

I was alone with the tiller.

Then the birds started to shadow the moon.

At first I thought it was clouds, shimmering against the pale light, shifting and dancing above the horizon. The moonlight seemed far away and remote. A shooting star fell rapidly beyond the summer horizon. Stars blinked faintly in the heat, as if they were too sick to shine. Then the cloud was moving towards us. It was birds, swarming out of the darkness. To welcome them, the sky was grey with exhaustion.

Then at dawn, it began raining.

Rain fell out of the sky and drenched the pine decks. Rain flooded into the companion and splashed and poured out of the scuppers and through the bulwarks. The sails shone with rain, reflecting the watery sky, and the grey, gentle sunlight. And in the torrent of rain, the birds started arriving.

The first of them fluttered into *Happy Jack*'s sails in complete silence, a pair of redshanks, a plover and one or two knots. A bar-tailed godwit flickered out of the rain and pecked eagerly at the decks as if they were sand-dunes full of food. A curlew stalked furiously up and down the main boom. Then the knots and dunlins started landing on the rigging and sails. They came in waves, thousands of them swooping from the sea, the knots in their reddish summer plumage, the dunlin plump and black bellied. The dunlin was the smallest of the common waders, the knot hardly visited the east coast at all during the summer. The sky was darkened by flying birds. They came in great clouds, huge flocks congregating briefly on the sails and masts, then lifting and swooping away again over the waves. I gripped the tiller and stared into the cloud of birds. I could hardly breathe for excitement. As more birds arrived, hundreds would leave the rigging and head off into the dawning sunlight. The more it rained, the more birds arrived. The whole sky seemed to be full of birdsong, the cool air drenched with the sound of birds, throbbing with noisy, wild life.

I closed my eyes and wanted to shout a welcome.

An hour later, the trawl snagged on the rocks at the edge of Southernmost Rough. *Happy Jack* gave a terrific lunge to starboard, and seemed to hang on the water like a dolphin, leaping for the waves. Then the net bit hard and the smack turned up into the wind, the sails weathercocking in seconds and hanging lifeless in irons as the smack rocked backwards and forwards. There was a snap as one of the ropes on the trawl net parted, and then complete silence.

Three

The net was shredded to bits. We had to sail the smack back on the course we'd been towing and then free the nets from the rocks. The trawl was beyond repair. Lowther stared at the ruined gear as if he was trying to wake himself from some drunken nightmare. A vein at the side of his forehead twitched jerkily. His face was mottled with drink, and there were tears in his eyes. He kept clenching his fists, unable to speak. When the gear was back on deck, he turned abruptly and went down to his cabin. Howard Martin gave orders to get hove-to. We worked without speaking. *Happy Jack* seemed to take the sluggish waters with a sullen, weary lift. Hove-to, she lay like the dead, drifting in the hot silence. The rain had stopped. The waders had disappeared into the morning sun.

We sat around on deck, listening to Lowther in his cabin. He broke bottles and yelled in sudden outbursts of rage. A chair splintered in the corridor outside the galley. Allen Hannah was too scared to go below to make drinks or meals, and Howard Martin had to take him, standing in the door of the galley while he prepared food. Frank Dawber kept watch while the rest of us waited on deck, making useless attempts to repair the damaged trawl net. It was torn to shreds, the whole of the cod-end ripped apart from the main net. As the midday heat got worse, we gave up and sat drinking tea.

The skipper climbed noisily up the companion later in the afternoon.

'Jonah!' he was bellowing. 'Where's my Jonah!'

I stood up and watched him warily. He was carrying a bottle of corn brandy, waving it unsteadily as he clambered out on to the deck. He glared round, blinking like a man emerging from the dark. When he saw me, he grinned and lifted the bottle, offering a mock toast of recognition, then lurched towards me.

'That you, Jonah?'

'Take it easy, skipper.'

I could smell the drink on his breath. His stubble was soaked with corn brandy and his vest stank of sweat and alcohol.

'You brought me bad luck, Jonah,' he said wildly, waving the bottle in my face.

'I brought you nothing. You charted the course.'

'You knew about those rocks.'

'I knew nothing.'

'You took us there deliberate.'

'How the devil . . .?'

'Hold him.'

I didn't understand what he meant. The other men stared at him for a moment and then Gatrill got up, watching the skipper nervously.

'I said hold him,' Lowther bellowed again.

I tried to move towards the bulwarks but Peter Watts was behind me and before I could turn round my arms were pinioned. I struggled to break free, but Peter Watts forced my arm up behind my back and then butted the side of my head where the cut was still aching. I felt the pain piercing between my eyes. As I lost my balance, Gatrill hit me hard in the kidneys with his fist, and the blackness flooded into my mind.

I must have been unconscious for seconds. When I came to, I could still hear Lowther yelling. I opened my eyes and tried to focus.

'Flogging,' Lowther was shouting.

'You what!' I began to shout, struggling to free myself.

'Flogging,' Lowther yelled again, stumbling close to me and spitting in my face. 'You heard first time, Jonah. You heard.'

He let out a laugh and took a long swallow from the corn brandy. I fought to get free but Watts butted me again and I felt myself going limp.

They tied me to the mainmast to do the flogging.

I could hear Lowther giving his orders, jeering as the ropes cut into my wrists. One of the men kicked me in the kidneys as I fought against the ropes and then they slammed my face into the mast, bruising my jaw and laughing as splinters of wood tore the skin on my cheek. In the struggle, for a brief second I saw Howard Martin at the tiller, his face white with tension, his eyes black and drained by exhaustion. I tried to shout his name, but he looked away. I saw Allen Hannah sitting on the fish hatch, weeping into his hands. Frank Dawber was at the bowsprit, staring ahead into the muddy sea.

'Now then,' Lowther was shouting.

The ropes tightened. Coming forward, Lowther threw a bucket of water on to the ropes, smiling gleefully at his work.

'Keep you comfortable,' he explained.

I knew the water was to tighten the ropes even more.

He stood back and glanced behind my shoulder. I couldn't see what they were doing. I heard the rope slice through the air but felt nothing.

'Get on with it,' Lowther ordered.

There was a pause.

'Not me, skipper,' Gatrill said. 'I don't have stomach for this.'

'Watts,' the skipper bellowed.

There was another pause.

I heard Peter Watts mutter something to Martin and then the rope fell across my shoulders. There was no sound, no weight behind the blow. Lowther's mouth was open. He tipped the bottle back and took a long swallow. Watts aimed again, and the rope flailed loosely on to my back.

'Do it!' Lowther roared, and next time the rope bit into my skin, tearing the flesh over the shoulder bone. I winced at the pain, and clenched my fists against the mainmast. Lowther took another swallow from his bottle and watched. The rope slashed again, whipping the skin above my waist. I knew the end of the rope was frayed, and the broken ends burnt like a fire. At the third lash, I yelled out with the pain and Lowther danced towards the mainmast, trying to see my face, slipping on the deck and dropping his bottle. 'Another,' he shouted hysterically.

At the fifth lash I lost count. I bit my own mouth until the flesh was open in the cheek. The rope was beginning to cut into the flesh. I could feel my spine wracking at each blow. The cut in my head was open again, and my eyes were full of blood and sweat and tears. The sky had turned red, black birds hawking above the becalmed vessel in screaming circles. I thought they were cormorants. I prayed for more rain but the liquid was my own sweat and blood. I was weeping blood.

'He's had enough,' somebody said brusquely.

'No,' Lowther grunted.

I couldn't see him, but I recognised his voice.

'I said he's had enough.'

I knew it was Martin giving orders. Lowther seemed to be on the deck on his hands and knees, retching and vomiting yellow liquid. Frank Dawber cut me down. As the ropes split I fell forward into Dawber's arms. My trousers were soaked with urine. Lowther went on being sick, a stream of thick fluid pouring out of his mouth. As Dawber and Martin carried me down the companion, I could see Allen Hannah scrambling after them.

I passed out as they lifted me into my bunk.

The last thing I saw was Allen Hannah standing in the doorway. He was weeping.

I drifted in and out of fever for two days. Allen Hannah bathed my back and mouth with cool water: they used the smack's supply of drinking water. My mouth was swollen and infected. Nobody complained about the drinking water. Howard Martin spread an ointment of sphagnum on the wounds every few hours, and forced a herbal ointment into my mouth: it was cool and tasted of peppermint. The flesh was hanging loose in two or three places on my back, but the rope hadn't cut to the bone. The shoulders were the most painful: they felt bruised and stiff. I couldn't move my neck where the rope had lashed into the tender skin.

In the filthy bunk, lying face down on the blankets, I saw birds flying through blood, a moon the colour of blood hanging over the Iceland horizon. As the moon dropped towards the horizon, huge icebergs drifted beneath the surface of the sea, and herring gulls dived and screamed at the water, picking at the bones of a fisherman's skeleton. In the tide, the skeleton floated slowly near the surface, revolving in slow circles, and when it turned over on to its back, I saw that it had my own face. I woke in terror and swallowed mouthfuls of cold water to calm my panic, and then slipped back into feverish sleep.

It must have been on the second day that Lowther came and sat beside the bunk in the cabin. The fire in the stove had been lit, I presumed to boil water for my wounds, but had now gone out. In the galley, I could hear Allen Hannah making drinks. I opened my eyes, feeling cooler for the first time in hours, and Lowther was sitting on the bunk opposite mine, his head forward in his hands, his shoulders shaking. I must have made a sound turning my head to change position. The pain in my neck and mouth was easing. My shoulder felt broken, swollen with bruises.

Lowther heard me and looked up blearily, trying to focus. His eyes were bright red. The stubble on his cheeks was black and flecked with spittle.

'Matthew?'

I didn't answer. I stared at him. For a moment, I thought he had come to finish the job: kill me and heave me over the side: write a lost life into the vessel's logbook. Nobody would be too worried about another drowned fisherman.

'Can you hear me?'

I closed my eyes, but didn't answer.

He waited for a second, then nodded, staring down at his hands.

'I reckon you can hear me,' he said quietly.

He must have gone away, or I drifted off into another sleep. When I came to, he was still sitting on the bunk, talking in a low voice. He was saying something about Henry Mundol, what kind of man he was to work for. There would be no pity for the ruined trawls. The best he could hope for was to keep his smack and have the cost taken from his own share of future trips. He talked drearily, without hope. He heard the change in my breathing and looked up. We stared at each other again, seeing each other for the first time: clearly, coldly. After a long pause, he shrugged his shoulders and stood up.

'They hanged my father,' he said, as if I would understand. 'For what he did.'

I stared at him blankly, uncomprehending.

'Murdering that woman,' he explained.

I tried to nod. I couldn't move.

'They hanged him, in 1847. July the third. I was thirteen. They left the body on the gibbet for a warning. He was there for years, I reckon. They do say birds built a nest in his mouth in the end, he was left in the open that long. I never saw him after the hanging.'

I felt a sudden choking panic rise in my throat, and then Lowther was gone and I was sinking back beneath the waves of pain, drowning in my own wet darkness. I was unconscious before he closed the door.

In one of my nightmarish dreams, I was back on Lindisfarne, standing at the edge of the beach in shallow water. A strange figure in black robes was walking towards me. Two otters ambled carelessly at his feet. I thought he was going to speak, but he waded straight past me and out into the cold sea. It was night, bitter with frost. I gasped as the water splashed against my flesh. 'Matthew,' a voice whispered. I tried to open my eyes but they were full of flying birds. The strange figure emerged from the water, and knelt down on the sands, where the otters dried his feet and blew warm breath on his hands. He talked to them as they ambled around him. I heard the herring gulls screaming over Lindisfarne, and the melancholy cry of curlews.

'Matthew!'

I finally managed to open my eyes, and Allen Hannah was standing beside the bunk, holding a bowl of weak broth. He piled soft pillows behind me, but I couldn't lean against them. I had to rest on my elbow and take the broth from a spoon. After a few mouthfuls, I collapsed back into the bunk, lying face down and watching the bedbugs crawl beneath the rough pillow. I slept again, but the strength was returning. I slept without dreams, and when I woke I heard Howard Martin's cry for Smeaton's Lighthouse. We were approaching the Humber Estuary.

I opened my eyes, and tried to sit up against the pillows. I drank some of the water left beside the bunk. I knew I couldn't stay on board *Happy Jack*. I had signed for the eight-week trip to the Dogger, but another trip with Lowther and I would be dead. The way he drank, we would all probably be dead. I had to get off the smack. He was obviously going into Grimsby to replace the ruined trawls, and the minute we reached the quays, I would have to make my escape. If it meant three months on the treadmill or oakum wards of Lincoln Prison, that would be better than another trip with Lowther. And they would have to catch me first. I shouted to Allen Hannah for another bowl of broth, and tried to sit up on the edge of the bunk to test my shoulder. The pain was unbearable, and my mouth felt ulcerated with pus from the wound where I had bitten in my agony, but I could hold myself upright. When Allen brought the broth, I forced myself to drink the whole bowl and then asked for another.

'You feeling better?' he asked, pleased and taking the bowl.

I shrugged.

'I'm sorry,' he said, his young face bright red, his eyes watering.

'Sorry?'

'About what happened.'

I closed my eyes and winced at the pain in my shoulders.

I didn't want to speak to him about that. I didn't want to speak to anybody on board *Happy Jack*.

'Get me some more broth, Allen,' I said through gritted teeth.

He went back to the galley and I tried to exercise my shoulder.

Four

I heaved myself out of the bunk. The deck seemed to lift to meet me. I could hear Howard Martin shouting the depths and guessed we were going over Binks Sands. Dozens of fishing smacks have been wrecked on the shallows over Binks Sands. I clung to the edge of the bunk and closed my eyes to stop the dizzying lurch of the cabin. I could smell the stale fug of tobacco smoke and my naked feet slipped on the cabin deck. When he was smoking in his bunk, Frank Dawber spat globules of tobacco juice on to the floor. What with the sulphurous fumes of the stove and the foul tobacco smoke, the hinges and brass fittings in the cabin were covered with scaly green verdigris. I thanked God the coke stove wasn't lit, filling the cabin with fumes.

I was still wearing my fearnoughts, the heavy cotton trousers you needed when working on deck, but nothing on top. The skin on my back and shoulders felt tight and inflamed. I tried to stretch and thought the wounds on my back were going to burst open. The sphagnum had taken the heat from the wounds and cooled the skin, but I hadn't had any ointment for several hours and the effect was wearing off. I couldn't do that myself. I had to get my knitted wool jersey from the locker and a pair of shore boots: the

leather boots were lighter than seaboots; I couldn't make my
escape in heavy seaboots. Everything seemed impossible.

I took a deep breath and got the jersey from the locker.
I waited a second, then dragged it over my head. The pain
of lifting my arms almost knocked me out. I had to lean
back against the bunk and close my eyes for several seconds, breathing deeply to get control. The smack rocked
and lifted on heavy waters, and I knew we were round
Spurn Head and into the dangerous waters at the mouth of
the estuary. There is always heavy water at the estuary, the
tide flooding into the brown race of the river and clashing
with the outgoing waters, and unless you are careful you
soon get swept on to Greedy Gut and Old Den, the shallow
sandbanks off Spurn. I hoped Howard Martin was on the
tiller. I got down to the floor and managed to pull my thick
socks and leather boots on and then heaved myself back on
to my feet. Sweat was drenching my face and I began to
fear I wasn't going to make it. I took a flask of brandy from
one of the lockers and swallowed two or three mouthfuls. I
waited, gathering my strength.

Getting up the companion was the hardest part. My
arms felt as if they were going to pull out of my shoulders
and the skin on my back stretched like a bursting boil. I
could feel wetness running down my back, and hoped it
was sweat, not blood. At the top of the companion, Frank
Dawber saw me and rushed across the deck to help. I got
out on to the deck hanging on to his arm and then stood by
the tiller. I pretended to stumble and reached for the mainmast. I needed them to think I was still weak.

'You all right, Matthew?' Dawber asked, bringing me a
mug of water.

'I'm fine. Needed some air.'

Howard Martin was at the tiller. The skipper stood at his
side, watching everything he did.

'That Spurn?' I asked, emptying the mug of water.

'That's right,' Lowther grunted.

I could see fires burning in the early evening light. The spit of land ran into the sea like the ends of the earth, a dismal jut of mud and sandbanks that gradually widened into the flat emptiness of Holderness. Hull was thirty miles away. The lighthouse, Smeaton's Light, stood at the end of Spurn, and the fires were dotted around the scrutty shores, men still working at their lines, women preparing food, lights burning in a huddle of poor houses. The lighthouse men and a community of worm-diggers lived on Spurn. A few fishermen. I could see longboats drawn up on to the shore. There were villages further up the coast, and gypsies and gangs of travelling labourers. On the fishing smacks, you heard all sorts of stories about Spurn. My last skipper called it devil's island because of the strangers who ended up living there, on the run from the law.

On the south shore, I could see the lights of Grimsby, flickering in the summer evening. It was a cool, quiet evening. The sky to the west was blazing orange for miles. Behind us, darkness and stars were already gathering at the horizon. I breathed the cool air thankfully and took another mouthful of brandy. Allen Hannah climbed up the companion and offered me a mug of hot tea and a chunk of freshly-baked bread. I refused the tea and forced myself to eat the bread. Frank Dawber stood at my side, lost for words, watching the lights along the coast. We were round the estuary and tacking under full sail for port. We had two ruined trawls and an empty fishroom. I didn't want to be there when Henry Mundol came aboard to check the damage.

I climbed back down the companion and went into the cabin. In the locker, I found my gutting knife and woollen hat. I pushed the knife through my leather belt and another knife down the side of my boot. I was drinking too much brandy but the alcohol eased the pain in my shoulder. My whole back felt inflamed now, and I knew I couldn't keep going much longer. I sat on the edge of the bunk and shouted for Allen Hannah. When he came, he looked scared. He wasn't much more than thirteen or fourteen.

'I need that ointment,' I told him.

'It's in the galley.'

'Get it.'

He was back in seconds, nervous, agitated, wondering what I was about.

'You're going to have to put it on, lad,' I told him.

He stared at me in panic. 'I can't do that,' he begged.

'Just do it, Allen.'

I stood up and leaned forward, facing one of the bunks. I stretched my arms and told him to lift the jersey. He must have seen the gutting knife. I winced as the cool ointment touched the wounds.

'I'm sorry.'

'Go on.'

'I don't know where to put it.'

'All over my back. Use it all.'

He rubbed the ointment into my shoulders and down my back. I felt the pain easing, the cool relief. Sphagnum moss is used on most fishing smacks in cases of accident. I was biting my teeth together against the pain. I took a dollop of the sphagnum on a finger and pushed it into my mouth. The natural saliva was already healing the flesh where I had bitten in agony during the flogging. I relaxed and breathed deeply, then stood up from the bunk, flexing my shoulders, forcing myself to keep moving. The herbs numbed the pain, so that I could move freely. I pulled the jersey back down and thanked Hannah.

'Get on deck now, lad.'

When he was gone, I took my money-belt from the locker and fastened it underneath my trousers. I had enough sovereigns to keep me going for a short while without earning more. I secured the belt, and then stood in silence in the cabin. I needed to prepare myself. I took a deep breath and listened to the sounds of the smack: the straining canvas, creak of booms. A swarm of gulls followed us as we neared land. I closed my eyes and listened to my own mind. I couldn't afford to make mistakes. I couldn't afford to make my move too soon.

The stillness calmed my mind, emptied it so that I could concentrate. 'Know when to sink the line,' my first skipper had taught me. 'Get the feel of the fish feeding.' It was a natural skill: feeling the cod on the bait, knowing when the green water was full of shoaling fish. You had to love the sea to work the liners properly. The sea was different wherever you sailed, and you had to know how to recognise the signs. Fleeing from *Happy Jack* was going to be like that.

I opened my eyes and was ready. I went through to the galley. I could hear men talking on deck. *Happy Jack* rode the turbulent waters off Sunk Island and I could hear gulls screaming after the offal: one of the crew was throwing the remains of gutted fish over the side. Another smack hailed us, and Lowther shouted something about damaged nets and misfortune. I could have told him all about misfortune.

I found the oil in the cupboard by the galley door and poured it all over the galley floor. My hands were soaked in oil. There were three containers. When I'd finished, I cleaned my hands and went back into the narrow passage. The skipper's door was shut but I knew he was on deck. I glanced into the starboard fishroom: there was nobody there. The crew's quarters were empty. As the smell of the oil sickened my nostrils, I climbed the companion and sat on the hatch, watching the crew handle the smack, the great redbrick tower of the docks floating towards us through the darkening evening. *Happy Jack* was working under the mainsail and foresail, the mizzen already reefed down. Arthur Gatrill and one of the young boys was busy getting the bowsprit run in. In the stern, Peter Watts and Frank Dawber were preparing the drogue, the heavy canvas that could be thrown over the stern to slow the smack if we went into the lock too fast.

'Reef the mainsail,' Lowther shouted at the tiller.

I had to get the distance right or ruin my chances of escaping. As *Happy Jack* slowed into the muddy waters a hundred yards off the lockpit, I slipped back down the companion and went into the galley. I struck a light from the coke stove and dropped the flaming taper on the oil. It flared up instantly. The deck was soaked in oil. I leapt back and made for the companion. The flames were roaring in the galley.

'Get the drogue,' Lowther was ordering.

A bell clanged on the lockpit and I heard men shouting on shore.

I waited ten seconds and then shouted as loud as I could: 'Fire!'

I was up the companion as the flames roared out of the galley door and something exploded in the narrow room. As I clambered out of the companion yelling my panic, I could hear the fire roaring behind me. I saw Lowther standing by the tiller, turning in confusion, Frank Dawber grabbing a bucket of water from the watertub and running towards the companion. I slipped on the deck and pretended to fall, crashing into the starboard bulwarks by the mizzen mast. I saw Howard Martin staring at me fixedly, struggling to control the smack. Lowther was suddenly yelling orders. Men ran for the companion and *Happy Jack* was running out of control into the lockpit. There was a thump as her starboard bows hit the stone walls.

I closed my eyes and prayed for good running.

As *Happy Jack* lurched further into the lockpit, crashing again into the stone walls with another sickening thud, I managed to stand and reach out for the iron ladders. There were iron ladders either end of the lockpit for repair work. The walls towered twenty feet above the smack. I glanced round quickly to make sure nobody was near, and then launched myself for the ladders. As my feet left the deck and *Happy Jack* bounced again into the walls, I could hear Lowther shouting furiously, then I was scrambling up the ladders as if the fires of hell were raging behind me.

'Don't let him get away,' I heard Lowther yell as I reached the top of the lockpit and hauled myself over the edge. 'Don't let him get free.'

A crowd were waiting on the lockpit: men and women, children looking for their fathers. A fisherman holding a bottle of corn brandy made a grab for me and I kicked him hard on the kneecap, sending him sprawling into the crowd. As he fell, he crashed into a woman holding a baby, knocking her and the child to the ground, and several people started to shout angrily. I pulled the gutting knife from my belt and threatened the nearest man, then ran for the darkness beyond the lockpit.

'Bastard,' one of the drunks was yelling.

'Hold him,' I heard Lowther ranting on *Happy Jack*.

But nobody bothered to follow me. They were too excited, watching the fire on board *Happy Jack*. At twenty yards I could hear the flames leaping into the sky, voices yelling in panic. On the quays, men were running and calling the alarm. In the huge fishdock, with a hundred smacks waiting to unload their catch, a fire could soon cause havoc. They were too busy to worry about me. I fled to the narrow lanes and cuts behind the fish market, and in the safety of darkness, collapsed to the cobbled ground. I was shaking with pain and fever. If I didn't get control of my body, they would find me at first light.

Five

I woke with a start. Something ran across my legs, heavy
and quick. I dragged myself to my feet and leant with my
back against the wall. The wall was slimy and blackened by
smoke from the curing houses, the grime covering my fingers. I could hear men shouting down at the lockpit, and
the sound of angry cries, footsteps echoing up the narrow
lanes. There was grass growing between the bricks of the
walls, nettles and dock-weeds on the ground. Men were
already beginning to search the alleys, flares from torches
blazing in the darkness. Along the quays there were flickering gaslights, but in the alleys there was no light at all. A
shroud of smoke hung over the pontoons, fog drifting from
the estuary, coloured flames from the streets around the
docks. I could hear sirens, and men shouting to each other.

It was more than time to move. I ran down the narrow
alley where I was hiding and round a corner. Glancing up,
I saw the name Ship Alley in crude lettering. I turned right
away from the quays and made for the lights I could see
ahead over the dismal buildings. I was at the back of the
fish market, in a cobbled street full of filleting sheds and
merchants' offices. It would soon be gone midnight, and
the lumpers came down to the fish docks at two o'clock to

start unloading the day's catch. I got to the end of another alley and heard the cries of street vendors and a hum of voices: there were crowds not far away, and I could hide in crowds until Lowther and his men got fed up of searching for me. I came out of the twisting maze of alleys and cuts and into the bright lights of the main cobbled street, the gaslight flaring and diminishing, casting a flickering glow across the streets, unreal, theatrical.

I knew where I was now: close to the top of the fish market and the district fishermen knew as Satan's Hole, a warren of dark and squalid streets, crowded with brothels and music halls, drinking houses and penny gaffs. You could get lost forever in Satan's Hole. I glanced behind me into the darkness, and then stepped out into the brilliant lights. There were gaslights and flares outside all the shops. I walked quickly into the crowd and made for the far side of a huge square. I went past a Lincoln Bank, jostled by gaudily-dressed women and housewives in thick shawls, and was soon outside a music hall, a bray of cornets blasting from inside the ramshackle building. The music hall was called Moody's. A horde of women lounged on the pavements outside, waiting for the customers to come out after the show, laughing and shouting at the crowds. I could smell the thick stench of laudanum. Several of the women were drinking Godfrey's Cordial, which was laced with laudanum. They stank of beer and gin. I had to fight my way through them, joking and pretending to be interested, keeping my hand on my money-belt.

I walked more slowly now, lost in the crowd, trying to ease my back. The jersey was rubbing against the lacerated skin, and I felt faint from pain and lack of food. I kept to the main street and crowded pavements. I didn't want to get lost down the yards and alleys where the girls and their friends waited for strangers straying in the dark. I passed another music hall, and heard shrieks of laughter from the sordid building, a sudden abrupt cry of pain, drunken shouts. On the far side of the road, I could see the entrance to a market, and a sign saying Newbiggin Lanes. I needed lodgings. I had to get some rest.

I crossed the street, stumbling in the ruts in the road. A fog of sulphur fumes hung over the streets clustered around the market. Two eight-year-old girls were flash-dancing at the entrance to the market, showing legs and knickers and giggling at the boys who applauded. As I approached the market, more children tried to grab my hand and lead me to the brothels. They screamed with laughter when I told them to leave me alone. I wondered if I was dreaming. Strange faces peered at me. Voices called in the smoky heat and I felt as if I was choking in hot fog. I plunged into the noisy market, hurling the children away from me with curses, ignoring the cries of pain of one of the girls.

The market was crowded despite the late hour. Gaslights flared at the gates but most of the stallholders had their own lighting: candles in turnips, fires burning in braziers, tarred flares, butchers' gaslamps streaming and fluttering. There were stalls selling everything you could want: pears, tea, onions, hot chestnuts, grapes, Yarmouth bloaters, bonnets, apples, red-edged mats, walnuts, boots, gaudy tea-trays, red handkerchiefs, cooked meat, flowers, oysters, cockles and whelks. At one stall, a tailor was working from his dummy, measuring a drunken fisherman for a blue suit. Married women jostled with the crowd, trying to get cheap food. One of the stalls had a fine display of pelts, the skins of strayed or stolen cats, flayed alive to get a better price. In cages, there were ferrets, rats, pigeons, guinea-pigs and cage-birds, all for sale.

In the main area at the centre of the market, entertainers worked the crowds for money: tumblers and pipe-players, jugglers, a magician, a conjurer, two clowns, an ancient drunk busking with a broken accordion, a man in a check suit doing card tricks for pennies. I paused for several minutes to watch a fire-eater terrify a crowd of children, and then turned away. I was free, but where was I going to go? As I made my way wearily among the crowds, beggars and dollymops tried to get me to listen, a child offered me a free ticket to a peepshow, I could hear music from the tingle aireys. A flower-seller held a bunch of delicate white flowers up to my nose and then asked me if I wanted to come down an alley with her. In the lurid darkness, music floated from the stalls: flutes and fiddles, a melodion playing a melancholy seachant. I stood by a baked-chestnut stove, and remembered my father playing his melodion on a Saturday night after days away at sea. I felt lost, and close to tears.

Then the rat-catcher appeared from nowhere.

'Ladies and gentlemen,' he was shouting, trying to attract customers, and as I turned to listen, he was in front of me, the rats running up and down his arms and inside his clothes, his mad face twisted in a wild grin. As I tried to step back he shrieked with laughter, pointing and laughing, his mouth open very wide. He had horrible yellow teeth with several black gaps and inflamed gums. He was a travelling showman, earning his living like the rest of us, but in my exhaustion I was terrified.

'I am the King of the rat-catchers,' he whispered as I began to retreat. He was stabbing his fingers into my chest. 'All others are humbugs,' he chanted. 'I am known throughout Europe, and challenge any to equal me. I go to a nobleman's house, or a farmer's stackyard, and I say to the rats and mice, "I want you," and out they come in thousands. They daren't deny me. No cure, no pay, that's my way.'

He stopped, holding out a cap for money.

I could feel the sweat standing on my forehead. I wondered if I was going to faint again. As I reached behind me for the safety of the brick wall, the rat-catcher grinned with amusement and took a rat from his pocket. He held it by the tail, swinging and kicking in the darkness. The light from a flare changed the rat's colour, so that it appeared to be red. It lifted itself in mid-air and tried to bite the rat-catcher's hand. He beamed with delight, and held it up to his mouth, still laughing, opening his mouth wide and showing me his teeth again.

Before I could look away, he took a rapid bite like a snake and bit the rat's head off, spitting it down at my feet and wiping the blood from his chin with the back of his tattered sleeve. It was so quick I wasn't sure I had seen it. I turned and grazed my face against the wall. I felt into my belt and took the gutting knife out. When I turned round, the rat-catcher was watching me with a friendly, relaxed smile. When he saw the knife, he shook his head with surprise.

I held the knife out in front of me but he could see that my hand was trembling. If he had made a move, I would have dropped the knife. I felt sick, as my boot crunched the head of the dead rat.

He took a step backwards and glared at me. 'I got food to earn, friend,' he said in a heavy, rasping voice.

'Keep away from me.'

'You watched, didn't you!'

'Keep away!'

I thought I was going to pass out. I felt dizzy with noise and heat. Then a hand had my arm trapped in a vice. The rat-catcher disappeared into the crowds. I lurched round, struggling to free myself, fighting the iron fingers. When I managed to turn, a weird face was staring into my own.

'What the hell . . .'

He was tall and incredibly thin and completely bald. His head was painted black, and his eyes were like lights in a dead ship.

He held a slate out for me to read.

'Praying Billy' the words on the slate said.

'You let me go,' I whispered, threatening him, struggling to keep my feet before I began sliding down the wall.

The weird figure had a bottle in his free hand. I could see a lump of pink flesh floating in the bottle. The smell coming from the bottle was of spirits. A cork was rammed into the bottle, tied with a filthy rag. I tried to read the words on the slate.

Praying Billy earned his bread from begging, the crude scrawled words told me. The lump of flesh in the bottle of spirits was his tongue. It had been ripped out by Indians in South America.

I closed my eyes.

But Praying Billy had my arm. Swaying and shaking in the lurid clouds of yellow smoke that were drifting across the market, he gripped my arm so hard I thought it was going to break. He opened his tongueless mouth and made a gurgling bubbling sound. He pointed a finger down at my knife and shook his head. Carefully, I put the knife back into my belt. He grinned happily. He was dancing in the light from the flares, shaking his head insanely. His shirt was open to the waist and the ribs jagged through the white hairless flesh. He opened his mouth again in a wet smile and started dragging me out of the market, making frantic warning signs and grunting, his grip more painful than the seeping weals across my back. But I was going with him. Even in the din of the market, I could hear the shouts of men pushing through the crowd. I had no idea why, but Praying Billy knew I was being chased, and he was trying to get me away.

Six

In an alley behind the market Praying Billy let go of my
arm and we both stood breathing heavily in the darkness.
The alley was like a tunnel, winding from the main street
through a maze of cuts and ginnels. In the darkness, all
sound was muffled, and I felt as though we had slipped into
some blind madness. I could smell urine and rotting offal
around my feet. In the darkness, rats scuffled about our
boots.

Suddenly, there was a scratching sound and a sulphur
match flared in my face. Praying Billy waved it in front of
my eyes, gesticulating, and then grabbed my hand and
made me hold the match. I held the flame up in the darkness so that I could see his face. He watched me, his eyes
blank and colourless, his black hairless head like some
savage skull from the African jungles. He had a white scar
running down his left cheek, and one of his ears had been
badly mauled. He was still shaking and shivering like a
creature with palsy. Carefully, he lifted the corked bottle
and pointed to the lump of flesh floating in white spirit: his
tongue, ripped from his mouth by savage Indians.

He grinned when he saw the look of revulsion on my
face. As the match flared and hissed, he put his hands up to

his mouth and pulled the lips right back. His mouth gaped like a black hole. I could see deep into the empty tongue-less dark. A rat scuttled heavily over my boot and I flinched, making the flame of the match dance. Praying Billy frowned and reached out for my wrist, holding it with dead fingers. I noticed the blue tattoos on each finger: tiny skulls decorating the bony knuckles.

To my horror, he plunged his hand into his mouth and rummaged about inside as if he was trying to find the ghost of his tongue. His eyes bulged. His face tightened and the scar on his cheek stood out a skeleton white. I started to say something, tell him to stop whatever he was trying to do in his insanity, when abruptly he brought his hand out of his mouth and held some grey coloured clay in front of my eyes. I pulled back instantly, pushing his hand away, and he roared with laughter.

'See the madman's tongue, fisherman,' a thin, whining voice jeered at me. 'See the madman's magic.'

I looked instinctively up and down the rotting alley but we were alone. I stared back in horror at Praying Billy. He grinned at me, his features relaxing but his eyes wilder than ever, like glass beads rolling in a jar. He held the corked bottle up again and roared with derision when I flinched from the swollen tongue.

'I got to earn a living, friend.'

'What?'

'I got to buy my food.'

He was talking. I pushed the match towards his face to get a better look but the match went out. We were plunged into blackness. I dropped the match and felt for my knife but his hand was already there, gripping my fingers and bending them viciously backwards.

'No need for knives, friend,' the whining voice told me.

I stayed silent. I didn't move.

'Is that you, Praying Billy?' I said after a long pause.

'It is, friend,' the high-pitched whine came back.

'I don't understand. Strike a match.'

His hand released me and seconds later another match flared.

'Take a look, friend,' he hissed.

I took the outheld match and peered into Praying Billy's face. He opened his mouth wide. For a second, there seemed to be nothing there, then abruptly he stuck a tongue out into my face and wailed with hysterical laughter when I fell back against the wall. He kept pushing his tongue out like a child, delighted by my reaction. The tongue was fat and red and as healthy as any human tongue I had ever seen. He kept glancing at the bottle and going into fresh fits of laughter. I held my breath and stared at him angrily.

When he had calmed down, he lifted his head and listened to the seeping darkness. A siren sounded on the river, and we could hear voices drifting from the market, women crying in the main street. Down at the end of the narrow alley, I could see the masts of vessels in the commercial docks, merchant ships waiting for the next tide, ice barques from Norway.

'I got to earn a living, friend,' he said again, as if explaining.

'Clever trick.'

'Not the first, friend. Beggar in Hackney taught us how. Touch the hearts of the rich and you won't be poor.'

He looked poor enough, jerking and swaying in the filthy alley, thin as a pauper, his face bony and colourless, his eyes drained of life. The clothes he was wearing were beggar's clothes: torn and second-hand, stained with God knows what filth. He looked as if he hadn't washed or eaten for years.

'I'm the one to help you,' he said suddenly, talking confidentially as if we were old friends.

'Is that right?'

'I'm the one knows Newbiggin Lanes.'

'I could run.'

'You could,' he giggled.

'So?'

'You wouldn't get far.'

'Is that so?'

'Try.'

He stepped back and watched me with his wolfish calculating grin.

I shrugged. The port would be crawling with Henry Mundol's men. That was why so few of the absconding apprentices ever managed to escape into the surrounding countryside: they were always picked up. How could I avoid the same fate, with my fisherman's clothing and wounded back. I didn't know Satan's Hole, and had no friends to shelter me. I was in a worse plight than a child, trapped in these endless lanes and tenements, surrounded by strangers. The thought of being taken back to Ben Lowther or sent to the treadmill at Lincoln Prison made me shiver.

'So you're going to help me?' I said warily.

'I might.'

'For love?'

He laughed. 'I don't like love, friend,' he said, grinning and then punching me savagely on the arm. I winced at the pain and his blank eyes followed my expression like a preying bird. 'Been hurt, have you?'

'How are you going to help me?'

He ignored my question. 'Been hurt on one of Henry Mundol's smacks?'

'That's right.'

'He's a vengeful man, Henry Mundol.'

I reached for my knife again and he watched impassively, not bothered now that he knew I was on the run from Henry Mundol, relaxed and prepared to wait. I had nowhere else to go.

'A vengeful man,' he said again after a long thoughtful pause.

'How much?' I asked briefly.

'A gold sovereign, friend.'

'I can pay that.'

'Now.'

'When we get somewhere safe, where I can sleep.'

'Now,' he said flatly.

I had no choice. I gave him the coin from my money-belt and waited. He bit the coin, pocketed it.

'All right?' I asked sarcastically.

'Fair enough,' he said with his vicious grin.

He started off along the alley. The match had gone out. In the darkness, I stumbled after him. I heard a siren on the river again and slipped over a pile of rubbish, rotting food and old sacks. I could hear the sounds of the market coming closer and then fading away as the alley twisted and turned. I could smell the river, and the stench of cess-pits. The August heat was unbearable in the dilapidated over-crowded streets, the pall of smoke from the curing houses so dense and acrid you could hardly see or breathe, fog swirling into the dingy alleyways and entries until a blanket of silence lay over every street and lane.

We emerged at long last into a narrow cut behind a row of dingy terraced houses. The houses looked derelict, weeds growing from the walls, a stench of damp rising from the ground. Pushing a gate aside, Praying Billy slipped into a tiny yard and knocked quickly on one of the doors. The yard stank of sewerage. From the row of silent houses lifeless windows stared down at us. None of the houses had chimneys. The buildings were huddled together so closely you couldn't see the stars. The door opened and I followed Praying Billy into a dingy kitchen where a

woman stood with a candle. She peered at us from behind
the flame. I could smell the aniseed whisky on her breath
and the grease on her apron. I had no idea why she should
be wearing an apron in the middle of the night, but didn't
ask. Plenty of old women in these lanes earned a few extra
shillings doing bloody abortions. She had a thick crust of
ulcers round her neck, and her hand shook as she held the
candle. She seemed a lovely sort of landlady. The two of
them had a fierce whispered argument for several minutes,
and then the woman held her hand out to me and I gave
her another of my sovereigns. They didn't need to explain
my position to me. I heard a drunk singing briefly down
the backs, and then followed the woman from the kitchen
into the tiny front room: there were just the two rooms
downstairs. There was a ladder in the front room to reach
the first floor. A sovereign for a night was a good price for
safety: assuming I got any safety. I stared angrily at the
woman and went to the ladder.

'You sleep well, friend,' Praying Billy said seriously, nodding his head and grinning.

'I sleep light,' I said, touching the knife in my belt.

He laughed uproariously. 'He's got a sense of humour,'
he told the woman.

'Good for him,' the woman said sourly.

She grunted and disappeared back into the dank
kitchen. I heard the sound of women in the street and then
a man harshly calling a woman's name. I climbed the
ladder into an empty room: there was no bed, no furniture,
just a pile of straw in a corner. The window was filthy. An
opening without a door led into the back bedroom which
was just as bare and smelt of laudanum. I noticed the hatch
into the loft. These rows of slum terraces had common
lofts, running the entire length of the street. I went back
into the front room and looked down into the street. You
could have reached out and touched the windows of the

terraces opposite. I guessed that the houses looked straight
down to the river and commercial docks. We had come
round the market and away from the fishdocks to the far
side of Satan's Hole. There were no lights in any of the
houses or in the streets. It had to be well past midnight by
now, though in the stillness I could hear singing in the
streets from the music halls, and men fighting and shouting. Every now and then a woman screamed, but I couldn't
tell whether that was pain or delight.

I lay down on a pile of cold straw, and fell into a deep,
nightmarish sleep, where I was tied to a burning pillar and
flogged until my blood quenched the flames while Ben
Lowther and Praying Billy danced around my body, howling with pleasure at my pain. It must have been dawn when
I woke from the horror of the dreams, and found my face
crawling with lice and a grey mouse darting from the filthy
bed of straw. In the pale, hot light, I struggled out of bed
and tried to open the window. It was jammed shut. I was
trapped. I stood shivering in the desolate room, trying to
grasp what had happened to me, and then suddenly heard
a whispered conversation going on in the room below. I
knew I wasn't dreaming then. I crept across the room and
knelt at the top of the rickety ladder.

'I told you, he's the one they want.'

'I ent staying alone in this house with none of that.'

'He can't hurt you.'

'Says you.'

'He can't get down.'

'He can climb up, he can climb down.'

'Move the ladder then you stupid old bitch.'

'You move it.'

I heard the woman gasp with pain and Praying Billy
whispering into her face. I could imagine his clawed hand
tearing into her arm. I breathed hard, trying to control
myself, listening to what they said.

'All right, all right,' the woman was gasping. 'You go.'

'You going to help shift the ladder?'

'Go on.'

A siren wailed incredibly close on the river and I jumped with fright, knocking the edge of the ladder.

'What was that?' the woman hissed.

'Shut your face, woman.'

'What was it?'

'Rats.'

'They ent rats in my house.'

'Not much else you daft tart. Come on, shift it.'

The ladder was suddenly jerked away from the hole in the floor and I heard it rattle down to the floor. Praying Billy was breathing heavily. The woman gasped for breath and cursed.

'That Henry Mundol better pay you well.'

'He always pays for runaways. You know that.'

'He better.'

They went on talking for several seconds, and then the door out into the yard opened and Praying Billy was gone. The woman locked the door and shuffled about in the kitchen for several minutes. She was making tea. Then I heard her snoring. She must sleep in the kitchen for the warmth. The house was silent. I sat at the edge of the gaping hole, crouched on the bare floorboards. My friend Praying Billy was off to see Henry Mundol. He was going to sell me twice. Another couple of sovereigns and he would be having a good night. I struggled to my feet and tried to think what to do. The window in the front room was jammed fast, and even if I broke the glass there wasn't much chance of surviving a jump down into the street. I wasn't going to get far with a broken leg, and my back was already painful enough to slow me down without that.

I went through to the back room and tried to reach the hatch into the loft. The room was tiny and had a low

ceiling. I could touch the hatch without straining. I got the
gutting knife from my pocket, wrapped my jersey around
my hand, and gave the hatch a good thump with the
handle. The thump seemed to echo through the house. I
listened, but there was no sound from downstairs. The
hatch hadn't moved. I braced myself for a leap, and hit the
hatch as hard as I could with the muffled handle of the
knife. The hatch lifted. Two more tries, and it slid sideways. I put the knife back into my belt and pulled my jersey
over my head. This was going to be my one chance. Sweat
was pouring down my face. I could hear the blood pounding in my head. I crouched down and braced myself.
Taking a deep breath, I launched myself up into the hatch
and was over the edge with one jump, clinging to the
wooden beams and flailing my legs to keep my balance.
With a crash, the hatch slammed back inside the loft, and
I was over the edge, scrambling among the cobwebs and
thick dust that choked the air. I took a deep breath and
prayed. I could see thin daylight through the broken tiles,
and smell the sea and acrid smoke of the curing houses. A
herring gull flew low over the shabby buildings, and landed
on the roof. It was time to go. I started to edge my way
warily along the cramped loft, terrified of putting my foot
through a ceiling, breathing nothing but filthy dust and
covering my face with a handkerchief as thick layers of
cobwebs matted my hair. This was my climb to freedom.

Seven

Fortune walked with me that morning. When I reached the brick wall that told me I was over the end house, I knelt down and searched for the hatch. It was in the middle of the floor. No sound came from the sleeping house. If the hatch was stiff, I couldn't escape without making a noise and waking the people in the bedroom. But I couldn't hear a thing. I knelt for minutes, holding my breath, trying to hear. A mouse scuttled across the rafters and a seagull landed on the tiles, but there was no sound from down below. I eased my gutting knife under the edge of the hatch, lifted it, and peered through. The room was empty. Thin dawn light drained into the room from a broken window. I dropped to the floor and waited for a sound from the other rooms or from downstairs. But there was nobody in the house. It was deserted. I ran down the narrow stairs and straight out into the back yard. I was free.

Trusting the light at the estuary, it had to be about four o'clock in the morning. I made my way slowly along the dilapidated rows of houses and courtyards, the warren of one-room tenements. There were lights still showing in some of the houses, lamps kept burning all night to discourage the bugs. In some of the narrow yards, doors had been torn off houses for firewood, and the inmates slept in the yards, preferring the cobbles to the stench and vermin inside. A cart trundled past me, collecting the night refuse for the nightman's yard, and at the end of one bleak street I saw the huge pile of dung and refuse, as big as one of the tenement houses, reeking in the dawn heat. Far away, I could hear shouts and cries: men working on the quays, lumpers unloading and preparing the catch for the market.

A couple of women passed me, staggering in the half-light, their faces pocked with smallpox scars. One of the women giggled and held on to my arm drunkenly. 'You lost your fancy, darling?' she whispered.

It might help if I had two women with me. I kissed the woman on the cheek and started walking on. She clung to my arm and her friend trailed behind, stopping every few yards to lean in doorways, belching and calling to her friend.

'Where we going, darling?' the woman at my side asked.

'You hungry?'

'I could eat you, lovely.'

'There's a market somewhere down these lanes.'

'Hold on, Cathy,' the friend shouted after us.

We waited for her. I showed them some silver and said I needed food. They seemed to find that hilarious, but stumbled along the street with me, stopping every few minutes to get their breath, laughing helplessly at my need for food. When we reached the market I gave them a silver coin each and pushed them away. I was gone before they could argue.

The market was beginning to come alive. Carts were unloading produce from the surrounding countryside, and a milk wagon was delivering fresh milk from the dairies. Several stallholders were drinking tea around a freshly lit brazier, and I bought a thick slice of bread and cheddar cheese and swallowed the food with hot tea. At this rate, I would soon have hardly any money left in the money-belt. When the food was finished, I walked on round the market, and at last found a stall that looked likely.

It was a vegetable stall, close to the entrance to the market. A couple of lads were unloading vegetables from a cart, and a woman was busy setting the goods out on display. There was no man in sight. I wandered up to the woman and bought an apple, paying her more than she asked. She glanced at me when I gave her the money. 'You come into money, stranger?'

'I earned every penny,' I said.

She stared at my fisherman's clothes and nodded. I must have looked filthy, and my back was throbbing with swollen pain. I guessed the wounds were infected after the night in the bed of straw.

'Earned it hard, by the looks,' the woman said and smiled. Her hair was grey, though she looked not much more than forty. She went on hefting the vegetables on to the stall and arranging them ready for the day's crowds.

'You bring your produce from outside town?' I asked.

'That's right. Marshchapel.'

'Is that far?'

'A few miles. Down the coast.'

She paused, taking a breath, watching me warily.

'I need a ride.'

'I thought so.'

'I can pay.'

'You in trouble?'

'I got flogged when my skipper snagged a trawl.'

'Oh yes?'

'It wasn't my fault.'

'They're expensive things, trawl nets,' she said thoughtfully.

'I told you. It was nothing to do with me. He was drunk.'

'Aren't they always,' she said bitterly. She paused, staring at her sons. They were just finishing unloading the cart. The horse pawed impatiently at the ground. The boys watched us without taking much notice. 'I don't want my boys getting into trouble,' she said quietly.

'A sovereign,' I said. I knew she wouldn't earn that much in a day. She would be lucky to clear it in several days. She blinked, her cheeks colouring slightly. I took her hand, and put the money into her palm. She said nothing, staring at the money in her hand.

'I'll tell them I hid if we get caught,' I said.

'Who's looking for you?'

'Henry Mundol. It was one of his trawlers.'

She blenched, glancing at me in quick fear, then nodded and turned away. 'That bastard,' she said under her breath. 'You better get under the sacks. Don't let anybody see you.'

I slipped beneath the sacks on the back of the cart and felt more sacks being thrown on top of me. I closed my eyes in the warm darkness, and said a prayer: I had not said so many prayers in all my previous twenty-two years. I couldn't do much about it if they weren't answered.

And then we were off. The cart rumbled round and the horse neighed against the reins. I could feel the wooden wheels turning over the cobbled ground of the market. Men and women shouted greetings to the boys. The cart seemed to spin and lurch in several directions at once as we got out of the market and into the main street, and then we were trotting at a great pace away from the busy noises. I could hear the sound of clogs as workers made their way down to the docks, and seagulls screamed overhead, but I had no clear idea where we were. We were heading rapidly out of town, and that was all that bothered me.

I suppose I was under the sacks no more than two hours. We stopped at one point for half an hour, and when I lifted the sacks and peeped out, I saw the lads having a beer at a pub. When they finally got back in the cart, one of them whispered to me that they always stopped at that pub and it would have looked strange if they hadn't. They delivered some potatoes while they were having a beer. I must have fallen asleep, trusting to the journey to bring me somewhere safe, because when the cart suddenly stopped, I had no idea where I was, only buried under piles of old sacks.

But I could hear the sea. I pushed the sacks aside and climbed out of the cart. The boys were standing a few yards away, smoking pipes. They had brought me along the coast, out to the dunes. There was nothing to be seen for miles. Herring gulls and curlews swooped and mourned along the shores. The sky was huge with cloud and pale sunlight. To the west, the range of hills lay low and dark on the horizon. Beyond the hills lay Lincoln, and the treadmill and oakum-picking wards of the prison. I stumbled, climbing down from the cart, and went up to the two boys.

'I'm grateful.'

'You paid our mother well.'

'She's an honest woman,' I said.

'This is Donna Nook,' one of the boys told me. He nodded along the coast southwards away from Grimsby. 'You keep going along the coast, you'll come to the cockle beds. You should be able to hide there safe enough. You know where you're making for?'

'No.'

'Just out of town,' the younger boy laughed.

'That's right.'

'We got to be going,' the first boy said without humour. 'We don't want to be seen out here with you. Henry Mundol's got friends. Our village is back there,' he added, nodding inland.

'Marshchapel.'

'You know?'

'Your mother told me.'

'She's too kind-hearted,' the older brother said angrily. 'You better forget we live in Marshchapel. We brought you as far as we dare, now we got to go.'

They got back into the cart and I stood and watched them leave.

I was alone now. I started out along the dunes, making towards the cockle beds. If I could get some sleep and walk at night I might stand a chance of finding my way south. I had some money left. In another port, I would have friends who could help me find a berth and I could forget all about *Happy Jack* and Henry Mundol's men. The papers I had signed had simply been for the summer trip to the grounds, and they could manage without me. They would soon find somebody else, and it wasn't like signing indentures when you sold yourself for years at a time. Nobody was going to bother searching for a fisherman for breaking his word on a single voyage.

I felt a strange excitement, being out on the dunes. The foreshore was deserted except for the thousands of waders, screaming and wheeling along the tideline, digging and diving for food. On the banks out along the shore, hundreds of herring gulls cried in the early sunlight. The dunes were soft and yellow, and thick with marram grass. I rolled down one of the dunes and forgot about the pain in my back. I still had some bread in my pocket, and ate it thankfully as I walked. Far out on the sandbars, the tide roared and heaved steadily, a great thundering background of noise to the endless cries of the seabirds. I reached the end of the dunes and stared out across the cockle beds. The dunes were high and full of tall grasses. I sat down and watched the sea for a long time. The sun was climbing in the sky now, and pink light splintered a grey mist far out at sea. I was exhausted. I lay down among the marram grass, closed my eyes, and went to sleep.

Eight

The sun was high in the blistering sky when I woke up, blood red in the cloudless blue. Brilliant heat dazzled my eyes and buzzed inside my head. I turned awkwardly on my side and felt the sand against my face. My skin was tight with sunlight. I was dozing, listening to the throbbing hum of the countryside, the dizzying racket of skylarks and crickets. Then I came out of sleep abruptly, hearing the melancholy cry of curlews, the squabbling racket of herring gulls, and another sound: a human voice at the tideline: a girl singing.

I eased myself up on to my elbows and parted the thick marram grass. I could hear the grass singing as a soft wind moved through the blades. But it was not the grass singing down at the edge of the sea.

There was a girl dancing on the water. She shimmered and hovered on the flat surface of the sea, her legs long and white, her blonde hair hanging loosely down to her waist. As she moved, her hair swayed and blew around her shoulders, and she seemed to be going deeper into the shallow water, away from a swarm of sanderling running busily along the edge of the tide, searching and bobbing for food. Further inshore, turnstones dotted the sands and curlews stabbed and dived for lugworms. The girl sang in a high, strange voice: a keening to the tumbling waves, a sound that came and went with the thundering of the tide so that I wasn't sure at first it wasn't the wind in the marram grass singing. But I knew it was the girl.

I stood up and waited until she saw me. She was collecting cockles or whelks from the tide. Now that I was awake, I could see the cockle rake in her hand. There were cockle beds the length of the estuary, and itinerant cockle-gatherers with their horses and carts worked from Grimsby out to Marshchapel and Horse Shoe Point and even to Donna Nook beyond the estuary limits, collecting and boiling their cockles during the week and then selling them round the farms and in Grimsby from pony and trap. The girl must be one of them.

She worked steadily along the tideline, gathering the cockles into the bag hung over her shoulder. The light and heat on the sea had given the impression that she was dancing, though she moved so gracefully she might well have been, long-legged and confident as she worked the shallow waters. When she turned in a wide circle to search for more cockles, she saw me and stopped abruptly, startled by the apparition. I lifted my arm in a friendly wave, knowing she would be frightened. I started my walk down towards the sea, going slowly so as not to scare her.

'I'm sorry,' I called as I walked. 'I didn't mean to disturb you.'

She said nothing: watching me warily, holding the cockle basket on her hip. The sun was behind her and her hair glistened in the sunlight. She was up to her knees in water, the tide washing around her legs, drops of water draining from the basket into the surf. She was wearing the kind of hessian apron the herring girls wear when they are gutting the herring, but her legs were bare. The bottom of her dress looked black where it had been soaked by the splashing waves.

She didn't move. She watched me cautiously, cool and reserved, self-controlled, her skin pale, her blue-grey eyes watchful, direct. I walked towards her, trying not to frighten her, desperate that she shouldn't suddenly turn and run away. She might go for help and raise the alarm. She might scream out loud. But she didn't move. She didn't flinch or take her eyes off my face. I reached the tide-line, and stood facing her. She was a few feet away from me, the plunging waves splashing around her knees.

Now that I was at the tideline, I couldn't speak.

I felt sickened with shock.

Her face was thin and bony, angular, and she had enormous grey eyes, like a seagull, watching me with a calm wary interest. Her pale skin had the pallor of sickness: drawn, unhealthy. Her hair fell to her waist and was wet at the ends where the waves had splashed her. I was surprised that her skin was so white, spending her life out on the shores. The salt winds should have tanned her lovely face dark brown.

I couldn't speak because of the sores on her face and neck: wet, seeping wounds of scrofula or something worse. I felt my throat going dry, and my face flushing red. They reckoned the swollen glands of scrofula were the first sign of consumption. The girl was thin enough for consumption. I swallowed hard and she smiled, her hand going quickly to her mouth, her eyes seeing everything that was in my mind. I couldn't take my eyes off the weeping sores. She was waiting for my reaction: judging me calmly with her quiet mocking eyes.

'I thought you were dancing,' I said foolishly.

'What would I want to be dancing for?'

'It was the light.'

'An illusion,' she said levelly.

She had a cool, remote voice, emotionless and sharp, without any accent I could recognise. It was reserved, withdrawn, as if she knew her superiority to the people around her. Her eyes were full of mocking laughter, a wild amusement shining through the shyness.

'Yes,' I said. 'I suppose. But it looked as if you were dancing.'

She studied my face for a moment, as if I might be daft, and then spoke matter-of-factly, dismissing my fantasy. 'I collect cockles for the trade,' she said calmly. 'Jacob sells them.'

'Jacob?'

'He's the cockler. He lives in Saltfleet. He boils them during the week and we take them round the farms and villages. Or in to Grimsby,' she added, without changing her expression. 'There's a good trade in Satan's Hole on Saturday nights.'

'You have a fine bagful there,' I said, nodding at the sack hanging from her shoulder.

She laughed. 'It's magic,' she said.

'Magic?'

'A magic gift. I sing them out of the sea.'

'Oh yes,' I scoffed.

'So people say,' she said nodding solemnly.

I couldn't tell if she was making fun of me, and felt a strange resentment: why should I care whether a cockle girl teased me about magic or thought me ridiculous. I had more serious things to worry about than magic. But I still couldn't concentrate. I couldn't fathom the expression in her eyes, the tight line of her smile. I wanted her to trust me, but we were like two birds, watching each other, alert and on guard for danger.

'Do you live nearby?' I asked.

She nodded along the shores, and I turned, noticing the small wooden house for the first time, a white-painted hut perched on the edge of the dunes. It must have been hidden by the slope of the dunes and the marram grass when I was sleeping. I looked back at the girl.

'You live there?' I said, surprised.

'Some of the time. And in town. I have friends in Grimsby.'

I wondered why she hadn't seen me if she had been in the wooden house overnight. I was suspicious suddenly. 'I was sleeping,' I told her, nodding towards the dunes. 'In the dunes.'

'I know.'

'You saw me!'

'You came at dawn. From the market.'

If she had seen me at dawn, there had been plenty of time to sound the alarm and Henry Mundol and his men would have been here by now. So she hadn't warned anybody, or gone to fetch help.

'I wouldn't,' she said suddenly, startling me with her soft words.

My suspicions must have been obvious from my troubled face.

'Wouldn't?'

'Tell anybody you were here.'

I seemed to be in a trance. My thoughts were incoherent, muddled. I kept wanting to sit down on the white sands and talk to the girl. I must be more tired than I realised, exhausted by my night in Praying Billy's filthy hovel in Newbiggin Lanes. My wounds were beginning to hurt again, the flesh tender, the cuts swollen and throbbing. I eased my shoulders and winced. I closed my eyes and then opened them suddenly.

I saw a longboat moving slowly out beyond the banks. It must have been there all the time, but the sunlight had blinded my eyes. It was half a mile away, and there was a single fisherman putting out his lines. As the longboat drew closer to the shore, I knelt down at the edge of the tide and cooled my hands in the water.

'I was trying to find my way south,' I explained, avoiding her eyes. 'Yarmouth maybe, Lowestoft. I work the liners.'

'You don't have to tell me.'

'It must have looked odd, finding me asleep in the dunes.'

'Lots of boys come this way,' she said. 'Not so many grown men. They don't like the fishing and try to get away. They rarely succeed. Henry Mundol's men usually catch them if they come this way.'

I stared at her, listening to the matter-of-fact way she described what went on: absconding boys fleeing from the fleets, grown fishermen trying to find their way south to happier ports. I felt like a child, caught out in some harmless dishonesty.

'I have food,' the girl said briskly. 'You must be hungry?'

'I had bread and cheese earlier,' I said.

'That won't give you much strength,' she said drily.

I seemed unable to string my words together. 'I'm tired,' I laughed ruefully.

I felt helpless, without willpower. I kept watching the girl's lovely face, the horrible sores on her cheeks and long neck. I could hear a bell clanging at the estuary. I smiled at the girl and she glanced over her shoulder. The longboat had dropped an anchor. The fisherman was standing in the bows, shimmering in the sunlight as the girl had shimmered, looking as if he was walking on the sultry muddy sea.

Then the fog started. It rolled in off the banks like a cold white mist, drifting across the surface of the water and then thickening and closing round us. A bell clanged far away, the sound drifting from the buoy in the estuary. It was a dense summer fog, lifting off the hot August sea and swallowing us in cold silence. I could hear the heat rising off the sea, and the bell ringing on the buoy, and then everything was gone, I could see nothing, I was alone with the girl.

'We should take shelter,' I said without much interest.

'Listen,' the girl said quietly.

In fogs along the coast you can hear every sound. Sound carries for miles. The girl was a few feet away from me, but I could hear her quiet breathing, the splash of gentle waves against her legs. The man in the longboat was testing his lines, weighing them in his hands, making sure the pull of the tide was right. I could hear everything he did. Yet the fog was like a silent wall, so thick I couldn't see my hand. I couldn't see a thing. Then I heard the fisherman talking. I heard him talking to a companion.

'Are you all right, Jacob?'

'Yes, I am.'

'What are you doing?'

'I'm laying my lines. Can't you see that?'

'Are there fish about?'

'There's always plenty of fish along these shores.'

'Lay your lines carefully, Jacob.'

'I do that.'

'Lay them to the right side.'

'I always do.'

There was a long silence.

I stopped breathing. I held myself still in the dense wet fog. I could feel it moving against my face.

Then the girl's voice came through the mist. 'Did you hear them?' she asked from the tide, softly, patiently, as if she had been waiting for my answer for a long time. I had no sense of time.

'Yes,' I answered.

The fog lifted as I spoke. A wind seemed to touch my face and thin light shivered through the whiteness. I could still hear the bell clanging on the fog buoy, but sunlight streamed down to the sands and suddenly there were hundreds of sanderling scurrying around my feet, plovers and curlews stalking up and down at the tideline. They had been there all the time, but making no sound. The fog drifted and rolled away and I stared at the girl. She was watching me, holding the basket in the same place on her hip. I stared out to the longboat. The fisherman was still there, standing in the bows, watching the movement of his lines.

'He's alone,' I said faintly, startled, suddenly frightened.

'Is he?'

'He was talking to somebody.'

'They must have been in another boat.'

'Yes.'

'Or further down the coast. Sound carries in these fogs.'

'Yes.'

I didn't believe her. I knew she was lying, waiting for me to speak.

'Did you hear them then?' she asked again.

'I told you,' I said angrily.

'Yes, you did.'

She was really smiling now, her face fresh and open, her eyes alive and kind. She reached her hand out towards me.

'Let me help,' she said.

I stared at the man in his longboat, still testing his lines, and then back at the girl.

'What do they call you?' I asked.

'Elizabeth Anstey.'

'Elizabeth,' I repeated, feeling the name on my tongue.

'What do they call you?' she said.

'Matthew Lidgard.'

Along the deserted shore, curlews cried forlornly. A cormorant scudded above the white surf. Above us in a suddenly piercingly blue sky, the blue of the soul and constancy, skylarks flashed and sang.

Nine

Suddenly the girl went very still. She seemed to be smelling the air, reaching for a sound I couldn't hear. She had her eyes tightly closed, and her head lifted to the stillness.

'What is it?'

'Can't you hear?' she whispered with surprise, opening her eyes with a start, concentrating on the horizon.

I tensed myself, straining to hear anything above the clamour of the seabirds and the roar of surf. I could hear nothing. I wondered if the constant roar of the sea was living inside my head, deafening me to all other sound.

The girl waded abruptly out of the water and knelt down on the ribbed sands. She put her ear to the wet sands, lifting her hair free with one of her hands. She knelt like this for several seconds, then leapt up.

'Horses,' she explained. 'You must swim.'

'Swim?'

'Out to the longboat.' She pointed, grabbing my arm and pushing me into the cold water.

'It's half a mile,' I protested.

'He's coming closer,' the girl hissed. '*Swim!*'

I saw that the longboat was moving quickly towards the shore, bobbing up and down on the rougher waves. I

paused for a second, glanced down the coast back towards
Grimsby, and then ran plunging into the sea. I could hear
no horses, see no cloud of dust rising from their hooves,
but I knew the girl was right. There were horses thundering along the foreshore and they would be here within
minutes. They could only be looking for me.

I forced myself through the rough waves closer to the
shore and then dived into the sea, swimming as hard as I
could. I thanked God my father had taught me to swim:
most fishermen don't bother learning; being able to swim
didn't save you from freezing to death when you were
fishing off Iceland or in the White Sea. I swam as hard as
I ever had in my life, and reached the longboat within
minutes.

The fisherman in the longboat had already dropped his
anchor and was pretending to lay fresh lines. As I floundered at the side of the boat, he stood in the bows, staring
down the coast, a broad-shouldered, bearded man with
tattoos on his arms and a gold ear-ring in his right ear. He
ignored me as I splashed alongside. 'Get round to starboard,' he said flatly, his voice thick with phlegm. I didn't
argue. I swam round the longboat and bobbed up and
down as the tide rocked the boat. I could see nothing from
here, and went underwater to get back to the stern. I lifted
my head from the wash of small waves and cleared the salt
water out of my eyes.

'Don't get yourself seen, lad,' the fisherman growled at
me.

I kept low in the water. The fisherman went on working
his lines. He must have had a second set in the bottom of
the longboat.

I could see the horses now. There were a dozen riders,
bearing down from the sand-dunes to the cockle beds. The
girl was working her way along the tideline, the cockle
basket on her hip, her back to the riders. As they galloped

through the surf at the tideline, I expected her to turn round, but she went on with her work, bending down and collecting shellfish, tossing the hair out of her eyes. I suddenly felt frightened for her. I had abandoned her on the foreshore, where Henry Mundol's men could find her with no trouble.

I saw the horses rein in and snort and stamp at the tideline, then I heard one of the riders shout. 'You been here all morning, girl?' The girl turned and seemed to chat with them, nodding and pushing the hair out of her eyes, showing them the shellfish she had in her basket. The men on horses were laughing.

'Search the hut,' one of them shouted.

Three riders spurred their horses back up the sand-dunes and towards the house. The girl watched them impassively. They dismounted and went inside the wooden hut. I could hear their laughter and there was a deal of crashing about, then a window glass broke.

The girl turned and spoke to the nearest rider.

'Hurry up, you lot,' the man shouted.

There was another crash from inside the hut and the three men emerged, one of them waving white clothing in the air and swinging it round above his head. Several of the men at the tideline burst out laughing. The girl shook her head. She didn't seem scared. She stared at the men, but I couldn't see her face. I felt for the knife in my belt and put my hand on the gunwales of the longboat.

'Get out of sight,' the fisherman said angrily, catching my fingers with his iron-nailed boots. I slipped back into the water, nearly yelling at the pain in my hand. When I came to the surface, two of the men at the tideline were getting off their horses and walking towards the girl, and the three men at the wooden house were stumbling down the sand-dunes to join them. I saw the girl begin to walk backwards into the sea. She was still holding the basket.

The next second one of the men had started to wade in after her and she dropped the basket and was crouching down, holding a knife in her right hand. The steel blade glinted in the sunlight.

'We have to help her,' I spluttered in the water.

I could see the fisherman hesitating. He had the iron hook used for recovering the lines in his left hand. 'You wait till I say, lad,' he growled unpleasantly.

'She's in danger.'

'She knows how to look after herself, our Elizabeth. She's had to learn. You keep yourself quiet.'

'For God's sake . . .'

I was about to lift myself out of the water and start back for the shore when there was a shout from the dunes. I cleared my eyes and looked. A new horseman had ridden out of the sunlight and was sitting at the top of the dunes. He was shouting something to the men. He was dressed entirely in black, and his grey hair looked cropped to his skull. His voice cracked in the silence, and the two men at the tideline went back to their horses immediately in panic. The men floundering down the sand-dunes turned round and went back to the wooden hut where they had left their horses cropping seagrass. The single rider spurred his horse down the dunes towards the tideline and the group of confused riders.

At the tideline, he reined his horse in and stood watching the longboat, a hand shielding his eyes from the sun. I went down into the sea and swam underneath the surface back to the starboard side of the longboat. I couldn't hear a thing until I lifted my head above the waves, and then I could see nothing.

'Is he here?' the hard-voiced stranger shouted.

'No, sir,' the fisherman answered. 'I reckon not.'

There was a pause, then the man shouted again, a crude warning. 'I know your face, fisherman.'

'Yes, sir, I reckon you do.'

In the stillness, I could hear the herring gulls screaming out on the sandbars. The tide thundered and roared as it turned. There would soon be deep waters flooding to the shore, carrying the longboat closer to the men.

'Don't prove yourself a liar, fisherman,' the hard voice shouted after a long silence. 'I know where you are, and I don't forget faces.'

'I know where you are n'all,' the fisherman in the longboat grunted under his breath. 'Evil bastard.'

There was another pause, and then the sound of horses moving off noisily through the surf. 'Henry Mundol thanks you for your help,' the man shouted as they left.

'Thank you, sir,' I heard the girl answering.

I hoisted myself on to the side of the longboat and watched the horsemen riding back down the shores. 'Who was that?' I asked when I caught my breath.

'Augustus Jackson,' the man in the boat told me. 'Henry Mundol's overseer. Looks after the fleets mainly. Does his dirty work for him.'

On the shores, I could see the girl making her way up to her cottage on the dunes. The riders had almost disappeared.

'You murder somebody?' the fisherman laughed coarsely, giving me a hand into the longboat.

'No, I didn't, but I might.'

'No offence, stranger. What did you do then?'

'I was flogged, on one of Mundol's vessels.'

'And ran for it?'

'That's right.'

'Which vessel?'

'*Happy Jack*.'

'Ben Lowther,' the fisherman said and nodded. 'Drunken fool. He's not fit to take the tiller, but Henry Mundol don't have much choice. He takes what he can get these days. Which means drunkards like Ben Lowther.'

'I didn't do anything,' I said, trying to dry my face on an old jersey he handed me. 'I was on watch . . .'

'You don't need to do anything. But Mundol can't let men run for it. Too many indentured boys trying to break free. He can't have grown men leaving their agreements. You'll be an example. He'll get you back or hurt somebody trying.'

I glanced towards the wooden house on the dunes. 'Elizabeth,' I said under my breath.

'Not this time.'

'Do you know her?'

'I'll take you ashore,' he said, ignoring my question.

'Do you?'

'You sure you didn't get a flogging for asking questions, stranger,' he said, and roared with laughter as he rowed the longboat closer to shore. When we were near enough, he told me to wade the rest of the way.

'I'll go on with my fishing,' he said with a grin.

'You were really after fish?'

'Some of us got to earn a living.'

'You haven't earned much today,' I said ruefully.

When we reached the shallow water, I climbed overboard and started wading ashore. By the time I remembered the strange voices in the fog, he was already working his way back out to sea. '*Are* you called Jacob,' I shouted, floundering in the white surf, but he didn't turn to answer. With a shrug, I walked across the sands to the dunes, and began to climb up to the wooden hut in my heavy, drenched clothes.

Ten

The girl came out of the hut as I reached the dunes. She watched me floundering up the dune through the fine sand, her hands on her waist, her hair now tied back behind her ears. I was sweating by the time I got to the top of the sloping dunes, sand cascading around my boots, my clothes beginning to dry in the afternoon sun.

She smiled and waited until I caught my breath.

'Did they hurt you?' I asked her.

'No.'

'I was going to come ashore.'

'That would have been daft after all my efforts. I'm used to Henry Mundol's men. They wouldn't have hurt me. They know me too well.'

I shrugged, staring out to sea where the fisherman had retrieved his original lines and was at last hauling fish on board. 'Have they done much damage?' I asked, nodding towards the hut.

She shrugged. 'No. I have some peppermint tea ready for you.' Before I could say anything she went inside and emerged seconds later with two china cups decorated with blue speedwell. The tea smelled spicy and delicate.

It had been cooling down and I drank it quickly, enjoying the refreshing taste. She poured me a second cup.

'I need to get dry,' I said. 'My clothes . . .'

'I have clothes inside.'

I stared at her, surprised, confused.

'They should fit you,' she said, ignoring the question in my eyes.

I drank the second cup of tea and couldn't take my eyes off her face: the lovely wide mouth, the scornful eyes.

'You shouldn't be out here alone,' I said gently, 'whatever you say about knowing Henry Mundol's men.'

She recognised the concern in my voice, but it seemed to amuse her, her grey eyes flickering with mockery, her mouth tightening into a suppressed smile. 'Do you think they would want me,' she said scornfully. 'Like this?' She touched the sores on her cheek with the tips of her fingers. I felt ashamed. I shook my head and looked down at the white sand. How could I say no woman would be safe with the kind of men who spent months at sea on filthy, crowded fishing smacks, no matter what she looked like. They could always shut their eyes.

I looked up, and was surprised to see the humour in her eyes. She was laughing at me. 'I would need to change,' she said teasingly, delighting in my embarrassment, enjoying her own good humour. 'I would need to transform myself into a mermaid.'

'I don't think so, Elizabeth,' I told her, saying her name for the first time, forcing her to pay attention.

But she ignored me. 'I *could* change,' she said thoughtfully. There was something taunting in her voice, but also a melancholy, a regret I didn't understand. She threw her head back and touched one of the sores on her neck. It was red and weeping. I wondered if she was suffering some kind of shock, or had added something to the peppermint tea. She seemed to be pulling at the sore as if determined to tear it off her skin, and I knew she was in despair, horrified by her own disfigurement, frantic with a wild longing for her real beauty.

'Don't!' I shouted, stepping towards her. 'Elizabeth! You mustn't!'

'Keep away,' she shouted at me, her eyes sparkling with laughter. 'Get back.' Then she pulled her hand away from her neck, and the weeping sore was gone, and she was flinging it gaily to the ground at my feet.

I stared at her in stunned horror. But there was no blood. There was no wound. Where the sore had been, the skin was slightly red and mottled, but there was no sign of blood. She took another of the sores and peeled it away, and then touched her cheeks with both hands and pulled at the pockmarked flesh until every sign of sickness had gone and her face was pale and clear and lovely as the face of a child, except for the rapidly disappearing red marks which faded as she massaged her cheeks and neck and waited for me to recover.

'It's a trick I learned from the beggars,' she told me after a pause.

'Beggars!'

I knew beggars used tricks to earn pity: soap and vinegar to look like yellow matter-filled blisters; lumps of raw meat under elaborate clotted dressings. But Elizabeth wasn't a beggar.

'I don't understand,' I said. 'You work the cockle beds.'

'Oh, I'm not a beggar,' she agreed. 'But I know some, in Satan's Hole. The town is full of beggars. I do it to protect myself.'

'From Henry Mundol's men?'

'From any men,' she said with a rueful laugh.

I thought briefly about Praying Billy, his tongue gummed to the bottom of his mouth, his quick hand freeing him into foul speech. But Elizabeth's transformation

was not into wickedness. Her transformation was into freedom and beauty.

'You seem disappointed,' she said gaily, running her
hands through her hair. 'Don't you prefer mermaids to
beggar girls?'

I laughed nervously, smiling at her. 'Mermaids lure men
to their deaths,' I pointed out. 'I like life.'

She grinned and fetched some more peppermint tea,
and when we had drunk the tea I went inside the wooden
hut and changed into clean trousers and a blue jersey and
a pair of leather boots. It was strange that she should have
men's clothing in the hut, and even stranger that it was all
fishermen's gear, including several pairs of fearnoughts
and three blue gansey jerseys. But I didn't want to ask
questions. I hung my own clothes out to dry in the sun,
and went back to Elizabeth at the tideline where she was
gathering her cockle baskets into a pile.

'We must walk down to the creeks and get some fish,'
she told me.

'We have no lines.'

She held up a wooden stave with a knife fastened to the
end with string. 'Butt-pricking,' she explained. 'The people
in the villages all do it. There's lovely plaice in the creeks.
We'll get ourselves some lunch and have a glass of corn
brandy.'

We walked along the tideline together. Elizabeth still
seemed amused by her transformation and kept laughing,
holding her hand up to her mouth and shaking her head in
apology.

'I don't mean to laugh at you, Matthew.'

'But you are.'

'Your face!'

'Thank you.'

'And you were so polite.'

I blushed and kicked at the sands, annoyed that she

should take me for a fool. 'I hope Henry Mundol's men don't come back,' I said, 'because I shan't protect you.'

'Yes, you will.'

'I shan't.'

'You're a natural born gentleman.'

We reached the creek and waded into the shallow water. Flatfish like the sandy or muddy bottoms of creeks. They lie flat and remain still when you start splashing about, and all you have to do is keep stabbing into the water with the butt-prick until you catch yourself a fine specimen. Elizabeth seemed to have the gift: she caught two huge flapping plaice and hoisted them over her shoulder in less than ten minutes. I just stood and watched her in admiration.

Back at the ramshackle hut, we lit a fire on the dunes and got the fish frying in a pan. Elizabeth had bread and fresh butter and a bottle of corn brandy. While the food was cooking, she insisted on seeing my back, and rubbed soothing ointment on to the wounds where the salt water had made them sore and white. The ointment was powerful and the pain soon eased.

'You must be a witch,' I told her, laughing as she dried her hands.

'I am,' she said seriously, and then giggled as she served the fish on to tin plates, the kind of plates we used on fishing smacks. 'I know about herbs, that's all,' she explained. 'You shouldn't go calling people witches round here, they're very superstitious. It's worse than being a Catholic.'

'Are you a Catholic?'

'I am,' she said simply. 'Why else do you think I live out here on my own?'

I glanced at her sceptically. There were plenty of Catholics living around the fishing ports: most of the work building the pontoons had been done by Irish navvies, and they brought their priests with them.

'I thought you had friends in town,' I said sarcastically.
She looked up at me with surprise. 'I do,' she said.
'Then why did you say . . .'
She smiled then and bit her lip. I thought she was going
to burst out laughing, but she shook her head and stared
down into the fire. 'I was joking,' she said quietly. 'Sorry.'

I finished the steaks of fried fish and mopped the plate
with the bread. The corn brandy was strong and cool. She
must have kept it in a stone bottle in the hut. I closed my
eyes and felt the afternoon sun gentle on my face now that
the heat was sinking to the west.

'Do you often hear voices?' Elizabeth suddenly asked.
I opened my eyes quickly. 'Voices?'
'In the fog, the men talking on the fishing boat.'
'That was an illusion.'
'Oh yes.'
'Another boat, further down the coast.'
'Yes,' she nodded, frowning, impatient. 'But do you?'
'I don't know what you're talking about,' I said, avoiding
her eyes.

She was quiet, insistent. Her voice made me look up.
She wasn't looking at me, but her whole body had become
still, concentrating on the fire, staring into the burning
embers. 'Yes you do,' she said softly.

I looked away and watched the fisherman in his longboat. He was sitting down, eating his own food. His boat
rode gently on the tide. 'I visited Lindisfarne earlier this
year,' I told her, trying to change the subject. 'I saw something strange there.'

'Yes?' she said, looking at me with interest.

I paused, listening to a herring gull, flying low over our
food, attracted by the fire. I looked out to sea, and saw a
cormorant riding the waves. For a moment, I seemed to be
somewhere else, listening to the immense underlying
silence of the shores, the sea slipping towards the estuary,

the sand shining and deserted, pools of water blinking like God's eyes, dazzling the cloudless horizon. I had listened to the silence many times before: curlews mourning all night at the tideline, terns with their haunting *keerree keerree*, herring gulls scrawling their wheeling sadness across the skies. It sometimes seemed to me that the foreshore was a constant dawn chorus, crying in my mind like the tides, mourning the desolation of our life at sea.

I closed my eyes briefly and then smiled at the girl. 'I saw a man wading into the water,' I told her, 'on the far side of the Island. And two otters, drying his feet.'

She snorted then, and reached across to slap my arm. 'You!' she said crossly.

'What!'

'I'm not stupid!'

'I don't know what you're talking about. I saw a man. It might have been in a dream but it was real enough to me and the otters were real . . .'

'That's St Cuthbert,' she almost shouted. 'Don't tell lies.'

'I'm not.'

'Did you think I wouldn't know?'

'I don't know anything about him,' I shouted indignantly.

'Oh, Matthew.'

'It's true. I'm not Catholic. I don't know about your saints.'

'They're your saints too,' she laughed impatiently, getting up and staring across the estuary to Spurn, shading her eyes from the brilliant dazzle of light off the sea. 'They're everybody's saints. St Cuthbert said his prayers in the sea, and the otters breathed on his hands and feet to warm them, and they dried him with their fur. He loved animals.'

I was still annoyed. 'Well, I don't know anything about

that,' I said. 'I know what I saw. I can't help it if you don't believe me.'

My words seemed to reach her at last, and she stared at me, her back to the light from the sea. She was serious suddenly, and interested, looking down at me as I lay comfortably beside the fire.

'Do you mean it?' she said in a quiet voice.

'Yes.'

She was thoughtful for some minutes, and then shrugged, and turned away. She seemed unhappy, and her eyes shone with tears. I struggled to my feet.

'I didn't mean to upset you.'

'If it was true.'

'It is true,' I insisted, taking her arm.

We sat down then and had some tea, brewed in a pot on the fire. I told her about my childhood in Staithes and how my father had drowned in a storm fishing on the Dogger Bank. 'He used to carry me on his shoulders,' I told her, 'telling me stories and showing me how to know the birds. He was always full of stories. He said the fish told them to him when he was working the lines at night, so that he wouldn't feel so lonely.' As I spoke, I felt the tears filling my eyes.

'And your mother?' Elizabeth asked gently.

'She couldn't manage without my father,' I said bleakly. 'She grieved until she died. I visited Lindisfarne because she'd been there. She went with her father. I think I went to try and find her.'

My face was wet with tears.

'So you're another orphan,' Elizabeth said sadly after a silence.

'Yes.'

'So many of the boys on the fishing are orphans,' she nodded. 'It's the only way the trawlers can get crews. Boys from orphanages and prisons, reformatories and workhouses. They take them to sea and they drown, if they don't go mad on whisky and disease. A lot of them escape to Satan's Hole, and hide with the women. Children who have to put a cross on their indentures because they can't even sign their own names.'

I listened to her clear voice: she was lost, abstracted, deep in some grief of her own, talking from a far place.

'Are your parents alive?' I asked her gently.

She shook her head and smiled sadly. 'My father was on the fishing. We lived in Yarmouth. They both died.'

She wasn't going to tell me how.

'And you live out here all alone?' I teased her.

'Some of the time.'

'Gathering cockles and buying fishermen's clothes and corn brandy.'

She glanced at me quickly and gave a rueful laugh. 'It's a good life,' she said firmly. 'Jacob sometimes catches sprats, and shrimps further up the coast. There are lots of shrimp boats working the estuary. He shares those with me because I help with the cockles. I like the work. I sometimes help on the stall or take whelks and cockles round to the farms in a basket. Like the Scottish girls. We get whelks, cuttlefish, crabs, lobsters. There are clams down Slate Run, if you have a spade to dig them out, and I sometimes find mussels. It's a good way of living.'

'But not what you really want,' I said dryly, watching her put on her fine performance.

She laughed. 'You *do* have the sight.'

'The sight! What's that?'

'You *see* things,' she said gaily, getting up to clear the plates and tea things. 'You *know* things.'

'I know you don't live out here on your own. You couldn't manage.'

'I told you, I stay in town sometimes. With the Sisters.'

'The Sisters?'

'In town. They have a Convent. I grew up there.'

'Is that the *friends* you were talking about?' I laughed.

'Yes. They brought me up.'

'Elizabeth Anstey!'

'It's true. They looked after me when my mother died, and they taught me about fishermen and beggars. I know how to survive. But I don't want to just survive,' she added quickly, her voice suddenly impassioned, her eyes wild with life. 'I don't want to live like this. I want to go to Lerwick. I want to know about the fishing. I bet you know about Lerwick.'

'Yes,' I said with surprise. Her rapid changes of mood were beyond me.

'And Iceland?'

'I've been to Iceland, yes.'

'On the summer season, long-lining?'

'That's right,' I laughed. 'Why on earth . . .'

'Because it's freedom. It's ordinary and it's freedom.'

'You don't know Iceland,' I said ironically.

'My father told me. He took me to Lerwick once, on one of his trips. The summer long-lining season. My mother rented a house on the lodberries and worked at the herring. I used to play on the quays, cartwheeling beside the water, helping my mother with the herring. She said I was never to work on the herring, but I loved it. Grey granite town on the edge of the green sea. My father coming back from the Faroes and Iceland. That was freedom. That was being free.'

'You have freedom out here,' I pointed out after a long silence.

'Not real freedom,' she sighed, breaking her own trance. 'Freedom is working for a living, away from all this sin and misery. Freedom is being allowed to earn your own food and build your own fire. That's what I want. Not being surrounded by orphaned children labouring to make riches for men like Henry Mundol. I want real freedom. I want to go to Lerwick.'

I had no idea what she was talking about. I stood and watched her, her fists clenched, her eyes shining with tears, her clear fine voice intense with hot passion. Then she turned to me and smiled. 'You do have the sight,' she said quietly. 'Whatever you say.' For the first time, I noticed that the man in the longboat had gone.

Eleven

Early in the evening, Elizabeth said she had to visit a friend in one of the villages. She wrapped a shawl around her shoulders and took a basket of shellfish. 'It would look odd if I didn't deliver as usual,' she said.

'Will you be long?'

'No. You must sleep. You need rest if we're going to get you away from here.'

She rubbed some more ointment into my shoulders and drying wounds. I could feel the scabs forming and the ointment eased the pain, making me feel drowsy. The salt air and heat of the day had healed my bruised face.

'Will you not tell me?' I asked as she prepared to leave.

'No, I won't. Now get some rest. I'll be back soon, I promise.'

The long summer twilight brought silence to the foreshore and the countryside. I could hear the liquid bubbling cry of the oyster-catchers on the dunes, and the hoot of an owl flying low over the empty countryside, but the herring gulls had quieted at last. To the west over the low range of hills the sun burned down the sky and then left darkness and shadows. The moon was rising slowly out of the sea over the estuary.

I slept for an hour or so, and when I woke the moon was high in the sky. Elizabeth was kneeling beside me, shaking my arm. 'It's time,' she whispered.

I got up urgently and glanced around. The dunes and foreshore were deserted. Lights shone dimly across the countryside from isolated farms, a cluster of village cottages. Far away up the coast, I could see the red light shining on the dock tower, the glow of gaslights like a shroud hanging over Grimsby. Across the estuary, fires flickered on Spurn.

'Come on, Matthew,' Elizabeth whispered, pulling my arm.

I followed her along the foreshore away from the cottage. The dunes sloped steadily downwards and eventually fell to the same level as the foreshore. Beyond the dunes, a large bonfire had been built. It was not visible from the wooden hut.

'When did you do this?' I asked.

'While you were sleeping.'

I saw a figure moving in the darkness beyond the bonfire.

'Is that Jacob?' I asked.

'He lives in Saltfleet, near Theddlethorpe Dunes. He helps us when he can.'

'So he is called Jacob?' I asked her innocently.

She glanced at me quickly, nervous and in a hurry. 'We haven't time for that, Matthew. Not now. We have to get you away. Augustus Jackson has put money on them finding you.'

'How much money?'

'Enough to interest starving men.'

At the bonfire, Jacob waited patiently.

'All right,' I nodded, sensing her urgency. 'What do you want me to do?'

'Wait here.'

She went over to the bonfire and whispered something to Jacob. Together, they started going round the heap of driftwood and dried seaweed, lighting sulphur matches and dropping them to the tinder. In the heat, there had been no rain for days, and the flames leapt instantly for the seaweed and then the cracking wood. Jacob watched the flames take hold and then began to throw fresh fuel on the fire. I joined him, working hard to keep the flames alive. Elizabeth gathered fresh armfuls of seaweed.

When the blaze was leaping to the night sky, we stood back and rested. Then I noticed that both Elizabeth and Jacob were staring across the estuary, not watching the bonfire at all. I looked up to see what they found of such interest. There were smacks in the estuary, some of them burning night fires in braziers in their sterns to warn other vessels. On Spurn itself, tiny lights shone from cottages and small fires.

Suddenly I saw a blaze towards the end of the spit of land, not far from the Smeaton Light. It must have been a huge bonfire. The flames sent a light burning across the estuary that nobody could have missed, and then within minutes the light had disappeared. Somebody must have doused it with sand or water. I turned, and found Elizabeth and Jacob doing the same, urgently throwing sand into our own bonfire, carrying buckets of water up from the sea and flinging them on the hot charred remains. Without a word, I joined them, helping douse the fire. I was sweating and feeling faint from the woodsmoke.

The fire was out at last.

'We have to hide,' Elizabeth told me.

We went up into the dunes and sat down at the highest spot. Jacob had slipped away, carrying the wooden buckets.

'Where's he gone?' I asked.

'To get the longboat. He often goes fishing at night. It looks better if he does what he always does.'

I took the flask she was holding out to me and drank gratefully: it was water, chilled from a stream. I cleaned my mouth and breathed fresh air. I handed the flask back to her but she shook her head, listening intently, watching the estuary. I could see her profile against the night sky, the faint moonlight rising from the sea. A plover rose in alarm not twenty yards from where we were sitting, and far away, I could hear a fox barking in the hills, and an answering bark from the nearer fields.

'Will they see the fire from town?' I asked.

'No, but maybe in Somercotes or Donna Nook. The isolated farms. They're always on the look out for smugglers.'

I knew there were smugglers working the coast: aniseed whisky and brandy, tobacco, cigars. The farmers collected the cargoes and carried them inland on carts. I began to feel nervous, glancing over my shoulder to the empty darkness, the silence that might hide any of Henry Mundol's men, or more dangerous characters, looking for something of value.

'Why do you do this, Elizabeth?' I asked abruptly, not thinking about the words, just saying them as they came into my head.

She didn't look at me, crouched and alert at the top of the dunes.

'Does it matter why?'

'You saved my life, but . . .'

'I haven't yet, and I would have done it for anybody.'

'Thanks.'

She turned, smiling in the darkness, regretting the haste of her words. 'I'm sorry, Matthew, but I would. Now be still, and let me listen. We need to be ready if they come.'

So we sat together in the darkness, the sky full of stars, the moonlight clear and shining on the calm sea. I breathed the rich scent of wild garlic, and heard animals rustling in the dunes. I closed my eyes, and felt the salt air on my lips.

In the quiet, I could not hear Elizabeth's breathing: she was like a stone, or a bird of prey, perfectly still, motionless, poised in her intent listening.

And then she was on her feet.

'Look,' she whispered, pointing out to sea.

I could see nothing.

'*Dancing Sally*,' she said with a clap of her hands.

'You're imagining things.'

'This side of the estuary buoy, a mile or so out to sea.'

I still couldn't see a vessel, but I took her hand and squeezed gently. She laughed, turning towards me, and then tensed suddenly, staring up the coast.

'They're coming,' she said in an urgent whisper.

She knelt down in the dunes and put her head close to the marram grass. She didn't need to listen for long. Leaping up, she strained her eyes to watch the sea. Her breathing was coming rapidly now, and when I tried to take her arm she pushed me away impatiently.

'Leave me!'

'Elizabeth . . .'

'They're on horses,' she said quickly. 'They could be here in minutes. You have to get out to the longboat.'

She was up and running for the foreshore. I followed her down to the tideline, floundering through the dunes and then out onto the firm sand. As we ran, I grabbed her arm and pulled her to a halt.

'Elizabeth!'

'There isn't time.'

'What about you?'

'We must hurry.'

She slipped free of my hand but I grabbed her again.

'I'm not going without you.'

'Don't be ridiculous, Matthew.'

'They can catch me.'

'After all this!' she said angrily. 'I shall be all right. They won't even see me. I have to get back inland or they will *know*, don't you see, they will find out about me and Jacob.'

'I don't care.'

I could hear the drumming of horses on the sands now. They must be riding directly along the foreshore. I tried to pull Elizabeth with me towards the sea but she suddenly bent towards me and the next thing I knew she had bitten my hand and was running away along the tideline.

'The longboat,' she shouted as she ran, and I glanced out to the white surf a hundred yards offshore where Jacob was waiting, standing in the stern of the longboat, waving his arm and shouting angrily.

'Come on, lad, come on.'

I turned away from Jacob and stared after Elizabeth. I could just make out her fleeing figure in the moonlight, running along the tideline, and then suddenly she seemed to change direction and made for the flat open fields behind the foreshore. There were no dunes here to hide her, only the open miles of the cockle beds and then the wide fields. I tried to see, but soon she had disappeared.

I had no choice. I plunged into the sea and began to wade out into the cold water. The horses were close now and I could hear voices shouting. I plunged into the water and swam as hard as I could, and within minutes was clambering aboard the longboat, Jacob's rough hands hauling me over the side and then thrusting an oar into my hands. We sat together at the rowlocks and rowed with all our strength.

'There they are!' a man yelled, and I heard the horses neighing and a great splashing at the edge of the tideline.

'Row,' Jacob hissed through his teeth. 'Row for your blasted life.'

I worked the oars until the blisters burst on my hands and my back felt like raw meat. Sweat was pouring down my face and into my eyes. I was soaked with seawater and sweat.

'I know you, fisherman!' a voice bellowed from the fore-shore. 'I shall make you sorry, you hear!'

'I know you n'all, Augustus Jackson,' Jacob muttered through his exertions. 'But you'll have to catch me first.'

We were half a mile offshore now, and Jacob eased the oars. He sat back on his pair, and gathered his breath. I turned round and looked to the shore. The men were visible at the tideline. There must have been a dozen of them. They sat for some minutes, watching us, and then I saw two of them turn and wheel away. They seemed to be making for the wooden hut where Elizabeth kept her few meagre possessions.

'She's not there,' I whispered thankfully under my breath.

It took the men minutes to fire the wooden house. They must have brought flares and tar with them. The house burned with brilliant flames, and I could see the horses at the tideline, stamping and splashing in the surf, frightened by the sudden fire. There was only one horse that seemed to be under control, the rider still and erect, staring relent-lessly out to our longboat. It was Jackson.

'He looks evil even at this distance,' I said in fear.

'He's an evil bastard fair enough,' Jacob agreed.

I prayed they wouldn't find Elizabeth: that she had made her way to safety, found friends in one of the villages.

'Will she be all right?' I asked.

'Aye,' Jacob nodded quietly. 'She can take care of her-self.'

'How do you know?'

'She's been doing it long enough.'

'But still . . .'

'She will have gone inland, to one of the farms.'

'You don't know that.'

He stared at me levelly, not speaking. He took his pipe from his pocket and started filling it.

'I know Elizabeth,' he said finally, dismissing me.

There was a shout suddenly from behind us, out at sea. Jacob spun round in his seat and grabbed the oars.

'Get working,' he said brusquely.

'I don't want to leave.'

He spun back and lunged out before I could move. The end of his oar hit me straight across the chest, knocking the wind out of my lungs, and I stumbled backwards into the bottom of the longboat.

'Elizabeth!' I managed to cry, struggling to get up, but the longboat was already skimming through the waters, making for the sound of the shout.

I lifted my head, and saw Jacob working at the oars. Then I heard the cry. A scream, carrying along the fore-shore, desperate in the summer night, chilling my heart with fear. It was a woman, calling for help, and then several men shouting together, and one man yelling in hard triumph.

Twelve

Before I could think what the scream meant, the longboat crashed into the sides of the smack and I was in the water. I went under, choking for air, swallowing great mouthfuls of salty water. I knew I was drowning, but I couldn't fight the darkness, the shreds of seaweed dragging me to a sandy grave. I opened my mouth to shout and another flood of seawater poured into my throat. Then I surfaced, and somebody was pulling at my shoulders, and I could hear a voice yelling 'Grab his arms.' My shoulder banged into the sides of the smack. 'Lift him over,' the voice was ordering. The sea was in my eyes, and a roaring of water in my ears. I felt the bulwarks crack into my legs and then I was on board.

I struggled to free my arms, vomiting water on to the deck. Two men were thumping me on the back, and I lashed out with my left arm, trying to stop them. I choked another mouthful of water out of my lungs and fought for my breath. The men at my side were laughing, but they'd stopped thumping me senseless. Another figure was crouched in front of me with a jug of water. His face blurred and then came closer: an angry, inflamed face with thin vicious lips and bloodshot, vindictive eyes. He was shouting something but I still couldn't hear for the roar of water in my ears. I gasped for air and focused on the face. The man's hair was scraped back off his pockmarked forehead and flattened with grease.

'You with us yet, friend?' he asked, his voice inflamed with some venom, rasping with almost uncontrolled fury.

'In a minute,' I managed to gasp.

'You ent got a minute, friend,' he whispered nastily, and as I spluttered for breath, he took a knife and held it to my throat. 'You ent got much of anything, by the looks of you.'

'Is this how you treat your friends,' I gasped when I could speak, trying to calm him down with good humour, but he ignored me, the knife blade jabbed painfully into my throat.

'What's your name?' he asked.

'Matthew Lidgard. What's yours?'

One of the two men at my shoulder laughed as though there was something hilarious in my question. I twisted, trying to see their faces, but they grabbed hold of my arms, forcing me back on to the deck. The one who had laughed was young and dark-haired. I couldn't see his friend.

The man with the knife leaned forward and pressed the blade firmly into my throat. I winced and fought to be free, but they were breaking my arms. I could hear shouts, men working the sails, other men on the ropes. I could see the mainmast and running bowsprit: we were fore-and-aft rigged with mainsail, staysail and jib, which meant the vessel was a small cutter, maybe forty feet by the feel of her, and ghosting the waters like a herring gull. She was a lovely smack, whatever kind of hellish lowlife lived aboard her. But she was churning through the muddy waters of the estuary with no warning lights on her masts. She was in complete darkness. I struggled to get free of the knife and the men behind me pinioned my arms again so that I gasped with the pain. I gave up struggling and sat back

against the transom stern. I could only hope friends of
Elizabeth Anstey would treat me kindly.

'You'll break my arms,' I said. 'I'm not going anywhere.'

'You can go over the side, easy enough,' the man with
the knife said, waving the blade in front of my eyes. 'Might
have to in the end. Best way with offal. Gutted and over the
side. You fancy that, friend?'

'Get on with it.'

'What you doing on *Dancing Sally*?'

'I was with Jacob,' I said wearily. 'You picked me up out
of the water. How the hell do I know what I'm doing on
your vessel?'

The knife prodded into my throat again.

'You know what I'm asking, friend.'

'No, I don't.'

'Why would Augustus Jackson be after you?'

'I was on one of Henry Mundol's smacks . . .'

'Which smack?'

'*Happy Jack*.'

'Ben Lowther's vessel?'

'Yes.'

'A sober man,' the man asking the questions said ironically.

'Not when I was on board.'

The knife was withdrawn and I heard a shout from the
bows. They must have sighted something, or reached a
point in our journey where a decision was needed. My
friend with the knife seemed to be the skipper, though
nobody had named him that. He stood up quickly and
glanced at me, his venomous eyes cold and worried, his
mouth tight and angry. Despite his sullen fury, he seemed
sly, crafty. He had taken the knife from inside his boot, a
strange place to keep a knife when you were sailing with
friends.

'I'll be seeing you in a minute, stranger.'

I saw him go forward to the bows where one of the crew was keeping watch. Another man was up the mainmast, hanging on and staring into the darkness. Out at sea, a breath of hot air touched the sails and we seemed to be heading straight for the estuary.

'Friendly type,' I muttered.

'Isaac Prusey,' one of the men told me.

'Your skipper?'

'Second hand.'

'Where's the skipper?'

'Isaac runs *Dancing Sally*, if that's comfortable with you.'

'As long as he treats me well.'

Both men laughed at this. They eased my arms and I managed to turn round. The younger man with the street accent winked at me. He had a broad, friendly face, and black fathomless eyes. His friend was older, with greying hair. 'Isaac knows who to trust,' the older one said, grinning at me toothlessly. I seemed to be finding my share of deformed cripples. The man grinned again, letting me see his black gums. 'I worry you?' he asked.

He was strong as an ape, and not much more than forty despite his toothless gums. I could smell the alcohol on his stale breath. 'I've seen worse,' I muttered.

He seemed to like that. 'I sold my teeth to a druggist,' he explained cheerfully. 'Shilling a tooth. You know how it is, going through a rough patch, need the money for a drink.'

'Not food then?'

'Drink,' he nodded firmly, enjoying his own good humour.

I thought briefly about Staithes. When I was a child there was a woman there who sold her teeth for food when her family were starving. The druggists who visited the villages made dentures from teeth they bought during famines. In good times, dentures were made from the teeth of the newly dead, or the dead in their graves if the diggers could find a deserted graveyard.

I lifted myself and tried to look astern. We were two or three miles offshore by now, but I could see a fire burning brightly against the cloudless sky. It seemed to be where the smack had picked me up. As I tried to make out the far shore, Isaac Prusey walked back to us and knelt down by the bulwarks. He glanced towards the shore.

'They set light to the cottage,' he said angrily.

'I heard a shout . . .'

'Did you now.'

'Scream more like,' one of the men muttered.

I nodded, watching Isaac Prusey carefully. He was still holding the knife.

'Why didn't Elizabeth come with you?' he asked almost casually.

'I don't know.'

I felt my arms being pinioned again. The older man without teeth jerked at my shoulder and I yelled angrily. 'I don't know, I tell you. You can break my arm but I still won't be able to tell you what I don't know.'

Prusey nodded at the man briefly, balancing the knife in his hand. 'Take it easy, Edward.' I felt my arms being freed.

'Thanks,' I muttered furiously.

Prusey stared at me for a moment, absent-minded, thoughtful. 'She should have come with you,' he said. 'I don't understand why she didn't.'

'Ask Jacob,' I snapped angrily, massaging my arms. 'He brought me out to the smack. I tried to go back, but he knocked me sideways. He won't get another chance. He was fishing inshore most of yesterday. And he was with us when we lit the fire. Ask him.'

The men with Prusey relaxed, sitting back against the bulwarks. Prusey was preoccupied, brooding, his eyes lifeless and unpleasant, his mouth tight with worry. He studied my face sceptically.

'Jacob went back to shore,' he said finally.

I felt a surge of relief, a sudden hope. 'Went back?'

'That's right.'

'Why?'

'Why do you think?'

I glanced towards the far shore again. 'If he could help . . .'

'Augustus Jackson's got her,' Prusey interrupted impatiently. 'He won't be able to help. But at least we'll know where she is. Jacob will find out what's going on.'

'Elizabeth,' I said miserably, staring unhappily into the night.

Even as I said the name I saw the expression change in Prusey's eyes: a contempt, a wildness. He leaned forward viciously and held his face close to mine. I saw the smallness of his eyes for the first time, smelt the cold breath. He was like the dead, cold and clammy and furious.

'I shouldn't be too free with that name if I was you.'

'She said . . .'

'I don't care what she said,' he sneered furiously, 'but I'd keep it off my tongue, if I didn't want it cutting out.'

'Fair enough.'

He stood up and was gone, going back to the tiller where two men were watching the sails and the estuary, whispering to each other in the silence. I wondered why everybody on the smack kept so quiet about their business. As we passed other smacks, nobody shouted a greeting. When greetings were shouted at us, they were ignored.

I managed to stand with the help of the man Prusey had called Edward, the one without teeth. He was shorter than me, and thick-shouldered. His hair was a mat of filthy grey curls.

'You going to try anything?' he asked warily.

'In the middle of the estuary?'

'Fair enough.' He held out his hand, grinning awkwardly. 'Edward Bannister,' he said, grinning as if he hadn't just been trying to break my arms.

I held my own hand out and then withdrew it just as he reached forward, gripping his fingers and crushing them until he yelled out. 'I don't like being knocked about,' I told him, whispering the words close to his face so that there would be no mistake.

The younger man watched us with surprise and then let out a bright hard laugh, grinning and enjoying Bannister's pain. 'He got you there, Edward.'

'Bastard.'

When I let Bannister go, I offered my hand to his friend.

'No thanks, Matthew,' he said. 'No offence, like.'

'What's your name. I like to know names.'

'Do you?'

'In case I ever need to find you.'

He laughed with delight, enjoying every word, showing me how much he cared about my threats. 'Charles Blow,' he said cheerfully. He looked to be in his twenties, black-haired and as broad-shouldered as his companion, but with muscles on his arms like iron, veined and bulging with several lurid tattoos of naked women. 'I come from the Hackney workhouse,' he went on gleefully. 'I don't reckon you'll have much trouble finding me, iffen you ever feels the need to.' I wondered whether I could have taken his grip. I stared him straight in the eyes but he was enjoying himself too much to notice, too amused to take me seriously. 'You can call me Charlie,' he added with a big grin.

'You hurt my arm, you bastard.'

'Take it easy, Matthew,' he smiled. 'You ent got many friends on this vessel yet. Might never have. A man always needs friends.'

I turned and looked to the far shore again. The fire was still burning. I felt the salt spray of the wake against my face, and heard a gull cry out of the darkness. *Dancing Sally* seemed to be heading straight out to sea, and Isaac Prusey was shouting orders to reef the mainsail. We would be passing the fog buoy soon where the great bell clanged during fog. I noticed the way the men kept clear of Prusey as he moved around the deck. He seemed restless, worried, and stared constantly into the darkness. There was something resentful and sullen about his face, the way he hunched his shoulders against the night. I decided to keep away from him.

'Take her out.' Prusey was hissing his orders to the man on the tiller, and *Dancing Sally* began the slow tacking away from the estuary and the fog buoy that swayed soundlessly in the clear night.

We seemed to be making away from Spurn, where I could see the fires burning clearly and the white shape of Smeaton's Light. I wondered where we were making for. There weren't many safe berths down the desolate Lincolnshire coast, and Prusey was obviously making for the open sea. It wasn't until we were out beyond Spurn Point that he gave his orders to tack back to port and make straight for Binks Sands. The men scrambled to the mainsail and staysail in seconds, and I stood in the stern, watching as Prusey took the tiller himself, guiding *Dancing Sally* back towards the far side of the long spit of desolation. We were half a mile offshore, and judging by the way the men at the port bulwarks were searching the darkness, looking for a longboat to take us ashore.

Thirteen

We plunged into rolling surf off the Spurn shore. The long-boat lifted up and down like a bird carried on enormous waves, and water deluged into the bottom of the boat, soaking us as we worked at the oars. 'Keep her head up,' Prusey shouted in the bows, and I saw Edward Bannister in the stern clinging to the tiller and trying to stand so that he could see the shore.

Dancing Sally was already tacking away from the dangerous waters. 'Where's she going?' I asked the man next to me at the oars, but he ignored me, and as the longboat plunged into another swamping cloud of spray, I saw Prusey turn and glare at me. I decided to hold my tongue. Maybe he was right about having it cut out. I had no idea what kind of helltown we were heading for on the bleak exposed spit of the Spurn.

With a mighty crash the longboat skidded into the sand and we were clambering ashore, a huge wave pouring down on top of us as we fought to drag the boat clear of the tide. Several men ran from the dunes to help us. In the deluge of water, I was struggling to keep my feet, but managed to note the fires burning around the flat dunes, figures moving in the darkness. I heard voices, and Isaac Prusey's name being shouted, then we were clear of the sea and Prusey was suddenly at my side, pushing his hair back out of his eyes, shaking his head and glaring at me.

'You still alive, friend.'

'My name's Lidgard. I don't reckon we're friends.'

'You got some sense.'

Now that I could see, I noticed figures standing around in the darkness, men and women watching us, children pushing forward and staring. Bannister was talking to one of the women, a child clinging to his arm. Prusey saw me having a good look round and punched me on the arm.

'Let's get moving.'

I followed him across the narrow spit of land, no more than a few hundred yards wide at the point where we had floundered ashore. I could see the lights of Grimsby across the wide river, and the fires of a number of smacks, riding at anchor in the safety of the Humber.

'Where's the smack gone?' I asked Prusey.

'You mind your own business, Lidgard.'

'Up the coast?'

He shrugged, ignoring me. I guessed they kept *Dancing Sally* moored at some inlet or creek. I had never studied the maps of this area: there was no need, unless you intended getting shipwrecked, and few survivors waded ashore off the graveyard of Binks Sands. I glanced over my shoulder to the north, but even in the cloudless sky with plenty of moonlight I couldn't see *Dancing Sally*. She must have gone at a good tack.

We reached the far side of the Spurn, and I could see the narrow hump of an island lying out in the river the estuary side of the spit. I knew that must be Sunk Island, a stretch of land that had once been part of Spurn but was now rapidly disappearing into the tidal waters of the river. A narrow strip of water separated Sunk Island from the Spurn.

'Go on,' Prusey snapped, jabbing me with his elbow.

I plunged into the muddy water which was not more than a foot deep and waded across to the grassy mound. Sheep grazed in the darkness. I could see the water moving all round us and the fires burning behind me. Sunk Island was only covered during spring high tides, and then the sheep were brought to the mainland. I walked up the muddy foreshore and stared around me. It was a strange, isolated stretch of earth, separated from the flat desolation of Spurn. I could see a figure, standing at the far edge of the island, staring across to Lincolnshire.

'He's here,' Prusey called at my side.

The figure turned and stared at us. He had been using an eyeglass, studying the distant shore. He must have watched *Dancing Sally*'s progress across the six miles of the estuary.

'Move,' Prusey muttered in my ear.

I crossed the narrow island. It was not more than fifty yards across and several hundred yards in length. The soil was poor and sandy and thirty or forty sheep cropped at the grass, moving out of my way as I walked through them. The figure at the far side waited patiently, like a lord of some lost kingdom.

I could see him quite clearly: tall and young, with long blond curly hair growing down to the shoulders and a pale, gaunt face, haunted by some grief that wouldn't let him rest. He lowered the eyeglass and stared at me calmly, studying my clothes and face. When he spoke, his voice was toneless, flat, with a soft accent I recognised from down south, Yarmouth or the Suffolk coast. He had a wide mouth and very high sharp cheekbones, giving his eyes an almost slanted look, so that he appeared foreign. He was wearing fisherman's gear and seaboots, the tiny tidal waters splashing at his feet as he studied me carefully.

'What happened?' he asked quietly, glancing at Prusey.

'They got Elizabeth. Burned the house. For this bloke.'

I started to protest, but the young man silenced me, lifting his hand. He was taller than me, and very thin. I guessed he was about the same age, maybe a little more: twenty-three or four.

'You don't know the truth of that, Isaac,' he said.

'They never burned her out before. Augustus Jackson was never interested.'

'That might not be due to this man. Was Jacob there?'

'Yes.'

'He brought him out in the longboat?'

'Yes.'

'Then he's probably all right.'

'If you say so, Nathan.'

Prusey turned away angrily, spitting with disgust into the river.

The young man eyed me levelly. 'Who are you, friend?' he asked.

'Matthew Lidgard.'

'You must have been on the run, for the fire to be lit.'

'That's right.'

'He says he was on *Happy Jack*,' Prusey said quietly.

The young man nodded, not looking at Prusey. He never took his eyes off my face. I could see his eyes in the moonlight: intense, fixed on my face as if trying to find his way into my mind, restlessly searching my expression to learn what he needed to know. He seemed to be in a sort of intense trance, his whole body directed towards mine, his searching look painful and disturbing.

'You were on one of Henry Mundol's vessels?'

'*Happy Jack*,' I nodded briefly.

'And absconded?'

'They flogged me.'

'For no offence, presumably,' he said mildly, without irony.

'For having a drunken skipper,' I said.

'Ben Lowther,' Prusey reminded his skipper.

'Yes, Ben Lowther. I know *Happy Jack*. She's a fine ketch. You were trawling?'

'Off Whitby and then the Dogger. We lost both trawl nets.'

'Both!' the young man laughed. 'That takes some doing.'

'The first was an accident. The second was on rough ground.'

'Still,' he said quietly, raising his eyebrows sceptically. 'No wonder Henry Mundol wants you. Are you a Jonah, Matthew Lidgard?'

'Lowther asked me that.'

'And you didn't like it. But I'm asking you now.'

He stared across the estuary towards the lights of Grimsby.

I took a deep breath.

'Elizabeth,' I began to say, but he looked up quickly, urgently, like an alarmed bird or an animal disturbed by some unusual sound. His eyes were dark with threat.

'You say her name freely.'

I paused. I was confused, not sure what I was going to say.

'You talked to her?' he asked with his searching look.

'She helped me. Of course we talked.'

'She helps anybody.'

He was abstracted, in his own world. I suddenly felt frightened: Prusey tensed at my side, and I could hear other men moving around on the mainland across the narrow strip of water. Where could I go from here: the river was the most dangerous in the world; a few yards out into the black tides, and I would be swept away forever, drawn down to the maw of the cold sea. Nobody would hear my cries in this desolation, and if they heard, there would be nothing they could do to save me. I wondered what kind of madman Elizabeth Anstey had delivered my soul to.

'Are you a Jonah, Matthew Lidgard?' the young man asked again.

'The girl who rescued me thought I had the sight,' I said abruptly, taking a terrifying risk. If he knew her, he would know what I meant: and it would be either my saving or my death.

He turned and stared at me searchingly for a long time. Standing very close, I felt his eyes like awful blank holes, pouring into my soul. I could smell laudanum on his breath, oozing out of his skin.

'Elizabeth wants us to leave for Lerwick,' he said suddenly, ignoring what I'd told him. 'Take the smack and head for Lerwick to work the Iceland summer voyage. Did she tell you that?'

'Yes.'

'Then she trusted you.'

'I don't know.'

'She trusted you. Do you know Iceland?'

'Yes. I've done the summer trip for years.'

'Long-lining?'

'Yes.'

The young man turned to Prusey with a brief laugh. 'Isaac doesn't approve of Lerwick, do you, Isaac?'

'Not my kind of fishing, Nathan.'

'No,' the young man smiled. 'Not your kind of fishing. What do you think about Matthew Lidgard, Isaac?'

'He's a Jonah.'

'Oh?'

'They've picked Elizabeth up, haven't they!'

'Yes,' the man said sadly. He seemed to be in a dream. He stared at me all the time Prusey was talking, studying my face. I was frightened. Then I heard splashing in the narrow strip of water between the island and the mainland,

and the sheep were being scattered again, racketing in the night silence. A short, heavily-built man with frizzled grey hair and a round face was striding through them, kicking them out of his way.

'They took Elizabeth, Nathan!' Prusey hissed urgently at the young man as if he wanted to persuade him before the newcomer joined us. 'They never did that before.'

'Yes, they took Lizzie,' Nathan said thoughtfully.

'He's a Jonah, Nathan, listen to me.'

I felt panic: was I a Jonah, or a scapegoat? Neither option seemed very attractive in this community of thieves. I had spent years working the east coast fishing communities and the green water grounds, and I had never had such bad fortune as during the past few days. I began to sweat, and felt the sweat running down my face and back. Nathan noticed this with fascination, reaching out his finger and touching my cheek. I flinched.

'What the devil's going on,' the newcomer asked angrily, storming up to us. 'What's this about Elizabeth?'

Prusey turned and almost snarled at the newcomer. 'Late as usual, Hubert.'

The man ignored Prusey, going straight up to Nathan and shaking his arm vigorously, jerking him out of his trance. 'God help us, Nathan,' he snarled. 'What kind of state are you in?'

'They have Lizzie, Hubert.'

'Who has her, in the name of heaven?'

'Henry Mundol,' Prusey said with a sneer. 'She tried to save this Jonah's life and ended up in Augustus Jackson's hands. You know what *he's* like. Walked straight into it, she did. We haven't got Jacob so we don't rightly know what happened. He says he was on *Happy Jack*, running away from a flogging. He could be working for Mundol for all we know.'

The younger man suddenly interrupted.

'Quiet yourself, Isaac. You're disturbing the sheep.'

'You know it's the truth, skipper.'

'I don't know anything yet. This is Hubert Caldicott, Matthew. He skippers one of our vessels.'

I glanced at the squat, urgent figure, the hunched shoulders and tightly curling grey hair shining in the moonlight. He had the same soft accent as Nathan. The older man was in his forties, and wore fisherman's gear the same as the other two. I guessed from his gait he had been on the smacks most of his life. His face was tanned as dark as mahogany, and his fingers were covered with tiny white scars from the gutting of the fish. He looked me up and down and nodded brusquely.

'You all right, friend?' he asked, shaking my hand.

'He's all right,' Prusey laughed. 'He brought his share of trouble for the rest of us though.'

'Hold your mouth, Prusey,' the new man said roughly.

'Why the hell should I!'

'Because we got things to do,' the older man said with the same rough indifference. He turned to me. He had keen, impatient eyes, a sharp stare under his rough manner. 'You say Augustus Jackson took Elizabeth?'

'That's right,' I said nodding.

'What do you reckon?' Nathan asked, staring at the older man, looking suddenly unsure and anxious.

'They'll try for a hearing the day after tomorrow.'

'Not before?'

'There isn't a sitting. Most of the magistrates are out of town. They'll hear her case in the morning, and send her straight to Lincoln. We have to get her out tomorrow night, before the hearing.'

'Get her out!' Isaac laughed.

'You heard.'

'Steady-as-she-goes-Caldicott!' Isaac suddenly jeered. 'You lost your mind, Hubert.'

'We have no choice. If they get her to Lincoln Prison, we'll never get near her.'

Isaac Prusey seemed to be choking with delight. 'Nothing good will come of it,' he jeered, and I guessed he was mimicking one of Caldicott's favourite phrases. It sounded to me close to the truth.

'We do as he says,' Nathan interrupted coldly.

There was an awkward silence.

Isaac glowered at the edge of the sands. 'You're both mad.'

'No,' Caldicott said quietly, shaking his head. 'There's only the police lock-up. There'll be one man on duty at the most. They've only got a couple of men to work the whole town at night.'

'And all Henry Mundol's men!' Isaac scoffed.

'He won't expect us to try anything.'

'That might be just what he *is* expecting,' Prusey shouted at him.

'Now what are you raving about, Isaac?' Caldicott said impatiently, beginning to lose his temper, but Prusey was already shouting over him.

'Don't you think it's strange,' he sneered, 'Henry Mundol wasting all this time over one man. Sending Augustus Jackson all the way out to the cockle beds just after one fisherman. You don't think he might be hoping we'll go looking for Elizabeth?'

Caldicott shrugged, and glanced at me. 'He don't look worth much to me,' he said ironically. 'But Henry Mundol can't keep losing men. Sets a bad example. Maybe our friend here was the last straw.'

'And if he's set us up?'

'Then we'll go prepared,' Caldicott said brusquely. 'You can come with us, stranger,' he added, turning to me. 'Been as she got caught on your account.'

'Right,' I nodded dumbly, almost losing the flow of what was happening around me.

'You think she's all right?' Nathan asked suddenly, talking to the older man. He sounded as though he hadn't been listening. He seemed tense, exhausted, his voice tight with nerves. He was staring across the estuary, his hands rubbing restlessly at his arms, his face abstracted.

'She'll be fine,' Caldicott said. 'You know Elizabeth.'

'Yes.'

'You get some rest,' Caldicott urged, touching Nathan's arm. 'I'll talk to some of the men.' He paused for a moment, and then turned and plunged back across the little island. Sheep fled from his angry boots. He waded through the shallow water and was gone.

'You brought us some trouble, friend,' Isaac said with venom as soon as Caldicott had gone.

'Leave it alone, Isaac,' the younger man sighed.

'But I'll be having my eye on you,' Prusey went on, turning and following Caldicott back into the night.

I stood for a moment, unable to understand what had happened to me. I had come to the estuary to learn more about my father's death, and ended up in this madness. At my side, Nathan stared across the river, and I could hear his harsh breathing in the silence. He rested a hand briefly on my shoulder and then looked up to the moon. There were tears shining on his cheeks.

'I need some laudanum,' he said with a croaking voice.

'I don't carry that stuff. I don't use it.'

He seemed not to hear me. He stared up at the moon and stars. He was crying. 'Is she all right, Matthew?' he asked through his tears.

'I don't know,' I said quietly.

'I pray she's all right,' he went on, his voice almost choking.

'So do I,' I muttered under my breath.

Across the six miles of the estuary, the fire that had once been Elizabeth's cottage had gone out. The coast was lost in darkness.

'Is she your girl?' I asked almost to myself, dreading the reply.

He didn't speak for several minutes, trying to get control of his breathing, wiping the tears from his face.

'She's my sister,' he said finally.

'Your sister!'

'That's right.'

'But she never said.'

'Why should she,' he said vaguely. 'Let's get back.'

He plunged into the shallow waters, and I followed him. On Spurn, fires were still burning, and groups of men were standing around in the darkness talking together. Several of them glanced in our direction as we climbed out of the water. In my confused terror, I knew they were talking about me: the Jonah.

I watched Nathan stumble off to find his laudanum, and then went and slept in one of the dunes by the warmth of an open fire. I wondered briefly whether I could escape, make a run for it in the darkness. But Elizabeth needed my help. I couldn't leave until she was safe. In the early hours of the morning I woke and she was in my mind: smiling from the bleak foreshore. Her smile was my only comfort in this deranged place. I went back to sleep, and slept soundly in her arms.

Fourteen

When I woke, the early morning sky was already pink with light, and I could hear laughing voices and the noise of activity all around me. I rubbed the sand out of my hair and sat up. Somebody had thrown a blanket over my body during the night. There was a fire burning a few feet away from me, and a couple of men preparing food. I rested my face on my knees for a moment, bringing myself awake, and then stood up and stretched gratefully.

'The hero awakes,' one of the men at the fire called, and I walked across to join them. He was short and bony, and wearing ancient fisherman's boots and a ragged jersey with holes in the elbows. He looked not much older than thirty. 'Have a drink, stranger,' he smiled, offering me a mug of tea. 'The food will be ready soon.'

I introduced myself and thanked him for the tea.

'Sidney Lill is my name,' the man went on cheerfully, 'and cook to this lot, for my sins.'

'Sins?'

'You wouldn't believe it, Matthew, but I hate cooking. It's a job for women, if you ask me. Actually ruins my appetite.'

His friend knelt at the fire, eating bacon and fresh bread.

'Don't take no notice, Matthew,' he said. 'Sidney always talks rubbish.'

'Yes, I talk rubbish,' Sidney Lill beamed, brandishing a wooden spoon. 'And this is Peter Loft. You may notice that he is eating. He eats all the time. When he was a child, his stepmother and father tried to starve him to death for the insurance money. He was seven years old. Wouldn't you think they'd take pity? He eats now because of the shock to his kindness his stepmother inflicted. He never blamed his father. He ran away to sea because of that woman and a broken childish heart.'

I drank my tea and knelt down to take a slice of bacon from the pan. 'And why are you the cook if you hate cooking, Sidney?' I asked, knowing I was going to get a daft answer.

He beamed at me cheerfully, wincing as hot fat stung his arms. 'My mother had an eating-house in Leicester, Matthew. Working men and serving girls. I had to help her because nobody else would. My father for one. He hopped it the minute I was born. She couldn't afford to pay for help. Not much profit in food in Leicester.'

'That's a fair way from the sea,' I suggested.

'It is indeed. I never heard of the sea until I was eleven. Then I ran away and joined one of Henry Mundol's smacks and because I was youngest they made me cook. I ran away from an eating-house full of drunkards and buckets of potatoes needing peeling and ended up on a trawler full of drunkards and more buckets of potatoes. So I broke my indentures, and joined Nathan, and Isaac Prusey made me cook on *Dancing Sally*. I cannot escape my fate. I am a doomed man. You wouldn't like a job, would you? Leave that!' he added with a thwack of the wooden spoon as Peter Loft tried to help himself to another round of bacon and sausage. 'There has to be some food left for the rest of the island.'

I got up and wandered away from the fire. I was restless,

wanted to have a look round. I took myself to the very end of the land, past Smeaton's Light and the cluster of shabby houses to the crown of the spit where the wind blew so saltily that my eyes ran, and I kept floundering on the moving ground, the dancing clouds of sand and weed. I stood at the very end of the earth, where the sand leaked into the sea and the low ripples of saltwater seemed to be eating the ground. To my right the enormously wide mouth of the river met the sea, angry breakers clashing furiously and then falling off, throwing up clouds of white spray. Close to the shore, I could see the rough waters surging over Greedy Gut and Old Den, the treacherous sandbanks off Spurn fishermen prayed to avoid. Away to my left the rocky deathbed of Binks Sands threshed and tossed spray into the hot air, and fishing smacks rose and fell on big grey waves, so close that I felt I could almost reach out and touch them. I was standing at the end of the world, and with a single step I could have walked out into the sea and drowned in the bottomless waters.

I heard a sound at my shoulder and turning sharply found Nathan Anstey standing behind me, shading his eyes from the sunlight. He had food with him, bacon and sausages sandwiched between thick slices of bread, and a fresh mug of tea. I took the food and drink and started to eat while he continued staring out to sea, searching the horizon and studying the vessels in the estuary.

'I don't know whether I can trust you,' he said abruptly while I chewed at the thick crusty bread.

I shrugged. 'I can't say much to persuade you,' I said. 'But your sister trusted me, and I don't work for Henry Mundol. I have more reason to hate him than most.'

'I saw your back,' Nathan said nodding. 'Ben Lowther?'

He must have brought the blanket to cover me in the night, and seen the drying scabs left by the flogging. 'That's right,' I said.

He studied my face for a moment, and then sighed and turned away, surveying the bleak spit of land on which we were standing, the distant haze of Holderness and the Yorkshire coast. He took a flask from his pocket and drank quickly, wiping the top with the sleeve of his jersey. I could smell the corn brandy and the laudanum.

'Leave it for now,' he smiled, relaxing. 'Enjoy your food. Did you know there'd been communities on Spurn for centuries, Matthew?' he asked. 'Long before our own time.'

'No,' I answered.

'There was even a chapel and religious community in the seventh century, though the land was further out to sea then. Spurn has moved over the centuries. There was a port out here at one time, Ravenser Odd, and villages over what is now Sunk Island: Tharlesthorpe, Penisthorpe, Orwithfleet and Frismersk. They say you can hear the bells ringing from the drowned churches at low tides. I like to stand on Sunk Island and think about the long-dead inhabitants of those villages. But I have never heard the bells. It is a strange place, my mad kingdom.'

'Kingdom?' I asked briefly, glancing at him in surprise.

He looked up, lost in his own thoughts, distracted by my question.

His face was almost white, lifeless and colourless, with dark bruises beneath the pale blue eyes. He studied me as if I were already dead, something washed up on the foreshore. When I met his eyes he looked away indifferently.

'That's how I like to think of it,' he said ironically. 'My mad kingdom, and with such lovely names,' he added in the same emotionless, cold voice. 'In the seventeenth century there was a lighthouse called Angell's, and in the fifteenth century, one called Reedbarrow's. I have no idea why they called them that, perhaps after the men who built them, but they are there on the old charts if you look.'

We walked back to the main camp and I left the mug with Sidney Lill. Nathan seemed to want to talk, show me round his mad kingdom. He was proprietorial, arrogant. As he walked, women shouted to him and brought their children for him to see. The men worked on the three or four longboats pulled up out of the reach of the sea, or sat around talking and playing cards. A group were playing chuck-hole, pitching half-pence into a hole in one of the sand-dunes and gambling on the results. They shouted and argued over the game, hardly noticing Nathan.

We walked for miles into the bleak wastes of Holderness. At the tiny village of Easington, we sat outside an inn and Nathan took several deep swallows from the flask he carried. He closed his eyes and his rasping breath eased. He seemed to be asleep. I wondered how he could stand the mixture of laudanum and corn brandy. On its own, corn brandy could make you delirious, but laced with laudanum it had to drive you out of your mind. I began to understand why Nathan seemed so maudlin one second, then wild with anxiety and energy the next, and wondered how long he'd been taking the damned mixture.

He started speaking abruptly. 'Do you have dreams, Matthew?'

'No, not often.'

'I have frightful dreams. Waking or sleeping.'

He was silent for some minutes, listening to the heat of the day, bees and insects swarming in the sunlight, a dove cooing on the thatched roof of one of the old houses.

'I dreamed last night about the sea,' he said suddenly. 'But not an ordinary sea. There was ash floating down from a copper-coloured sky, and fires smoking on the horizon. A boiling cauldron. Real witches' brew.' He laughed curtly, dismissively, resting his head back against the wall of the inn, his eyes still closed. 'I think there was a woman in my dream: fat, bloated, a red-haired harpy who breathed disease into my face.' He laughed again, savage, angry. 'She was catching hold of my right eye and trying to pull it out. I grabbed her arm but the arm was wet, spongy, and when I woke this morning my hands were covered with blood and my right eyelid was swollen.'

He fell asleep then, snoring slightly. I felt the sun on my face and tried to force myself to relax, keep calm. I edged away from Nathan along the bench. Was this the moment to make a run for it? I was sure I wasn't safe with Nathan: he seemed unpredictable, violent, with his moods and his strange dreams. He carried a long knife in a sheath at his waist. He might decide to kill me at any moment. But I couldn't stop thinking about Elizabeth, waiting for us to come to her in Satan's Hole. I didn't want to leave Elizabeth, and even if I made a run for it, Nathan was surrounded by friends, he might even have friends in this village. I breathed the salt air and wondered how I was ever going to escape and get back to my journey south to find a berth in Yarmouth. I hadn't mentioned that fact to Nathan.

I was lost in my own thoughts when I noticed a figure standing in the shadows outside the church. The church was at the far side of the market square, opposite the inn. The man was watching us, motionless by the church porch. I wondered if he was one of Nathan's men, and reached out to touch Nathan, but when he saw my movement, the man suddenly turned and walked rapidly through the porch and into the churchyard. I stood up, but he was gone before I could call. He glanced over his shoulder as he reached a corner, and then disappeared. On the bench, Nathan went on sleeping. When he woke, I did not mention the man.

As the sun rose, we started to make our way across to the far side of Spurn. The landscape around us was flat and hunched and wind-whipped. The fields were small, the dark earth scored with scratches of sand blown from the foreshore. The hedges were scrawny, grown tightly into each other, and there were no tall trees, only a few thorns with their arms flung up in horror, as if the earth groaned with the nightmares of the sea.

At Patrington Haven, Nathan pointed to a dismal huddle of huts and shacks, shelters of wood and stone with straw for roofs, rough and squalid lean-tos. Women and children crowded outside the huts, some of the women with children at the breast, older children chasing each other and throwing stones at a snarling dog tethered to a post. One or two elderly men lounged on the grass, playing cards or drinking, red-spotted neckcloths round their necks.

'This is Irish Green,' Nathan explained.

'Bothies,' I nodded.

He smiled with mock surprise. 'You're a well-informed man, Matthew.'

'Reclamation work?' I asked casually.

I knew reclamation gangs were working on Spurn, embanking, draining and warping, reclaiming land from the relentless efforts of the sea.

'I'll show you,' Nathan grinned.

We walked past the muddle of ramshackle bothies to the edge of the river. A dozen men were working up to their waists in mud. They were trapping the retreating water as the tide ebbed, adding mud to the black embankment which would slowly turn into soil. They worked with heavy, sharp-edged spades, their bodies black in the morning sunlight.

'A wild travelling life,' Nathan said ironically.

'They earn good money.'

'They do. And terrify the people of Easington and Patrington.'

'But not you?'

'They're my friends,' he said with raised eyebrows. 'They don't pillage my orchards and hen-roosts, or accost my women. They have women of their own: flocking to them, so I hear, after the easy money and romantic life. But we have an understanding. They buy my finest whisky, I buy their pheasants and hares. It's a business arrangement.'

One of the men waded out of the mud and came across to us. We couldn't see his face for the black mud.

'This is Duffy,' Nathan said, introducing the man.

'A fine day for a dram,' Duffy said, insisting on shaking my hand.

'I haven't a drop with me,' Nathan grinned at him.

'You're fooling, man.'

'Sorry.'

Duffy put on a big show of scowling, winked at me, and went back to his work. 'We'll be needing something tonight, Nathan,' he shouted as he went. His men lifted their excavating spades and shouted their farewells to Nathan, throwing handfuls of mud and jokes after us as we continued along the tideline back to the end of Spurn.

I wondered why Nathan was showing me all of this: perhaps he didn't have a reason, was bored and restless, or perhaps he wanted me to know how hopeless it would be to run.

We had just got back to the camp when the gypsies started to arrive. There were half a dozen of them, with a string of dishevelled ponies. Isaac Prusey immediately started arguing with their leader, and several of the men joined him. Nathan stood by one of the fires and waited while Peter Loft brewed some fresh tea. The gypsies seemed indignant, dangerous: they weren't frightened of Isaac Prusey and his men. One of the gypsies was carrying a shotgun which he held casually across his shoulder.

'What are they doing here?' I asked Nathan.

'They bring tobacco and aniseed whisky.'

I glanced at him in surprise. 'Smuggling?'

'Trade. We take the supplies out to the fleets.'

'You use *Dancing Sally* as a coper?'

'That's right,' he said amicably.

The copers were trading vessels which sold adulterated alcohol, shag tobacco and pornographic pictures to the men in the fleets. They usually came from Holland, but some of them worked out of isolated east coast ports, bringing their foul goods to the floating helltowns, fetching mayhem and tragedy to the fleets. Nathan's mad kingdom by the sea was a community of smugglers and dealers. I wondered whether my father had come across them during his brief days on the fleets.

'How long have you been here?' I asked, trying to hide my feelings.

'A couple of years. Not long.'

I didn't reply.

'You don't approve,' Nathan said softly at my side, and I glanced into his eyes, watching me with their cold, drugged indifference.

'I don't like the trade,' I said bluntly.

He smiled, nodding to himself. 'You talk bravely.'

'I haven't got much to lose. If you're going to kill me . . .'

He turned away, smiling but annoyed. 'Matthew! You're a guest. Take some food and rest.'

I walked unhappily back to the main fire and sat down with a group of men. Sidney Lill was handing out soup and bread and cheese and several of the men were drinking corn brandy. Isaac Prusey was still arguing with the gypsies who were also drinking from flasks of brandy. The atmosphere was wild and tense, but the men round the fire didn't seem bothered.

'Matthew was on *Happy Jack*,' Peter Loft was telling the men round the fire. 'He got flogged for ruining their trawl.'

'I got flogged for nothing, more like,' I muttered.

'We all been flogged, friend,' one of the men grinned at me. 'One time or another. I been flogged frequent. Edgar March is the name.' He leaned forward and shook my hand vigorously and then went on talking. 'I was on the Harwich liners from the day I was born, almost: 1837 first trip. That was a blower. I'm fifty now. You wouldn't know it, would you, mates?' He grinned round at all of us and we all agreed he didn't look a day less than forty. He didn't. 'I know Iceland better than my own garden,' he said cheerfully. 'I been there more often.' Finishing his food, he took a melodion from beside him and started playing. Two or three of the men lit pipes and settled back in the dunes.

'You ever been to Iceland, Matthew?' Sidney Lill asked me.

'Every year since I signed up. A dozen trips I reckon. You can't call yourself a fisherman if you haven't worked the liners.'

'I'd like to go to Iceland,' a young lad said dreamily, staring up at the sky. 'I'd like to serve the Lord in barren places. Go into the desert of floating ice and do the Lord's will.'

'That's Luke Hobbins,' Sidney told me with a confidential wink. 'He was going to be a preacher but his parents went and died. Thoughtless couple. He used to preach in the Harwich workhouse, going up and down the wards. They were pleased to be shut of him, I hear tell. His grandmother brought him up. She taught him the Bible and a few hymns and then she died. Inconsiderate family on the long view.'

Behind us, Isaac Prusey and the gypsies seemed to have come to some sort of agreement, and the gypsy leader was now talking to Nathan. I couldn't see Hubert Caldicott anywhere on the spit. Men were coming and going all the time, carrying bundles, bringing food or drink, standing around and idly chatting. Nathan finished talking with the gypsies and turned to look at me. He seemed unsure, pre-occupied, listening while Isaac Prusey whispered something at his side. I saw money change hands, and then the gypsies left, refusing the food they were offered.

Nathan waved to me, and I joined him on the estuary side of the mainland. He waded into the water and out to Sunk Island. I followed him.

He stood at the edge of the low island, staring across to Grimsby. The estuary was six miles across at its widest and a smack could take hours to get from the lockpit in Grimsby to the Spurn headland. They did say you could see Lincoln Cathedral on a clear day, but I couldn't imag-ine that. I had no time for Lincoln: there was only the treadmill and oakum wards in Lincoln for fishermen. I shaded my eyes from the blinding sun, and all I could see was water and a shimmering heat haze. I was beginning to feel dizzy with all the sunlight and sea, light dazzling off water. I felt lost and confused, as though any minute I might fall off the edge of the world. The world moved and then steadied, and when I opened my eyes, Nathan was watching me with a quizzical, hard smile.

'Do you know why I hate Henry Mundol?' he asked.

'No,' I shook my head.

'He ruined my father. I only went on the fishing because of my father, and Henry Mundol destroyed our business. He left us orphans. He wrecked our lives. We were children when he did that.'

I waited. I couldn't judge his mood, didn't know whether to say what Elizabeth had already told me. I held my peace.

'Are you as passionate?' he asked abruptly.

'Passionate?'

'For revenge?'

'I don't have much reason to like the man,' I said jokingly.

But he wasn't in the mood for my humour. 'Are you passionate?' he repeated brutally.

'Yes,' I nodded, agreeing promptly.

There was such loathing in Nathan's voice I didn't dare tell him what I really felt. I didn't want an argument with a madman, and on that lonely spit of land caught between the flooding estuary and the gang of men at the fires, I had no doubt Nathan was mad. I had nothing to thank Henry Mundol for, but I didn't hate the man: I had never met him. I simply wanted to get away and leave the estuary behind me forever, with its savagery and strange communities. I agreed with Nathan to save my life.

He laughed weirdly, gazing up into the blazing sun, the veins in his neck tensing like iron, his fists clenched in white fury. 'Good,' he said, 'I'm glad,' then shouted his sister's name, 'Elizabeth!' to a flock of circling herring gulls. I glanced over my shoulder. The gulls screamed and wheeled above us, and I saw Isaac Prusey and several of the men on shore turn and watch. 'I love my sister, Matthew,' Nathan said fiercely.

'I know.'

'You can tell?'

'It is in everything you say and do.'

He smiled, touching me briefly on the shoulder.

'Maybe you do have the sight. Isn't that what Elizabeth said?'

'Yes.'

He seemed interested for a moment, then dismissed the thought with derision. 'She talks nonsense, sometimes,' he said with a bored yawn.

'I don't know,' I shrugged warily. 'I don't know her.'

He smiled. 'That's a clever answer, Matthew.'

'It's the truth.'

'Well, I don't believe,' he said bluntly. 'I had religious parents. Did Elizabeth tell you we were Catholics?'

'She mentioned something about the Sisters helping you.'

'The Sisters!' he scoffed.

'In town.'

'Yes, they help. But their help isn't religious. I don't call it religious. I don't believe in their religion. My father died holding a cross. It didn't save him. I believe in revenge. I want revenge. You can help me get it, Matthew, then I might start believing you tell the truth.'

He gripped my arm fiercely while he said this, glaring into my eyes with an intensity I had never met in anyone before. Then he released my arm, and plunged through the shallow waters back to the Spurn mainland.

Fifteen

In the late evening, we set out along the sea foreshore. As I had guessed, *Dancing Sally* was kept in a creek at Old Hive, just up the coast. At Easington, the huddle of thatched cottages around the church were silent as the grave, and the streets, cobbled with stones from the beach, deserted. We could see the sea all round us, flat and calm, pink light draining out of the horizon to the east as the stars twinkled and blistered the night sky. The beach was deserted. When we reached Old Hive, Hubert Caldicott and several of the men started to haul longboats down to the sea and we clambered aboard. Nathan had brought a dozen men with him, with Hubert leading the way. Isaac Prusey had stayed behind to watch the camp.

We rowed out to *Dancing Sally* and climbed aboard over the port bulwarks. A tiny cluster of houses lay inland of the creek, but none of the houses showed a light. It was as if the whole community on Spurn knew what we were about and preferred to stay indoors even this early in the evening. From the stern of the vessel I could see across the flat fields to the ventilated spire of Patrington Church shimmering above the endless fields of wheat. The church clock wheezed and struck nine: the notes wandering out over the fields and fading in the last of the evening light.

'Mainsail halyards . . .' Caldicott was shouting his orders. 'Get the anchor up, Bannister. Haul out the jib.'

I saw a couple of lads I didn't recognise running the jib-boom out ready for the jib, and Bannister heaving and sweating at the anchor. Two more men worked at the mainsail halyards and then sheeted the sail out and secured the ropes at the tack, clew and head cringles. The mainsail took the wind immediately, like a girl waiting for her lover. Everybody worked without fuss or hesitation, and *Dancing Sally* rode gaily with the tide as the wind filled her sails and she began to tack to starboard and leave the shore. We were obviously going to keep a wide berth of Binks Sands.

I leant at the tiller post and watched as Caldicott took the smack out to sea, quiet and confident, happy with the tiller in his hand. Nathan had gone below to the aft cabin, but emerged within minutes with a flask of brandy and a chart. One of the youngest lads, Joel Cross, followed him with mugs of hot tea. Joel looked no more than twelve, and had left home for a trawler because his mother was so peevish. Now that he had broken his indentures, he didn't dare go back. He handed the tea round and went down to fetch more.

'Ease the shrouds and forestay,' Caldicott shouted to one of the men in the bows, and the man leapt to his work.

'You know about smacks, Hubert,' I said admiringly, seeing the way he adjusted the stability of the sails.

'I've been on them all my life,' he said indifferently. He was not a man to waste time talking or listening to compliments. He kept his eyes on the burgee at the mainmast and listened to the swell of the rough water, alert all the time to the movements of *Dancing Sally*.

'Hubert sailed with my father,' Nathan said mildly, lounging at the transom stern, perched dangerously on the low bulwarks. One unexpected swell of the tides and he would be lost overboard. I thought he probably liked the idea of the danger. 'He was my father's favourite companion.'

Caldicott ignored the remark and went on with his work. We were soon under full sail and tacking hard round the rough waters of Spurn. Where the sea met the outflowing river, there was always surf and turbulence, and *Dancing Sally* rode the clashing waves like a bird, lovely and free under Caldicott's firm hand. I drank my tea, and enjoyed the salt spray on my face.

It took us into darkness to sail up the river and past the yellow lights of Grimsby. A dull haze of gaslight lay like a shroud over Satan's Hole. In Cod's Kingdom, where most of the fishing families lived in houses built along the fore-shore, there was less gaslight, and individual lights burned and glowed in the hundreds of houses. Out in the river, dozens of fishing smacks lay at anchor with fires burning in their sterns, but Caldicott kept well to the centre of the river away from the vessels waiting to enter the lockpits. He seemed to know the river like his own hands, and never once glanced at the chart Nathan had brought from below.

Suddenly, Nathan stood from the bulwarks and pointed to the shore. There was a lighthouse beyond a cluster of houses, but no lights. Caldicott grunted some-thing to Nathan and then shouted for the mainsail to be close-hauled, the sheets pulled in as close as they could be. We were on a starboard tack and heading straight for the darkness of the shores.

'Where are we?' I whispered to Nathan.

'Haven Creek,' he whispered back. 'The Freedom Tree.'

'The what?'

'Keep it quiet,' Caldicott hissed at us from the tiller.

'The Freedom Tree,' Nathan said again as if I was a fool for not knowing, then went for'ard to the bowsprit to watch Bannister and another of the young boys, John

Parnham, haul the wooden spar aboard. The next minute, the drogue was over the stern, and without any orders, the anchor dropped and the longboat swung over the side.

'You stay in the main channel,' I heard Caldicott telling two of the crew as he clambered over the bulwarks down to the longboat. 'Watch for us in the morning.'

I made a move towards the tiller but Nathan was back beside me before I could make myself scarce. 'You come with us,' he said. 'You can help us in Satan's Hole.'

'I don't know the place.'

'You don't need to,' he hissed close to my face, his hand gripping my arm.

Caldicott was already in the longboat, and I climbed down in front of Nathan and took a set of oars. We lurched away from the smack and ploughed ashore through the shallow muddy water, leaping out and wading into mud when we finally beached. I could smell the mud on my boots and clothes. I was wearing a pair of seaboots Nathan had got for me from *Dancing Sally*'s stores. The mud went almost to the top.

Once on shore, we watched the longboat heading back for the smack.

'One thing,' Caldicott whispered, gathering us round him. 'When we're in town, we don't use names. You understand that?' Several voices agreed. 'Right,' Caldicott grunted. 'Make sure you remember. And keep close.'

Then we were off, moving in a single file along the foreshore, our boots slippery on mud and then crunching through broken shells and gravel. Shallow streams meandered through the marshes and down to the shores. I tried to keep an eye out for where we were heading, but I could see nothing in the darkness except for the distant glow of lights over Grimsby. I had Caldicott right in front of me, and Nathan keeping close behind. I couldn't have found my way to freedom even if I had made a break for it. I walked blindly, wondering what they meant by the Freedom Tree, wondering even more about the trouble that might be waiting for us, wherever Mundol and his men had imprisoned Elizabeth Anstey. But I knew we had to set her free. One look at Augustus Jackson had told me that: I wouldn't rest until she was free.

It was midnight when we found our way through the backstreets of the town, a dingy straggle of houses built on the marshes, narrow lanes overgrown with grass and weeds, the air dank with rot and disease. At one of the houses, Nathan knocked on a window and waited for ten seconds, then knocked again. At the second knock a door was opened and a man peered out briefly. Nathan disappeared inside. He was gone for several minutes. When he came out, he was with a girl, and a light flickered briefly from the dingy house. Nathan and the girl had a whispered conversation with Hubert Caldicott, and then turned to say something to the man. I saw his face as he listened to them: it was Jacob. Then the door closed and we were off again along the alley. The girl came with us, pulling a shawl over her head. She kept close to Nathan, and I could see she was carrying something: a bundle wrapped in cloth or brown paper; it smelt like food.

'Jacob,' I said under my breath, and the man at my side heard me. It was Edgar March, breathing heavily as we made our way through the darkness.

'That's right, lad,' he whispered back.

'He got away.'

'Looks like it.'

It must have been Jacob who passed on the news about Elizabeth. I wondered what else he had passed on. And what he would do now. He could hardly return to the cockle beds with Augustus Jackson looking for him. Maybe he would join us on Spurn, or travel further down the coast: there were plenty of cockle beds further south. He would be just one more stranger who had helped Nathan and Elizabeth Anstey.

We went on in silence, our feet making no sound along the lanes which were mostly earth and grass. Ahead of us, gaslights were sending up a yellow glow. Nathan and Caldicott slowed down. There was more whispering. I had no idea where we were but they waved to us to take it carefully and we followed them into cobbled alleyways, our boots clattering on the cobbles, our shadows leaping up the high walls of warehouses. I could hear the sounds of the docks: ropes knocking against bollards, a dog yapping, nightwatchmen calling to each other. The main commercial docks seemed to be over to our left towards the river, and we veered to the right and were suddenly in a dingy street that led along the edge of the old Haven docks and timber yards. We stopped, and clustered in the shadows of a narrow alley, the windowless walls looming above us like a prison.

'There it is,' Caldicott whispered.

There was a low brick building across the road, round and humped like a beehive, with barred windows. A single light burned through a grid in the wooden door. There was no sign of life.

'She'll be shackled,' Caldicott told us. 'But we've got a key.'

'How the hell did Nathan get that?' one of the men whispered.

I guessed Nathan had friends all over the town. Or maybe it was Jacob. There would be plenty of locksmiths working on the docks who could turn their hands to most things. The woman was probably Jacob's girl, or one of Nathan's friends from Satan's Hole. She was still clutching the parcel. I watched as Nathan and Caldicott whispered together with the girl. Nathan seemed to have come alive now with the excitement of doing something: he was quick, alert, arguing with Caldicott, showing him something about the building, asking the girl questions.

Then we were off. We crossed the narrow cobbled road, and got round the sides of the lock-up. Caldicott waited, breathing hard. 'No names,' he whispered once, then hammered on the door.

There was a pause, then a light flickered briefly at the grid in the solid wooden door. 'Who's that?' a voice called nervously from inside.

'Henry Mundol sent you some supper,' the girl shouted cheerfully.

'Nobody said anything about supper.'

'And a beer. He thought you might like a bit of company. Dark night like this.'

There was a pause, and then the door opened. Caldicott was nearest the door, but Nathan was the first inside. By the time I got into the building, the policeman was on the floor, blood streaming from his mouth, Bannister and one of the lads kneeling over him. Nathan was busy unfastening Elizabeth. She had been shackled to the wall, and was seated on a low bench. A newspaper was spread out on the table, and cards.

'Hurry,' Elizabeth was whispering to Nathan in a frightened voice.

The lock clicked back and she was free. She held her arms round Nathan's neck, burying her face in his shoulder. Her hair was dishevelled and her clothes looked filthy. There were no shoes on her feet.

'Get these on,' Caldicott said urgently, finding her boots in a corner. The man on the floor stirred into life, and Bannister gave him a savage punch in the stomach. 'And leave him alone.' There was another gasp for breath. 'Shackle him,' Caldicott said quickly.

Bannister grunted and made a move to lift the policeman to his feet, but Nathan turned swiftly and gave a harsh whisper. 'Not him,' he said, his voice croaking in the narrow cell. He glared straight at me. 'Him.'

Before I could move, Charles Blow was behind me with a knife and Bannister was moving towards me. I was too surprised to fight. They had my arms wrenched backwards and were dragging me to the shackles.

'Make a nice present for Mundol,' Nathan said viciously, seizing the first of the shackles and grabbing my arm.

I fought free and heard Caldicott shout angrily.

Elizabeth had my arm before Nathan could fasten the lock. 'Are you mad, Nathan!' she hissed at him.

'He works for Mundol.'

'Mundol would kill him.'

'We don't know that.'

'*I* know!'

'Lies, it's all lies, he works for Henry Mundol.'

Nathan tried to get the shackle round my wrist again and this time I was ready. I kicked backwards and got my elbow straight into Bannister's throat. He choked for breath, and I spun to my left, trying to slam my right fist into Charlie Blow's face.

But Elizabeth was between me and Nathan. She had a knife, grabbed from one of the men. 'You leave him be, you hear me,' she hissed.

'Keep out of this!'

'If he stays, I'm not going.'

Caldicott was suddenly shoving Nathan aside, slamming the shackles out of his hands and roaring at Bannister and the other men. 'Let him free. We don't get out of here soon, we'll all be wearing irons.'

I thought Nathan was going to go for us with his knife, or start crying. His face crumpled like a child's. His eyes were closed and he was gasping for air. We all watched him.

For a moment, Hubert seemed irresolute, puzzled, not

knowing who to believe. He glanced at Nathan and then back at me, confused by Nathan's passion. Then he frowned, grabbed the shackles and told Bannister to chain the policeman to the wall. The policeman started to move backwards across the floor, pulling himself on his elbows. Bannister hoisted him to his feet and fastened the lock. The policeman slumped between the shackles, sweating, trembling with fear.

'You must come now,' Elizabeth was telling Nathan.

We were alone in the cell. Everybody else had followed Hubert and Edgar. I stood by the door, listening to the retreating footsteps, the night sounds of the fishdocks. A siren wailed on the docks, and another siren answered out at the estuary.

Nathan seemed to be asleep. He had lost his energy and wildness. He had given up, slumped into a drugged apathy.

'Please,' she begged, touching his face.

He looked up at her and then at me. 'You trust him?' he asked.

'Yes,' she nodded firmly.

Nathan let Elizabeth take his arm and lead him out of the cell. As we locked the door behind us to delay the discovery of the escape, she looked at me directly for the first time.

'Thank you,' she said.

'For what?'

'For coming.'

'I wasn't given much choice,' I laughed.

She smiled, but her eyes were full of tears.

I felt like crying myself, stunned by Nathan's savage change of mood.

Sixteen

We left the dangerous streets of Satan's Hole behind us and crossed the marshes. There was no sign of anyone following us. As we struggled through the mud and marram grass, a curlew lifted from the shores and carried its alarm out over the river. The moon was high and bright in the sky. Millions of stars blinked and shimmered, dense clusters of milky light. I could hear the sea lapping against the foreshore, the liquid piping cry of the turnstones along the sands. The sky over Grimsby was yellow with gas flares and smoke from the curing houses.

I was really worrying now about how I was going to make my escape. If Henry Mundol and his men caught me with Nathan I would end up suffering the same fate as the rest of Nathan's gang. You didn't get kind treatment for breaking into a prison house and seizing somebody awaiting the magistrates' pleasure. And I could well imagine the sort of magistrates there would be in Grimsby: they were the talk of the east coast fishing communities: every one of them close friends and relatives of the biggest vessel owners, the men who owned and ran the fleets. They would be delighted to hear how I had been forced to take part in the night's adventure against my better judgment.

Even without Henry Mundol on the bench, I could count on several months in Lincoln Prison.

But what was the point of trying to make a run for it? The marshes were all around me, and I had no idea where I was. If I headed back to town, I would be caught without fail, and if I made for the open country, where would I find help? The money-belt that had been round my waist had disappeared during the first trip on *Dancing Sally*, and I was pretty sure Isaac Prusey had made short work of that. I had no money, no friends, and not a hope in hell of getting across country on my own. I would starve to death on the journey.

I plunged on with the rest of them, cursing my luck, keeping my eye on Nathan and Elizabeth.

'We have to keep low,' Caldicott whispered after several minutes, working his way back along the line. 'Don't make a sound.'

I looked ahead through the darkness. Elizabeth was following Caldicott, coming to join me. 'Are you all right?' she asked.

'More or less.'

'I'm glad you got away.'

'For this!' I said with a harsh laugh. 'I might have been better off getting caught when Augustus Jackson was looking for me.'

'Don't be stupid. You don't know him.'

She said this with such bitterness I kept quiet.

I saw a fire burning ahead in the darkness, and pointed it out to Elizabeth.

'Yes,' she nodded. 'The gypsies. They camp on the marshes.'

'There were some gypsies on Spurn,' I told her.

'Yes. It's the same ones. They cross further up the river. Nathan knows them. They help us.'

'I saw,' I said steadily.

She took in my words. 'You know he's my brother?'

'Yes.'

'And the copers?'

'Yes. He told me. It's a nice trade, Elizabeth.'

She said nothing, walking at my side when she could, stumbling in the rough marram grass or the drifts of soft sand, slipping in pools of mud. The horizon over the sea was still dark, but the noise of waking seabirds rose like a cloud of sound along the shores, lifting and falling through the dawn stillness. A glow of faint moonlight hung at the estuary, and in the dim light of the stars I could see the shapes of the smacks on the river, the outline of the gypsy camp ahead of us.

'These dunes,' Caldicott whispered back down the line, 'we rest here,' and we came to a halt at last. I knelt down and caught my breath. Elizabeth went forward to see Nathan. I closed my eyes and tried to calm my breathing. All around me, men were slumping on to the ground and groaning, complaining. Several of them had flasks of cold tea or corn brandy and started passing them round. Salt air touched my cheek. I could hear the river. The tide was going out, the low slap and gurgle of the water washing the riverside. A screech owl hunted over the marshes.

I felt restless, worried. I walked away from the dunes and found an old, flooded brick-pit, the souls of the drowned lost in the black water. I walked along the edge of the pit, stepping carefully over the treacherous bindweed. I could have plunged into the brick-pit and drowned. Drowned like my father, only not at sea. Below me, I could hear the water sloshing and gurgling in the darkness. The pits were a hundred years old, graveyards for the men, women and children who worked there, labourers starving on low wages, dying slowly in the pits rather than drown on the fishing. I couldn't get my mind clear of the ghosts. I couldn't hear what I was thinking. I went back to the men and lay down.

I must have slept for two or three hours. When I woke, and lifted myself on my elbow, I could see that we were not fifty yards from the river. Its great flat brown expanse flooded past with swirls of wrack and eddies of faster water. At the tideline, I could hear the low piping of the turnstones, the *pink-a-pink-a-pink* of the oyster-catchers, the musical clamour of the curlews. They knew dawn was coming. They heard the faint rustle of light breaking across the sea. At the estuary, the sky was a delicate pale pink, and the birds along the foreshore were clamouring for food. There were dozens of fishing smacks out in the river, cutters working for the cockles that the long-lining smacks used as bait for their lines, ketches heading for the estuary.

Half asleep, I peered at the marshes around me. A dead elm was standing a hundred yards from where we were resting, not far from the gypsy camp, its branches whitening and naked in the dawn light. Reed warblers *jag-jag-jagged* harshly in the weeds around the old brick-pits where a thick undergrowth of dead men's fingers and dog roses smothered the ground. The rosehips were already deep orange and beginning to turn scarlet because of the heat. They didn't usually change colour until September. The ground was thick with ragged robin. The brick-pits had been abandoned when the waters from the marshes broke through the diggings. The whole area was treacherous with bindweed. I sat up and rubbed my eyes clear of sleep. A kingfisher flashed along the shores, its blue feathers shining against the thick black mud of the foreshore.

Elizabeth came and sat on the dunes beside me when she saw that I was awake. 'You needed your rest,' she said with a smile. She was still combing her hair, tying it back behind her ears. She seemed pleased to see me again, touching my arm and kneeling down beside me.

'I've never had so much exercise,' I said with a grin.

'I'm glad you came.'

'Nathan wanted me with him,' I said. I couldn't keep the sarcasm out of my voice. 'I didn't feel like arguing.'

She blushed. 'You don't know him.'

'That's true.'

'You should give him time.'

'Fair enough.'

I could see Nathan making his way across the marshes to the gypsy camp. I didn't recognise any of the men talking with him, the women and children swarming around the brightly-painted caravans. The gypsies already had their fires burning. Several ponies grazed at the grasses, and I could see men sitting in the dunes all around us, keeping a watch.

'Is that the Freedom Tree?' I asked sarcastically, nodding at the dead elm.

'Yes,' Elizabeth said without hesitation.

'Is it a joke?'

'No. It's the tree that was here when the Pilgrims left for the New World.'

'Don't be daft.'

'Please yourself, Matthew.'

'That was Plymouth.'

'And here. They left from here for Holland and then America. You can ask. Or go and look in the churchyard. Francis Hawkins is buried there. They say he was trying to escape in search of religious liberty. You could be driven from the country for not worshipping in the Anglican church in those days, and executed if you came back.'

'What were they doing here?'

'There were whole families of them, from all over Lincolnshire.'

'But why?' I asked, intrigued, fascinated, settling back in the sand and simply enjoying listening to her voice whatever romantic nonsense she might be telling me. 'Why here?'

'They decided that the women should travel by water to Bawtry, down the Idle and the Trent. This was a pretty deserted part of the river in those days. The menfolk were to travel overland and meet them at Haven Creek. They were supposed to be meeting a Dutch vessel. They were going to travel to Holland, and then on to America.'

'What went wrong then?'

'The small boats arrived first and sheltered in the creek. Early the next morning the ship arrived and the menfolk managed to clamber aboard, but those in charge of the small boats with the women and the children got stuck fast in the mud. They couldn't get free. It was going to delay them until the tide rose again. They had to wait hours.'

'And they got caught?'

'There is something written about it. The alarm had been sounded in the surrounding countryside. Horsemen and men on foot with guns and staves came across country after them. Because he'd got a fair wind, the Dutch skipper weighed anchor and sailed. You can't blame him for that. The men already on board must have been in great distress for their wives and children left behind, but they could do nothing to help them. The women and children were abandoned, and left to survive penniless.'

I glanced up and saw the smile in her eyes. 'You are telling stories?' I said cautiously.

'Not really. It's all perfectly true. But the women and children were allowed their freedom in the end. I suppose it was too embarrassing to keep them in prison. The men eventually reached Holland and the authorities here let the families free after a few months.'

'There you are then, kindness prevailed,' I said. 'And the Freedom Tree is where the Dutch vessel was supposed to collect the families? Let's hope we have better fortune.'

'We don't need fortune,' Elizabeth told me solemnly.

'Oh no?'

'We have Nathan.'

I thought briefly about the way Nathan had behaved last night, his sweating panic in the police lock-up, but kept my peace: I didn't want to upset Elizabeth.

There was a shout from the gypsy camp, and I saw Nathan waving his arms. Half a mile offshore, *Dancing Sally* was tacking towards us. But Nathan was pointing down the coast. I stood up and shaded my eyes from the sun which was climbing over the estuary by now. I could see horses moving across the marshes. They shimmered and danced in the heat, and I wasn't sure I was seeing clearly, but then for a moment they suddenly seemed much nearer, and I could make out the riders.

'Let's go,' I shouted to Elizabeth, grabbing her hand and helping her up from the sands. 'Before we all lose our freedom.'

We ran down to the muddy foreshore and kept turning to watch the approach of the men on horseback. There was a heat haze over the foreshore, and the black mud shone blue in the sunlight. Waders darted and stabbed for shells and lugworms.

Elizabeth hurried away to Nathan's side.

I could see the longboat being lowered from *Dancing Sally*.

'We're going to have to swim for it,' Nathan shouted to us, and several of the men were already wading into the muddy water.

I saw Nathan put his arm round his sister and turn to look back towards the riders. Elizabeth turned round and searched for me. 'Pray, Matthew,' she shouted, when she saw me.

I was already diving into the water, sinking up to my knees in mud. The mud felt cold and slimy around my feet, going over the top of my boots.

Far away down the foreshore, I could see worm-diggers

at work, wrapped in old sacking, filling their metal buckets with long black worms. The worms were used for bait by some of the fishermen. There were dogs barking on the marshes. As I plunged deeper into the water, I thought I saw the gypsies moving their caravans along the foreshore away from the galloping horsemen, but I was soon too busy trying to drag myself out of the sucking drowning mud to worry about what was happening on shore.

Seventeen

I got back to *Dancing Sally* in the longboat, and collapsed in the stern while Caldicott took the smack back into the main channel and down the river. We could see the riders on the shore, watching us from the desolate marsh. Several of them had gone in chase of the gypsies. I could just make out the black outline of Augustus Jackson, motionless on his horse.

At my side, Charles Blow offered me his flask. 'Sorry about the rough stuff,' he said ruefully. 'You don't argue with Nathan.'

I took the flask and half-drained it, swallowing hard and rubbing my eyes as they filled with tears. The brandy was like hot molten honey. 'You don't have to be so quick with your fists,' I said.

He held the flask lightly, weighing how much I'd drunk and grinning with amusement. His squat ugly face was drained from lack of sleep, and he had dark bruises underneath his eyes. 'You learn to use your fists,' he said after emptying the flask. 'Growing up in Hackney.'

'We all grow up somewhere, Charlie. Doesn't mean we have to enjoy hurting people.'

'You didn't grow up in Hackney,' he said, then roared

with laughter at this, and punched me on the shoulder.

I smiled ruefully. You couldn't resist Charlie's good-humour.

'Don't tell me. You had a hard time?'

'Nah,' he said grinning. 'It weren't that bad.'

'You're naturally evil then?'

'More or less. Weren't the workhouse, anyways. Worst bit was before the workhouse. At least I learnt to fight in the workhouse. Farthing a broken nose. Halfpence a torn ear. Full penny if you gouged an eye out. I got a living for life in Hackney workhouse. Worst bit was before. Isle of Dogs. Growing up there. I never had a mother. She was on the tarting. Didn't want kids. Couldn't understand what they was for. My old man was a gravedigger. He used to take me with him digging the graves. You couldn't put the spade in without hacking into somebody's head. Dead-on-dead they piled 'em. I hate the smell of rotting flesh. You ever been in an overcrowded graveyard, Matthew?'

'Leave off, Charlie, it's been a rough night.'

'No, I'm telling you, they fight for room to rest, the dead do. They shift around for a bit of peace. It was like a battleground some mornings when my old man finished digging new graves. Limbs scattered everywhere. Bits of bone. Blood soaking into the ground. No wonder they had grave robbers a few year back. Corpses must have been glad to get out of my old man's way.'

I listened to Charlie until I fell asleep, and when I woke, we were going over Stony Binks and Nathan was shouting for the longboat. At his side, Elizabeth was leaning on his arm, a tall slender woman in a blue silk dress, tight at her waist and with a white collar. Her hair had been washed and brushed, and hung loose over her shoulders. She smiled at me when I got to my feet, and there were delicate hints of pink rouge on her cheeks and lipstick on her lips. She had a blue ribbon tying her hair back behind her ears.

'Welcome to sanctuary,' she said, still leaning on Nathan's arm.

'Sanctuary?'

'That's what I call it.'

Nathan glanced at me quickly, busy watching the men, indifferent to my waking. He seemed to resent my presence, alert to anything I said to his sister. His face was drained of colour and his eyes dark with hollows. I guessed he hadn't slept all night after the panic in Satan's Hole.

'I've been here before,' I reminded her.

'Yes, but not with me. This time, I'll be able to show you round.'

We got ourselves ashore, and for a while I was busy with Caldicott, checking the longboat and supplying *Dancing Sally* with fresh drinking water and food. Despite his age, Caldicott seemed to be inexhaustible.

'I never leave her short of supplies,' he explained as we worked, checking the galley stores with the boy, Joel Cross.

'In case you have to sail suddenly?' I suggested.

'That's right, lad.'

'Seems a tiring way of life to me, Hubert.'

He hardly gave me a glance. 'It's a life,' he said brusquely.

When he was satisfied, he took *Dancing Sally* back to the creek at Old Hive, and I went ashore. I found Prusey at the fire with Sidney Lill, helping himself to a mug of tea, watching my approach with his sullen, crafty eyes.

'You did all right then, friend?' he said unpleasantly.

'We got her freed.'

'So I see.'

He drained his mug and walked away, spitting in the sand as he went. I saw him making his way to the cottages near Smeaton's Light where Nathan and Elizabeth were standing together, talking. One of the cottages seemed to be kept for Nathan, and Elizabeth had gone straight there. Isaac joined them and started talking and waving in my direction.

'He's a friendly sod, Isaac Prusey,' I muttered.

Sidney Lill shrugged and handed me a plate of food. 'He's got his job to do,' he said in his inoffensive way. 'Same as the rest of us. He doesn't know you yet, Matthew, and this is a good way of life. He doesn't want to lose it. Eat this. You had a rough night by all accounts.'

I finished the food, and kept my eye on Prusey and Nathan. They were arguing about something and I guessed it must be me. Elizabeth listened, and then said something sharply to Isaac, stabbing her finger into his chest and turning away. She went inside the cottage briefly and then came out and made directly for where I was sitting at the fire.

'Keep me company, Matthew,' she said.

'You trying to make me popular!'

'Just keep me company,' she said impatiently, and walked off towards the shallow channel of water that separated Sunk Island from the mainland. I followed her reluctantly. I didn't want to get embroiled in her fights with Nathan. Nathan was nowhere to be seen. Prusey stood alone outside the cottage, brooding.

'Does Prusey still think I work for Henry Mundol?' I asked.

'It doesn't matter what he thinks.'

'Nathan listens to him.'

'You know that, do you?'

'You were arguing. The three of you. I saw.'

She stopped and looked at me, her eyes quizzical and amused, her bad temper gone. 'We weren't arguing about you, Matthew,' she said. 'We were arguing about me. They're angry, because I have to go back.'

'Back?'

'To Satan's Hole. To go on with my work.'

'I don't understand.'

'Then don't judge what you don't understand. Nathan listens to *me*,' she said emphatically. 'He listens to what I tell him. You don't have to worry about Isaac Prusey. He always complains about things and then does what he's told in the end.'

I shrugged. 'Fair enough.'

'Shall we walk down the foreshore? I want to show you something.'

We set off along the narrow stretch of sand and rough grass. On the river side of the Spurn the ground was muddier, the water less rough because it was protected from the sea by the main spit. We walked parallel to Sunk Island and on towards Hawkins Point, a jut of land further up the river beyond the Island. You could see the dark outline of several sandbanks through the murky depths of the river.

'Why do you call this place sanctuary?' I asked.

'Because it is a sanctuary.'

'From what?'

'Oh don't be difficult, Matthew. Use your imagination. From Henry Mundol and the other owners. From the brutality of Satan's Hole. From the fleets. It is our sanctuary before we depart for real freedom.'

'Right, absolutely, I understand,' I said brightly.

'And don't mock,' she laughed, hitting me sharply on the arm and warning me. 'I hear your tone.'

'I wouldn't dare . . .'

'You would, and you won't.'

'Where are we going?' I asked when we had walked in silence for some minutes, following the curving shore of the river, watching the vessels out in the main channel and the smoke rising from the curing houses on the far coast. From Spurn, the Lincolnshire countryside looked radiant with green fields and dazzling sunlight, a lush rich landscape spreading away from the crowded slums of the fishing port. I felt free, and strangely elated. I could have kept walking with Elizabeth for the rest of my life, out of the nightmare I had wandered into, away to some different kind of life.

'Stone Creek,' Elizabeth answered my question.

'Where's that?'

'Up the river a way. I want to show you something.'

We saw isolated farmhouses on the Spurn mainland: white buildings shining in the summer sun, men working in the flat fields. Whole families were gathering the August harvest, men toiling at the wheat, women and children busy with the gleaning.

'So many children,' Elizabeth said quietly to herself.

'On the farms?'

'Working everywhere.'

'At least this is healthy,' I pointed out. 'They aren't orphans, and they get enough to eat without being beaten for it.'

'The boys on the fleets get enough to eat,' she said dryly.

'I know,' I said, understanding her sarcasm. 'But that isn't freedom.'

She nodded, her arms folded across her blue dress, her eyes blue with some intense unhappiness. 'There are so many,' she said quietly. 'The fleets can't put to sea without apprentice-boys. Nobody cares what happens to them. It seems impossible, when they die so far away and nobody *sees* what happens. You can't make people understand.'

'I know,' I muttered.

I felt oppressed by her unhappiness, disturbed by the intensity of her feeling. She was staring across the desolate river as if she longed to make it disappear, dry up and become black mud in the hot summer sun so that no vessels could make for sea and the nightmare of the fishing fleets.

She sensed my concern, and smiled quickly, touching my arm, reassuring. But she couldn't keep the indignation out of her voice.

'The Sisters do what they can,' she said. 'Helping the families. Getting in touch with families out of town, where the boys come from. But there isn't much they *can* do. Most of their time is spent fighting the brothels and the disease. And do you know, Henry Mundol gives them money for that. He is the town's great hypocrite. He gives them money to take the women off the streets, because the women give his crews disease. Some weeks he can't get his vessels to sea there are so many boys needing treatment for syphilis. Can you imagine that, children with syphilis.'

I blushed, shading my eyes from the glitter of the water. I had come close enough to the disease myself on a few occasions, visiting friendly girls in the stews of other ports. I had never visited the brothels in Satan's Hole, though they were ripe with sickness for visiting seamen.

'But what about the fleets?' I asked. 'He doesn't do anything to stop the copers? His skippers trade with them freely.'

The copers took more damnation to the fleets than the stews of Satan's Hole. Men drowned when they were drunk on aniseed whisky or wild with laudanum dreams. They didn't drown in the arms of prostitutes, whatever the sickness they bought for their money.

Elizabeth laughed tightly, angrily, her cheeks flushing hotly. 'It suits his purposes,' she said bitterly.

'His purposes?'

'For the men to be addicted to alcohol and tobacco. Addicted men need his cash. He has such twisted religious scruples you see. Close the brothels because the women give his men sickness but leave the copers free to trade. His vessels need men who can't afford to leave the fleets, they are in such debt to alcohol and drugs. He couldn't keep crews otherwise. He is a fine Methodist, a pure-souled man.'

I waited, thinking about Nathan. Did I have the courage to mention Nathan, and the community of thieves on Spurn, earning their livelihood selling illegal drink and tobacco to the fleets? Elizabeth knew all about that. She must be ravaged by the pain of seeing how her brother earned his living. I was silenced by my confusion, suddenly conscious of the deadly conflict in this world Elizabeth called a sanctuary. My mind said Henry Mundol was not the only one with twisted religious scruples, but my heart knew better. There was more in this than answered the calmness of logic.

'You are quiet,' she said after a long silence.

'I don't understand everything.'

'You mean my brother Nathan?' she said calmly, matter-of-factly.

She seemed to see straight into my mind. I shrugged, and avoided her eyes, but she went on looking at me, her quietness like a rebuke. I turned at last, and spoke directly.

'There has to be a reason for all this,' I said, nodding back towards Spurn, the camp where we had left Nathan busy with his men. 'What he does. I don't understand, but I don't judge. It isn't my business. But you realise Nathan has a problem?'

She flinched at that, stepping back briefly and turning away.

'No!'

'Lizzie . . .'

'No, no!'

'It is only the truth, Lizzie . . .'

'No! Nathan does not have a problem. No! You do not call me Lizzie. Nobody calls me Lizzie.'

'All right, I'm sorry.'

'Nobody!'

We paused for breath, Elizabeth flushed and angry, my own mind racing with doubts and fears. If she turned against me, what would happen to Isaac Prusey's sly insinuations. I couldn't trust Nathan to keep a clear mind, especially after the violence in the lock-up, and without Elizabeth I hadn't many friends on Spurn. Her sanctuary would not be a place of escape for me, unless it was escape into death.

'I am your friend,' I said urgently. 'I am grateful.'

'Then never talk about Nathan.'

'I won't.'

'Never.'

'I promise.'

We stood face to face, gathering ourselves, calming down. Our voices had alarmed waders along the foreshore, and they rose noisily around us.

'I am your friend,' I said again, reaching out and touching her arm.

'Yes,' she said finally.

'I promise.'

'Yes.'

We walked on at last, past the huddled bothies of Irish Green, and reached Stone Creek in silence. Then I saw what she had wanted to show me: another vessel, a ketch moored in the shallows, her sails reefed down and her hull gleaming against the mud. She was a lovely sleek vessel, eighty-foot long and with a fine carved tiller. On the bows, her name gleamed in the sun: *Waterwitch*.

'She's beautiful,' I gasped, going forward to look at the name.

Elizabeth stood on the higher ground, her arms folded, her eyes shining with pleasure. She looked young again, the haggard pain gone from her face, a fresh youthful excitement gleaming in her eyes.

'What does the name mean?' I called from the side of the smack.

'I will tell you one day,' she said and laughed.

Then I saw Nathan, coming towards us from the dunes.

Eighteen

'Are you telling him about our *Waterwitch*?' he shouted as he stood at the top of the sandy dune overlooking the creek. 'Telling him our secrets?'

'Don't be childish, Nathan.'

'She's a fine vessel, isn't she, Matthew Lidgard?'

'She is,' I said. 'I bet she handles beautifully.'

'She does indeed. You should let Hubert show you round. *Waterwitch* is Hubert's special secret. His love affair. He found her in a salvage yard. He's been working on her for months, trying to get her right.'

'Right?'

'She was damaged in the hull. He's repaired that, with some of the men. He's tried her on the banks a few times. She is his great joy.'

Elizabeth seemed suddenly impatient, restless, wanting to leave. 'Matthew doesn't want to know all this,' she said resentfully, pulling at my arm. 'Let's get back, Matthew.'

'You haven't walked all this way for nothing,' Nathan laughed.

'Have you been following us?' Elizabeth said.

'No, why should I? You're free to go where you will.'

'Thank you.'

'Now he's proved himself,' he added with a glance in my direction.

'Stop that, Nathan,' she told him angrily.

I watched them, facing up to each other, furious, determined. I might as well have not been there.

'Have I?' I asked, interrupting their fury.

Nathan glanced at me irritably. 'You still here, Lidgard?'

'Have I proved myself?' I said calmly, not worried by his tone, not frightened now that there was just the two of us out on the dunes away from the rest of his men. I climbed up the steep bank of the creek and stood in front of Nathan. He watched me, gathering himself, amused by my threat.

'He's a dangerous man, Lizzie.'

'Don't be foolish. I was telling him about the Sisters. All the money Henry Mundol provides for the fallen women.'

Nathan laughed bitterly. 'A righteous man,' he scoffed.

They seemed to be having their own private conversation, but I was determined not to be thrown off my guard by Nathan Anstey. I stared him out and went on as though there was no tension between us.

'I know why I hate Henry Mundol,' I said. 'I have good reasons.'

'Indeed,' Nathan smiled coldly. 'A flogging is a good reason.'

'But he never flogged you.'

'He might like to,' Nathan said with an icy derision.

Elizabeth scrambled up the bank after me and stood in front of Nathan, touching his arm, trying to pull him away. He shook her free.

'He hurt your family?' I went on relentlessly.

There was a tension between the two of them I couldn't grasp. She pulled at his arm again and then turned away impatiently, glancing at me.

'This is stupid,' she said angrily.

'Is it?'

'You don't need to know anything about us, Matthew.'

Nathan glowered at the two of us. 'Stop calling him Matthew.'

'It's his name, isn't it! If you're going to tell him all our business I might as well use his name!'

'You don't have to use his name!'

They were silent, glaring at each other. His fists were clenched. I thought he might strike out at her, hit her with his clenched fist.

Suddenly, Elizabeth turned on me with her wild anger, her eyes full of tears. '*Waterwitch* was my father's vessel,' she said furiously. 'Henry Mundol bought it. He bankrupted my father. He ruined us. Do you need to know that? Do you need to hear that?'

She was shouting, and I stepped back involuntarily, ashamed of my questions. I glanced at the beautiful fishing smack, delicate on the black mud of the dry creek. The water of the tide was already flooding into the creek, washing against her hull, but she was still lying to port against the mud, waiting for the tide to lift her. She should be out at sea, and any fisherman would have felt that.

'I'm sorry,' I said, embarrassed, awkward.

But Elizabeth had turned to leave.

'Lizzie,' Nathan called.

'I have to prepare.'

'No, wait.'

'I can't wait. I have to get back to the Sisters. I have things to do. They need me.'

Then she was going, stalking back along the foreshore, her arms folded across her chest, her hair free and blowing in the slight wind. We watched her go, and then we were alone.

Nathan was chewing the inside of his mouth. He glared across the estuary towards the dull haze of Grimsby.

'How will she get back?' I asked after a long silence.

He glared at me, resenting the words, the intrusion into his own thoughts. He took a flask from his pocket and swallowed the brandy.

'Hubert has to run up the river for a delivery.'

'A delivery?'

'Yes. Is that all right with you?' he asked derisively.

'Is it safe, I mean going back to Haven Creek?'

'They won't be going there. The delivery's to a farm we sometimes use, beyond Barton. Off Pudding Pie Sand. Three tons of tobacco.'

I was surprised at the amount. Nathan spoke in staccato bursts, his voice harsh and unnatural, his eyes lifeless and grey. Water in the creek lapped around *Waterwitch*. We stood in silence as the afternoon burned around us. I took my time, letting him calm down.

'Is she really going back to Grimsby?' I asked.

He nodded curtly.

'Isn't it dangerous?'

'The Sisters will look after her.'

'In the Convent,' I mused.

'That's right.'

'She told me about them.'

He was irritated, annoyed by my questions.

'She is going back,' he said with a sneer. 'She tries to help. Put right what Henry Mundol puts wrong. She thinks she has to do that. A good Catholic you see. The priest tells her all that nonsense. She must help the fallen women.'

His voice was filled with loathing, a wild hatred.

'You're both Catholics,' I reminded him.

'We were. When we were children. I've grown up.'

I kept my voice quiet, trying to calm him down. 'I thought she wanted to leave for Lerwick,' I said, trying to change the subject.

He laughed. 'Another dream. She lives in dreams. We all

go to Lerwick and live by the fishing. Be a family again. We have *Waterwitch* and *Dancing Sally*. Why not. Why not live by dreams!'

'I don't know,' I shrugged, as if his rhetoric had been a genuine question. 'You tell me.'

He scoffed. 'We can't leave, Matthew. We can never leave. Henry Mundol has the papers, the indentures. Half the men with us signed indentures with Henry Mundol. As long as he has those, he can send the law after us wherever we go. He doesn't mind us selling whisky and tobacco to his fleets. That keeps his men happy. But if we tried to leave Spurn and start earning a living from the fishing, he'd get the law after us in days. Him and his overseer, Augustus Jackson. He'd not let us free. He couldn't afford the bad example. Other fishermen might get ideas. He would follow us to the end of the seas, and Elizabeth will never understand that.'

I waited for a moment, amazed by his vehemence, his wildness. When he was calm, I tried another question. 'Then why don't you get them back?'

He laughed. 'Get what back?'

'The indentures.'

'Are you trying to be stupid?'

'No. You could buy them. Or steal them.'

'He wouldn't sell. And we couldn't steal them. He has copies at the Custom House and in his own home, locked in a safe. He would never sell, and there isn't a chance in hell of breaking into his safe, even if we could get the copies in the Custom House. You think we haven't considered even that? We're not without imagination, Matthew.'

'So that's why you hate him?' I said roughly.

'What?' He frowned. He glanced at me, his eyes blank with tiredness. His anger had burned out into a dull resentment, a confused bitterness.

'Why you hate Henry Mundol.'

He stared at me, the incomprehension flickering across his dull eyes, his mouth working as he chewed his lips. Then he took a deep breath and collected himself. He stared down at the sand around his boots.

'No,' he said bleakly.

'I thought . . .'

'No.'

He looked up and his eyes were red with broken blood vessels and exhaustion. He hadn't slept all night. He looked as if he was living in a delirium where sleep was more dangerous than living nightmares.

'He ruined my father,' he said suddenly, his voice drained of any human feeling, almost croaking with anger. 'Lizzie told you that.'

'He's ruined a lot of fishermen,' I pointed out.

'Yes.'

'They don't hate.'

'You know that do you?'

'They don't want revenge.'

He flinched, glancing at me quickly. 'Did I say I wanted revenge?'

'You live your life for it.'

He thought about that, chewing the inside of his mouth, reflective, holding my eyes. It wasn't me he was seeing.

'And that matters to you?' he said quietly. 'How I live my life? You want to go back and tell him?'

'I'm not working for him, Nathan.'

'So you say.'

'I have never even seen the man.'

But he didn't seem interested in hearing me out. He took a decision and kicked at the sand. 'Let's walk back,' he said quietly.

I followed him, and he talked as we walked. I didn't interrupt.

'I'll tell you,' he said briefly. 'We had two long-liners in

Yarmouth. *Waterwitch* and *Eliza*. *Eliza* was named after my mother. She helped on the market and looked after the crews: the boys and the younger men who were not married. We had twenty-two men working for us. I went on my first trip when I was eleven. My father did the summer season to Iceland and worked the coastal waters the rest of the year. He was a good fisherman. He knew the grounds.'

He paused to take a drink from his flask, staring blindly across the wide river towards the estuary. He put the flask back into his pocket and went on talking, ploughing through the soft sand with his foot.

'Henry Mundol got him into debt somehow. Took a catch for the Grimsby market and then refused to pay, claimed the fish were rotten. My father was an honest man. He wouldn't have lied to save his soul. He went to see Mundol and wasted more time arguing. There was nothing he could do. But the dishonesty got into his mind. He gnawed at it, couldn't let it go. He sold another catch to a friend of Mundol's without knowing it and the friend pulled the same trick. My father mortgaged *Waterwitch* to keep us going. He lost his touch. He couldn't sleep. In the end we had a run of bad trips and had to mortgage *Eliza* as well and then she went down off Harwich in a bad storm. We lost everything. We were bankrupt.'

He walked on in silence, his eyes fixed to the ground, his mouth working in furious emotion. Suddenly, he came to a halt and turned on me. There were tears pouring down his face.

'My father hanged himself,' he said, choking on the words. 'He used the long-lines. The lines cut right through his neck, nearly decapitated him. It was my mother who found him, covered in blood. He had a cross in his hand, a crucifix. He was praying as he died. There was blood still trickling out of his mouth. He hanged himself, and my mother died of grief a year later. She couldn't forgive herself

for not going to the yard to see if he was all right. He never
went to the yard on a Sunday afternoon. She wouldn't
believe it wasn't her fault. Henry Mundol took *Waterwitch*
in payment of the debt. We didn't see her again until
Hubert found her. Mundol never said a word to my mother
for comfort. He killed her. He killed them both.'

Without another word, Nathan turned and walked off.
We were within sight of Sunk Island, and he waded
through the shallow water of the channel and climbed up
on to the isolation of the island, surrounded by water and
grazing sheep. I was left on my own on the foreshore, with
just my fears and the curlews to keep me company, and the
sight of Nathan Anstey, standing alone on his wretched
island, dreaming the nightmares of revenge that seemed to
keep him alive.

When I got back to the camp, Isaac Prusey was organising the men. They were carrying loads of tobacco to the
longboat and rowing it out to *Dancing Sally*. Elizabeth was
watching them, standing alone on the shingle, wearing her
grey cotton dress again and leather boots. She ignored me
when I walked up to her.

'You have to go back?' I asked.

'Yes, I do.'

'I talked to Nathan about your parents . . .'

'Don't tell me.'

'Elizabeth . . .'

'I don't want to hear. I'm going back to see Father
Hobart.'

'He's your priest?'

'Yes,' she said nodding. 'There is a lot to do. There are
new girls in one of the brothels. I have to do something
useful.'

'I understand that.'

There was a brief pause. She kicked at the sand and
stared down at her boots, then glanced restlessly towards

Dancing Sally.

'Nathan wants you to go on the fleets,' she said abruptly.

'What!'

'He told me.'

'I don't know what you mean,' I said, confused, glancing round to where Prusey was organising another load of tobacco for Pudding Pie Island.

'He wants you to help with the next trip to the fleets.'

'He can go to hell!'

'Well,' she said angrily. 'If you see how we earn our money, you may understand why I want to get my brother away.'

And answering a shout from one of the men, she walked off to the longboat and climbed aboard for *Dancing Sally*.

Nineteen

The next day, we were sailing for the Dogger Bank and the fleets. The heat had grown torpid and humid, and *Dancing Sally* responded sluggishly to the tiller. Nathan went down below the minute we were off Old Hive and Isaac Prusey took the helm. There was nothing to do on board once the tobacco and alcohol for the trip had been loaded into the hold, and I spent the first watch at the tiller with Prusey. He handled the smack lightly and easily, enjoying himself, relaxing and smoking a pipe. He kept a mug of tea beside him on the tiller post, shouting down to the galley for more as soon as one mug was drained.

'We making straight for the Dogger, Isaac?' I asked as *Dancing Sally* ploughed through green water and clouds of white spray sparkled over the bowsprit.

'Clay Deeps,' he nodded. 'Fenners and Gamecock's will be further north. We always go for Mundol's first.'

'Oh?'

'Nathan's orders.'

There were a dozen fleets working the Dogger grounds, but I knew I would never go back on the trawlers after my few days on *Happy Jack*. They could talk about all the money in the world, but it didn't seem a likely trade to me.

The men worked eighteen hours a day, gutting the fish when the trawl nets were down on the bottom, then hauling the trawl again for a fresh catch as soon as they had finished. If the hauls were good they never got any rest, but if the nets came up empty, they fought and argued and bought drink from the copers. And whatever hell they were living through, it went on night or day, summer and winter, for months on end. In storms, they were lucky to get back to port alive.

For the men, slaving at the nets without rest, the copers and grog-ships selling tobacco and alcohol were the one glimmer of light, the one chance of comfort. A skipper only had to hang an oilskin over the stern of his smack, and the grog-ship would round up into the wind and await his longboat. Shag tobacco at a few pence a pound was a real temptation, and the drams of free drink soon tempted men to buy whole bottles, until drink-crazed crews ended up selling their catch or even the trawl nets to buy more of the rank poison. If a trawl net was reported lost overboard, you could bet your week's wages it had been sold for drink.

It felt grand to be taking part in such a trade.

'You like this work, Isaac?' I asked casually.

He glanced at me quickly, his eyes narrowing with suspicion. At the tiller, his hands flexed nervously. 'You think I have a choice?' he said sarcastically.

'You could stay on the fishing?' I suggested.

'Yes, but not earn the same money.'

I kept my silence. He drained his mug of tea and shouted for more, Joel Cross clambering up the companion and filling the mug from a tin teapot. They kept an urn of tea on the boil round the clock, filling the urn with fresh tea leaves and sugar and milk when it was emptied. The tea was dark brown, and sweeter than syrup.

'Were you born to the fishing?' I asked, trying to keep him talking.

He lit his pipe again, stuffing the black tobacco into the bowl, and then sucking the smoke into his lungs with his eyes closed.

'No,' he said after a pause. 'I grew up Caistor way, just outside Grimsby. My father was a farm hand. He drank. When there was typhoid in the village, my mother went round helping folks. Stupid bitch. She died of the fever. My father drank all the time after that. Got himself caught in a threshing machine when he was drunk. Cut his leg off. He didn't stand much chance after that. I signed indentures with Fenner's when I was twelve, and when they laid men off, Henry Mundol bought the indentures.'

He had grown sullen, resentful, talking about the past. His skin was inflamed, and he pushed his fingers back through his greasy hair. Lumps of grease hung at his collar. He concentrated on the tiller, watching the canvas of the mainsail, draining his mug of tea. It was hot enough to burn the skin off your mouth but he didn't seem to notice.

I climbed down the steep companion ladder. Sidney and Joel were in the galley, drinking tea and chatting, preparing the midday food: fried fish and boiled potatoes. Joel washed the potatoes in a bucket of sea water, scrubbing them with a wire brush and then throwing the dirty water over the side. While he was doing this, Sidney was baking bread, the unleavened busters always ending up with his grubby thumbprints baked into the crust. I chatted for a few minutes, and then went into the cabin. Bannister and Charles Blow were fast asleep. John Parnham, a boy of fourteen who clambered everywhere on the smack in sheer terror, and frightened of even looking at the water, was writing to his mother. I got my pipe, and went through from the passage into the starboard hold where the goods for the trip had been packed. I needed some fresh tobacco.

In the hold, I found Michael Hart. He jumped when the

door slammed back. He was twelve, maybe thirteen, and had been on the smacks since he signed indentures at eleven in Whitby, a visiting skipper giving him drink and getting him to sign without even reading the details. He had been on Mundol's for a year, working as a galley boy, before running away.

He cringed when he saw me, and then smiled his false, mincing smile. He had learned to please everybody on Mundol's smacks: following the older men, wincing and placating, trying to be friendly. He stood up and stared at me, his eyes full of fear. He had been kneeling beside the shelves, staring at a stack of picture cards.

'Let's have a look, Michael,' I said, reaching out my hand.

He held the cards out, smiling. 'You'll like them, Mr Lidgard,' he said quickly, grinning with a sudden excitement.

'Will I?'

'They make you excited,' he said, licking his lips.

I stared at the crude pictures: men and women together, men with two or three women, a couple with women wrapped around each other. I glanced up at Michael's pale face, the boils on his neck, the white pustules clustered at the sides of his mouth. He licked his lips again and held his head on one side. 'I can do things, Mr Lidgard,' he said.

I handed the cards back and told him to put them where they belonged. He flinched nervously, kneeling down again and stuffing the cards into the packages as quickly as he could. When he stood up, he tried to smile again but stayed well away from me.

'Get out,' I said angrily. 'Find some work on deck.'

He hesitated for a second, glancing at the door behind me, then turned and made for the for'ard door up to the bows. The door shut behind him and he was gone. I waited for a moment, controlling my anger. I glanced at the shelves: we carried a ton of tobacco and racks of aniseed whisky. The pornographic pictures were on the bottom shelves, three packages, hundreds of cards. I wondered angrily what Nathan charged for the cards. It was certainly easier work than being a fisherman.

In the corridor, Nathan was standing outside his cabin, listening. As I came out of the starboard hold, I walked straight into him. He leaned against the door of his cabin, smiling his strange, withdrawn smile. He had been drinking again, swallowing the sweet laudanum which filled his eyes with dreams.

'Your outrage is commendable,' he said with his cold derision.

'He's twelve years old.'

'Too old for some tastes, Matthew.'

'You bastard.'

'No,' he shook his head with amusement. 'Not me.'

'You prefer laudanum.'

'I *do*!' he said with outrageous delight, a lethal deranged mockery.

'Very funny.'

'You understand.'

'That boy . . .'

'Gives pleasure where he can. You should have let him show you.'

The contempt in Nathan's eyes was frightening, chilling. I pushed past him and went into the galley. As I helped myself to a mug of tea, he went back into his cabin and closed the door gently. The gentleness seemed like an insult: the indifference, the brutal calm.

I climbed the companion with my tea and went to the bows. Luke Hobbins was sitting on the bowsprit, his eyes closed, a Bible in his hands. He heard me, but kept his eyes closed until he had finished his prayers. I saw his childish lips moving, the spray wetting his cheeks, the movement of the smack lifting his fair curly hair. He was seventeen, but looked years younger, unlike most of the orphan boys who worked the corrupted fleets.

'Hello, Mr Lidgard,' he said pleasantly, talking like an old man.

'You can call me Matthew, Luke.'

We both grinned at the conjunction of names.

'And we have a John on board,' he said with delight, 'John Parnham. But no Mark. My favourite Gospel.'

'Is it?'

'Yes. Although my mother named me Luke because she loved the Nativity stories. Not the way the Catholics love them: not idolatry. But simply as stories.'

He always made me want to laugh, with his seriousness and sombre religion. He sang hymns when he was working, and read the Bible whenever he found a moment's rest.

'Were you Methodists?' I asked him, settling on the bowsprit and enjoying the little fresh air there was from the turgid seas.

'Independent Methodists,' he answered. 'My father was born with the Methodists, but saw the corruption of the truth. He became an Independent when he heard the Word being preached in Harwich.' I tried not to show my amusement, but he seemed to sense it even with his eyes closed to the blinding sunlight. 'There are so many false shepherds,' he said nodding, as if reading my thoughts. 'Even within Methodism. Magic Methodists, Methodist Unitarians, New Connexion, Primitive Methodists. The Primitives have some of the truth, but they distort the Word. There were Quaker Methodists in Newlyn. And Tent Methodists, and Welsh Jumpers.'

'They're all Bible Christians,' I pointed out.

'But they don't read the same Bible,' Luke insisted,

turning and drilling me with his intense, immature eyes, as if he would convert me by the blaze of his belief. 'They don't read the *same* Bible.'

I let him calm down and then told him about Michael. 'I found him in the hold,' I said quietly. 'Looking at the stock.'

I had no idea why I was speaking: why should I burden Luke with the misery of another child. Yet he seemed to invite the confidence.

He nodded solemnly. 'He goes to study the pictures,' he said calmly.

'You know that?'

'He is a sodomite, Matthew.'

I shook my head hopelessly. 'No, Luke. He isn't a *sodomite*, he's a *child*. He isn't old enough to be what you call him. He doesn't know.'

'We all know,' Luke said with his relentless cheerfulness. 'We are born in sin. We know that. There isn't any excuse. I have told Michael.'

'Told him?'

'He knows the danger to his soul.'

'He's *twelve*, Luke. You're seventeen, aren't you? You can understand. You know the truth. He's a child.'

Luke glanced at me, concerned, worried. 'You care about him?'

'I can't speak to him,' I said. 'I tried . . .'

'But he smiled at you,' Luke said quickly, seeing what I was saying immediately, looking away.

'Yes,' I said, 'he smiled at me, if you like. You're more his age. Why don't you talk to him?'

'I have.'

'Again.'

'No.'

'Why not?' I demanded.

He turned and shook his head sadly. 'He came into my

bunk one night,' he said with a sigh. 'He is beyond anything I can tell him. He doesn't hear my words. You came
to us too late to be of help to Michael. He sleeps with the
devil already, Matthew. Without grace, we cannot save
him. Without grace, he is a wretched sinner.'

In Luke's generous, good-hearted mouth, the words
seemed to come from the devil himself. How could a boy
of seventeen believe such things of a child of twelve? I
didn't know which of them was the more lost.

I was silent after that. *Dancing Sally* seemed to hang
motionless on the sluggish waves, although the horizon
lifted to our starboard side and the sun gradually slipped
behind us. I thought we might be touching two or three
knots, although it was difficult to tell in such calm. The sky
seemed to be gathering at the horizon like a boil, pulsing
with immense heat, threatening the vast grey seas. The
German Sea, my mother had always called the North Sea:
something dangerous, without age.

For some reason I thought briefly of Nathan: dangerous,
and without age: the words seemed right for Nathan.

At my side, Luke started to sing one of his favourite
hymns: 'Come, O my guilty brethren, come,' he sang, his
childish voice sounding sweet and clear as we churned
with our hellish cargo through the afternoon heat. At the
tiller, Isaac Prusey remained motionless, like a figure
carved from wood. Edgar March joined in the singing,
and then Sidney Lill, climbing up from the companion
with fresh tea. Luke led them as if they were in church, or
on the quays on a Sunday afternoon, trying to convert the
drunken crowds.

> 'Come, o my guilty brethren, come,
> groaning beneath your load of sin!
> His bleeding heart shall make you room,
> His open side shall take you in;

He calls you now, invites you home;
Come, o my guilty brethren, come.'

After the first two verses, I turned away and went back
down below to the aft cabin where I slept a restless couple
of hours before waking to Sidney Lill's clamour for the
day's main meal. I struggled out of my bunk, and felt as if
I would never rest again.

Twenty

We sighted the fleets on our third day out. Dotted across the seas, a hundred trawlers were working a north-east tack along the Clay Deeps. The smacks all had their flags hauled down, which meant they were trawling and would be on the move for another hour or so. It was a heart-churning sight. The smacks sailed so close together that their jibs and topsails seemed to form terraces of red and brown canvas. Watery streets and tenements of sail over-lapped in the bustling confusion, and a dozen collisions seemed on the cards as the vessels ghosted up to each other and the men shouted greetings over the bulwarks. We had to hope there were plenty of fish around. If the fishing was bad and the nets were empty, the fleets might cease their work and sail to new grounds.

Nathan came on deck for the first time since we left Spurn.

'Get the gear on deck,' he told Isaac as *Dancing Sally* dropped her anchor. 'You check the alcohol, Edgar.'

In the bustle, I went down to the hold and helped Edgar lift the jars of corn brandy and aniseed whisky up the com-panion to Edward Bannister and Sidney Lill. They were arranging the jars of alcohol on the deck while Nathan watched. In the hold, we sweated in the sullen heat, our arms aching from the heavy jars of drink. Charles Blow and Joel Cross were dealing with the tobacco.

As we worked, I asked Charlie about the cargo. We were carrying cigars, tobacco, corn brandy and two hundred gallons of aniseed whisky. It was the aniseed whisky which was the dangerous stuff. Liquid darkness, some of the religious skippers called it, or chained lightning, sent from the devil. It caused a sad havoc on the fleets. Poured down the throat, it was so potent men couldn't hold a rope after a few glasses, and many of them drowned on their way back to their smacks. One crew poured aniseed whisky over a violent skipper when he was asleep and set light to him for a joke, intending to throw him overboard before he got hurt, but he burned to death in seconds. It was actually cheap adulterated whisky, with aniseed added to disguise the poor quality. The aniseed gave it such a strong taste you couldn't tell that it wasn't real whisky.

'How long will this lot last?' I asked Edgar.

'A couple of days maybe. In this hot weather. If they're catching fish it goes quicker. They have money to waste then.'

'You sound cheerful.'

He stopped to wipe his forehead, staring at me glumly. 'It's not a friendly place to be, Matthew,' he said dismally, 'when you've got alcohol on board and drunken fishermen looking for a bit of pleasure.'

'You can sing to 'em with your melodion, Edgar,' Edward Bannister shouted from the deck. 'That'll keep 'em happy.'

'I wouldn't waste my gifts,' Edgar grunted back.

It was the first time since I landed on Spurn that I had seen Edgar in a bad temper. His irritation made me feel nervous, edgy.

It took us an hour to get enough stuff on deck to satisfy

Nathan. He was pacing the deck, watching the fleet as the skippers began to drag their trawl nets in, staring anxiously through the eyeglasses to see whether they were bringing up any fish. At the tiller, Isaac Prusey kept an eye on the stores we were sorting out, securing the tiller with a tie-rope so that he could help with the trade when the fishermen came on board.

'They're hauling,' Nathan exclaimed suddenly, pointing to a red-sailed ketch that had hauled its trawl over the side and loosened the rope that secured the cod-end, deluging the contents out on to the heeling deck. The deck was wet with spray and gleaming with fish slime, and even at this distance, we could see the crew standing round in their brown oilskins, scarlet neck-ties and heel-to-hip leather boots, staring miserably at the catch.

'It's rubbish,' Nathan shouted excitedly.

As we watched, the crew on the trawler began the work of gutting, and Nathan turned his attention to other vessels. He studied the fleet with an intense, furious concentration. He seemed to come alive as each trawler hauled a poor catch. The men on *Dancing Sally* began to cheer as Nathan shouted each haul. They were excited, making bets on the next haul.

I sat alone at the stern and watched the trawlers backing their staysails and riding the lifeless currents while the crews gutted the handfuls of sprawling, flapping fish. It was a hot, bronzed day, the sky leaden with yellow cloud at the horizon, storms breathing in the fetid air. I had my jersey off, letting the sun heal the scars on my back. The cuts had not been deep: they would leave faint white scars which would soon fade with the salt air and sunlight.

'You reckon there's weather about?' I asked Isaac as *Dancing Sally* rocked steadily against the anchor.

'You can't tell,' he said sourly. His good-humour was gone. He looked agitated, impatient, keeping his eye on the fleet, the horizon, the gear on deck. He seemed restless, unable to stand still, his hands on the tiller though we were motionless in the brutal heat.

In the bows, Charles Blow suddenly shouted. 'Longboats coming!'

We all turned to the starboard side and saw three long-boats, lifting and ploughing through the choppy water.

'Haul the trading flag,' Nathan shouted excitedly. 'Prepare to welcome customers.'

I had not seen him so exhilarated since the day I arrived on Spurn. He was like a child with blazing red cheeks, feverish eyes, too worked up to sleep before a party or treat. He seized my hand and shook it hard.

'You're going to see us do business, Matthew.'

'Looks that way.'

'See how we earn our fortune. You can forget about Lerwick. You can forget what Lizzie told you. She doesn't see the work we do. We are bringing pleasure to these men, helping them endure the unendurable. She will never understand that. She thinks we can simply sail to Iceland and catch fish and that will earn our living. She has no knowledge of the fleets, the hundreds of men who depend on us for their sanity. They would go mad without the pleasures we provide, Matthew, they would not survive the long hours of the night without the comforts we bring.'

He sounded insane to me, his eyes wild with fantasy, his lips wet with spittle. He turned away, lurching against the mainmast and dragging his flask of laudanum-laced brandy from his pocket. He lifted the flask and poured the golden liquid down his throat, his throat working desperately to swallow the sudden rush of poison, the brandy running down his neck and soaking his blue jersey.

'Take a drink,' he said, thrusting the flask in my face.

'No.'

'Drink!' he threatened.

He would have forced me to take the brandy if one of the longboats had not arrived, crashing into the side of *Dancing Sally* as the man on the tiller misjudged the waves. We heard the splintering of an oar and curses.

'Give them a hand,' Nathan yelled, rushing to the starboard bulwarks.

Edward Bannister and Charles Blow were already leaning over the side, dropping ropes to the men in the longboat and shouting encouragement. Nathan rushed to the jars of whisky and pulled a huge cork from one of them, going back to the bulwarks to welcome the first customers. Even as they clambered aboard another longboat had crashed into our stern.

'Welcome, welcome,' Nathan was shouting. 'A free drink for welcome.'

The men from the longboat looked dazed and wet through. One of them had a huge shaggy beard, and he took the jar from Nathan and lifted it to his mouth. He poured the liquid straight into his open mouth. We all watched, Nathan laughing excitedly, signalling to Bannister to open another jar. As more men clambered over the sides, Bannister and Sidney Lill were soon busy handing out mugs of corn brandy and aniseed whisky. Joel Cross and Luke Hobbins started handing tobacco round. Nathan was everywhere, shouting his welcomes, giving the first free drinks, pushing the visitors towards the deck crowded with goods. Even as we took the money from the men in the first three longboats, I could see more boats launching from the smacks and beginning their perilous journey towards *Dancing Sally*. Then Nathan seized my arm again and breathed fiercely into my face.

'Get down below and bring some more gear,' he hissed.

I went with Edgar March and found John Parnham already in the starboard hold, hoisting a package of postcards. Edgar ignored him and went straight for the jars of alcohol.

'Did Nathan tell you to bring those?' I asked Parnham.

'Yes,' he nodded, his eyes frightened, his young face pale with anxiety. He was fourteen, a country boy who had been brutally beaten on one of Mundol's smacks. He seemed to expect the same treatment from every man who spoke to him. 'He told me, just now.'

Edgar saw my face, and grunted at the boy. 'Get on with it then, John, don't keep him waiting.'

I met Edgar's eyes. He shrugged, let the boy out of the hold, and then followed him with two jars of corn brandy. I got some tobacco myself and went after them. I heard the shouts on deck before I got to the top of the companion ladders. The fisherman with the long beard was holding one of the cards, showing it to his mates. They all roared with crude laughter. I saw Michael Hart standing beside Nathan, and felt a sickness in my heart. I climbed on deck and pushed into Nathan, knocking him sideways into the tiller and apologising.

'Sorry, I lost my sea legs.'

He glared at me with frenzied eyes, his hand going straight to his knife. 'You be careful, friend.'

'I said I was sorry.'

'You be careful.'

I could feel Isaac Prusey at my side, trying to take the package of tobacco. He pulled the package free and glared at me.

'We got enough to be getting on with without you losing your sea legs all of a sudden,' he said angrily.

I slumped against the tiller post and watched as the trade went on. I kept close to the companion, so that Michael Hart couldn't disappear down below with one of the visiting fishermen. He seemed to be drunk, dancing around like a puppet, jerking at the sides of the dozen or so men who crowded the deck around the mainmast. I noticed Bannister and Charles Blow pushing codbangers through their belts, the long wooden staves that line fishermen used for stunning the cod. The codbangers would make useful coshes if our visitors turned nasty.

In the heat, I hardly noticed the clouds. I was sweating, and had to go down into the galley for a break. I drank a mug of hot tea, listening to the row on deck. They were singing songs now, 'Daisy, Daisy' to the lilt of Edgar's melodion, more raucous songs as the drink took hold. I heard another longboat crash into the stern of *Dancing Sally* and wondered how long it would be before one of the boats sank to the bottom with her entire crew. The tea made me sweat even more, and my head ached with the fumes of alcohol and shag tobacco. I climbed back up the companion.

Several men were dancing around the mainmast, Michael Hart clapping his hands and Edgar wearily playing the melodion. The fisherman with the beard was slumped unconscious on the deck. As the wild dance went on, one of the younger fishermen grabbed Michael's arm and pulled him into the circle, keeping his arm round the boy's waist.

'Dance, boy,' I heard the fisherman shout, and several of his friends started clapping their hands.

'You show 'em, Michael,' Edward Bannister roared with sneering laughter.

Michael didn't seem to understand what was going on. He thought they were applauding his frantic leaps and jerks, the drunken skips he took as he stumbled round the mainmast. I saw Nathan watching from the tiller, his eyes glazed with laudanum, a meaningless smile on his open mouth. Isaac Prusey stood close to him, watching Nathan, watching everything that was going on. He had seen me climb back on the deck. Even as the wild dancing went on, another longboat arrived at the starboard bulwarks and men shouted for a rope. Nathan saw me, and staggered towards me.

'You see now,' he shouted in my ear.

'I see.'

'They can't sail without crews like this.'

'Dregs, you mean.'

'If you like. But legally bound. Signed up for years at sea. You want to tell them they can't have whisky? You want to tell them that?'

I stared at him, frightened. He was perfectly capable of starting a brawl right here on deck. I shook my head and he grinned, delighted, triumphant, touching my arm in a sneering friendly way. In a drunken parody, he winked, and then staggered back to the tiller to watch Michael fall, sprawling, on the deck, face down in the scuppers as the visitors cheered and poured alcohol over his half-naked body.

I made a move forward, but Edgar March was at my side. He gripped my arm. 'That sky means weather,' he said, shouting above the din.

I glanced to the horizon and saw the banks of black cloud rolling towards the fleet, the grey, unholy light glimmering through the clouds. The horizon seemed to be lifting up and down. I looked back to Michael. I saw one of the fishermen bending over him and trying to lift him while his friends stood round watching. Nathan and Bannister shouted encouragement. Isaac Prusey looked on warily. Two of the drunks were trying to pull Michael's trousers down.

I stepped forward again but Edgar held my arm in a vice, his fingers bruising and hard.

'I have to help him.'

'Watch,' Edgar said with a hiss.

I thought the men were going to strip Michael on deck

and start their rape, but suddenly Isaac stepped forward and whispered something to one of the men. I saw the man look up, annoyed at first, and then smiling with the puzzled frown of a drunk. He stood free of the body, and Isaac nodded to Bannister and Charles Blow. They lifted Michael and carried him down the companion, pushing past me and winking at Edgar. I could hear Michael gasping hysterically, his eyes wide open, his body drenched in alcohol.

'Let them love me, let them love me,' he was whimpering.

There was a thud as they struggled down the companion, and I heard Bannister cursing. 'Shut your filthy mouth, boy. We could have left you with them sweethearts.'

I stared at Edgar, but he was ignoring me. Isaac was back at the tiller, and more drink was being handed round. I helped with the tobacco. Dozens of the postcards were littered around the deck. Men lay in drunken stupors at the bulwarks, and Sidney Lill and Joel were going round feeling in men's pockets. I felt exhausted. Nathan seemed to be asleep, standing at the tiller, swaying drunkenly in the silence. I slumped against the mainmast and lowered myself carefully to the deck, and closed my eyes.

Then the rain started. It fell from the sky like water from a mountain stream, cold and clear, washing our bodies. I opened my eyes and let the rain wash my face and hair. I lay back, propped against the mainmast, swallowing the cold rain. It grew steadily heavier, pouring from the black skies like a gift from heaven. The clouds were black with rain, and there was no wind, no movement in the sea: just the steady sound of torrential water and silence.

Luke Hobbins sat down beside me. He looked exhausted, his young face drained white, his eyes darting around the deck with nervous terror. 'The Lord sent us this rain,' he said wearily.

'Did he, Luke?'

'Don't you believe me?'

'I think I do, yes,' I smiled. 'It's more than welcome.'

'It's to save our souls,' Luke said. 'But we won't listen.'

I closed my eyes and let the rain clear my brain. The feverish pain in my head had eased. I felt relaxed, tired, bathed in water.

'What did Prusey say to the drunks?' I asked Luke.

He shrugged. 'He tells them Michael has syphilis,' he said calmly.

'Is that true?'

'No.'

'Thank God for Isaac.'

'Isaac is an evil man,' Luke said. 'But good comes of his evil.'

I scoffed. 'You do sound like an old man, Luke.'

'I am old.'

'In your soul.'

'Wisdom is a gift, Matthew, not something you learn.'

He left me then and I finally made my way down to the cabin. At the tiller, Isaac Prusey was wearing his waterproofs, and he watched me with scornful knowing eyes when I said good night. The deck was littered with sleeping bodies, soaking in the downpour. At Isaac's side, Nathan stood bareheaded and motionless, the rain running in torrents down his face, his hair plastered to his head. I made a move to go towards him, but Isaac stopped me with a look of furious warning.

I had no energy left to argue. I went below intending to sleep. At the bottom of the companion, I clung to the ladders, feeling the smack sway with the seas. I could hear Michael crying in the cabin. The galley was empty. The door to Nathan's cabin was banging backwards and forwards against the jamb.

I went to the open door and stepped inside. A lamp was

burning on Nathan's desk. The desk was littered with papers and drawings of smacks, cuttings from old newspapers. I could hear no sound from the deck. I went to the desk and glanced through the press cuttings. They were all about Henry Mundol: news items about his smacks, stories of losses, details of catches and prices. I searched through the papers: more press cuttings, reports of council speeches, copies of indentures with his signature. There were several crude oil paintings on the walls, I assumed vessels from Mundol's fleet. On the desk, I found a page of dates, meaningless to me, and several sheets of handwriting, an endless list of scrawled signatures: a litany of *Henry Mundol* written and scrawled repeatedly in black ink across white paper.

I went back to the crew's cabin and slept.

It was on our fourth day that John Parnham drowned. He had gone with one of the trawler longboats to deliver three jars of aniseed whisky and a package of tobacco. A dozen pornographic postcards had been tied in an envelope to the tobacco. John sat in the stern of the longboat, and as the men rowed away towards one of the smacks, I saw him turn and wave at a call from Luke Hobbins. I hadn't realised the two were friends until I saw Luke reading the Bible to the shivering lad the morning after our first night's trading, John holding his head between his hands, crying with terror at the drunken nightmare.

'He is going to turn to the Lord,' Luke told me, standing at my side at the stern, watching the longboat.

'You must be pleased.'

'Why should I be pleased?' Luke said, genuinely puzzled.

'To have helped your friend.'

'That would be vanity,' Luke told me solemnly, and turned to get on with his work. We were preparing the decks for another day's trading. Nathan was down below, asleep at last, exhausted by his night in the rain, when he had never left Isaac Prusey's side.

I could see the longboat riding the swell as she approached the trawler. The trawler was a large ketch with a transom stern, and the longboat took one of the swells and pulled towards the port side, where men were leaning over the bulwarks, throwing ropes and shouting orders. The men in the longboat seemed slow about their work, sluggish after a night's drinking. I saw the longboat hit the hull of the smack and take water in her bows, tilting away from the side of the smack and then running out of control as the smack rode to starboard. The sudden movement of the smack brought her stern up and round, and the next second there was a scream as the longboat went under the stern, and the huge weight of the transom came down on the struggling men. The smack came down, there was a crashing noise of splintering wood, and then the smack was free and the longboat had gone, all the men taken down with the wreckage. I saw no sign of John. He was gone before we could see, his heavy seaboots dragging him down into the relentless water without a chance of swimming free.

That night, I kept the midnight watch. Nathan had traded all day, and then hauled the trading flag. We were going home in the morning. I asked Prusey if I could take the watch, and he agreed silently. He was drained, ashen-faced and tired. He looked like one of the dammed.

In the empty midnight, I stood at the tiller and felt a wind on my face. The rain had brought wind and a drop in temperature. I could hear Luke crying in the for'ard cabin where the boys slept: or I thought I could. Maybe it was a herring gull, mourning across the waves.

We had a fire burning in a brazier at the stern. On the seas, the trawlers were working again, hauling their trawl nets through the dark hours of the night watch. Several of the smacks had fires burning in their sterns to warn the other vessels. In the darkness, I was surrounded by lights, bobbing up and down on the restless seas.

'The fleets can't sail without men like these,' Nathan had said. And they couldn't get men without kidnapping and treachery, decoys with exaggerated stories of money to be earned, men like Augustus Jackson with silver coins and papers to be signed that tied men and boys for years. There were no real fishermen left, and the fleets were floating helltowns, nightmarish cities where the men were lost for months on end and the only relief was the visiting copers with their aniseed whisky and pornographic pictures. 'The dregs,' I had said angrily, and Nathan had laughed, his eyes bright with delirium as Michael Hart began his lurid dance and the drunken fishermen watched him, imagining what he would be like if he were a woman.

I felt the tears in my eyes. This was the world where my father had died, drowned like John Parnham in the unforgiving seas. My father was lost forever, and the loss ached in my mind. He had drowned, and I would never know how. I swallowed hard and stared up to the night sky, brilliant with stars now that the rain had ended. I thought about Elizabeth, back in Satan's Hole, where other children were living in the filthy overcrowded streets, the stews and drinking houses, music halls and brothels. I had no idea what she was doing, how she was trying to help. I saw her face, and my eyes were blinded with tears.

'I love you,' I whispered to the immense empty night.

In the silence, I could hear the fire in the brazier flaring. I turned, and stared into the flames. I felt the warmth of the fire on my face. I could hear the sea, and the crackling of coke. I stared into the flames, and saw a sudden blaze of white heat, and papers dancing in the fire, blackened fragments floating across the deck. I blinked and then reached out to catch at the charred remains, but there was nothing there. I grasped the tiller and tried to stop the vision. But the flames went on leaping to the skies, the papers went on burning, dozens of them, then hundreds, yellow scrolls of paper flaring and blazing in the silence of the night watch, drifting over the sea like a cloud of black smoke from the curing houses. It was the indentures, burning in the tiny brazier. It was a massive bonfire of indentures, lighting the night sky.

Twenty-one

We arrived back at Spurn after five days at sea. The weather had turned cooler with the rain, and a steady breeze brought us home quickly. Hubert Caldicott was waiting for us. We got ashore, and Isaac took *Dancing Sally* up the coast to Old Hive with a couple of the crew. Hubert waded out to help beach the longboat, anxiously looking for Nathan.

I thought Nathan had gone mad during the trip. He was white bone, sitting erect in the stern of the longboat. He hadn't been on deck since we left the fleets. In the watery sunlight, his face shone with a bleached, drawn unhealthiness, his skin stretched on the cheeks and translucent, burning, his eyes black with fatigue. I wondered if he had slept at all.

'How did the trip go?' Caldicott was asking Edgar March as we pulled the longboat up on to the shingle away from the tumbling surf.

Edgar had his melodion over his shoulder. 'We lost John Parnham,' he shouted above the surf, glancing back at Luke Hobbins who was wading ashore behind us, a blank misery on his young face. I was surprised by Luke's despair: I hadn't thought he had the imagination for such suffering. He seemed to be mourning his friend with a blind, animal unhappiness, clutching the Bible like a life-line strung across a heaving deck during a storm. Caldicott studied him carefully for a moment, the waves crashing around his knees, and then turned back to Edgar.

'How did that happen?' he asked.

'In the longboat. Taking whisky to one of the trawlers.'

Hubert was white. 'No trouble?' he asked, studying Edgar's face.

'Not with John,' Edgar told him ironically.

Hubert was frowning with concern, his eyes taking in everything Edgar said. He nodded briefly and then followed Luke up the dunes.

The rain had brought fresh life to Spurn. The grass had grown inches during the time we had been away, and there were pools of water between the rocks and among the dunes. Along the foreshore, seaflowers shone red and pink and yellow in the pale sunlight. It was a clear still day, the seabirds making their racket on the sand-dunes, but the air quiet, calm, nobody making a noise. I followed Caldicott up to the cluster of houses and saw him talking to Luke. When Luke went away, Caldicott turned to me.

'You had a bad trip, I reckon?'

'Aren't they all like that?'

'I don't go,' Caldicott said glumly. 'I got duties here.'

'But you profit from the money Nathan brings home.'

He studied me for a moment, as if seeing me for the first time. He rubbed his hand through his grey grizzled hair and shook his head. 'I can't rightly make you out, Mr Lidgard,' he said good-humouredly. 'You could have run for it several times. Nathan let you have plenty of rope.'

'Was that deliberate then?'

'You could have walked for Patrington the day Elizabeth showed you the *Waterwitch*.'

'I wouldn't have got far.'

'But you could have tried.'

I nodded, dropping my shoulder bag to the sands and pushing my hands back through my hair. The earth felt strange after a few days at sea.

'Nathan was there too,' I pointed out quietly.

'Still.'

'And I like Elizabeth.'

'Do you now?' he smiled.

'She seems to trust you,' I added tiredly.

'I knew her mother and father,' he said after a pause. 'I grew up with the family.'

'Is that right.'

'She did tell you, Mr Lidgard. Do you have a poor memory as well as a weak sense of direction?'

I shrugged. 'I didn't want to walk,' I told him. 'I'm not going anywhere. At least, not this side of the river.'

'You wanted to find a berth down south,' Caldicott reminded me.

'She told you?'

'Yes,' he said.

I thought for a moment. 'That was my plan, when I left *Happy Jack*. But I didn't get away. I ended up here. I'm not a man to fight his fate,' I smiled warily. 'I thought this place might be interesting.'

He laughed sardonically. 'I can imagine.'

'I don't just mean Elizabeth. I have to earn some money. I lost most of mine. And my money-belt. I think Isaac Prusey took that.'

'You will get it back,' he said stiffly.

'But there isn't anything in it,' I said.

He stiffened again.

'I don't mean Prusey emptied it. I paid good money to get away from Mundol's men. I need more if I'm going to make it down to Yarmouth and a new berth. I reckon I'll give the trawlers a miss. Go back on the liners where I belong.'

'You didn't enjoy your experience on *Happy Jack*,' he laughed.

'I didn't.'

'Might be wise then.'

'Are you going to trust me?'

'For what, Mr Lidgard?'

'To stay around for a few days. Earn my way. Get a bit of money before I strike out again?'

He seemed uncertain, reluctant to trust me, studying my face and scratching his chin slowly. 'I might.'

'Isaac Prusey doesn't.'

'Isaac doesn't trust anybody,' Caldicott muttered. 'Let's walk back to the camp. There's somebody waiting to see Nathan.'

We walked back to the huddle of houses and small fires and found Sidney Lill busy preparing a meal, the men sitting around talking and smoking. Nathan was nowhere in sight: he must have gone into one of the cottages. A stranger was sitting by the fire with the men. When we got up to the fire, I recognised Duffy, the man working on the mudflats, but without his thick coating of black mud.

'You had a good trip, my friend?' he asked cheerfully.

'We survived.'

Caldicott went into the hut and after a few minutes came out with Nathan. I saw Isaac making his way back along the foreshore towards us.

As Nathan came out of the hut, Duffy stood up. 'Matthew was saying you'd had a fine trip,' he beamed, shaking Nathan's hand as if he was trying to break it off, grinning at me pleasantly. Nathan hardly seemed to see him, his eyes bleary and sore. Before he could speak, Isaac strode up to the fire and grabbed a mug of tea from Sidney.

'What you doing here, Duffy?' he said brusquely.

'Delivering a message, Mr Prusey.'

'I bet.'

Duffy didn't seem perturbed by the rudeness. He winked at me and helped himself to a pipe of tobacco. Nathan slowly lowered himself to the ground and sat forward, his chin resting on his knees.

'What is it, Duffy?' Nathan asked.

'They want two ton of tobacco down Sleeping Sands. You know the place, Mr Anstey.'

'I do.'

'They say tomorrow night if you can manage that.'

'Is it Bridey again and his friends?'

'They'll have a cart waiting for you if you can run the tobacco ashore. Shouldn't be any trouble. Money in the hand as before.'

Nathan nodded slowly, watching Duffy, but Isaac seemed irritated, swallowing his tea in great gulps, holding his temper down. 'What about the fleets, Nathan?' Isaac said suddenly, glaring at Duffy.

'We can go back after Bridey.'

'We can earn more money on the fleets . . .'

'Is there anything more, Duffy?' Caldicott interrupted.

The Irishman bowed towards him gaily, and winked at me again. 'A boy to be collected,' he said, speaking directly to Nathan. 'On the run from Mundol's. Been on the run several days. Needs to travel south urgent they say. Urgent family difficulties. I haven't been told what they are.'

Isaac hissed with impatience, but Nathan was watching Duffy. 'Is this the truth?' he asked.

'It's the message we got down Irish Green,' Duffy said. 'Came with one of the carriers from Holderness. They reckon Bridey sent it himself personally. I don't know if he knows the boy.'

'We have business with the fleets, Nathan,' Isaac said again angrily.

I could feel Caldicott tensing at my side.

Nathan seemed to be lost in his own thoughts.

'We have another trip to the fleets to make,' Isaac went on furiously. 'And since when has Bridey sent messages through Irish Green?'

I saw Nathan react to that: he glanced up at Duffy. 'Money in the hand, you said?' he asked the man.

'Money in the hand,' Duffy said and grinned at him. 'Those were the exact words I was told to tell you, Mr Anstey, money in the hand promised.'

Isaac protested angrily. 'You going to listen to that, Nathan!'

'I might,' Nathan said very quietly.

'You going to listen to some Irish drunkard . . .'

Nathan looked up and silenced him. For a second, I thought there was blood in his eyes, but it was only the flame of the fire and the tiny broken blood vessels of his tiredness.

'No,' he said firmly: calm, decisive. 'Not the fleets. We can go on with that when we get back. We have to make the delivery down the coast. Keep Bridey sweet. Two tons of tobacco: that won't repay badly. *Dancing Sally* will be ready in a few hours, Duffy, and we can do a round trip to the Lincolnshire coast easily. Shouldn't take more than an overnight drop. You can tell your friends in Irish Green we'll be leaving tomorrow afternoon, after a rest.'

Isaac was about to start arguing again, but Nathan got to his feet and walked away. I saw him tell one of the lads to fetch a horse. He talked with Duffy for a few minutes then Duffy left the camp and Nathan mounted the horse. He rode off across the dunes towards Easington.

In a second, Isaac turned furiously on Caldicott. 'You planned this, Hubert.'

'I planned nothing.'

'We got customers out there waiting for our goods,' Isaac snarled at him. 'We got business to hand. You think this is more important, Hubert? Wasting our time with a cartload of tobacco?'

'It will fetch good money, Isaac,' Caldicott pointed out calmly.

'Yes, but it isn't that, is it? You know as well as I do. It's the boy. We shouldn't be wasting our time chasing after boys. Let 'em take care of themselves. We got better things to attend to. They shouldn't sign indentures if they don't want to go to sea.' He seemed bitter and furious and I couldn't see why. He stared at me with sudden anger, as if noticing me again for the first time. 'Funny how this happens when you arrive on the scene,' he sneered.

'I don't know anything about Irish Green,' I protested.

'Seems to me there's too many things you don't know anything about, friend,' he sneered again.

'Maybe, but it's the truth.'

Caldicott watched Isaac with interest, a flicker of amusement in his eyes. He looked solid as a piece of oak, standing in front of the thinner man, his hands resting casually on his belt, his gutting knife safely to hand. He didn't seem remotely worried by Isaac's outburst.

And then Isaac suddenly lost his passion, and with a sneer at both of us, walked away. It was as if a breath of wind had taken his fury away. He gave up and simply walked.

When he'd gone, I helped myself to food and sat down at the fire. Hubert Caldicott stood for a long time, watching Isaac talking to Edward Bannister and Charles Blow, then he shrugged and crouched down beside me.

'Is it true, what Isaac said?' I asked.

'About the message? Yes. True enough. We usually hear from the gypsies if Bridey needs anything. But there's no reason why he shouldn't send a message through Duffy. They are friends.'

'You know this Bridey?'

'He works with a gang in Lincolnshire: farm labourers. He hires labour. We knows most of what's happening down the coast and he always pays, money in the hand, as Duffy said. That's what made Nathan trust him. He used Bridey's words. Exactly.'

'You trust Duffy then?'

'No reason not to. He runs the gang with a man called Gannan: about forty men, with their women and children. They're kept busy on the reclamation most of the time, but they do the odd bit of trading. There's another man called Hagan who sometimes goes on trips with us.'

'Then why is Prusey so worried?'

Caldicott shrugged and raised his eyebrows. 'Maybe it's what he said. Maybe he isn't sure who *you* are. Maybe he thinks you know more about Irish Green than you're pretending. You might even be working for Henry Mundol for all we know.'

I saw that he was having a good laugh. 'Maybe I am too,' I said. 'It couldn't be more trouble than working for Nathan Anstey.'

I spent the rest of the day hoping Elizabeth would come back, but by the time *Dancing Sally* was ready for the trip to Lincolnshire the following afternoon, she had still not returned, and I would have to keep my heart to myself for another long night. In the yearning of the hours, I knew I could wait forever for Elizabeth Anstey. What I didn't know was whether I could trust her brother Nathan. He had not come back until the early hours of the morning. Did he have a woman, or other business to arrange? I remembered the stranger in the square in Easington, slipping into the churchyard when I saw him. He had not returned. I had never seen him again. I knew I could wait for Elizabeth: I just hoped I wasn't going to be overtaken by violence before she made her return journey.

Twenty-two

We left Spurn early the following evening, heading south down the desolate Lincolnshire coast but keeping close to the shallow waters. The evening was warm and still, the sticky heat of the previous weeks gone. Inland, I could see mist on the fields and distant hills, and the lights of isolated farms shining in the twilight. *Dancing Sally* moved gaily in the cool breeze. Over the starboard bows, I saw the salt pastures at Horse Shoe Point, and the cockle beds where Elizabeth had lived in her single-roomed cottage, then the dangerous sands off Theddlethorpe and Bleak House.

'We going far?' I asked Hubert, who was on the tiller.

'To the Wash.'

'That's dangerous water.'

'Not if you know what you're doing,' he said mildly.

I watched the featureless coast sliding past to our starboard. Out at sea, I could see a few smacks, still working in the gathering darkness, fishing deeper waters. There was something restful, timeless, watching the seas race past from the deck of a fishing smack. We could have been travelling anywhere, bound on some great adventure. I always felt that when I put to sea. It had been the excitement of voyaging that had first drawn me to the fishing smacks, and the excitement was still there on every trip, despite the brutalities I had seen. In the quiet of *Dancing Sally*'s wake, there was a smell of rain or mist in the cool air.

'Is there much of this going on still?' I asked Hubert.

He took his time answering, concentrating on the tiller. 'Not a lot,' he said casually. 'Tobacco and spirits, brandy and cigars now and then. There used to be a regular trade along this stretch of coast when I was a boy, before the revenue got steam cutters. A smack can't outrun a steam cutter. It's mostly casual stuff now, merchant seamen bringing a few bottles ashore, and some of the smacks carrying a cargo from Holland.'

'Why does Nathan bother?' I asked.

Hubert shrugged. 'Bit of danger,' he suggested with a dry laugh.

'There can't be much money in it.'

'No. The real trade is in supplying the fleets. That's where you find the big money. My dad did it for fun more than anything. He used to bring a load across every now and then from France. Kegs of whisky mostly. The revenue never caught *him*.'

'They're pretty rough on anybody they catch,' I said apprehensively, thinking about our own trip.

'Don't worry, Matthew, we won't get caught.'

'But they are.'

'Yes, if you like to think about it.'

I fetched tea for Hubert and myself as we slipped down the darkening coast and chatted with him at the tiller. There hadn't been time for much conversation before. He laughed when I asked him about the community on Spurn, why the revenue hadn't bothered to clear them out.

'There's troops in Hull,' he said cheerfully. 'They'd enjoy a day clearing us out, especially if the gypsies were visiting. Or the Irish. They'd like to have a go at them. They're always being called to Irish Green when Gannan and Duffy get arguing over Mary Herring.'

'Mary Herring?'

'Duffy's woman. Causes more trouble than aniseed whisky.'

'But why no troops?' I insisted. 'Why do they leave Nathan alone?'

Hubert shrugged. 'Nobody's that bothered. We don't break any laws taking our trade to the fleets. They don't know about trips like this. And it suits Henry Mundol and his kind. You already know that. It suits them fine. Men aren't going to be happy paying twenty shillings for a jar of corn brandy when they've got used to paying five. That's only human.'

He had to be right. I gave up asking, and concentrated on the trip. It seemed a sin to ruin a pleasant night's sailing with such miserable thoughts. We went down the coast as far as Seacroft where the land began to curve inland to form the huge muddy bowl of the Wash. Hubert was relaxed, smoking his pipe, at ease with the tiller. He wasn't mithered by my questions. As we approached the Wash, he called all hands on deck and Isaac Prusey came and joined us. Nathan came up from the aft cabin. We were heading for dangerous waters, where the whelkers sought for bait and the sandbanks were treacherous: Outer Dog's Head, Inner Knock, Wainfleet Sands and Friskney Flats. Caldicott handled the tiller as if the wrecking sands were as familiar to him as his own garden. The whole of the Wash is a nightmare for fishermen, haunted by sudden drifting fogs and murderous with shifting sand-banks: Wrangle Flats and Long Sand, Butterwick Low and Black Buoy Sand, Herring Hill, Gat Sand and Roaring Middle, Thief Sand and the miserable Bull Dog Sand. I knew them all. Caldicott took us south of Long Sand and made straight for shore. I thought he was going to take us up the Haven into Boston, but he sought Black Buoy Sand

and then turned north again for Butterwick Low. It seemed a dangerous course to me, but Caldicott never blinked and Nathan seemed to trust him with his life.

We dropped anchor off Butterwick Low and hauled the longboat over the side, working urgently as *Dancing Sally* rose and fell with the sluggish movement of the tide.

'This is it,' Nathan whispered.

'Butterwick?' I said, glancing to port.

'You been here before?' Isaac Prusey asked suspiciously, working at my side.

'I worked a whelker one season,' I explained. 'Out of Boston.'

'You certainly been around, Matthew,' Isaac said sourly.

I studied the immense deserted foreshore, the miles of sand curving away to the north. Nothing moved. In the moonlight, the shadow of *Dancing Sally* leapt on the water, but inland there was mist and brooding silence, trees growing in isolation, flat featureless dunes. I felt the loneliness of the place, the emptiness.

'Let's get moving,' Nathan said impatiently.

We loaded the longboat with tobacco and then rowed for the muddy shore. Hubert stayed with *Dancing Sally*. Isaac was in charge of the tobacco. I wondered briefly if Nathan didn't trust him to stay with the smack once we were ashore, but then had to concentrate on what I was doing. You could have been stepping out of the boat into ten feet of water or ten feet of mud, the surface was so flat and shining in the moonlight. A thin mist hung over the low shore. We could hear our own breathing.

Making several trips, we got the cargo ashore in the longboat, and as we finished hefting the last load a group of men emerged from the dunes, trundling a cart down on to the beach to the tideline. They started to load the tobacco without a word. Nathan helped; I had never seen him lift a hand before.

'It's good tobacco?' one of the men asked in a whisper.

'Best you'll see in these parts,' Isaac said unpleasantly.

'Got to be good, friend,' the man said stupidly, his accent broad and soft Lincolnshire, his grin as wide as the Wash. 'They like a nice strong pipe these parts.'

When we were done, Isaac glanced back towards the longboat. 'Right,' he hissed. 'That's us. You can manage the rest of the job on your own.'

'Are you not going to lend a hand?' one of the men asked, surprised.

'We are,' Nathan said brusquely. 'Get your shoulder to it, Isaac, and stop fretting. We've got a job to do.'

We pushed the cart back up the sloping sands. The mist was heavy on the ground, soaking the marram grass and our feet and trousers. In the long grass, the wheels of the cart slipped and got stuck and we had to put our shoulders to the wheels to lift the cart forward.

A horse was waiting behind the dunes, tethered to a post.

'Bridey not with you?' Isaac asked one of the men, leaning against the cart and catching his breath.

'He's waiting at the farm.'

'With the boy?' Nathan asked.

'That's right.'

We harnessed the horse to the cart and the strangers started to lead her along a narrow rutted lane. Pools of water stood in the ruts after the rain. We followed close behind, stumbling in the muddy holes.

'This is idle madness,' Isaac muttered at Nathan's side.

'Keep it quiet, Isaac.'

'We're going to get caught.'

'Not if you keep your mouth shut, friend,' one of the strangers called angrily down the line.

I saw Isaac falling back, talking to Edward Trevitt. Trevitt was a thin, gangling man with weak eyes and spectacles he wore perched at the end of his nose. He said his weak eyes were due to starvation as a child, but he was quick and lithe at sea, malicious in the way he mocked Caldicott and Luke Hobbins. He was another of the gang from Yarmouth, with the same slow drawling accent. I began to think about Yarmouth, longing for the narrow lanes, the soft burr of the Suffolk voices.

The shot crashed into my mind, startling me out of my thoughts.

I stumbled into Edgar March who was in front of me, and heard Nathan curse further up the line. The men with the horse dragged her to a halt, yanking at the halter. In the silence, I could hear Nathan's rasping breathing, Isaac Prusey's muffled curse. There was a shout, and then another shot, and then a third.

The men with the horse suddenly leapt for the sides of the lane and scrambled into the ditches. They were gone in seconds, all of them, disappearing in the tall reeds of the dykes. Nathan turned and hissed at us to get back to the smack. There was a fourth shot, further away, and then more shouting, the sound of men fighting and somebody hurt. A man started screaming, his cries piteous in the stillness. We stood in the lane, unable to move. In the darkness, I saw Charles Blow easing his gutting knife out of his belt.

Nathan was suddenly at my side. 'You come with me,' he told me in a harsh whisper.

'Where?'

I felt a knife jabbing into my ribs. Isaac Prusey was stumbling back towards me, looking for Nathan.

'You take the men back,' Nathan hissed at Prusey.

'You're taking him with you?'

'Do it!'

'What the hell you playing at, Nathan . . .?'

'I said do it!' Nathan said again angrily, getting loud.

Several of the men round us started to run and stumble back up the lane towards the coast. Another shot rang out, a long way off now, and Nathan grabbed my arm. 'You coming?' he said again, as if I was deaf or stupid.

I stumbled after him.

It took us half an hour to find the barn. It was a huge rambling building, on the edge of a farm. Lights were burning in the farmhouse.

'You wait here,' Nathan whispered.

'What are you going to do?'

'Find the boy.'

'You're mad, Nathan.'

'He's why we came.'

'We came for the tobacco.'

'We *came* for the boy,' Nathan said through his teeth, grabbing my shoulder and pulling me so close I could feel his breath on my face. 'One of Mundol's boys. One of Mundol's *victims*. We came for the boy. I'll not let Henry Mundol have him.'

Then he was gone.

I was frightened. Alone in a ditch, I tried to control my breathing. I was somewhere close to panic. If they got hold of Nathan I would never get back to *Dancing Sally*, and if I did, they would never believe I hadn't betrayed Nathan: with Prusey's incitement, they would probably kill me. I glanced around, trying to see in the darkness. The sound of pursuit had faded across the countryside. I could see the lights burning in the farmhouse but there was no movement, no sound of voices from inside.

If I made a run for it now I might reach Boston and then find some means of travelling south to Lowestoft. But I had no money. I was wearing fisherman's gear and I hadn't a coin to my name. That would take some explaining. I glanced towards the farmhouse and wondered whether I could steal enough money there to buy new clothes and get me on my way, but the thought of breaking in and searching for hidden coins froze my nerve. I couldn't do that, whatever the rights and wrongs.

Then in the stillness, I began to think I was hearing things. A weasel shrieked with terror in the long grass, and a rat slithered across my boots. I heard a harsh whispering noise, like a voice trying to attract my attention. I strained my body to hear, but the voice was gone. The weasel shrieked again, and an owl flew low over the barn, its white wings fluttering like a ghost over my head.

'Matthew,' a voice called softly from nearby, husky in the night terror.

'Over here.'

Nathan came scrambling out of the ditch. He was alone. I saw his face briefly in a glimmer of moonlight. He was struggling to breathe, his breath rasping in harsh painful gasps.

'Are you hurt?'

'No.'

'What happened?'

'The barn's empty.'

'He must have got away,' I said. 'Or been caught.'

Suddenly, Nathan was gripping my wrist, bending it backwards. His strength was like a nightmare: a relentless, lethal violence. He held the knife in his free hand, the blade close to my neck.

'Or maybe he was never there?' he said, still gasping for breath.

'Nathan!'

'You hear!'

'I heard you. How the hell would I know?'

'How *would* you, Matthew?'

He held my wrist so that I couldn't move for a long silence, and then abruptly he let me free and scrambled up out of the ditch. 'Let's get moving,' he whispered urgently.

'I know nothing about the lad, Nathan.'

'So you say.'

'Nothing.'

'Right.'

I followed him back across the fields towards the huge skies over the sea. He seemed to know his way instinctively, never fumbling in the dark, sliding across the fields and ditches without pausing to get his bearings. I knew if I tried to make a run for it he would be after me without a second's delay, and in this wilderness I wouldn't stand a chance. He was mad enough to kill me even if it meant the revenue men caught him doing it. But I had heard the venom in his voice. When we returned to *Dancing Sally*, he was going to let his venom loose.

Twenty-three

But Nathan said not a word.

The longboat was waiting for us on the flats. 'Get in, quickly,' he ordered, not bothering to keep his voice low now that we were away, triumphant that we had escaped. I climbed into the longboat and took the oars. Nathan heaved the boat into the surf. Edward Bannister was already in the water with him. 'We did it,' Nathan laughed aloud, thumping Bannister on the back. 'We tricked the bastards.'

'They get the boy?' Bannister asked between plunges at the oars.

'Mind your own business, Edward. Just get us back to *Dancing Sally*.'

Isaac Prusey was ready with the same question the minute we got on board. But to my stunned amazement, Nathan ignored him. 'Get the mainsail out, Hubert,' he shouted to Caldicott, and while Prusey glared at him with mistrust and disbelief, went down the companion to his cabin. We could hear him telling Sidney Lill to break out a bottle of brandy, and then his door slammed shut.

Prusey turned on me immediately, his eyes darting suspiciously across my face. 'You see a boy?' he asked angrily.

'No.'

'You think there ever *was* a boy?'

'Lend a hand, Isaac,' Caldicott interrupted, trying to distract him.

'I have no idea,' I said, staring Isaac out.

'Well I do, friend. I have an idea. I have a nasty idea you're going to bring us all to ruination, and you don't fool me with your damned innocence.'

'Foresails, you idle sods,' Caldicott shouted for staysail and jib, and Prusey glanced over his shoulder, always fisherman enough to keep his eye on the vessel, furious with Nathan for leaving everything unsaid.

'There's questions need asking,' he muttered furiously.

'You going to do any work tonight, Isaac?' Caldicott suddenly roared, his clenched anger terrifying, and Prusey gave up, turning away with a contemptuous snarl and helping Edward Trevitt secure the mainsail sheets.

Free of the man's relentless questions, I went to give a hand with the jib, and when we were under full sail and the ghostly coastline was slipping past on our port like a dream you can't quite remember, I went down to the aft cabin to try and rest and keep out of Isaac's way. I was exhausted. My hands were trembling. I thought I would be haunted by my fears, but I went to sleep as soon as I reached the bunk, and didn't wake until I heard the cries and shouts of alarm.

I grabbed my boots and clambered up the companion to the deck. There were fires burning all over Spurn. In the darkness, I could see two of the cottages burning, and down towards Patrington a huge blaze lit the sky. We were hove-to just off the Spurn mainland, and Nathan was clambering into the longboat. Isaac Prusey went after him. I turned to the tiller and asked Hubert what was going on, but he was too busy trying to secure the smack before joining the rest of the men in the longboat. His face was shining with sweat. He glanced at me angrily when I spoke, and his look told me to leave well alone. I quickly followed them into the longboat.

From the longboat, we could see figures moving around the dunes in the light of the fires, men carrying buckets of water from the sea, trying to put the fires out in the two cottages, women rushing around searching for children, other women carrying armfuls of clothes away from the blaze. There were shouts and cries drifting through the night, and the sound of crackling timber and roaring flames. Further down the spit of land, away from the camp, the great blaze towards Patrington was filling the dark sky with a lurid red light.

'It's Irish Green,' I heard Nathan shout, pointing in the direction of the blaze. 'They've set fire to Irish Green.'

We clambered ashore through the surf and I grabbed a bucket from one of the women who was standing up to her knees in water, staring and weeping at the confusion. I filled the bucket and ran towards the first of the cottages. The heat was blistering the air. I threw the water hopelessly into the burning inferno and turned away, the skin on my forehead scorched. I plunged back into the sea and stumbled forward with a second bucket.

'It's no use,' a man already on the line shouted to me. It was Peter Loft, one of the men we had left behind. 'It's got too much of a hold.'

I saw groups of women fighting smaller fires, throwing buckets of water ineffectually into the flames. There seemed to be furniture and clothing on the bonfires, as if somebody had deliberately ransacked the cottages. I noticed men lying on the sands, with women kneeling beside them, trying to help them. There was blood, and as I ran to fetch another bucket of seawater, I heard somebody moaning: a man's cries. Children were weeping in the darkness.

In the end, the fires in the cottages burned themselves

out. It took all night. We sat on the sands, drinking tea or alcohol, helping the wounded. None of the wounds were serious. One of the women had a broken arm, several more had bruised faces. For hours, Nathan went round the camp, offering his flask, asking questions. He comforted the children. As a grey opal dawn lifted out of the sea, we saw the blackened ruins the fires had left behind, the charred remains. Women sat around on the ground, huddled with their children, too exhausted to cry. Wounded men lay on blankets. Hubert Caldicott was still going round trying to help them, giving treatment, offering drink from a flask of water. He had a medical box he fetched from *Dancing Sally*. His face was grey as ashes, and he looked worried, puzzled.

I was sitting on the dunes, staring out towards Grimsby, wondering what had happened to Elizabeth, whether she had been here on Spurn during the attack. I hoped she hadn't returned. I was too exhausted and worried to rest. When Isaac Prusey and Nathan came and stood beside me, I looked up wearily, knowing what they were going to say, too tired to argue, or resist Isaac's furious accusations. Isaac had a wound on his forehead where a beam in one of the cottages had fallen and burned his face. Nathan looked like death: his cheeks sucked in, his face a sickly grey.

'They set fire to Irish Green,' Nathan said tiredly, his voice lifeless with depression.

I nodded. I couldn't speak. I felt as though my throat was caked with ashes and fire. My lips were cracked and bleeding from the heat. I hadn't had a drink of water all night.

'A mob, from Holderness,' Nathan went on. 'Angry about the land reclamation work being done by foreigners. They reckon the work should be given to local people. They went to Irish Green and chased the men into the river, then fired the houses with tarred flares. Went after the women. Mary Herring ran down here for help and they followed her, set about our people. They knew what they were about. They knew what they were after. They brought tarred flares with them.'

I still couldn't speak, licking my lips, trying to find some moisture in my mouth. I realised I was frightened.

Nathan didn't look at me. His tiredness was like a wound, draining the life out of his voice. He held himself rigid, staring at the muddy turbulent waters of the wide river, forcing himself to stay awake.

Isaac was biting his lips, swallowing with difficulty and struggling to hold his fury. 'Did you know about this, Lidgard?'

'No,' I managed to croak.

'We get lured away after some fairy-tale fisherboy and when we get back Irish Green has been burned out and our own people set on, and you know nothing about it!'

Nathan lifted his hand wearily, touching Isaac's shoulder. 'Let it rest, Isaac,' he groaned.

'No, I won't let it rest.'

'He isn't going to tell you even if he knows.'

'He can learn to talk,' Prusey said, spitting in the sand, clenching and unclenching his fists. I noticed how blackened his hands were: the palms pink and the backs like scorched earth.

I saw Hubert Caldicott walking tiredly towards us from the camp. He was still carrying his medical box. He reached us and stood listening to Isaac.

There were tears in Prusey's eyes, and his voice shook with exhaustion. Nathan squeezed his arm. 'Leave it, Isaac, for God's sake.'

'No.' Prusey shook his head. 'Everything's gone wrong since this Jonah came among us, and you won't even see it.'

The bitterness in his voice made him choke, racking phlegm, and he coughed on to the beach, Caldicott punching him on the back. When he'd recovered, Caldicott took one of his hands and got some ointment from his medical box.

Isaac pulled free. 'Leave us alone.'

'You got burned hands, Isaac, don't be more stupid than you must.'

'I can manage.'

Caldicott ignored him, and went on rubbing the ointment into the burns. Prusey made no attempt to struggle free.

We were silent.

I wondered if I was in a dream, waiting to wake from the long night. I had no idea why Nathan was defending me. With one word he could have let his men loose. After the fiasco at Butterwick Low, how did he know I wasn't one of Henry Mundol's men? I had come to them from one of Mundol's smacks. I had brought them bad luck according to Isaac. I stared at the restless river, and could fix my mind on nothing but Elizabeth, somewhere in the rotting stews of Satan's Hole, or lying somewhere injured in the riot. I couldn't think about my own terror.

Nathan seemed to gather himself and look around. 'It's a beautiful day,' he said quietly, watching the light climb up the opal sky, the curlews and oyster-catchers swarming along the deserted tideline.

Hubert had finished with Isaac's hands. 'We have to do something, Nathan,' he muttered. 'We must talk to Duffy.'

'He's here?'

'At the fire. Sidney's giving him some food.'

Nathan looked as if he could scarcely think. 'I thought they'd all gone,' he said wearily.

'Most of them are back,' Hubert told him. 'They're sorting their things. Gannon's disappeared.'

'And Hagan and Mary Herring,' Isaac added.

Nathan groaned.

'They'll be all right,' Caldicott said. 'They must have got off in one of the longboats. We seem to have two missing.'

'And two more caved in,' Isaac said bitterly.

We were silent again. I could see Sidney Lill beginning to prepare breakfast. I couldn't smell the food on the air: it still reeked of fire and ashes.

Nathan suddenly turned to me. His eyes were a lurid glaring red. His cheeks had sunk into his mouth. He wasn't looking into my eyes: just staring at my face as if I were a lump of wood or a stone carving.

'You must get to Father Hobart,' he said very quietly.

'Across the river?'

'Take Duffy with you. Father Hobart can help Duffy. They're going to need help to rebuild the bothies. And he will know what is going on. He will have heard things.'

'Why should he . . .'

'Because they're Irish,' Caldicott said brusquely, contemptuous for the first time since I'd come to Spurn. 'He's a priest, and they're Irish. He can tell us what's going on.'

I shrugged, turning back to Nathan. He was watching me steadily. He seemed to understand my confusion. 'Father Hobart will know if Mundol was involved,' he said. 'Or the police. If it was just a mob then we have nothing to fear. If it was Henry Mundol's men, we might have to leave Spurn. They might have been looking for me.'

'While I was luring you down to Butterwick Low?' I said angrily.

The sarcasm wasn't a good idea. Nathan stared at me for a long time while the other two men waited uncomfortably beside us. His eyes were like dead ice. I saw a spot of feverish colour coming to his cheeks. He spoke very slowly, forcing the words out of his mouth, spitting them in my face.

'You will take Duffy to the Freedom Tree, and go to Father Hobart. Duffy will show you the way. Hubert will make the trip across the river. They won't be expecting that. You will ask Father Hobart what is going on. Tell him I sent you. He knows Duffy, so he will trust you. Then you will make your own way back to Spurn, and tell us what you find out. If you don't come back, we will know what that means, and we will find you.'

The words sounded ridiculous, but not the way Nathan said them. He would journey to the end of the earth to find me if I proved myself a liar.

'All right,' I said finally.

One of the men went and fetched my shoulder bag, and when Duffy and Caldicott were ready, we started our journey back to the Freedom Tree.

Twenty-four

We made the journey to the Freedom Tree later that evening. Caldicott was busy with the smack and Duffy sat in the stern, smoking a pipe. He hardly spoke. His face was badly bruised from the rioting and he was worried about his friends Gannon and Hagan, about Mary Herring. My throat was still sore and inflamed. As we hove-to off the shore, Caldicott told me he would bring *Dancing Sally* back at midday the following day, and again the day after. Duffy was the only one going with me.

We waded ashore through the black mud and made for the Freedom Tree. In the twilight, I could see the twisted, gnarled branches, black against the pink sky, the sun dying in the west. White, leafless, the tree creaked in the heat, light stretching through its bare branches. There was something hanging from one of the branches of the tree. Duffy came up behind me and stopped, staring in alarm at the white bark of the dead tree. I went closer to the trunk. A mangled hairy mess was hanging from one of the leafless branches: it was the jaw of a dog, torn off and tied to a length of tarred fishing line.

'What does it mean?' I asked Duffy as he stood beside me.

'That's bad news, Matthew.'

'Bad news?'

'For us.'

'It *is* the jaw of a dog?' I asked, staring at the mangled flesh.

'It is. Must have been in a rare fight. We run the dog-fights on Spurn and in Holderness. The gypsies run them over here. It's our bit of sport. And for the money like.'

I turned away and searched the marshes. There was no sign of life, not a sound in the still evening apart from the wash of the river against the mudflats. I shuddered, wondering who had hung the torn flesh on the tree. I hadn't the nerve to take it down.

'They'd know we'd seen it,' Duffy said when I suggested we bury the jaw. 'Best be on our way.'

'No, we bury it.'

He opened his mouth to argue, then shrugged, and looked around. He took his knife from his belt and cut the mangled flesh down from the tree. 'Best dig away from the tree,' he muttered, and found some earth a few yards away. We buried the mauled remains quickly, covering the grave with sand and rough grass. It would be easily found if anybody was looking. 'That ease your feelings?' Duffy asked when we'd finished. I didn't waste words with an answer.

Duffy led the way across the marshes, avoiding the fore-shore and going past the ruined brick-pits. He moved like an animal, sure-footed and quick over the treacherous ground. I followed him, and kept my eye on the foreshore and the river. I didn't want to be surprised.

It took us an hour to reach the straggle of houses on the outskirts of the town. Duffy relaxed in the narrow streets, stopping to light his pipe. He glanced around cheerfully, trying to seem casual.

'We'll be safe now.'

'You know where the priest lives?'

'I do. St Joseph's. It's not far from here, on the edge of Satan's Hole, overlooking the fishdocks. You can see the lockpit from the presbytery gardens. Father Hobart will put you right. He knows everything that goes on in this town.'

A couple of young women came out of one of the houses and started down the cobbled street towards the docks, and Duffy fell in beside them, chatting and asking their names, telling them we were strangers to the town looking for work on the fishing. They glanced at my jersey and seaboots with derision, laughing at Duffy's outrageous humour.

'You have the smell of the sea on you already,' one of the women told me as we made our way through the winding, narrow streets and lanes.

'And what about me?' Duffy asked indignantly, putting on a great show of wounded feelings.

'The beerhouse,' the women said together, roaring with laughter at his mock hurt expression.

We left them behind the market and Duffy promised to see them when they finished work. He was glancing round him rapidly even as he joked, and I saw the way he took his time lighting his pipe. Around the market the evening streets were crowded, and as we emerged from an alley and turned into the main street, we could hear music coming from the music halls, laughter in the dark courts and yards behind the shops.

'We're out for an evening's entertainment,' Duffy told me with a wink, and we made our way up the street, talking loudly and cheerfully as if we had nothing to fear from being heard, even stopping at one beerhouse to buy a couple of beers and ask about berths on the trawlers. Duffy acted the buffoon, but his eyes never stopped watching his shadow until we reached the edge of Satan's Hole and I saw a high church steeple, standing at the top of a low hill, with a cross looming out of the dark garden, and lights shining in the presbytery windows. Even as I saw the buildings, a bell started to ring from the tall tower, the immensely high steeple.

'That's it,' Duffy said with a nod. 'They'll be ringing for Rosary. The Litany of Loreto. We should go in and sit in the quiet for a while. Father Hobart will know we're there. He'll see us soon enough.'

I had never been inside a Catholic Church. Duffy crossed himself with Holy Water and we slipped into the back of the pews. There were thirty or forty people kneeling inside, mostly to the side of the church where there seemed to be a chapel. There was an altar in the chapel, with curtains of pearls and gold thread and with angels kneeling at each side. Candles glimmered in the darkness. A statue of the Virgin Mary was surrounded by hundreds of candles. I saw a young priest come in from the right of the church and genuflect before kneeling with the congregation. There was a moment's silence. The air was thick with incense. Then the priest started leading the prayers. As far as I could follow, they seemed to be saying the Lord's Prayer and then a prayer about the Virgin Mary. 'That's the Hail Mary,' Duffy whispered at my side. 'They're saying the Rosary: the Litany of Loreto.'

We stayed where we were until the prayers ended, and the priest left as quickly and silently as he had entered. I made a move to get up, but Duffy held my arm, his head still bowed as he pretended to pray. The rest of the congregation were already leaving. We waited until the church was empty, then Duffy got up.

We found the young priest in a tiny room at the rear of the church, a room hung with vestments and crucifixes. He nodded a brief greeting to Duffy and led us through a long passage to a sitting-room to the rear of the presbytery. I could hear voices coming from several of the rooms, and another priest passed us in the corridor, hurrying on some business. We had passed from the church straight into the presbytery. The priest showing us the way knocked at one of the doors and showed us inside to a book-lined study. The large windows were open, letting in the night air, and a much older priest was sitting at a desk, writing on a pad. He glanced up and smiled at Duffy.

'Are you well, Duffy?'

'I am, Father.'

'And is this your friend?'

'Nathan said you can trust him,' Duffy explained condescendingly. 'I wouldn't know myself, Father, he seems a bit of an innocent to me, you know, but you like innocence, Father.'

'You could do with a bit more of it yourself, Duffy,' the older priest said smiling. 'Though I suppose it would be a hindrance in your line of living.'

'Oh it would, Father, it would,' Duffy said, turning to me and grinning broadly. 'You'll be fine now, Matthew,' he told me, punching me on the arm.

'Where are you going?'

'Father Corcoran will look after me. You have a talk with Father Hobart.'

Duffy and the young priest left the room, and I heard them going down the corridor. I could hear laughter coming from another part of the presbytery upstairs, and voices singing. There seemed to be endless rooms and corridors, and people coming and going.

'So you are Matthew,' the older priest said affably, crossing his fingers in front of him on the desk.

'Matthew Lidgard, yes. You know me?'

'Elizabeth has talked about you.'

I went up to the desk, and shook the priest's hand, his palms like sandpaper, his eyes a startling deep blue. He looked fifty but could have been sixty, his hair cropped and very white, lines crinkling around his sharp blue eyes.

'Have you eaten?' he asked kindly.

'I'm fine, thank you. I need to find Elizabeth.'

He watched me carefully as I spoke, leaning forward gently, patient and at ease. 'Is that why Nathan sent you?' he said quietly, his eyes perfectly direct, not questioning my words. He knew perfectly well it wasn't.

I blushed quickly. 'No,' I admitted. 'He needs to know why we were attacked. On Spurn. I'm sorry.'

'No need to be. I'm sure he is concerned about his sister as well. You said "we"? I thought it was the community at Irish Green?'

'They burned two of our cottages. Ransacked them first. Hurt three of the men.'

'Is anybody badly hurt?'

'No.'

'Hubert can look after them?'

'Yes. Was it Henry Mundol?'

He thought for a moment, studying my face. 'No,' he said firmly. 'I think it was pure wickedness. No doubt about that. But a riot. A thing of the moment.'

'But nothing to do with Henry Mundol?'

'I'm sure not.'

'Nathan thought . . .'

'Nathan should leave Spurn,' the priest said firmly.

'Maybe. He's worried that Mundol is going to bring more men.'

The priest shrugged. 'Maybe he will. He was not responsible this time. He isn't interested in what Nathan does. Nathan is the man with the obsession. I doubt whether Henry Mundol even knows who he is.'

I stared at the priest, wondering how much he knew. He stood up and went to the open windows. I could see the gaslights of the docks down the hill, and hear the distant racket of Satan's Hole. It seemed a strange place to have a church to me, but perhaps not. The priest opened the French windows behind his desk and led me out into the garden.

'It is a beautiful night,' he said, looking up at the stars.

All the windows in the presbytery were lit up, and in the garden I could hear more clearly the singing and the sounds of conversation. There appeared to be activity in every room in the presbytery.

'We are a busy community,' the priest smiled, noticing my surprise. 'The Men's Sodality, the Boys' Guild of St Stanislaus, the Women's Sodality of Our Lady of the Immaculate Conception, the Altar Society, the Guild of St Agnes for the young girls, the Brotherhood of St Vincent de Paul. We have several Masses a day, and schools for boys and girls providing food as well as education. There is so much work to be done.'

'I'm not a Catholic,' I told him.

'No,' he smiled. 'I know that.'

'But I am worried about Elizabeth,' I added, unable to keep my peace. But he was not a man to be hurried.

He nodded, folding his arms across his chest, studying me keenly but with a friendly smile.

'She tells me you've been to Lindisfarne,' he said.

'That's right.'

'And St Cuthbert's Farne?'

'No,' I said. 'Not there. But the fishing is very good in those waters.'

'It would be,' he said obscurely. 'A beautiful island, Farne.'

'Is it?' I said, wondering what he was after.

'Yes indeed. But they do say devils with hideous faces rode round the island on black goats, at least when he was there.

'When who was there?' I asked simply.

'St Cuthbert.'

I nodded, beginning to understand.

'That's the kind of story Elizabeth likes to hear,' I said.

'Is it?'

'Oh yes.'

'And do you despise her for that liking?'

'No,' I answered frankly. 'I love her.'

He showed no surprise. 'Do you now?'

'Yes,' I said, shocked by my own words, alarmed that I was talking so freely. This priest might be a friend of Nathan's. 'Yes, I do.'

He let me live with the words for several minutes, the two of us staring out to the lights of fishing smacks on the estuary. I had never talked to anybody so simply or directly. I suddenly realised that I didn't want to leave. I could have gone on talking to him for hours.

'What do you make of such things, Father?' I asked suddenly, blushing at my own words, hesitating, feeling a fool.

He smiled, seeming puzzled, or pretending to be. 'What things?'

'What you said. Ghosts, devils on black goats.'

'Ah, the dead, you mean?'

'If you like.'

'The dead are right beside us, son.'

'Devils riding on black goats!' I scoffed. 'You don't believe in them, do you, Father?'

'Oh no, no, no,' he laughed uproariously, throwing his head back and enjoying the cool night air. 'I don't believe in them,' he agreed. Then he stared at me suddenly with cold mocking eyes, enjoying himself, enjoying the effect his laughter was having. 'But I've seen them,' he said emphatically, and turned and went back into his study.

At his desk, he scribbled a note and rang a handbell.

'You wish to find Elizabeth?' he said.

'If you trust me.'

'She trusts you herself. She is with the Sisters. This boy will take you,' he added as a brief knock sounded on the study door. 'Come.'

I tried to thank him but he stood up and bustled around from behind his desk, telling me that there were people waiting to see him.

'You will be safe with the Sisters,' he assured me.

'Am I to tell Nathan anything?'

'He knows all I would say to him,' the priest smiled, shaking my hand. 'God be with you.'

I left, not knowing what else to say, not wanting to go.

The boy led the way down a dark corridor, and we were out in the garden to the front of the church, walking past the tall wooden cross that threw a shadow on the sloping lawns.

Twenty-five

'You make sure you keep close, mister,' the boy told me cockily as we left the walled grounds of St Joseph's and plunged back into the raucous crowded streets of Satan's Hole. 'We've got to cross the stews,' he added, 'and you can't get lost in there. We'd never find you in there. Nobody would.'

'The stews?' I said with some surprise.

'Satan's Hole,' he said cheerfully. 'That's the quickest way.'

I followed him close, but I wasn't thinking clearly. I couldn't concentrate. I had been confused and caught unawares by the priest, thrown off my guard. I had never talked to a priest before: the simplicity, the directness, unnerved me. He seemed to welcome me and take what I said on trust, and the welcome made me feel oddly ashamed, as though a lifetime's dishonesty fell away in his presence. I kept trying to imagine him talking to Elizabeth: and Elizabeth telling him all about me. Why had she done that? My heart leapt at the thought.

'Do you know the priest?' I asked the boy, grabbing his shoulder as we went down an alley behind the main street and were lost in shadows and flitting darkness. I could smell rotting food but we were too far from the market for it to be that. I guessed we were near to the shambles of lodging houses and eating-houses where there would be plenty of rotten food waiting to be thrown out, or fed to the impoverished customers. A woman's voice shrieked angrily close to my shoulder from one of the tenement windows and I almost jumped out of my skin.

'Course I know him,' the boy laughed. 'Father Hobart. He took me in. He gave me this berth.'

'How do you mean?' I insisted, hanging on to his arm.

'We're in a hurry, friend.'

'I want to know.'

'Please yourself. I was working the lodging houses. Kelly's Kitchen when he found me, though I'd been in worse. Vermin infested. There weren't no kitchen neither, just brothel beds. I was supposed to fetch the drink and turn the beds once in a while. You couldn't turn 'em for the vermin running underneath. I worked there three month then Father Hobart found me and drove me out into the street and gave me a lashing with his tongue. He said I was turning my soul into vermin. I never went back. I'm sleeping at the presbytery until they can find me something better. I don't reckon there *is* anywhere better, not in this world.'

'Does he help other boys?'

'Don't you know?'

'I'm not a Catholic.'

'You don't need to be. He helps everybody. He helps the girls mostly, him and the Sisters of Mercy. That's where I'm supposed to be taking you now if you'd let me. He helps the fisherboys on the run. They can't get out of town without somebody helping them. Wearing fishing gear. Everybody knows them. And the gaffers pay a reward: name a boy and you earn a few coppers. I turned a few in myself until Father Hobart took me on board. You a fisherman?'

'Yes.'

'I reckon you know what I mean then?'

'Yes.'

'So can we go now?' he asked sarcastically.

We went on in silence for some minutes and then reached the end of an alley where the boy held his hand up in warning. I waited. I could hear the sound of a fight and dozens of men and women cheering and howling with laughter. There was a squawking flapping noise and stones thudding into something soft.

'Where are we?'

'Brute's Corner,' the boy whispered. 'Take a look.'

I crept forward and peered round the corner. We were in an alley leading into an enormous yard, high buildings all around with darkened windows, a great crowd gathered in the yard. At the centre of the yard was a post, and I could see several chickens suspended by their legs from a rope, being stoned to death by the mob.

'They pay a shilling and win a pint of beer if they get a kill,' the boy whispered. 'Wait until there's a kill, then we go straight through the crowd. They'll be too worked up to bother us.'

There was a huge roar even as the boy spoke, and he was darting forward, pushing through the dense crowd and shouting and joining in as he made his way. I tried to follow him. The crowd was packed tightly into the yard and the cobbles were slippery. I saw his coat a few yards in front of me, and then he was gone and I was forced towards the front of the crowd where a man was tying fresh hens to the line and another man was collecting coins in a hat. A woman cursed me for shoving and pushing and I had to fight my way towards the far side of the noisy crowd, reaching the brick walls of the houses that surrounded the dingy yard. There were weeds growing out of the walls, and the windows were broken.

'Let Gaff-hook have a go,' the crowd were roaring, and then there were fights breaking out all over the yard.

'Jacky Mousetrap,' somebody else yelled and there was another roar for Jacky Mousetrap.

'How about Sweep-crack,' a woman's shrill voice called.

Then I saw Praying Billy. He was sitting on a window-ledge on the first floor of one of the houses, his legs swinging free, a bottle of corn brandy in his hand. His bald head shone in the light of a gas lamp at the top of one of the passages leading into the yard, and his bottle of spirits containing his tongue stood on the window-ledge beside him. He was hysterical with delight, waving his arms and kicking his legs violently against the brick wall. At his side on the window-ledge a woman clung to his arm, blind drunk and shrieking abuse at the crowd.

'Give him Typhoid Annie,' the woman was shrieking incoherently. 'Give him Cholera Kate.'

The crowd replied with yells of derision and the woman worked herself up into a frenzy, yelling abuse, shaking her fists. A brick hit the wall close to the window and some of the stones that were supposed to be for the hens. I saw rotten fruit smash into the window, and Praying Billy laughing with slobbering excitement.

'A shilling for Stew Sally,' a man in the crowd shouted out, and several more joined in immediately.

'A tanner, more like.'

'Thruppence if you kill her.'

'Farthing for a tooth.'

Bricks and stones and rotten cabbages hailed through the air, and Praying Billy started to clamber back into the window, giving the woman a push. She seemed demented, screaming at the crowd and balancing on the narrow window-ledge. I tried to move away towards one of the passages, seeing that she was going to fall. She fell with a sickening thud right at my feet. I heard the crunch of her arm as she tried to shield her face, then she lay perfectly still. A pool of blood flowed from her mouth.

The crowd went silent. Instinctively, I looked up, and at that minute Praying Billy got back out on the ledge and peered down to see what had happened to the woman. He saw me straight away. His eyes lit up. He pointed and then the next minute plunged his hand into his mouth. I could see him tearing at the gum which held his tongue down to the bottom of his mouth. From the yard, it looked as if he was clawing at his own mouth, trying to tear the flesh, and several people gasped. Then he had the sticky grey gum free and was over the window-ledge, shouting, shrieking in his high-pitched evil whine.

'You robbed me, you bastard. You cheated me.' The crowd turned and stared at me in amazement. Above me, Praying Billy was clambering over the window-ledge, getting ready to drop to the ground. 'Hold him,' he shrieked, his voice like a screech of chalk down a blackboard. 'Don't let him get away. He owes me money, the bastard. He's one of Henry Mundol's men.'

I knew the last was thrown in to get the crowd on his side. I turned and fled before they had a chance to think about it. I went straight up the alley into the main street and collided with a couple kissing in a doorway. I knocked the man sideways and the woman lashed at me with her fist. I turned left and fled across the main street, the road full of collapsing holes and clouds of dust, carts nearly colliding with me as I barged through the late-night shoppers. I knew I had to get away from the lights, and went down the first alleyway I could find.

It led into a yard. Paradise Row a sign said at the entrance to the yard. I slipped under some open wooden stairs and got down behind a bale of straw. I could hear the crowd in the main street.

'Cry havoc,' a man was shouting.

'Cry havoc,' another voice joined in.

I couldn't make out Praying Billy's thin strident fury in the chanting of the mob. I crouched lower behind the bale of straw. It was rotting. There was a pump in the middle of the yard, and the stench of polluted water. In the darkness, I could make out the wooden stairs going up to a door. It looked like an old barn, and I guessed it was a bakery from the smell. They must have kept the corn down below, and done the baking somewhere in the street. I could smell fresh bread.

'Try Paradise,' a woman called at the top of the passage. I tensed myself. I could see no way out of the yard, and it would be pointless to go up the wooden stairs, the door was bound to be locked. I crouched lower behind the straw and tried to force myself underneath. The bale was loosely packed, and I found the ropes tying it. I got my gutting knife from my belt and cut the ropes. They were thick but dried out and cut easily. I could hear footsteps in the passage and see lights casting long eerie shadows into the yard. 'Try Paradise,' the woman shouted again, and several people laughed crudely.

'Not in the yard, Polly,' a woman protested.

'I don't mind,' the first woman laughed coarsely.

I was under the straw now. It stank of stale urine and fever. I wondered how many couples had made love on it in the putrid darkness. A rat moved against my leg and I clutched at my trousers, preventing it going up inside the cloth. The rat squirmed and then bit me savagely. I nearly cried out. I hit my own leg with the handle of the gutting knife and the rat stopped squirming, crushed by the blow. I could feel blood wet on my leg.

'Nothing in Paradise,' a male voice yelled up the passage. 'He must have got away.'

'Try Sunshine Row,' one of the men in the yard suggested.

They were gone.

I lay in the darkness trying to breathe, my leg throbbing where the rat had bitten into the flesh. God knows what disease and foulness I had in my blood now. I could feel the dead rat against my flesh.

I waited until I couldn't stand it any longer, and struggled to my feet, throwing the straw in all directions, shaking the rat from inside my trouser leg. It fell with a thud to the cobbled ground. I wanted to plunge myself into cold water. I felt filthy, rotten straw down the back of my jersey, my face smeared with something that felt like wet mud and stank of the bakery. It must be stale dough, thrown out of the bakery. I stood up, and started to retch, a thin fluid of bile pouring out of my mouth. Then a door in the yard opened, and a flood of light illuminated the corner where I was hiding, a roar of flames coming from inside the room where I could see women coming and going, moving through the light of the flames like the damned dancing in hell.

Twenty-six

A girl darted across the yard before I could make a run for it. 'Come, quickly,' she said urgently, glancing over her shoulder in fright, pulling at my arm in her panic.

'Who the hell are you?' I cried, pushing her off.

'There isn't time for arguing, you fool,' she hissed. 'You'll get us both caught.' She seized my arm again and started to drag me towards the open door. She had a loose shift on and was bare-footed, and her hair was hanging loose down to her waist. I heard voices in the main street, heading back towards the yard, and went with her.

I thought I had walked into one of my own nightmares.

The girl fled through the door and into an enormous kitchen, dragging me with her. She slammed the door behind her and leant panting against it. Several women were in the kitchen, throwing old clothes into a massive coke burner, preparing food and drink at a long table, joking and talking with the boys who sat at the table. 'Lock the door,' one of the women shouted. Women came and went all the time, lounging into the room and sitting down at the table, fetching food and drink or just standing in the doorway, watching what was going on and shouting comments. The air was thick with alcohol and tobacco fumes. The boys at the table were half-naked.

'Sit down a minute,' the girl at my side gasped.

But I didn't want to sit down. I wanted to get out. I looked round quickly, apprehensively, wondering what kind of hellhole I had wandered into. The boys at the table were all young, none of them more than twelve or thirteen, some of them covered with bruises and cuts. One of them had an eye like a rotten balloon, and another was crying while a girl bathed his feet: his feet had no skin on.

'What the hell's going on here?' I said through my teeth.

'They need help, dressings, clothes,' the girl told me.

The room was like a furnace, the flames of the stove leaping up the chimney, streams of condensation running down the walls. As the clothes on the fire burned to ashes, one of the women took more from the pile and added them to the flames. I saw a pair of heavy seaboots going into the fire, and began to feel a kind of panic, a nightmarish fear. What were these women doing? Ash floated up to the arsenic green ceiling, and I began to shiver: exhaustion and fear. This was like my vision: the indentures being burned, the flames leaping and blinding. Only here the fisherboys were waiting, the naked boys waiting for freedom.

A wave of nausea flooded into my mouth, and I stumbled back against the door, knocking into the girl who was still trying to catch her breath. 'Watch him,' a woman called, and then I was on the floor, the cold stone pressed hard against my back, the room reeling inside my head. I passed out as the naked boys stood up nervously at the table, white faces peering at me in fright, flames dancing and shimmering on the ceiling behind their heads. I could hear voices calling for help, and a chair was knocked over. Then darkness swamped my mind.

I woke up in an airless, cold room. I thought at first I was waking in my own room in Staithes, a rime of winter frost on the window, but the pale light coming from the hatch in the ceiling was gaslight, and the window was thick with dust not frost. I was not in my own familiar bed of childhood. I came awake instantly, hearing a cry of violence. It was from downstairs, a woman's shriek and then a man's sudden yell of anger and pain. There was scuffling on the stairs and another yell. I sat up, terrified. I was naked. I started feeling around the mattress for my clothes, and found them heaped at the bottom of the bed. Somebody had washed them, and washed me at the same time by the feel of it. The wound on my leg had been bandaged. I got dressed as quickly as I could. The only thing they hadn't left was my boots. I couldn't find my leather boots. I was on a single bed, and the mattress was full of holes and dirty straw. I got up and went to the window. I could see the lights of a music hall next door, hear the faint sounds of laughter and cheering. I went and tried the door to the room, and to my surprise, it opened.

I stepped out on to the landing and heard voices down the darkened stairs, women talking together, brief laughter. Somebody said something and there was a louder burst of laughter, then a door opened. A girl came up the stairs to the landing, carrying a candle. It was the girl who had fetched me from the yard. She saw me and flinched.

'Don't *do* that,' she gasped, reaching for the bannister.

'What?'

'You keep giving me turns.'

'*I* keep giving *you* turns!'

'You do. Come down and have a drink.'

'I thought I was locked in,' I said stupidly.

'What?'

'The door.'

'It isn't locked,' she pointed out as if I was a bit slow on the uptake.

'No.'

'Otherwise you wouldn't have been able to get out.'

'No.'

She shook her head and went ahead of me down the stairs. At the first door on the next landing, she turned and looked at me. 'Are you all right?'

'I'm fine.'

'We were worried.'

'I haven't eaten for a while,' I said.

'Come on then.'

She opened the door and I followed her into the room. It was a lounge, with sofas and a large table, several hard chairs. The walls were covered with a lurid, velvet red paper embossed with roses. I blinked in the light from the lamps. There were gilt-framed mirrors on all the walls. Several women looked up and stared at me with interest.

'Come in, fisherman,' one of the women shouted cheerfully, sitting at the table cutting thick slices of bread and cheese. There was a ham on the table, and jars of pickle. Some of the women had glasses of beer. 'Take a seat, make yourself comfortable. We don't know your name.'

I sat on a hard chair by the door. I kept as close to the door as I could. I stared round at the women, the gaudy room.

The woman at the table laughed, noticing my hesitation with my name. 'Tell us your name, sweetheart,' she said with an easy smile.

There didn't seem any point lying. If they were going to hand me over to Henry Mundol, they would. 'Matthew Lidgard,' I told them.

'That's a nice name,' she said with a grin. 'I like Matthew. Feels comfortable and sort of reliable, if you know what I mean. You can trust a Matthew, don't you think girls?'

Nobody spoke. The woman doing all the talking was thin and bony and looked tall even sitting down, her face long and angular, a pair of round gold spectacles perched on the end of her nose. 'I'm Mary Plumtree,' she said with her hard smile. 'Do you like pickle on your cheese, Matthew?' She spread pickle on the cheese without waiting to hear my answer, and handed me the hunk of bread.

The girl with the candle blew it out and offered me a glass of beer. 'I'm Susan Ackrill,' she said with a quick smile. She had her long hair tied back behind her ears now but was still wearing the cotton shift and a blue shawl draped around her shoulders. She saw me staring at her bare feet. 'I was having a bath,' she said with a quick laugh, 'when we heard the racket you were making.'

'It wasn't him making the racket,' the older woman corrected her. 'It was Praying Billy crying havoc.'

'What's it mean?' I asked, munching at the bread and cheese.

'Henry Mundol puts money out for lost boys,' the older woman said. 'And men,' she added dryly.

'Absconded, you mean.'

'If you like. We thought he might be paying money for you. Fisherman on the run, like. You hear the cry havoc and you know somebody's up for grabs. Why'd they want you, Matthew?'

I filled my mouth with food and stared at her, chewing slowly. I kept my eye on the door. The girl who said her name was Susan Ackrill was helping herself to food, listening to us talk. There was a sudden roar of noise down the stairs and a lot of banging and thumping, but at the table, Mary Plumtree went on preparing food. She saw me listening, alert to the sounds of the house.

'Don't worry,' she said. 'We got Freddie and Louis down there.'

I finished the food and took a swallow of the beer. It was cold and tasted fine. I drained the glass.

'You didn't tell us why Mundol wants you?' the older woman said.

'I didn't know he did.'

'Be more friendly if you told the truth, Matthew.'

'So's you can turn me in?' I suggested.

'We wouldn't do that.'

'Course not,' I said with a sneer. 'I'm a lumper,' I went on, making it up as I went along. 'Lost my place in Hull. Looking for work.'

The women grinned at each other, and Mary Plumtree let out a loud barking laugh of derision, hacking at the last of the bread. She waved the knife in my face jokingly. 'You could make me angry.'

'I could?'

'But you ent like that.'

'No?'

'No.'

I got up and went to the table. They had taken my boots but I had my thick waterproof socks on. The carpet underneath my feet felt about six inches thick. I helped myself to some more cheese and another glass of the cold beer. I sat down again. I wasn't going to get far with naked feet.

'I was on *Happy Jack*,' I said.

'Ben Lowther.'

'You know him?'

'We know him, don't we girls?' Mary Plumtree said and laughed.

'Fucking bastard,' one of the younger girls said. She had a weal across her cheek, livid white, and a squint in one of her eyes. She looked no more than seventeen or eighteen.

Susan Ackrill sat down in one of the chairs opposite me and crossed her legs, the shift slipping up her thighs. She saw me looking and smiled. 'We heard there was trouble at Spurn,' she said.

'I wouldn't know about that,' I shrugged. 'I always avoid Spurn. Too many sandbanks.'

Mary Plumtree sat forward in her chair, watching me

suspiciously. 'We heard Henry Mundol was after some-body from over there.'

'Not me.'

'You might as well tell us.'

'I told you, I was on *Happy Jack* . . .'

'Because you won't be leaving here without you do.'

There was an awkward silence. I thought for a moment and shrugged. 'Freddie and Louis?'

'That's right, Matthew.'

'How do I know you won't send for Mundol?'

'He's trying to close us down. We don't do him any favours.'

'Close you down?'

'Get us off the streets. Make us illegal. He wants to bring the law here and have licensed brothels, only his Methodist friends won't let him. They won't speak to him if he tries that. Giving the town a bad name; condoning sin, like. So he can't do it. But we're bad for business. Too many of his crews end up with us instead of going to the fleets. They seem to like it here. It's very frustrating for him, and frustrated men get nasty. He sets his boys on us every now and then. Buys leases when he can and turns us out. We don't have any reason to help Henry Mundol.'

I listened to this, watching her face as she spoke: the anger, the resentment in her eyes and voice. She finished, and raised her eyebrows.

'All right,' I agreed. 'I was on Spurn. There was a riot, men from Holderness. They burned a few houses, attacked Irish Green. There wasn't anything organised. It wasn't Henry Mundol.'

Susan Ackrill glanced at me quickly. 'You know that?'

'I saw somebody who knows.'

'At St Joseph's,' Mary Plumtree said.

'Yes, at St Joseph's.'

'Was Nathan hurt?' one of the girls asked.

I shook my head. 'No, he wasn't hurt.'

'And Hubert?' Mary Plumtree asked.

'You know Hubert?' I said with surprise, trying to hide the way it came out.

She laughed. 'Yes, I know Hubert. He's a man, you know. Same as you. And what do you want us to do for you?'

'I need to get to the Convent,' I said. 'I was going there when I got lost. The fight in Brute's Corner. That was when Praying Billy saw me and started the chase.'

'Why the Convent?' Mary asked.

'I have to see somebody there.'

Susan Ackrill sighed. 'Elizabeth Anstey again,' she said. 'She wins all the best ones.'

'Is it Elizabeth?' Mary asked.

'Yes.'

There was a knock on the door, and Susan went and opened it. An immensely fat man with a huge jovial face peered through the door. He was wearing an eyepatch and his fists looked like boiled hams.

'Las one done, Misses Plumtree,' he said.

'Thanks Freddie.'

'You wan me shut doors?'

'Please.'

When he was gone, Mary Plumtree stood up and stretched. When she came round the table, I saw that she had a wooden leg. She grinned at my surprise, standing in front of me with her hands on her hips.

'Don't you fret about me, pet,' she said. 'I have a wooden leg, and a lark for company. What more could a woman desire? You worry about yourself.'

The door opened again and two more girls came into the room, glancing at me in surprise, going to the table to help themselves to food. They ignored me. Mary Plumtree was talking to Susan Ackrill but I couldn't hear what they were saying. Susan disappeared for several minutes, and when she came back she was wearing a grey cotton dress and leather boots. She had a black shawl around her shoulders. She touched me on the arm and nodded upstairs. I went with her out of the room on to the landing. Mary Plumtree was busy with the food once more as another couple of girls went into the room, arm in arm and talking tiredly.

'We going somewhere?'

'If you like.'

'Susan?'

'You wanted to see your loved one.'

'I didn't say . . .'

'How could you *not*,' she said with a fine display of scorn, then giggled. 'Don't listen to me.'

I followed her up the stairs and she showed me where my seaboots were hidden outside the door. She had the candle with her again. She pulled a shawl round her shoulders and waited until I had the boots on.

'What next?'

'Back downstairs.'

We went down three flights of narrow stairs and then a wider carpeted stairway to a hall. At the back of the house, a light was still burning in the kitchen. At the table, an old man was sleeping with his head on his arms. He sat up the minute we walked in. He was wearing a brown shirt stained with sweat and filth and ragged trousers and a long red coat with wooden buttons. His shoes had the toes cut out. He stared at us, blinking, his eyes sunk deep in his head, his cheeks drawn in. The naked boys had all gone. The beggar went back to sleep.

'Who were the boys?' I asked Susan as she got a key from beside the door.

'Lads on the run.'

'You were burning their clothes?'

'They wouldn't stand much chance in fishing gear.'

She put the key in her pocket and pulled a shawl around her shoulders. 'Ready?'

'Yes.'

She opened the door into the yard, and we stepped out into the quiet of early dawn. Susan had put rouge on her cheeks and her eyes shone with amusement as she saw me glance at the pile of rotting straw by the back door of the bakery. 'Come on, Matthew,' she whispered, taking my arm. 'You can pretend to be my feller for a few minutes. If that won't hurt your feelings.'

'No,' I laughed, pulling her closer. 'I don't mind.'

She tried to push me away. 'Let's hurry.'

As we walked, I took her arm again, and felt her lean against me.

'I wish we could burn Henry Mundol's indentures as easily as the clothes,' I said casually.

She laughed briefly, but looked puzzled, not understanding. 'Why do you want to burn them?' she asked.

I shrugged in the darkness. 'Something about freedom.'

'Oh yes?'

'It would be good to find freedom.'

She nodded bitterly at that. 'It would,' she said. 'But you'll never get free if burning the indentures is your only way of doing it,' she added quietly.

'I know. They're in Henry Mundol's safe. Don't tell me.'

'They're not in a safe,' she said. 'But they might as well be.'

I stopped, pulling her round in front of me. I wasn't sure what she had said. The light from a gaslight shone on her young face.

'What did you say?'

'Let go, Matthew, you're hurting me.'

'You said they weren't in a safe?'

'That's right. You needn't be so rough. They're on a

shelf in Henry Mundol's study, if you think that's any better. I used to work there. I was a downstairs maid, cleaning and dusting, until one of his friends tried to have a go at me. Selfish pig. Henry Mundol wouldn't believe what I was saying so I was thrown out without references.'

I stared at her, listening intently to what she said. 'You're sure they're not in the safe?' I said eagerly, not sure what use the information was, but certain it was important.

'I said so, didn't I? How would he ever get them in a safe, there's hundreds of them. But what difference does it make? They're in his house!'

I wasn't sure. I didn't understand my own excitement. I pulled her close to me and hugged her with a sudden passion, lifting her feet off the ground and swinging her round gaily. She gave a little shriek, thumping my shoulders and hissing at me to put her down.

'Do you *want* somebody to hear!' she whispered crossly when I calmed down. 'What are you so worked up about, a few silly papers!'

'I don't know,' I said, holding her hand and smiling at her stupidly. 'I'm not sure. I'm sorry you lost your job.'

'Some job.'

'Still, I don't understand why you have to be here,' I said, my arm still around her shoulder. 'In Satan's Hole.'

She was angry instantly. 'Oh don't you!'

'Susan . . .'

She laughed brightly, resentfully, turning on me. There were tears suddenly filling her eyes. 'Don't you!' she almost shouted. 'When a visit to the workhouse gets you a bed and a hunk of stale bread for fourteen hours' labour in the oakum sheds,' she hissed furiously, 'and that means sitting on the floor with a hundred other tarts, stripping oakum from piles of tarred rope and taking the skin off your fingers until you can't use them. You don't

understand why I prefer Mary Plumtree looking after
me!'

'Susan . . .'

'Maybe I do prefer Satan's Hole, but it doesn't mean I
ent got feelings, so you can keep your hands for Elizabeth
Anstey, she might like it, but I don't have to.'

She walked ahead of me then, and I followed silently,
shivering with tiredness in the cold dawn, ashamed of my
crude familiarity.

Twenty-seven

We left Satan's Hole and made our way along the edge of an enormous park, tall trees rustling eerily in the night breeze. In my tiredness and nervous strain, I thought I could hear a restless sighing music drifting from the trees, and the abrupt calls of the screech owls were like ghosts signalling their alarm. Between the dense foliage I could see pale moonlight glimmering on water, a large ornamental lake in the centre of the park. We kept to the shadows for safety. There was no sign of life in the stillness.

After a few minutes, we left the park, and crossed a narrow cobbled lane, hidden behind a row of terraced houses. The houses had long gardens, and Susan led the way from garden to garden, slipping past the backs of the houses to avoid the gaslights of the street. Dogs barked. A light shone dimly in a downstairs room of one of the houses. Susan climbed easily over fences and gates and we hid among trees and prickly foliage. The houses were enormous, their spacious gardens running down towards the old part of the town where we could see the spire of the medieval church just beyond the cattle market.

'This is it,' Susan whispered when we reached a tall

fence. 'You go through the garden to the back door. They're expecting you.'

'How do you know that?'

'The boy Father Hobart sent will have told them.'

I started to climb the fence, then dropped back down to the ground and held out my hand. Susan laughed nervously, and then took my hand, shaking it formally. I lifted her fingers and kissed them gently.

'You're a fool.'

'If you hadn't helped me . . .'

'I did it for Elizabeth,' she said quickly.

'Still.'

I climbed the fence then and dropped down into the garden. I didn't hear Susan leave. The garden was long and surrounded by elms and horse chestnuts. I walked up towards the Convent. It was difficult to see in the garden. There were small clearings of lawn with statues standing in the shadows. I thought they must be of the Virgin Mary, or holy saints. It was still too dark to see properly.

A light was shining at the rear of the Convent. I went up to a kitchen door and tapped lightly on the window. They must have been sitting in the kitchen, waiting. The door opened quickly, and I went inside. Two nuns stood in the kitchen, and a young boy I didn't recognise.

One of the nuns stepped forward. She was elderly, and wore tiny round spectacles, but I could hardly see her face for the black veil. She smiled briskly. 'Matthew?'

'You knew I was coming?'

'Yes.' She turned and whispered something to the boy and he left the kitchen in a hurry. The second nun bowed to me briefly, keeping her hands inside the sleeves of her habit. She was smiling, offering me a chair. 'Father Hobart sent a message,' she explained.

I could hear a quiet chanting going on somewhere towards the front of the Convent, and then saw the first nun filling a kettle and hanging it over the fire in a huge black range. The nuns busied themselves making tea, not saying another word, and I sat at the kitchen table, wondering how to ask about Elizabeth, what I was doing in such a place. I wondered if the boy had gone to fetch Elizabeth.

A clock in the hall chimed the hour: five o'clock. A door opened faintly somewhere downstairs, and suddenly I heard the chanting more clearly. It was some kind of prayer.

The tea made, the nun who had spoken to me first sat down at the table and filled a single cup. She did not pour a drink for herself. She crossed her arms on her lap and spoke quietly, matter-of-factly.

'You came with Susan?' she asked.

'You know them?' I said, surprised.

'Of course. Mary Plumtree helps us with our work.'

I couldn't understand what she was saying, and shook my head, trying to hide my thoughts. They probably didn't know how Mary Plumtree and her girls earned their living. I drank my tea and kept my patience.

'You need to see Elizabeth,' the nun said calmly, nodding quietly, as if sensing my impatience. 'I know.'

'Is she here?'

'She's busy,' the nun said. 'She'll come as soon as she can.'

I finished the tea and stood up. I couldn't hold my tongue. 'I have something very important to tell her,' I said abruptly. 'She must know.'

The nun standing by the door kept her eyes on the floor, her hands buried in her sleeves. The elderly nun sitting with me smiled quickly and nodded her understanding. 'She will come,' she said firmly. They seemed almost to feel sorry for me, as if my urgency were to be pitied. I sat down again and tried to control my temper. The chanting went on.

It was another hour before somebody came into the kitchen, and then it was not Elizabeth. A much younger nun suddenly appeared, gliding into the room and bowing to the two nuns who were sitting with me.

'I'm Sister Clare,' she smiled at me, introducing herself. 'I am sorry you've been waiting so long. We had something we needed to do.'

'Is Elizabeth here?'

'Of course. You can come now.'

I followed her into the hall and down a passage to a large room at the front of the Convent. The ceiling was high and white, and the walls were lined with religious paintings and crucifixes. A candle burned over the orange fireplace. Elizabeth was standing by the fireplace.

'I was beginning to think you weren't here,' I said rudely, then glanced at the nun, instantly regretting my words.

'I was busy,' Elizabeth said calmly.

'I'll leave you alone,' the young nun said, avoiding my eyes, closing the door behind her as she left.

I didn't get a chance to apologise. I turned back to Elizabeth, angry with myself and with the stupid way I had behaved. I wanted to go after the nun and tell her I was sorry.

'God,' I muttered, 'she must think I'm ill-mannered . . .'

'Perhaps you were.'

'I was.'

'Then say you're sorry when she comes back.'

I stared at her: she was relaxed, smiling at me, her arms folded across her chest. But her eyes were tired. She looked drained.

'Are you all right?'

'I am.'

'I was worried about you,' I said, smiling at her.

She seemed placid, surprised by my concern. 'You needn't have been,' she said quietly.

'Did you know about Spurn?'

She nodded. 'Duffy was here.'

'Nobody was hurt. Not really.'

'I know.'

I felt relieved, glad she hadn't been fretting, waiting for news, and yet irritated by her calm, her lack of excitement. I thought she might have been pleased to see me. 'What were you doing?' I asked quietly, forgetting my own haste and impatience. I simply wanted to know. 'Just now, I mean. I've been here a long time.'

'Finding clothes for three children.'

'I don't understand.'

'A woman from Cod's Kingdom came early this morning. Her children had been seized in the street and stripped of their clothes. It happens sometimes, among the poorest even. They steal the clothes for selling, or for their own children. She had to wait until the early morning when her husband went to work. He is a lumper on the fish-docks. She couldn't let him know the clothes had been stolen. He would have beaten the children.'

She talked perfectly matter-of-factly, looking down at the carpet as she spoke. When she had finished, she looked up and smiled. She seemed almost cheerful, content. 'Would you like some breakfast before we leave?'

'No. I have something to tell you.'

'Oh?'

'The girl who brought me here . . .'

'Susan.'

'Yes. She told me something about the indentures.'

She seemed not to understand. 'Indentures?' I could see her bringing her mind back to the fishing, to the community in her sanctuary on Spurn. 'You mean the fishing indentures?'

'Of course I do,' I said irritably, annoyed that she was not interested, not listening to what I was saying. 'What else would I mean?'

'I'm sorry, Matthew. I'm tired.'

'Susan told me that the second set of indentures are kept at Park House.'

'We already knew that, didn't we?'

'But they aren't kept in a safe.'

'Oh,' she said blankly, staring at me. 'I see.'

'They aren't kept in a safe, Elizabeth, don't you understand?'

'Nathan thought they were,' she said vaguely.

'They're filed on shelves above the safe in the study. Susan says she worked as a maid in the house until she was sacked. One of Mundol's friends kept pestering her. She was forced to leave. She used to dust the study.'

Elizabeth was watching me now, her attention fully on what I was saying. 'And what does all of this mean?' she asked seriously.

'We can get the copies.'

'Get them?'

'Steal them, destroy them.'

I began walking up and down the large room. There were chairs positioned around the walls as if the room was used for meetings of the nuns. I stopped in front of a crucifix and paused briefly.

The hammering on the door startled me.

I turned quickly from the crucifix and stared at Elizabeth. She unfolded her arms and took a deep breath, collecting herself. 'I see what you mean,' she said.

'The door . . .'

'We must tell Nathan.'

'There's somebody at the door, Elizabeth.'

I heard the door opening and a whispered conversation.

'You mustn't worry so much,' Elizabeth said, coming across the room and touching my arm. Her face was long and pale, the cheekbones shining without any kind of make-up. Her eyes were almost watery with a grey, cool searching look. She squeezed my arm. 'You worry too much,' she said with her grave, quiet smile.

'I thought you would be excited.'

There was a tap on the door. Sister Clare came in and closed the door behind her. I noticed how pretty her face was, the calm quiet of her expression. She held her arms folded in front of her.

'We are going to have a visitor,' she said. 'Henry Mundol.'

'What!'

'It is nothing unusual,' Sister Clare said and smiled at me. 'He often visits us.'

Elizabeth came and stood at my side and took my arm calmly. 'It's true, Matthew. He brings money. To help with our work.'

'I don't believe this.'

'I thought you knew. I told you.'

'He comes *here* in the middle of the night . . .'

'It's just after six o'clock,' Sister Clare said sweetly, laughing at me.

'In the morning.'

'He's a busy man. He likes to see how we use his money. He visits us once a month on his way down to the fish-docks.'

'This is ludicrous,' I said angrily.

'But we use his money for good,' Sister Clare explained, still laughing at me. I thought they were both insane.

'And if he finds me here?'

'He doesn't know you, does he?'

I stopped. 'No, he doesn't know me.'

'Then it will be a fine opportunity for you to meet.'

I saw that Elizabeth was laughing at me openly now.

'What!'

'You look so foolish,' she said.

'You want me to *meet* Henry Mundol?'

'Why not. Will he be here soon, Sister Clare?'

'In a few minutes.'

I followed them back to the kitchen where a place for breakfast had been set at the large table. Elizabeth sat down and smiled at me, relaxing at last. There were tiny bright flushes of colour in her cheeks. When the food came, bacon and sausage and tea, I couldn't touch it. I was trying to understand what was happening. I was confused, upset. Elizabeth seemed to be in a world of her own.

When the nuns left us alone, I banged my knife and fork down. I couldn't keep my peace. 'I thought Henry Mundol killed your parents,' I said angrily.

Elizabeth stared at me in alarm, shocked, coming out of her trance. She flinched before my anger. 'What?'

'He destroyed your family . . .'

'No . . .'

'You said . . .'

'Stop it!'

She stood up, pushing her chair away. She was flushed, shaking her head.

'I thought . . .'

'I don't want to know what you thought.'

'Nathan told me, Elizabeth,' I said, jumping up from the table and seizing her arms before she could leave the kitchen.

'Let go of me.'

'How can you sit down with such a man.'

'You don't know me,' she said, struggling to get free. 'You don't know anything about me. How dare you!'

'He ruined your family.'

'You think I don't *know* that!' she choked.

She was weeping now, leaning against my shoulder and sobbing, her face hot through my jersey. I tried to soothe her, but she broke free and glared at me, wiping her eyes furiously.

'You know nothing!' she said in a fury.

'I know your father hanged himself and your mother died in grief,' I said coldly, determined not to let her get away from me.

'Oh yes,' she scoffed.

'Yes.'

'Is that what Nathan told you?'

'Well isn't it true?' I said, shouting.

'If Nathan said so,' she said, glaring at me sarcastically.

I stopped again, confused, puzzled by her sarcasm. '*Isn't* it true?' I asked, freeing her shoulders.

'If that's what Nathan says,' she repeated fiercely.

'Oh damn you,' I said angrily, sitting down again, but she wasn't moved by my anger, she wasn't interested. She closed off, biting her lips, turning away from me. She stood by the door, refusing to move, lost in her own thoughts. I stared at my plate. 'You're mad, both of you,' I said bitterly. 'You and your damned brother.'

I saw that she was crying again, the tears running down her face. When I stood up, regretting my words, she held out her hand, fending me off, warning me through her tears.

'Elizabeth . . .'

'No . . .'

'I didn't mean to hurt you . . .'

'I don't want his revenge,' she said fiercely. 'I don't want it. It is revenge which is eating Nathan up. He can't see that. Revenge is destroying him. I don't want it.' Then the knocker on the main door hammered into our silence. 'I must go,' Elizabeth said quickly.

'I thought you wanted me to meet him?'

'Yes, you stay. I can't. He might recognise me. I shall be in there.' She nodded to the pantry to the rear of the kitchen and disappeared, closing the door behind her.

I was left alone in the kitchen, and heard the nuns

opening the front door, welcoming the stranger. I couldn't hear what they were saying. It was a man's voice, quiet and cheerful, polite. After a moment, the front door closed and there was some more muffled conversation, then he came through to the kitchen, pausing at the door. Sister Clare was with him.

'Good morning,' he said with a brief nod of greeting. There was no courtesy in it. 'Don't let me disturb your breakfast,' he said smiling.

I sat down again, and tried not to stare at him. He was wearing a grey linen suit and waistcoat, with a mauve silk handkerchief in the pocket of the jacket. His hair was sleeked down with oil. Across his broad chest a gold watchchain hung loosely, and he was carrying a silk top hat. His button boots shone with polish. He looked hard, complacent, and I could see the muscles in his hands, the energy in his restless eyes. He held a black walking stick in his free hand.

'That looks very good,' he said, nodding at the food on my plate.

'It is,' I told him. I hadn't touched the food.

Sister Clare remained quietly in the doorway.

'Are you looking for work?' he asked me.

I shrugged. 'I'm not long in town,' I said, clearing my throat.

He smiled. 'My overseer can always use good men,' he said. 'Ask around the pontoons. They all know me: Henry Mundol. You buy fine bacon, Sister Clare,' he added abruptly, as if I wasn't sitting there.

'We put your money to good uses, Mr Mundol,' the young nun said and bowed.

'I thought I gave it for saving the souls of the street girls.'

'This young man was hungry. We feed the poor. You don't object?'

'No,' he said with a dismissive laugh. 'You know I don't.'

I looked up, and he was staring at me. There was contempt in his steely eyes. I had no doubt he recognised me. Ben Lowther must have given Augustus Jackson some kind of description, simply to help them catch me. He knew who I was, and nearly laughed in my face with his knowledge. He had the whitest teeth I had ever seen.

'Enjoy your breakfast,' he said complacently, getting up from the table. He left the kitchen without another word. As Sister Clare followed him, I heard them discussing money, and the clink of gold coins. His voice echoed in the hall after the main door closed behind him, and his clean lifeless smell polluted the kitchen. And I knew now: he wouldn't have known my father's name. He wouldn't have known the names of any of the men and boys who died on his vessels. And even if he had known, he would never have cared.

Twenty-eight

When Mundol had gone, Elizabeth came out of the pantry. She was restless and agitated, her eyes bright and feverish, her lips tight with worry. In her drawn, nervous exhaustion, she paced up and down the kitchen while Sister Clare rushed off to arrange for our escape back to the marshes.

When Sister Clare returned, I stood up and told her I wanted to say something. She glanced at me, surprised, in a hurry to get us away. 'There isn't much time,' she said quickly, then gathered herself and folded her arms into her black sleeves, only her eyes showing her concern.

'I know. Please. I have to apologise.'

'All right,' she smiled.

'I was rude. Discourteous. I need to apologise.'

'Thank you for that, Matthew.'

Her smile was direct and simple, then she was hurrying again to tell Elizabeth what had been arranged. I gathered my things and prepared to leave. I felt exactly as I had done with Susan: ashamed.

We left the Convent through the garden, making our way to the main road out of town and then joining a carrier, hiding in the back of the cart. The cart was empty, returning from the market. At the marshes, we crossed the wild terrain hand in hand, Elizabeth leaping from tuft of grass to tuft of grass like an animal fleeing from a fire. The ground was dense with bindweed and wild flowers. Birds scared up from our clumsy escape, clattered into the hot air. We reached the Freedom Tree, and collapsed on the ground. Looking up at the tree, I remembered the mangled remains I had found with Duffy when we landed, and was glad I had insisted on the burial.

Elizabeth closed her eyes and rested. There was a fine line of sweat on her forehead, and her mouth was slightly open as she tried to breathe. I stared down at the hard-baked ground, listening to the mourning curlews.

'I should have taken my time,' I said eventually.

She opened her eyes, shielding them from the sun, looking at me. 'Time?' she asked quietly.

'Telling you. About the indentures.'

'Oh.' She sighed and closed her eyes again. 'You worry about things too much, Matthew. You should say what you mean and then forget it.'

'I thought you would be excited.'

'I am.'

'You don't seem it.'

She sighed again and sat up, leaning forward and resting her chin on her knees. She stared at the river, the fishing vessels working the main channel, the grain barges going up and down the wide brown waters. She was looking for *Dancing Sally*, searching the estuary with her sharp clear eyes. She smiled at me. 'I was tired,' she said. 'We were up late with the woman, finding clothes for her children.'

'I realise now. I'm sorry.'

'You don't have to apologise, Matthew. Whenever I'm with the Sisters there seems to be plenty of time for things. They seem to live in a different time. You won't understand that. They get things done but don't seem to hurry. It isn't a simple thing to explain.'

'I understand. At sea, time seems to be different.'

'Yes,' she nodded thoughtfully, watching a curlew stabbing into the firm sand. 'I help when I can,' she said after a moment, 'and get lost in the work. You forget what it's like outside then: all the noise and violence. Satan's Hole. The way Nathan lives. I desperately want to get Nathan away from that: from Isaac Prusey and Spurn, the fleets, the life he's living. It will kill him in the end. But I forget, when I'm with the Sisters. I find another way. Or I think I do.'

She hardly acknowledged my presence. She sat back and held her face up into the morning sunlight. It must have been ten or eleven o'clock, and the sun was climbing in the sky, but not hot, fine and pleasant. Birds flew all around us, herring gulls screaming at the tideline. We could hear the curlews and oyster-catchers on the mud.

She turned to me suddenly, smiling as she rested her face on her knees. 'So I did understand. I think. About the indentures. You wanted to tell me about the indentures.'

I nodded. It somehow seemed less important now. A sudden vision: then gone. I shrugged. 'I thought we could burn them,' I said.

She laughed. 'That would be wonderful, yes.'

'Freedom.'

'Burn both copies.'

'I suppose.'

Suddenly, the idea seemed farcical: we couldn't just steal legal documents from the Custom House and from Mundol's own study and burn them. I realised how farfetched the idea must have sounded to Elizabeth in the middle of the night when she had just come from sorting new clothes for three starving children. I looked down at the grass, trying to see why I was so excited by something so unrealistic. Then I knew it was the vision.

Elizabeth was watching me. 'What is it?'

'You'll think it even madder.'

'I don't think anything you've said *mad*.'

'Breaking into Mundol's house and stealing his indentures. It seems ludicrous in broad daylight.'

'The best things always do,' she smiled sadly.

'Not to a reasonable person.'

'Go on, Matthew, please say what you want to say.'

I glanced at her, and took a deep breath. 'I saw the indentures burning, on the fleets.'

She nodded briefly, listening, trying to take in the words. 'Yes?'

'I was on night watch. The fire in the brazier was lit. I suppose I was tired. I seem to have been exhausted ever since I saw you on the cockle beds. I was on watch, and suddenly I saw papers being burned, ashes blowing across the surface of the sea, scattering everywhere in the flames. And then in the brothel, they were burning clothes in the kitchen and there were naked boys at the table, and I thought it was the same vision . . .'

'Boys on the run. There are always some in hiding.'

'Yes, hiding. The women were burning their old clothes, fishing gear and seaboots, finding them something new they could wear in town. I saw the flames, the ashes . . .'

I was beginning to be upset without knowing why.

'It's all right, Matthew . . .'

'And I knew I had to tell you . . .'

I stopped, closing my eyes. I felt as though I were betraying something, saying words that shouldn't have been said. I was having difficulty controlling my voice, my emotions. I wanted to sink into her arms, bury my face against her grey dress, feel the comfort of her stillness, her calm voice soothing my terrors. I bit my lip, despising my weakness, hating what was happening to me.

Elizabeth reached out a hand and touched me gently on the shoulder, smiling her grave, tender smile. 'Go on.'

'It's insanity, or exhaustion. I need a good sleep.'

'You saw something.'

'Yes, you would like that,' I said crossly.

'No,' she smiled. 'It has nothing to do with what I might like. You saw something and you must tell me.'

'The words don't sound right now,' I said, almost choking.

'I can tell that. It must be something important.'

'Is that it?' I said and laughed sceptically, trying to force a hardness into my voice that wasn't there.

'You fight too hard, Matthew,' she smiled. 'You don't want it to be happening to you. You saw the man with the otters at Lindisfarne and refused to believe your own eyes . . .'

I stood up and walked away, angry with myself and with Elizabeth. 'This isn't anything to do with that nonsense,' I shouted back at her. 'I had an idea. Burn the indentures. Get rid of the damn things. Then Nathan won't have any excuse for staying on Spurn. That's what you want, isn't it? He won't be able to say Henry Mundol has the power to follow us. I wanted to tell you. I thought you would be pleased.'

She stood up, watching me cautiously, not coming towards me. In the shadow of the Freedom Tree, her face was obscured, I couldn't make out her expression. She lifted her hand, as if beckoning me back to her side.

I turned away. 'It's going to sound wonderful to Nathan,' I said brutally.

'He will listen.'

'He thinks I'm a Jonah already.'

'No. It isn't true. Isaac Prusey thinks that, but not Nathan.'

'No!' I scoffed.

'No, you are going to take us to freedom, across the river to freedom. Into the promised land. That's Exodus, not Jonah.'

I laughed bitterly. 'Don't be daft, Elizabeth.'

'Taking us to freedom isn't daft.'

'To exile more like.'

'No, Matthew, freedom. Like the Pilgrim Fathers.'

We were silent then, standing apart, waiting. A herring gull landed on the Freedom Tree with a raucous screech, and pecked at the cloudless sky. A dog barked far away across the marshes. Turning, I glanced along the shore and saw a curlew lying motionless in a pool of water, watching the retreating tide. Its long curved bill groped at the air, searching for insects, its streaked and patterned plumage shining in the bright sun. I walked across the sands, and as I approached the bird its melancholy cry bubbled along the foreshore, like a song for the departing tides, a chant of distress for the community of waders. I knelt down beside the bird. Its wings were broken. I cradled it in my hands, and it lay still, its sharp eyes closed. When it was dead, I laid it on the sand, and watched as the sunlight dazzled the broken wings into rainbows, splintering the glazed heat and stabbing at the bright sunshine. I closed the broken wings around the curlew and it lay very still and silent. Along the foreshore, other birds began to sing, the sounds gradually swimming back towards me.

I walked back to the spot along the shores opposite the Freedom Tree. Elizabeth still refused to come and stand beside me. She had been watching me, but said nothing about the bird.

'When I was a child,' she said eventually, 'I used to have dreadful dreams. Full of devils and awful punishments. I think the priests used to half frighten us to death with their talk of hellfire and what would happen if we made the slightest little mistake. You seemed to be walking close to the edge of the pit all your waking hours, and when we went to sleep, the terrors must have drawn closer, coming alive.'

She laughed briefly, and I tried to make out her face in the shadow from the tree, but I still couldn't see her properly. There was something warmer, more normal in her voice now. She was laughing at herself.

'I had a dream one night, that I was being chased down a garden by a squirming mass of worms. Can you imagine! They were all over the garden. I could feel them on my feet and ankles. I was bare-footed for some reason. Hundreds of very long, fat worms with dozens of tiny legs. I suppose they were lugworms. I'd seen enough of them on the foreshore. I woke up crying out for Nathan, but he was away with my father, working the Tea Kettle Hole, north of Smith's Knoll and Ribs and Trucks. Have you fished there?' she asked vaguely, and smiled sadly when I nodded. 'I always hated Tea Kettle Hole after that dream,' she laughed. 'It has such a lovely name. But Nathan was there, and I needed his help. When he came back, they had lost an entire catch to a swarm of dogfish, nursehounds feeding off the lines. The line was dancing with the skeletons of cod. As far as I could tell, the night they lost the catch was the night I was having my dream. So I don't think your dream is foolish. I don't laugh at dreams. I must save Nathan from the community at Spurn. I must get him clear. Your dream might be the way for us to do it. Together.'

I listened to her words, and a great silence gathered around us. She was tense, remote, concentrating on what she was saying, frowning at the hard earth as she spoke, forcing herself to remember the dream. A curlew mourned at the corner of my mind. The words were like sadness, holding us apart, sweeping us together: a kind of dancing stillness at the heart of what she was trying to say. I wondered if this was madness: the madness of my own vision of fire on the smacks; but her voice was perfectly collected and calm, reasonable in the shadow of the Freedom Tree, quiet on the remote edge of the wild marshes.

When she finished speaking, she looked up, and our eyes met. There was nothing disturbed or emotional in her expression. She seemed perfectly happy. After a few seconds, she shrugged briefly, and held out her hand. I went and stood beside her at the Freedom Tree.

'I love you,' I told her.

'Yes.'

'Ever since that first day.'

'Yes.'

She held my hand very lightly, smiling at me.

'Do you feel the same?' I managed to ask.

'Yes.'

'You do?'

'Yes.'

I held her in my arms for a long time. Brilliant flashes of sunlight dazzled my eyes as I stared across the marshes, the sun shining on pools of water. I felt no panic, no urgency: there was just this for now. We both turned and looked out to the river, shielding our eyes from the sun, searching for *Dancing Sally*.

Twenty-nine

Nathan was at the bulwarks when we climbed aboard *Dancing Sally*. He was in a fine mood, busy helping us climb over the bulwarks, hugging Elizabeth and shaking my hand. 'This is becoming a habit,' he joked as Isaac Prusey took the smack back out into the main channel, Hubert Caldicott leaning against the tiller post smoking his pipe. 'You two needing rescue.'

'You *are* all right, Nathan?' Elizabeth asked him, forcing him to take notice, holding his arms.

'Of course I'm all right.'

'Matthew said some of the men were hurt.'

'Only Isaac over there. He never could look after himself.'

'But you weren't hurt?'

'No, I'm fine.'

As *Dancing Sally* headed into the breeze, the sails filled and Joel Cross brought us tea to the deck.

'We should celebrate,' Nathan said, getting his flask from his pocket, but when he saw Elizabeth's quick frown, he made a low, exaggerated bow and put the flask away again. I thought he was drunk already, or hysterical. But his face looked fresh and his eyes had lost their blank violence. He looked as if he had slept for hours.

'Did you see Father Hobart?' Caldicott asked as we drank our tea.

'Yes,' I nodded.

'And did he tell you anything?'

I could see Isaac frowning at the tiller, concentrating on the mainsail but trying to listen. A ketch went past our stern much too close, and Nathan lashed out at him, telling him to watch what he was doing. There were dozens of smacks in the river, several of them showing Mundol's purple flag at the mainmast. At any moment, smacks would be coming and going from the fleets, crews taking a few days' rest, smacks needing repair work in the shipyards.

I finished my tea and settled on the edge of the companion.

'Well?' Nathan said, laughing to disguise his impatience.

'He said there was nothing organised, nothing to do with Mundol. Just wickedness, I think those were his words.'

'That sounds like a priest,' Isaac Prusey said sarcastically.

'But no rumours?' Nathan persisted.

'No.'

'No word about another attack?'

'No, nothing. He was certain.'

Nathan clapped his hands loudly together and gave Elizabeth another hug. His eyes were shining. He turned to Joel and told him to fetch another mug of tea. I don't think I had ever seen him drinking tea before.

'Then we're all clear,' he said with his pleased smile.

'Sounds like it,' Caldicott said, knocking his pipe out on the tiller post. 'Well done, Matthew.'

'Yes, well done, Matthew!'

'I'm just the messenger.'

'But you brought our Lizzie back to us,' Nathan said,

refusing to listen to my protestations, putting his arm round Elizabeth's shoulders and squeezing her affectionately. 'You brought my sister home.'

Elizabeth frowned at him unhappily, trying to break free. 'This isn't home, Nathan.'

'It's the only one we've got.'

'It isn't *my* home.'

'You want to watch out, Nathan,' Isaac said unpleasantly, 'she'll be running away to the nuns soon.'

Nathan turned on him savagely, poking him in the chest with his finger. 'You keep your thoughts to yourself, Isaac.'

'Fair enough.'

'You hear!'

'I said fair enough,' Prusey snarled, turning towards Nathan and letting go of the tiller. *Dancing Sally* almost went dead into the wind, but Hubert grabbed the tiller and Prusey collected himself, relaxing as Nathan glared at him. In the scuffle, I saw Elizabeth go white, her face draining of colour. I reached out to her, but she shook her head quickly, warning me off. Then she gave me an imperceptible nod, mouthing the word indentures. She wanted me to tell Nathan.

I stood up from the companion.

'I did hear some interesting information,' I said.

Prusey went back to the tiller and Nathan glanced at me, furious, indifferent, still angry with Isaac. 'What was that then, Matthew?' he said without much interest. His moods seemed to change like the weather.

I tried not to look at Elizabeth. Hubert Caldicott was watching us with interest, and I knew he had seen the way I reached out to Elizabeth, the way she had passed her message on. 'I had a few words with a girl who used to work for Henry Mundol,' I said. 'In his house, as a maid.'

'Oh yes,' Nathan said, suddenly watching me with intense interest.

'She had to leave.'

'Got caught, did she?' Prusey laughed.

'One of Mundol's friends was making her life a misery,' I said.

Prusey laughed nastily, dismissing what I was saying before he'd heard it, muttering under his breath. Caldicott was still watching me, but it was Nathan's eyes that unnerved me: he was like a weasel or a stoat, hypnotising its prey. He came close, waiting for me to go on.

'She used to clean downstairs, in Mundol's study,' I said. 'She says the safe is in the study. You couldn't break into it. It's too big.'

'So?' Nathan said, searching my eyes.

'She said the indentures aren't kept in the safe. There are too many of them. They're kept on a shelf over the safe. In files. She thinks there are hundreds of them, just stacked on the shelf.'

I managed to hold Nathan's stare, until finally he turned away and looked at Elizabeth.

'Has he told you this, Lizzie?'

'Yes, Nathan.'

'And you think it's true?'

'It seems likely. Henry Mundol wouldn't expect anybody to break in to his house, and they probably wouldn't fit into the safe anyway.'

'What do you think, Hubert?'

'Interesting,' Hubert said noncommittally.

Nathan was pacing up and down the deck now, rubbing his mouth with the back of his hand, restless as if he had an itch inside him. Finally, he pulled the flask from his pocket and took a long swallow. He stopped in front of me abruptly and studied my face as if he was thinking of buying a piece of meat. 'You believed this girl?' he asked.

'I don't know,' I shrugged. 'How would I know?'

'Did you trust her?'

'Yes,' I said, 'I suppose.'

'Why's that then, Matthew?' Prusey asked sarcastically. 'She tell you this between the sheets.'

Nathan glared at him impatiently, and nodded towards Elizabeth as if she was some innocent child listening to the foul talk of men.

'I trusted her,' I said levelly. I wasn't going to explain how she saved me from Praying Billy and his cry havoc. To have crossed Praying Billy's path twice would have beggared anybody's belief. 'I thought she was telling the truth,' I went on, 'and she didn't really have a reason not to. She isn't interested in the damn indentures.'

'No, but we are,' Nathan said grimly.

'Yes, we are,' I said. I was beginning to lose my temper. 'They keep us here. At least, that's what you told me. They mean Mundol and his men can follow us anywhere. If we've signed them, we're as good as his property. It's the indentures that stop us leaving.'

Nathan listened to all this with his eyes following my lips, as if he could find the truth of my words in the way I spoke. When I finished, he nodded slowly, watchful, thinking. 'You didn't sign indentures, Matthew,' he said quietly.

'No, I didn't.'

'You signed for the summer fleeting.'

'That's right.'

'But you said "we",' he said smiling bleakly.

I shrugged. 'I was talking about you,' I said grimly.

He nodded again and turned away. *Dancing Sally* was round Spurn by now, heading into the choppy waters over Binks Sands. He went to the port bows and leaned against the bowsprit. Nobody spoke.

'He needs time to think,' Elizabeth managed to whisper as we crossed the Binks. I nodded. She went to talk to Nathan, and I helped the rest of the crew get the smack hove-to and the longboat over the side. Still nobody spoke.

We rowed ashore and Nathan crossed the camp and waded out to Sunk Island by himself. Prusey took *Dancing Sally* up to Old Hive. I tried to talk to Elizabeth, but she was worried, preoccupied. She kept glancing across to Sunk Island and frowning.

'He's thinking about it,' I said, trying to persuade her, repeating her own words.

'I'm not sure.'

'It'll be all right, I'm telling you.'

She went into one of the cottages that hadn't been damaged and changed her clothes. When she came out, she was wearing a long blue dress with leather boots and had her hair tied back behind her ears. She let me hold her hand briefly then told me we had to wait before we said anything to Nathan. 'When this is sorted out,' she said. 'Then we'll tell him.'

'It isn't anything to do with Nathan,' I tried to argue. '*We* aren't anything to do with Nathan. I love you.'

'He's my brother,' she said quietly. 'You must be patient. I'll go and talk to him.'

It wasn't until Prusey got back that we gathered around one of the fires and Nathan joined us. He had been drinking all the time he was alone on Sunk Island. His cheeks were feverish with colour but his eyes dull. 'Tell us what you had in mind, Matthew,' he said with a harsh smile.

'We get the indentures,' I said. 'Then burn them.'

Prusey scoffed. 'That's easy said.'

'I didn't say it would be easy, but if we destroyed all the copies of the indentures, you could leave this place and go north, start earning a living on the fishing.'

'We already have a living,' Isaac pointed out.

'A dangerous one.'

'You think fishing isn't dangerous,' he sneered. 'I don't see the point, and I don't trust you, Lidgard. We don't know who the hell you are. We're supposed to trust what you say on the word of a whore who lost her job because she was fooling around with one of Mundol's visitors. It don't make sense to me, not when we've got a perfectly good way of living already.'

'I don't think good is the word,' I said contemptuously.

I saw Hubert move nervously, glancing at Elizabeth, pretending to look out to sea where a couple of smacks were crossing Binks Sands. He pulled his pipe from his pocket absent-mindedly. I was beginning to think everything Hubert did was calculated to hold things together, calm things down. 'If we had the indentures we would be free,' he said thoughtfully.

Nathan nodded. 'That's obvious, Hubert.'

'But it would be awful damaging to Henry Mundol,' Hubert went on as if the thought had just occurred to him. I wondered just how crafty he was being.

Nathan stared at him, his dull eyes dangerous with passion. He shook his head briefly, almost unable to speak. 'Yes, it would.'

I could see Prusey on the other side of the fire furiously clenching his fists. He seemed to resent any suggestion that we help the boys.

'Most of his crews are on indentures,' Hubert finished flatly, stuffing his pipe with tobacco and lighting it from a flame in the fire. 'He wouldn't have many men left if we burned them.'

There was a pause. Nathan took a deep breath and looked directly at me. 'That your notion, Matthew?'

'I don't care what happens to Henry Mundol,' I said, 'but if he can't get crews for his smacks I shan't lose any sleep over it. But there is a problem.'

'No,' Prusey sneered in disgust.

'We need to get *both* copies,' I went on, 'the ones in the Custom House and the copies Mundol keeps at home. And we need to get them at the same time. If we go from one place to another there will be time for an alarm to be sounded. How do we get both lots of copies at the same time?'

'We haven't enough men,' Prusey said instantly. 'Forget it, Nathan.'

'Is that how you see it, Matthew: the problem?'

'Yes,' I admitted.

'We wouldn't need that many men,' Hubert interrupted mildly.

'Go on,' Nathan told him.

'We could get hold of the clerk at the Custom House. I know where he lives. Just pick him up at home and he'll help us. He lives alone. That would take two or three men. Nobody would know what was happening. Then we could go on to Henry Mundol's house. If that's what we agree.'

Isaac Prusey emptied his mug into the fire and walked away. Nobody commented. I tried not to look at Elizabeth. She was staring into the fire, watching the flames. I began to talk without thinking, blurting out the words, carried away by my own belief. 'I had a vision,' I said, 'on *Dancing Sally*, when we were on the fleets. I saw papers being burned in the brazier. I saw the indentures being burned. I know it was that.'

There was a silence.

I thought for a moment I had wrecked the whole thing.

Nathan was shaking with laughter, and Hubert was staring at me as if I had gone insane. Elizabeth looked at me angrily.

'I'm listening to a man who has visions,' Nathan said through his gasps of laughter. 'I'm trusting a visionary I don't even know.'

We all watched him, waiting for him to stop. When he managed to get control of himself, he touched my arm in apology, wiping his eyes free of tears. He seemed completely good-humoured and relaxed. 'You know what they say about visions, Matthew?' he asked dryly.

'No.'

'That they only come to the unhappy?'

I was too tense to listen properly, hear what he was saying. 'Is that so?' I answered angrily, still worried that my big mouth had ruined our plans.

'So they say,' Nathan smiled sadly.

He almost looked as though he regretted his words, felt sorry for ridiculing the afflicted. Then he shrugged, and punched me cheerfully on the shoulder. 'You lead us to the promised land, Matthew,' he said ironically. 'You lead us to freedom.'

I glanced quickly at Elizabeth, but she was already walking away towards the cottage where she would sleep. My mind was in turmoil over the words. But I couldn't follow her. We all settled round the fire and began to make our plans.

Thirty

The following evening, *Dancing Sally* ghosted down the Lincolnshire coast for several miles and then tacked back close to the shore until we reached the salt marshes just south of Grimsby. The smack was crowded with Nathan's men, everybody excited and whispering, Nathan rushing around the deck excitedly, checking that everybody knew what they were doing, making sure they had knives and codbangers. Elizabeth refused to go below, but stayed on deck at the tiller, chatting with Hubert. Isaac was in the bows, using the lead to check the depth of water. This close to shore, *Dancing Sally* had to be careful.

'You certainly get things stirred up, Matthew,' Charles Blow told me with a grin as we stood together in the stern watching the low coastline glide past our port. He had been with me ever since we left Spurn. 'Never been the same since we picked you up off the cockle beds,' he said and grinned.

'Did Nathan tell you to keep close to me?' I asked good-humouredly.

'Isaac dropped a hint.'

'Worried is he?'

'He's a worried man, Matthew. Ulcerous. Can't you tell: his breath smells like rotten vegetables.'

'I don't know as I want to get that close.'

'A wise man. But I'm telling you: ulcerous. I remember my old father. You couldn't get near him towards the end, he stank so appalling.'

'Horse Shoe Point,' I heard Isaac calling hoarsely from the bows.

Hubert acknowledged the sighting, and *Dancing Sally* tacked a point to starboard as we ghosted towards the low-water mark off Tetney High Sands.

'Take it steady, Hubert,' I heard Nathan whisper, coming back to the tiller. 'We're nearly there. Get the long-boats ready.'

We had two longboats on deck ready for going over-board. Luke Hobbins came and joined us at the stern, rubbing his hands together and looking up to the sky. 'It's a good night to meet the Lord, Matthew,' he said cheer-fully. He had been quiet and withdrawn for days after the death of John Parnham, but seemed all right now: resigned, accepting. 'A fine clear sky,' he told Charles with a grin.

'Give over, Luke, I don't want preaching at as I go down.'

Edward Bannister shambled up to us, tightening the belt on his fearnoughts and grinning awkwardly. I had hardly spoken to him since the night in the police lock-up. He punched me hard on the shoulder. 'No hard feelings, Matthew,' he said with his big toothless grin.

'Why should I have hard feelings?'

'People hang on to grudges. T'ent friendly, but you know how it is.'

'I can't imagine,' I said sourly.

Hubert was getting *Dancing Sally* hove-to now, and as the longboats were hoisted over the side, Nathan came back to the stern and told me to stay close. 'I want you, Hubert and Isaac with me, and Edward and Charlie. We should be able to manage Frears.'

Frears was the clerk who worked at the Custom House in the indentures office. It was his job to prepare the indentures and see that they were legally signed and witnessed. He got paid a shilling for every signature.

'Who's staying with the smack?' I asked.

'Sidney Lill, Luke, Edgar and Joseph Ablett. We need them to bring the smack round and keep her ready, in case we need to leave in a hurry.'

The rest of the gang had remained behind on Spurn.

'What about Elizabeth?' I asked.

'She's staying with *Dancing Sally*.'

'I'm not,' Elizabeth whispered at his shoulder.

Nathan turned and glared at her. 'Lizzie . . .'

'I know this town better than any of you, Nathan.'

'You're staying with *Dancing Sally*.'

'I shall swim ashore,' she said with a tight smile.

Nathan glanced at the moon, thinking about the time. He took my arm and led me aside to the mainmast. 'Will you tell her, Matthew?'

'Tell her?'

'Ask her then?'

'I'll try,' I said. 'But she does know the town . . .'

He glared at me. 'I thought you cared,' he said unpleasantly. 'This isn't going to be a friendly evening stroll through Satan's Hole. Somebody could get hurt. We might need to force Frears to come with us. You came up with this midnight adventure, so you persuade her to stay where she's safe, with *Dancing Sally*. She knows where we need picking up. Tell her to do what I ask for once.'

I went back to Elizabeth and as the last of the men climbed overboard into the longboat, I told her what Nathan had said.

'It's because I'm scared of the violence that I want to be there,' she said unhappily.

'I promise to take care.'

'Of Nathan?'

'I won't let him hurt anybody, or get himself hurt.'

She bit her lip, staring out over the moonlit foreshore, shivering slightly with apprehension.

'Stay, for me,' I whispered, holding her and kissing her cheek.

She nodded reluctantly. 'If you promise to take care. Not just of Nathan.'

'I promise.'

'Come back safely.'

I climbed down to the waiting longboat and unfastened the painter. As the longboat plunged into the waves towards the shore, I saw Elizabeth leaning over the stern, waving and watching us go. I waved back, and then turned to concentrate on the oars. Ahead of us, the beach was deserted. You could see for miles in the moonlight. We plunged into the surf and scrambled ashore, then pushed the longboat back into the waters. Joseph Ablett was at the oars, ready to take her back to *Dancing Sally*. I watched the smack for a moment, trying to see Elizabeth, but the moon went behind a cloud, then we were crunching up the pebbles and broken shells away from the tideline, clambering up the dunes to begin our mad adventure.

We had to cross the salt marshes and make our way along the coast to the district where the Custom House clerk rented a house, the miles of crowded tenements built along the foreshore called Cod's Kingdom. It was in Cod's Kingdom where most of the fishing families lived, some of the houses built on sand, others on wooden joists over grass so that grass grew through the floors and rainwater or snow came through the joists during bad winters. There were dozens of chapels and corner shops, public wells full of stinking yellow water and alive with maggots, and whole tenements rented out as single rooms with five or six people sleeping together. The better off fishermen might be lucky enough to get an entire house, with a kitchen and a bedroom of their own. During the day, the streets would be crowded with net-makers, women baiting lines outside their houses. The children could run wild on the foreshore facing the houses. At night, the streets were dark and menacing: gas lighting hadn't reached Cod's Kingdom yet.

It took us an hour to reach the sprawling huddle of lanes. 'This is the place,' Hubert said as we slipped down an airless alleyway and reached the end of a dingy row of dilapidated houses. There were no back doors to the houses, and we followed Hubert round to a tanyard at the side. The front doors faced the foreshore and the river, but you had to get round a tanpit to reach the houses, and the ground was littered with scrapings from the skins left out by the tanyard workmen. Hubert showed us the house, and we hid round the corner while he knocked gently on the rickety door.

After a long time, the door creaked open, and Hubert lunged inside, slamming the door back against the wall and knocking the man aside. There was a brief scuffle, and then we were piling in after Hubert. There was no light in the narrow kitchen, and I could hear somebody whimpering in the darkness. 'Get a candle,' Hubert whispered. There was a thump, and another whimper, and then a candle flared into life and we could see Frears cowering on the floor, trying to get underneath his kitchen sink. In the tiny damp kitchen, there was little room to move, and Nathan quickly told Edward and Charles to get outside and keep watch.

'What do you want?' the clerk hissed at us, cringing when Nathan turned and looked at him by the light of the candle. 'Leave me alone,' Frears begged, 'please, you leave me alone.'

Nathan stared at him with contempt. 'Shut up, Frears.'

'I work for Henry Mundol,' the clerk started to say, struggling to get up off the floor, pretending indignation. 'He won't let you hurt me.'

Nathan lashed out with his boot, making the clerk whine with fright and try to press himself back against the wall under the sink, which was running with water.

'Get out from there, man,' Hubert said impatiently. 'We ent going to damage you.'

Frears scrambled out, darting nervous glances from Hubert to Nathan, licking his thin mean lips. He was a cringing, jerking little man, with boils on the back of his neck and a dirty crunched skin grimed with filth. He flinched when Hubert grabbed hold of his arm.

'You got the keys to the office?' Hubert asked him.

'What office?' Frears asked in a shriek.

Hubert bent his arm backwards. 'You know what office, Frears.'

'You said you wouldn't hurt me.'

'You got the keys?'

'Yes, yes.'

The keys were in his coat pocket. Hubert threw them to Nathan and then pushed Frears back against the kitchen wall. The wall was covered with brown stains and I could see fungus growing along the floor. The houses must have been rotten with damp and there were white salt marks on the brick where the sea had flooded the foreshore during winter storms. The houses closest to the foreshore were flooded every winter, and nothing would move the white salt stains.

'We're going for a walk,' Hubert whispered into the clerk's face.

'Yes, sir.'

'You're going to show us your office.'

'Yes, yes, I will, you promise not to hurt me.'

'I'll break your slimy neck if you make a sound.'

'I won't,' Frears said desperately.

'A whisper.'

'I won't, I won't.'

I heard a noise in the house next door. The walls must have been as thin as paper. Nathan heard the sound too and told Hubert to get going. Isaac was leaning against the sink, staring at the clerk with loathing. We left the house, locking the door behind us, and moved in a group along the foreshore, making for the fishdocks and the north wall. Frears stumbled between Hubert and Isaac. He was weeping.

But no fisherman would be too upset to see the Custom House clerk in trouble. He was paid well for what he did, and wasn't too bothered about legalities. If a boy cried and begged, Frears went deaf. If a boy claimed to have been cozened or decoyed from his home, Frears laughed gleefully at the joke. If a boy could barely stand from blows or trembling with terror, Frears lost the use of his eyes. He was like a grey rat scuttling along the quays, searching for boys and eagerly bribing them to try a life on the seas, lovely bribes of excitement and money, although the money never got paid and they were lucky if the excitement ever meant much more than being cuffed round the ears, or being frozen sleepless on the deck of some wretched fishing smack. If they were really lucky or brutal enough to survive, they might even work their indentures out and end up with their own smacks. Most of them weren't that fortunate, or brutal.

We reached the north wall of the fishdocks and went round behind the shipyards and sailmakers and curing houses, keeping to the alleyways and darkness until we worked our way round to the market and then hurried to the grim red-bricked buildings of the Dock Offices and Custom House. It was a dark silent night, the darkness somehow threatening, and judging by the height of the moon, getting on for midnight. We hadn't seen a soul.

We were dragging Frears by now. His trousers were soaked where he had wet himself, and a constant whimpering sound came from his throat. Isaac hit him with the heft of his gutting knife to make him walk but he whimpered like an animal, too scared to respond even to pain.

'Let him be,' Hubert hissed, and we made our way round the side of the Custom House and down some dark steps to a black hole beneath the main building. The indentures' office was off the main corridors. Hubert fiddled for several minutes with the key, and then we were in the building.

Frears was weeping helplessly by now like a child. Without candles, we couldn't see what we were doing, and Hubert had to bang the helpless creature back against the wall to make him understand.

'You aren't going to get hurt,' Hubert hissed repeatedly in the man's face. 'We aren't going to touch you.'

With a grunt, Isaac suggested locking him in the cellars; and while Nathan went off with Hubert, Charles Blow and Bannister, I helped Isaac carry the clerk along the corridor and round to the back of the building. We found the kitchens easy enough, and the boiler room, and then got the door unlocked down to the cellars. In the darkness, we kept stumbling into chairs and stoves but the moonlight was bright through the high kitchen windows and it took minutes to drag Frears down into the cellar.

In the darkness, I heard Isaac kick the man as we let him drop to the ground. I could smell sea water and when I bent down to find Frears, I could feel the wetness of the ground. There were rats scuttling in the corners of the cellar, and Frears let out a yelp of fear.

'Don't leave me down here,' he begged.

'Shut up,' Isaac snarled, kicking at him again.

'Please, don't leave me.'

'It smells wet,' I whispered to Isaac.

'Sea water,' he said. 'Disease. The ground is rotten with water: that's what undermines the foundations, brings the disease. Can't you smell it: typhoid, scarlatina, dysentery, smallpox, enteric fever. You got a nose. It seeps through the air. Comes with the sea water. The high tides always flood this building. Bad weather waters.'

Frears let out a cry, and I turned, trying to see in the darkness.

At my side, Isaac gave me a push. 'Let's go, friend.'

'You can't leave him.'

'Can't I!'

'He's terrified.'

Isaac seemed to be shaking with fury. I felt his knife sharp in my ribs. His voice scraped in the darkness like poison. 'He signed my boy on one of Henry Mundol's smacks,' he hissed close to my face, his breath bitter and ulcerous as Charlie had told me, his voice shaking with violence. 'He signed my boy, and pocketed Mundol's coins. But he never bought flowers when my boy drowned. We never heard a word from him. Let him whimper now. Let him drown, if the rats don't poison him.'

I could smell the oil Isaac used to grease his hair back, the stale sickness of his stomach. I remembered the night on Butterwick Low, when he had lost his temper, shouting furiously about the boy we had tried to rescue: we shouldn't be wasting our time chasing after boys . . . they shouldn't sign indentures if they didn't want to go to sea. It made no sense. I hesitated on the stairs.

Isaac seemed to know what I was thinking, his eyes bitter

with pain and derision, his lips twisted with resentment. 'You think I should care about the others?' he said with a sneer.

'I don't know, Isaac,' I told him.

'You don't know!' he sneered.

'Isaac . . .'

He shrugged me off. 'Nobody cared about my Daniel.'

I thought he was going to cry, his face twisted in a seizure of pain, his breath coming in short hard gasps.

'All right,' I whispered quickly. 'Let's get out of here.'

We were at the top of the stairs. I wanted to get away. I was beginning to panic in the enclosed scuffling darkness. We ought to take our good fortune and make a run for it before somebody came. I knew there were nightwatchmen on the docks, and they might check the Dock Offices. I felt the clerk's terror breathing in the damp silence down below us.

Isaac turned at the top of the cellar steps and whispered down into the darkness where we could hear Frears sobbing uncontrollably. 'Don't worry, Frears,' Isaac laughed. 'The tide comes in soon. You'll get a nice swim with the rats. Then you'll know what it feels like being on one of Henry Mundol's smacks.' As the clerk cried for help, Isaac slammed and locked the door. 'Bastard,' he muttered under his breath.

We made our way out of the kitchen, and meeting Nathan and the rest in the corridor, hurried out of the building. Hubert and Charles were both carrying sacks over their shoulders. Edward Bannister followed behind.

'Did you find them?' I asked as we hurried for the darkness beyond the Dock Offices.

'We found them,' Nathan said, his voice trembling with excitement.

'So far so good then,' I whispered.

'So far so good,' Nathan agreed.

Behind us in the clammy darkness of the dock buildings, I thought I could hear a voice screaming, but it was only a disturbed herring gull, flying low over the faceless buildings.

Thirty-one

The large houses of the owners were in the old part of town, not far from the medieval church. Hubert knew Henry Mundol's property: a gloomy, shadowy pile, surrounded by trees and bushes, with turrets and castellated walls, stained-glass windows and roofs sloping in every direction. We crossed a park and slipped into the rustling, shimmering garden that surrounded the house, moonlight glimmering on the foliage, fireflies flickering in the undergrowth. 'The souls of the dead,' Charlie Blow said close to my ear as we slid on our bellies through the dense undergrowth.

We reached the side of the house and stopped outside a small window, smothered by bushes and ivy. Charlie and Hubert were still carrying the sacks, Edward following close behind. They knelt down and waited. Nathan crept up to the window and with his knife eased the catch. I saw the blade glitter in the light from the moon, moving suddenly from behind a cloud. I heard the catch open with a snap.

Nathan gave a little sign of triumph. 'Hubert,' he whispered, 'you stay here with Charlie and Edward and keep watch. Whistle if anybody comes. You got the sacks safely?'

'Yes.'

'Be ready to run. You know where to head for?'

'Yes,' Hubert whispered impatiently. 'Get on with it, Nathan.'

Nathan turned and looked for Isaac in the darkness. 'You got the other sacks, Isaac?'

'Yes,' Isaac muttered.

'Come on then, you two. Let's go.'

I followed Nathan through the window, Isaac bringing up the rear. We climbed into a tiny cloakroom, shawls and coats hanging on the pegs, the floor tiled. Our boots clattered on the tiles.

Nathan eased the door open. I could hear my own breathing, the blood pounding in my ears. We stepped cautiously into the hall. It was massive. I had never been inside such a grand house. A sweep of stairs went up into the darkness above us. There were pictures on all the walls, and a huge stained-glass window casting moonlight into the hall. There was a table in the middle of the hall, draped with a heavy cloth, and another long table with vases of flowers. I could smell the scent of flowers and rosewood polish, and the carpet was bouncy beneath our feet, thick with pile. Up above us, on the first landing, thick drapes hung from the bannister, and an enormous chandelier shimmered where the glass caught the moonlight.

Nathan went down the hall and we followed. A dark stuffy passage led off the hall down to the back of the house. Nathan opened two or three doors before finding the one he was looking for, and waved us inside. I closed the door after me. The room was smaller than the hall, but still bigger than most of the houses in Cod's Kingdom. It was at the side of the house, and the large window had stained, coloured panes decorated with patterns of flowers and figures in gorgeous clothing. There was stained glass everywhere, lurid with bright colour, like a church celebrating wealth and power. This room smelled of flowers and rosewood polish, like the hall, and was full of heavy ornate furniture and drapes and thick curtains. Nathan went to the curtains and pulled them back silently.

'Must be the study,' Nathan said, going over to the iron safe standing in a corner, a heavy drape flung over the top casually to try and disguise its purpose. The room was walled with bookcases, and there was a large grand piano and a great stone fireplace. The wallpaper was heavy and red, and there were more pictures on all the spare bits of wall. On the mantelpiece, I recognised figures of Wellington, Tennyson and Victoria, and there were Minton figures of Narcissus and Dorothea. 'We preach not ourselves but Christ the Lord,' I read from a gold-framed card.

Nathan was checking the shelves over the iron safe. 'Looks like your friend was right, Matthew,' he whispered.

I went over to the shelves. There were files stacked neatly in rows, and Nathan was flicking through them, checking the contents.

'Is that them?' Isaac hissed.

'Yes.'

'Let's get it done then.'

We started filling the sacks with the files. Each file had a thick sheaf of indentures, and there must have been fifty files going back years. I couldn't imagine Henry Mundol throwing anything away. When the sacks were full, Isaac went to the study door, but Nathan was going round the study, picking up vases and pottery figures, looking at the paintings. There were several paintings of smacks in the estuary or out on the Dogger, and two wooden models on the walnut desk. The desk was covered with magazines and accounts books. There were two armchairs and four or five studded chairs. It looked like a room that was meant for business, every inch cluttered with ornaments and decoration, brilliant with the loud colours of corruption.

'So much stained glass,' Nathan said under his breath.

'Like a church,' I agreed.

Isaac snorted, waiting by the door, his hand on the handle.

'Yes,' Nathan muttered, 'like a church, only a Methodist wouldn't approve of glass like this in a real church. Mundol keeps it for himself. Makes his wealth into a religion. This house worships wealth. Every stone and fancy picture. It smells of rotten money.'

'We got to leave, Nathan,' Isaac said impatiently, still standing by the study door.

Nathan went on prowling round the room.

'You go,' he said in a strange excited voice.

I glanced at Isaac. We had been in the house a long time now, maybe half an hour. I could hear owls hooting outside.

'I think we should go, Nathan,' I said urgently.

He turned on us, and pulled a gun out of his jacket pocket.

Nobody spoke.

I could hear the clock in the hall chiming the hour: half past two. We had to get out of here before somebody was roused. I could feel the sweat on my forehead, running down my back. I clenched my fists, keeping my eyes on the gun.

'You leave,' Nathan said quietly.

'Not without you.'

Nathan raised the gun and pointed it directly at my face. He smiled strangely, watching me with a kind of vicious fascination, his lips almost pitying. 'You take your orders from me, Matthew.'

I shook my head. 'I promised Elizabeth.'

At the door, Isaac suddenly turned the handle and pulled the door open. Nathan glanced quickly round. Isaac pointed with his finger, indicating the open door and then raising his eyes to the ceiling, showing him that we could easily be heard with the study door wide open.

Nathan lifted the gun level with my eyes and moved it slightly, indicating that I should leave. I took a step forwards, and saw his finger tighten. Isaac had already gone, taking one of the sacks with him. I thought I heard him in the tiny cloakroom, easing the window open again. It must have taken seconds, and then my nerve broke: I grabbed the second sack and followed Isaac.

The silence of the house was like a tomb.

'What the hell's going on?' Hubert demanded when I clambered clumsily out of the small window and fell into the dense undergrowth.

'He won't come,' I gasped.

'You left him!'

'He's got a gun, Hubert,' Isaac hissed at him, shaking his arm. 'He's going to kill somebody.'

'Don't be stupid.'

'He's got a gun!' Isaac said again, gritting his teeth.

I thought instantly of Henry Mundol.

Hubert was gazing at Isaac as if he was mad.

'You left him in that house with a gun!'

Isaac was furious and agitated, his voice rasping as he tried to whisper, the anger lashing out of him as he pushed his fist into Hubert's face. 'You want to get yourself shot, friend, that's fine with me,' he hissed, 'but I'm getting out of here now.'

An owl flew low over the bushes where we were hiding, and I flinched, my face soaked with sweat. I had promised Elizabeth that I would look after Nathan, and now he was alone inside Henry Mundol's house with a gun. I had to do something. I had to go back inside and force him to leave with us. I made a move towards the window. Hubert jumped nervously at my side, grabbing hold of my arm.

'We got to think, Matthew,' he started to whisper, hanging on to my arm.

Then we heard the shot.

It came from inside the house, deadened by the thick walls.

'Jesus,' Isaac whispered, 'what the devil was that?'

Then Isaac was gone, stumbling through the bushes and making for the front of the house, leaving the sack on the ground behind. Crouching in the darkness, Edward Bannister hesitated a second, then crashed after him, making no attempt to keep quiet.

A dog started barking furiously.

I stared at the window, praying that Nathan would climb out.

At my side, Hubert took one more look at the house, and then took his decision. 'We got to leave,' he said fiercely.

We followed Edward through the garden. Charlie Blow was already at the low wall, waiting for us. 'What's going on?' he asked urgently.

I could see Isaac disappearing among the trees into the park in front of the house. A light had gone on upstairs, and the dog was still barking frantically. 'We can't leave him, Hubert,' I tried to argue, but Hubert wouldn't listen.

'We can't help him if we get caught in there ourselves,' he said bluntly.

'But the gun.'

'No.'

There was no arguing with Hubert. He set off across the park with one sack, and I followed, hefting the sack Isaac had dropped over my shoulders along with my own, Charlie Blow running at my side with the fourth sack. In the darkness, I stumbled and almost fell, and Charlie reached out his hand to help me. The moon was shrouded in cloud, and we could hardly see where we were going.

Hubert seemed to be making straight for Satan's Hole.

'Where the hell are we going?' I gasped.

'*Dancing Sally*,' Charlie said easily, running without effort, glancing back over his shoulders to make sure we weren't being chased. There were half a dozen dogs barking now, and lights blazing from Mundol's house, but we could hear no sound of pursuit.

'She's down the marshes,' I managed to gasp, but Charlie grabbed one of the sacks from my shoulder and told me to save my breath.

I ran on towards Satan's Hole, Hubert not far in front of us, Isaac slowing down now that he heard our pursuit. The dull glow of yellow light hung like a fug over the narrow streets and alleyways of Satan's Hole. I gave up trying to see where we were going. Wherever it was, the rest of them knew. I was the one Nathan had decided not to tell.

I could think of nothing but Nathan's face now: the blind hatred, the frenzy in his grey eyes. I could think of nothing but his passion for revenge. And the promises I had made to his sister. I had promised to look after him, and now we were stumbling back to *Dancing Sally* alone and Elizabeth was waiting to greet us.

Thirty-two

I caught up with Hubert in the deserted main street. It was eerie and silent, our boots echoing between the dreary shops and houses, a cat bounding in front of us as we slowed our pace. Gaslight shimmered dimly up alleyways and in smelly courtyards, and ahead of us the dock tower loomed out of the early dawn light. 'Where are we going, Hubert?' I asked.

'*Dancing Sally* is down on the docks.'

'What!'

'Elizabeth has taken her there. They wouldn't expect that. We painted the name out before. Nobody will recognise her.'

I noticed Bannister wasn't with us. 'Where's Edward?'

'He went ahead. Give her time to get the smack ready.'

We reached the square of drinking houses, banks and music halls outside the docks and crossed the road. There was still no sign of life. Hubert led us down to the south end of the docks and into the narrow lanes behind the quays. The lanes were a maze of ropewalks and boat-builders, sailmakers and shipwrights, smithies, coopers, blockmakers, caulkers yards and twine spinners, ice-houses and sail-barking yards, dozens of smokehouses. The air was thick with the fug of the curing sheds. We reached the end of the lanes and Hubert told us to wait. He disappeared along the north wall, his boots echoing on the cobbles. We huddled together in the darkness, hiding in a yard piled with ropes and chains, anchors and old sails. There were broken oars on the ground, and lengths of chain-cable.

At my side, Charlie eased one of the sacks to the ground and told me I could carry it now. He had been carrying the two sacks ever since we left the park. 'I could carry it before,' I muttered, panting for breath.

'Sounds like it,' Charlie laughed.

Suddenly, Hubert was back, whispering beside us. 'She's ready,' he said. 'The lockpit's open. Come on.'

We followed him along the quays. He had warned them we were coming, and as we hurried along in the shadows of the sheds, I saw *Dancing Sally* ghosting away from the bollards and moving along the harbour wall. There was a creak of the boom as Edgar March and Joseph Ablett hoisted the sails, and I saw the great mainsail swinging against the night sky. We kept pace with the smack, staying in the shadows as she tacked towards the lockpit.

When she was halfway through the lockpit, Hubert whispered 'Now,' and we raced across the open ground, reaching the sides of the lockpit together and leaping down to the swaying deck of the smack. I managed to land while still hanging on to the sacks and the papers broke my fall. I heard Charlie land with a curse, and Hubert came sprawling after him. Isaac was the first to his feet, grabbing the tiller and shouting to Joseph Ablett to get the jib and staysail out. I couldn't see Elizabeth anywhere on the deck.

Then she was in front of me. I staggered backwards as she seized my arms. She had been halfway up the mainmast, trying to see us as we ran along the quays. She was breathing heavily, clawing at my arms with her nails. 'Where's Nathan?' she cried angrily, shouting in the stillness, not bothering about who might hear us. 'Where is he?'

Hubert got to his feet and tried to grab her hand. 'Elizabeth . . .'

'You promised, Matthew!'

'He had a gun,' I told her, holding her hands and trying to make her understand. 'He wouldn't leave . . .'

She yelled straight into my face. 'Liar!'

'It's the truth, Elizabeth,' Hubert said, helpless to intervene.

I stepped back, freeing her hands. She lifted her hand to hit me, then suddenly turned on Hubert.

'You as well?'

'He had a gun, Elizabeth,' Hubert kept shouting.

'How do you know?'

A flash of doubt crossed Hubert's face, then he went on regardless. 'I heard the shot.'

She blenched. For a second, I thought she was going to fall, but she stepped back and held on to the tiller. Isaac was busy trying to get *Dancing Sally* out of the muddy waters close to the shore and away to safety in the main river. On the lockpit, there was no sign of life. The merchants would be coming to open the market soon, but we would be gone long before anybody noticed our departure.

Suddenly, Isaac spoke furiously from the tiller. 'There was a gun, Elizabeth. So what! He was probably fearful of this bastard. But I thought he was going to shoot one of us. When he told us to get out, I didn't stop to argue.'

'Get out of where?' Elizabeth asked hopelessly, as if she already knew the answer.

'We were in Mundol's study,' Isaac said flatly.

In the silence, I could hear Joseph Ablett securing the jib

and Sidney Lill down below arguing with Luke Hobbins.
Dancing Sally rode a tidal wave and we passed a string of
barges, winding their way slowly down the river, not a sign
of a watch being kept on the flat decks.

'I see,' Elizabeth said quietly. She glanced at me, and
then at Hubert. 'He had a gun in his cabin,' she said. 'I
never thought to check. If it's gone, I will believe you.'

She went down the companion, and was below a long
time.

I couldn't move.

The force of her venom had shocked me, leaving me
stunned and miserable. There had been nothing I could
have done to persuade Nathan to leave, let alone force
him. Not unless I'd been prepared to take a bullet right in
the face. Every instinct had drawn me to go back, but the
same instincts had made me leave. If he had shot Henry
Mundol, it wasn't my fault.

Hubert eventually sat down at the tiller post, shaking his
head, trying to get control of his breathing. Charlie Blow
and Edward Bannister sprawled on the deck, drinking the
tea Luke Hobbins brought for us all. Isaac worked the
tiller, lost in his own thoughts. I was still standing at the
bulwarks when Elizabeth climbed back up the companion.

She walked straight up to me. 'I'm sorry.'

I shrugged, my eyes smarting suddenly, my hands
trembling.

'Matthew?'

'Yes.'

'You are all right?'

'I'm fine.'

'The gun's gone. He took it with him. He was the only
one who had a key. It's just that he swore he would never
touch it again . . .'

She stopped, confused, uncertain.

I gazed at her.

'I told you he had a gun. What do you mean, never use it again?'

She looked at me, and then shrugged, avoiding my eyes. 'It doesn't matter,' she said. She turned quickly and glanced at Isaac. 'Are you all right?' she asked.

'Yes,' he nodded indifferently.

We were out in the main channel now, gliding down the river towards the estuary. There were faint pink flecks in the sky to the east as the sun rose from the horizon. Elizabeth sighed, once, her whole body seeming to shake, and then she turned and smiled at me, touching my arm. 'I hope I didn't hurt you,' she whispered.

'He's not that pathetic, is he?' Charlie Blow laughed.

'I'm fine,' I smiled at Elizabeth.

We made the rest of the journey back to Spurn without talking about what had happened. Everybody needed time to think. Elizabeth stood at the tiller and watched what Isaac was doing. I knew she could have taken the smack round Binks Sands herself any day, but she left Isaac free to do it himself. He looked haunted in the thin daylight. I remembered his voice in the cellar at the Custom House as the clerk screamed for help. I sat down finally by the main-mast, and tried to get some sleep.

We didn't talk until we were safely back on Spurn. *Dancing Sally* was left offshore so that we could use her if need be. Just the four of us crouched beside a fire, drinking tea, talking: Elizabeth, Hubert, Isaac and myself. I felt like a ghost, haunting their conversation.

'I don't see as there's anything we can do,' Isaac said, staring at his hands, his face pitted with acne, his eyes red with fatigue.

'We have to go back,' Hubert said bluntly.

'Go back?'

'Find out what's going on, what happened last night.'

Isaac shrugged. 'We could always ask our friend here.'

Elizabeth cut him off. 'Leave it, Isaac.'

'Well I'm hardly out of place. I nearly got caught last night fetching his wretched indentures.'

'I never signed indentures,' I said tiredly.

'They're your *idea*,' Isaac sneered.

'Let it alone, Isaac,' Hubert grumbled. 'We ent going to get anywhere chasing that line of argument. He was there with us. We can't keep calling him a liar.'

'I don't see why not, when he is,' Isaac said angrily.

'I think we should burn the indentures,' Elizabeth said quickly, standing up and going to the sacks.

There were four sacks of the papers. She hefted one of them closer to the fire and unfastened the rope. The papers burned quickly on the hot fire. Ash floated on the air. Hubert went and fetched a second sack and flung it on to the flames without unfastening the rope. I watched. The air was full of ash and floating fragments of parchment. Several of the men and women of the community turned and watched, and children ran up to the fire to help. Hubert untied the third sack and gave them handfuls to throw into the flames. The children clapped and danced round the fire, enjoying the blaze. The final sack was unfastened, and Hubert asked me if I wanted to help. I shook my head. Isaac watched me sourly. 'Maybe we should burn him n'all,' he said bitterly.

'Give it a rest, Isaac,' Hubert laughed.

The last sack of indentures was thrown into the blaze. We all watched in silence. A refreshing breeze was coming off the sea, and ash floated away across the river, drifting on the wind, dropping to the waves. Our clothes and hair stank of ash. There was a smudge of grey daubed on Elizabeth's pale cheek. At last, the indentures were all burned.

'Freedom,' Elizabeth said with a sigh. There were tears in her eyes, tears running down her cheeks. 'Freedom.'

Isaac stood up and yawned. 'Yes,' he said sourly, bitter to the end. 'That's right: freedom. Except that Nathan isn't here. We don't know where the hell he is. He's probably in Mundol's cellar, or in prison if he's lucky. Or maybe he's dead. I don't reckon that's much of a freedom. I'm going back to *Dancing Sally*. Got to get her geared if we're heading back across the river. Got to do something to pass the time.'

He walked off without another word.

Elizabeth sat for some minutes, staring after him, not bothering about the tears running down her cheeks. Finally, she shook her head and coughed slightly, turning away when I reached out my hand to comfort her. She got up and wiped her eyes on the sleeve of her dress. 'I'm going to change my clothes,' she said briefly. 'Be ready when I get back.'

I was left alone with Hubert. 'It wasn't me,' I said quietly.

'I know.'

'Do you?'

'You get to tell about a man, working the fishing for so many years. You don't seem the dishonest kind. Besides, it was Nathan who ordered you to leave. Isaac said that. You weren't the one with the gun.'

We sat in silence for several minutes. I could see Isaac rowing out to *Dancing Sally* in the longboat. Elizabeth had gone into one of the cottages to change her clothes. I closed my eyes and yawned. 'I'm tired.'

Hubert grunted at my side, lost in his own thoughts. 'She's just like her mother,' he said finally, staring at the hut where Elizabeth had gone to change. 'Strong willed, knows what she wants to do. She's got her mother's temper too.'

I gazed into the embers of the fire. The indentures had burned to ashes now. There was nothing left. Herring gulls wheeled over the camp, circling for food. Curlews and oyster-catchers cried along the foreshore. I felt a strange sense of timelessness, as though we were all waiting for something to happen. But the sky was perfectly blue, cloudless. The string of barges we had passed earlier had just reached the estuary and were heading south down the coast. Fishing vessels came and went busily.

'Did you know them both?' I asked Hubert.

'Yes. I worked for Richard Anstey. He was a fine fisherman. He knew the grounds better than any man I ever knew. And how to work them. I worked the summer voyage with him for years.' There was a roughness in his voice now: tiredness, or emotion. He shook his head briefly. 'They were a fine couple.'

'Yes?'

'A fine family. You don't get many like that these days, what with the fleets and the drinking. Henry Mundol ruined that. Him and his greedy friends. They wanted more than the sea can readily give. Now they've got it. Richard Anstey wasn't made to survive that way. Nor his wife, for all she tried. And she did try. She tried till it broke her heart. But she wasn't meant to live like that.'

He gazed into the fire for some minutes longer, and then stood up. I could see Elizabeth coming towards us from the cottage. Hubert wiped his eyes roughly with the back of his sleeve. He coughed and spat down into the seagrass. 'You say nothing,' he told me brusquely.

'No.'

'*Nothing.*'

He walked off abruptly, shouting to Elizabeth, and I was left alone by the dying fire. All I could think about was the gun, and Elizabeth's strange words: he swore he would never touch it again. As they came towards me, I stood up and brushed the sand from my trousers. We were ready to get back across the dangerous river.

Thirty-three

The gypsies were waiting for us at the Freedom Tree. Hubert had decided to take a trip into town with Isaac to try and find out what had happened to Nathan. The rest of us would have to bide our time. *Dancing Sally* was hove-to offshore and I heard Hubert giving brief instructions to Edward Trevitt and Joseph Ablett. They were to wait on board the smack, and if there was any sign of trouble, get the longboats over the side to pick us up. In the meantime, we could mingle with the gypsies.

'Do you think there will be trouble?' I asked him as we climbed into the longboat together, but he shook his head.

'They've got Nathan, one way or the other,' he said bleakly, resigned to the mess we seemed to be in. 'You'll be safe enough here, and if not, *Dancing Sally* can soon get you away.'

Most of the men were already ashore, settling down in the dunes, talking together in small groups.

'You read your Bible, Matthew,' Luke Hobbins told me, sitting at my side in the stern of the longboat. 'All the answers are there.'

'I'm more worried about the questions,' I said with a tight smile.

When we reached the shore, I clambered out of the longboat. Elizabeth was standing by herself at the Freedom Tree. The Freedom Tree had been cut down and hacked to pieces. Branches lay scattered all around in the bindweed, strewn across the mud. The main trunk had been sawn up and then chopped apart in a frenzy.

'The gypsies?' I asked, coming to her side.

'Why would they do this?'

'For firewood?'

She shook her head scornfully, pointing to the scrawled sign that had been pinned to a white branch.

Nathan Anstey: this is what will happen to you.

The words made me shiver, and then laugh, they were so melodramatic. 'That must have been written before this morning,' I pointed out.

She looked puzzled. 'Why?'

'It's a threat. They knew we used the Haven. But they've got Nathan now, they don't need to make threats.'

She watched me for a moment, considering what I said, thoughtful, then she shrugged dismissively. 'Does it make any difference?'

I didn't know. If it was Henry Mundol's men, it meant they knew what was going on on Spurn, but that didn't amount to much. Most people in town knew about the trading Nathan did from Spurn. It was more likely Mundol had lost patience with boys running away to join Nathan's community. He wouldn't need to worry now, assuming he wasn't dead: he had Nathan.

I decided not to bother Elizabeth with my thoughts.

'Not really,' I admitted.

Hubert came up to us, staring glumly at the wreckage of the tree. He rubbed the side of his face, frowning.

'What do you make of it, Hubert?' Elizabeth asked.

'Kept somebody busy,' he said. 'We got to get on, Elizabeth.'

She looked at him, reaching out and touching his arm quickly with nervous affection. 'Take care, Hubert.'

'You know me. Joel Cross and Luke Hobbins are going with us. They might be able to mix with the crowds more easily than me and Isaac.'

I noticed Joel and Luke had both changed out of their jerseys and seaboots and were wearing shirts and serge trousers. Luke was carrying his Bible very prominently underneath his arm.

'Still, you be careful,' Elizabeth insisted.

'We got Luke's Bible,' Hubert said dryly.

The four of them set off across the marshes, going slowly over the hard ground, sunlight glinting on the stretches of stagnant water. The rest of the men were making their way up the marshes to the gypsy camp where a string of horses seemed to be arriving from down the river, half a dozen men walking with them. The gypsy camp was noisy and busy, children running after the horses, women sitting by the fires smoking or preparing food. Elizabeth watched Hubert crossing the marshes until she could see him no longer, then she turned and stared out to *Dancing Sally*, hove-to in the brown waters off the shore. 'I never dreamed my life would be like this,' she said absent-mindedly.

'I don't suppose you would.'

She laughed slightly hysterically: bright; harsh. 'My mother would have been shocked,' she said, 'living with all these wild men.' There were tears in her eyes. 'Selling alcohol and worse.'

'Elizabeth . . .'

'It's all right. I'm all right.'

She turned away from the Freedom Tree and sat down suddenly on the white sand, burying her face in her knees, her long blonde hair falling around her face like a shroud. She was perfectly still. I knelt down beside her, running my hands through the white sand, watching *Dancing Sally* ride the low wash of the tide. I could see Joseph Ablett in the stern, smoking his pipe, gazing at the brown water, dreaming his own dreams. If you hadn't known, you would have thought *Dancing Sally* was waiting for a tide, or had her fishing lines over the starboard side.

'I wanted to ask you something,' I said quietly.

After a moment, she looked up, brushing her hair out of her eyes and smiling weakly. The morning sunlight shone directly into her face, making her shield her eyes. She had the longest eyelashes I had ever seen.

'Nathan said something about the promised land. You lead us to the promised land. You lead us to freedom.'

She nodded, smiling briefly. 'I told you he doesn't think you're a Jonah.'

'It isn't that,' I said.

She looked puzzled, frowning. 'What then?'

'He used the same words.'

'Yes?'

'The words you used.'

She thought for a moment, then bit her lip, surprised, hurt, taking a quick breath. She glanced at me, and her eyes were shining. 'You think I talked to him?' she said indignantly.

'You used the same words. Exodus and crossing the river.'

'Yes.'

'Exactly the same words.'

She shook her head, saddened, not knowing what to say. 'We grew up together, Matthew,' she said unhappily.

'I know.'

'Of course we use the same words. He's my brother. When we were children we were never apart. We grew up listening to stories from the Bible.'

I felt ridiculous, ashamed of my suspicions. She was crying now: dry, bitter tears. I took her in my arms and she rested her head against my shoulder, not resisting, tired. She cried for a long time, and then dried her eyes, trying to be cheerful. 'I'm fine,' she said, when I tried to comfort her. 'It's Nathan, he behaves so wildly, he unsettles people. He was like that as a child. He destroys everything. He had a model of a fishing vessel my father gave him. My father spent hours making it, crouched over the kitchen table, working by lamplight. It was a beautiful boat. I don't think Nathan ever loved anything more. When my father died, he burned it.' She was crying again, dry, aching tears. She brushed my hand away when I tried to hold her. 'Burned it,' she said sadly.

'Elizabeth . . .'

'We should get some breakfast,' she said quickly, standing up and brushing the sand from her grey dress. I followed her. We walked across to the gypsy camp, and Sidney Lill brought us plates of bacon and fried potatoes and mugs of hot sweet tea. The tea made us feel better. We ate our food and then walked along the foreshore, watching the waders, paddling in the shallow water where the tideline was not muddy.

Elizabeth was sad, preoccupied.

'I always had to look after Nathan,' she said as we sat on a bank of grass and watched the turnstones working their way along the higher shore, sanderling swarming at the tideline. 'He was always in trouble.'

'Isn't that what sisters are for?' I asked gently.

'He was supposed to look after me,' she said with a short laugh. 'My father thought so anyway. But he was always in trouble. He used to fight the children from the chapel. Pick the biggest boy and go and start a fight. They burned his face once, two of them, holding him over a brazier. He broke a chapel window. But they used to throw stones at us, if we cut through the churchyard to go to Mass. We lived just outside Yarmouth then, and had to walk miles to Mass, every Sunday. My mother never flinched.'

'Don't distress yourself.'

She glanced at me vaguely for a moment, lost in her own thoughts, almost surprised to see me sitting there. 'I'm not distressed by that,' she laughed. 'It was lonely, that was all, going through crowds of chapel people. But they never bothered me, with their taunts and hymns. We just thought they were foolish. They used to stand outside during Mass and sing hymns. I never could stand your hymns.'

'They're not mine,' I protested innocently.

'You know what I mean.'

She gazed down the river towards the estuary, blinking in the brilliant sunlight. 'I always thought my mother was an angel,' she said with a brief laugh, her smile full of regret. 'Childish really, but she seemed so good, calm and gentle. She could always make things better. Even Nathan: she was the only one who could handle Nathan. My father hadn't any idea. He just used to shout and lose his temper. And now all this nonsense . . .'

She broke off, biting her lips, avoiding my eyes.

'Elizabeth . . .'

'He's such a *fool*,' she said bitterly. 'He's such a child. He knew it was Henry Mundol's house, but still he went. Obsessed with revenge. I should have gone with him, I should have insisted.'

'I don't think he would have let you,' I said, trying to calm her down.

'Oh, what do you know, Matthew, you don't know us at all.'

'I know about your parents, Nathan told me.'

'Did he!' she said with savage mockery.

'I know revenge is a sickness, all this obsession, but you can understand why any man would feel like that.'

'Oh yes!' she scoffed her derision.

'Yes!' I insisted, beginning to lose my own temper. 'It's fair enough, after what happened. I just wish we hadn't . . .'

'He didn't tell you the truth.'

She spoke perfectly calmly, quietly, watching my reaction.

I nearly went on, shouting, venting my anger, but then the words sank in.

'What do you mean?'

'He didn't tell you the truth. That's clear enough, isn't it?'

I looked at her, trying to understand. I thought she was laughing at me, but her smile was tired, beyond derision. She looked deathly, the colour draining from her cheeks. She shivered suddenly, and then got control of herself.

'What about the truth?' I asked finally.

'Henry Mundol didn't destroy our family,' she said tiredly. 'My father did that. Oh, Henry Mundol ruined the business. He wrecked that all right. But he wrecked lots of men: got them into debt, bought their smacks. He built his fleet on other men's bad luck. But they didn't all fall apart like my father. They didn't all go on the drink until they were too stupefied to handle their own vessels. My father drank himself into a stupor because of Henry Mundol, but other men didn't.'

She was silent for a long time, picking angrily at tufts of grass, glaring across the river sightlessly. She was not crying now. Bright spots of colour flared in her cheeks, and then faded again as she talked. She was relentless, unforgiving.

'He started drinking after we lost *Eliza*. What I didn't understand was why the drink had such an effect. Unless he had been drinking all along. But some men can't take alcohol. He collapsed so fast . . . Hubert tried to help him, tried to run the business. He's always been loyal. He worshipped my father. But my father didn't want saving. He wanted utter ruin. And then he started hitting my mother. We could hear him, shouting downstairs, breaking furniture. He broke most of our furniture and we had to sell the rest for food. We were starving.

'My mother died of loneliness and a deranged mind because of what my father did: he started drinking, then going with women; he said he hated the Church; eventually he hit her, then hit her again. One night Nathan came home and found her unconscious on the floor. He came to me and woke me. He was eleven, he didn't know what to do. I was nine. My father had gone off with one of his women, down the drinking houses. We had to carry her to bed and bathe her face. There was blood all down her cheek, and a great bruise on her forehead. She never mentioned it next morning. She refused to talk about it.

'In the end, my father lost *Waterwitch*, and started hitting me as well. He attacked me one night with a gutting knife, because I hadn't any food to cook for his supper. I had a tiny white scar on my arm for years. You can't see it now. One Sunday afternoon, I was playing in the yard, and he came home drunk and started smashing things in the kitchen, not that we had much left. He broke the window. It was the breaking glass brought my mother downstairs. I thought he was going to kill her, but Nathan got in front of him. He had a gun. I have no idea where he found a gun. He must have bought it on the market or from one of the gypsies. He pushed the gun in my father's stomach to hit him and it went off. He bled to death. He lay on the kitchen floor and bled to death while my mother ran for help. All that nonsense Nathan talks about him dying with a cross in his hand. There was no cross. There were flies buzzing in the kitchen. A lot of blood. I can remember standing there: as if it went on forever, as if it is still going on: me in the doorway, Nathan in the middle of the kitchen, watching my father die on the floor.'

She was quiet for a long time: thoughtful, rocking slightly against her knees. When she spoke again, her voice was rough, angry.

'We told people it was suicide. My mother died of grief, but it wasn't the grief Nathan told you about. It was much deeper than that; it was grief for her whole life. She was never going to recover. Nathan was eleven years old.'

I could think of nothing to say.

We sat together, and I held her briefly in my arms, but she needed to be on her own. I wandered down to the tideline, and listened to the sounds of the sea, the teeming life of the river.

I remembered what Nathan had said about visions – the gift of unhappiness. I had visited Lindisfarne to look for my memories: my mother, my father. What I found on Lindisfarne was a man stumbling in the sea, a wild figure plunging into the icy waters. Was that a vision, or a waking dream? A figure walking out of the wastes of my loss? I had never thought about it. A fisherman doesn't have much free time for thinking. I had lived my life and never known the deep unhappiness that sang in the background like the sea. But I knew it now. I heard it, and it was breaking my heart.

We spent the rest of the day together, walking on the marshes, eating a huge dinner with Sidney Lill and some of the gypsy women, talking to Charlie Blow. Charlie could cheer most people up, and he told Elizabeth stories about his father and the Hackney graveyards which had her weeping with laughter, but her eyes didn't lose their shadow all day, and she kept close by my side, holding my hand, leaning on my shoulder as we watched the evening sunlight fade over the western hills.

It was late evening when Hubert got back. Isaac and the two lads had stayed in Satan's Hole, and Hubert came along the foreshore, shouting out when he saw Elizabeth that Nathan was fine and safe, taking her in his arms when they met and giving her a big hug. 'He's safe,' he kept telling her. 'Nobody was shot. We're not too certain what happened in Mundol's house, but it looks like the gun went off by mistake or in a struggle. He didn't shoot anybody.'

'Thank God,' Elizabeth cried into his shoulder. 'But where is he? What's happened to him, Hubert?'

'Hold your horses a fraction, girl, let me get my breath. I'm an old man, you know.'

We settled down by the fire, and Hubert told us about their day. They had spent most of it hiding in various houses in Satan's Hole, and latterly at the Convent. It hadn't taken long to find out that Nathan was being charged with housebreaking and that the magistrates were hearing the case late in the afternoon. One of the nuns went to the court, because they were trying to help a girl who was being charged with streetwalking. Hubert spent the afternoon fretting in the Convent garden, talking to Sister Clare and trying to keep his patience.

'Henry Mundol gave evidence,' Hubert told us. 'Said he heard a noise and went downstairs to look around. Found Nathan in the study trying to open the safe.'

'The safe?' I asked, surprised.

'That's what he said.'

'But what about the indentures?' Elizabeth asked.

'Mundol never mentioned them. But then he wouldn't. He doesn't want news getting around that they've been stolen. He wouldn't have a boy left on his vessels if that news got around.'

'He must have guessed we'd burn them,' Elizabeth said.

'Course. Playing for time probably. Hoping to find copies.'

I was still puzzled. 'Didn't Nathan get a chance to say anything?' I asked.

Hubert laughed briefly. 'He had his say, all right. Bold as brass he was. He claimed Mundol invited him to the house to discuss business. Fresh supplies for the fleets. That changed Mundol's face I can tell you. He went green. And the magistrates. They weren't too comfortable. But they didn't ask: they didn't want to know.'

'And the gun?'

'According to Nathan, he was in the study when Augustus Jackson attacked him. Started an argument about something. That's when the gun went off. I reckon everybody in that court room knew he was lying, and not one of them raised an eyebrow. Too scared to ask questions.'

'So what happened?'

'They're sending him to Hull tomorrow for the Assizes.'

'Why not Lincoln?' I asked.

Hubert laughed, acknowledging my point. The local courts hardly ever sent cases to Hull to be heard. They got better results in the cathedral city. 'It was going to be Lincoln according to what the magistrates said,' he said. 'But then I got word that they'd changed their minds after the hearing. Just to confuse us a little maybe. Send us chasing after the wrong tack. He'll go by train first thing tomorrow morning to New Holland and then by ferry across the river. That's when we get our chance.'

Elizabeth looked eagerly at Hubert. 'You've something planned?'

'Isaac thought we should try and set him free off the ferry.'

'That sounds dangerous,' she said.

'From the train,' Hubert agreed. 'That's my thought.'

'But where?' Elizabeth asked.

'When she stops at Ulceby. It's an hour from the river at most. We can free him and be gone on *Dancing Sally* before they know what's hit them. Try the ferry, and we'll be done for piracy, with dozens of witnesses naming

Dancing Sally. From the train, they'll never prove who freed him.'

Elizabeth couldn't stay still. She paced up and down by the fire, firing questions at Hubert. She wanted to know where Isaac and the two lads were, why they hadn't come back, and Hubert explained that they were busy passing the word: we were going to need all the help we could manage. At one point, she clapped her hands like an excited child, rushing to Hubert and giving him a warm embrace.

'You're a lovely man,' she told him.

'I know that lass.'

'If I didn't love Matthew . . .'

'Well, well, don't let's bother about all that. We should get ourselves out to *Dancing Sally* and let the lads know where to meet us tomorrow.'

We spent the night planning and talking. The fires in the gypsy camp burned through to dawn, men kept coming and going, *Dancing Sally* hoisted her mainsail and set off up the river towards the waters opposite Ulceby. In the hush and excitement, I thought Elizabeth was like a young girl, busy planning a holiday. I wasn't convinced it was going to be such fun.

Thirty-four

At dawn there was a thin mist, cold and creeping over the fields and pools of water, dank with the wetness of the river. The fog bell was ringing on the buoy at the estuary, and the sound carried over the lonely countryside. Nothing moved. In the fields, cows munched at the grass. We couldn't see a thing. We lay in a ditch, ten or eleven of us, our clothes soaked with dew, our hair wet through. Elizabeth kept close to Hubert.

'This is a right game, Matthew,' Charlie Blow whispered at my side. 'Another of your ideas, was it?'

'Not my choosing.'

'I believe you. I wasn't born for fields and dew. North Sea's wet enough for me. I was born for cities and wild women.'

A pheasant chortled in front of us, the noise racketing from field to field in the dense fog, startling Charlie. He looked around as if he had heard a weird creature from his dreams. The fog seemed to be getting thicker instead of lifting with the dawn. It was like the fog from the morning on the cockle beds, when I heard Jacob talking to a ghost. I still wasn't sure whether I had been imagining things then, but this morning there were no ghostly

conversations. We were on our own in the desolate countryside.

'You like having women aboard?' Charlie whispered,
making sure Elizabeth didn't hear us. 'Trip like this?'

'Why not?'

'They bring bad luck I reckon.'

'You should have told her,' I said ironically.

'Be quiet,' Hubert hissed down the line, and we kept our
peace.

I wished I was still in my bed, waking from a pleasant
dream. But I wasn't. Edgar March and Joseph Ablett had
taken *Dancing Sally* up river, Michael Hart and Joel Cross
going with them because they were too young to be of
much use on our venture. Edgar was too old and whimsi-
cal, though Hubert didn't tell him that. The rest of us
were supposed to be fit and lively and eager for a bit of
train-robbing.

In the long grass at the bottom of the ditch, I tried to
think of something happy to cheer myself up. A few days
ago, I had been planning to make the journey south to
find myself a comfortable liner for the rest of the season.
That was proper work for a fisherman. Since the morning
I found Elizabeth, wading up to her knees in the surf, nothing seemed to have gone right. Except that I was in love
with her, and had learned a new trade of housebreaking
and running adulterated alcohol to the fishing fleets. My
own good-humour made me laugh, and Charlie jerked
awake at my side, glaring at me for disturbing his peace.
But then we heard the sound we were listening for. I held
my finger up to Charlie.

The train was coming. Out of the dense fog, a whistle
shrieked like a knife scraping metal, and we heard the rattle
of the wheels. It must be seven o'clock. Without waiting for
a word from Hubert, we climbed out of the wet ditch and
ran across the field. The field was full of grazing cattle. I

heard Charlie crash to the ground and an animal let out a bellowing groan. I could see Hubert ahead of me, with Elizabeth, and Isaac running to my right. As we ran, the mist began to lift, and suddenly the station was there right in front of us, a low, wooden building, painted white and green, with a long, deserted platform. There was nobody in sight. We could still hear the train, rattling down the track. I was out of breath. I plunged on after Hubert and Elizabeth, and saw Edward Bannister and Luke Hobbins to my right, stumbling after Isaac in the long wet grass. I wanted to shout and urge them on: anything was better than waiting.

Then we were down the low bank and crossing the track. The train was to our left approaching slowly, steam adding to the mist. The mist seemed to be swirling and thickening in patches, and beyond the station we could see nothing but fog. I stared at the platform in panic. I had expected it to be still deserted, but a dozen or so men and boys had appeared from behind the station and were already lounging against the walls, sitting on the wooden seats. I wondered if they were Mundol's men.

'It's all right,' Hubert shouted as he clambered up the low wall and on to the platform, turning to wave us on, 'they're with us.' I followed the rest of them, crossing the metal tracks, glancing at the men waiting for us. I slipped on the bricks, climbing the wall, and hoisted myself up on to the platform. Hubert was already down at the far end, talking to a couple of the men, lighting his pipe and trying to look unconcerned. Isaac lounged casually further up the platform, where the engine would come to rest. Soon Bannister and Luke Hobbins joined us, and then Charlie, Sidney Lill and Peter Loft. Edward Trevitt was the last to scramble up on to the platform, still fastening his trousers after urinating in the field full of cows. Elizabeth was standing with Hubert, leaning on his arm as if they were a father and daughter out for the day.

'Who the hell are these characters?' I asked Charlie nervously.

'Isaac spread the word last night, in Satan's Hole. Told a few friends the indentures had been burned and we needed help. News like that soon gets around, Matthew.'

Some of the men looked like fishermen, but the boys were children, none of them much older than eleven or twelve. They were obviously taking Isaac's cry for help as a chance to make their own escape across the river.

'This is turning into a pilgrimage,' I said bitterly, wondering how much could go wrong with a train full of armed policemen and us standing on the platform surrounded by children.

At last the train pulled into the station. I thought for a moment the driver was going to take her straight through. He leaned out of the cabin and stared at the crowded platform and then turned and shouted something to his fireman. But it was too late. Edward Bannister was in the cabin before they could change their minds, and the next minute the driver stumbled down the cabin steps and fell sprawling to the platform. Hubert was leading half a dozen of the men into one of the rear carriages. At the engine, Isaac Prusey climbed up into the cabin and helped Bannister persuade the fireman to climb down to the platform.

I ran along the platform to the rear carriage, and saw Hubert inside, struggling with one of the policemen. There were two more policemen fighting at the carriage door, trying to kick Edward Trevitt out of the carriage. I opened another door and came up behind them, getting my arms round one while Trevitt seized his chance and lunged at the second man's legs. They both went down with curses, and then Charlie and Peter Loft were weighing in, thumping the men on the floor and threatening them with their gutting knives. I had my own knife in my hand, and managed to get to my feet. I was wet through with sweat, and it wasn't heat but fear. As I struggled to my feet, the man on the floor lashed out with his fist, and I stumbled backwards, cracking my head against the metal edge of the door. I passed out, collapsing into somebody's arms.

When I came to, Hubert was talking to me and I was still inside the carriage. Nathan saw me and waved. He was unfastening the chains around his ankles with the key they had got from the third policeman. Absconding apprentices on their way to Lincoln Prison were always kept in chains as they were marched through the streets of the cathedral city. When Nathan had his own chains free, Peter Loft started unfastening the rest of the prisoners. There were five of them, all boys, on their way to the treadmill at Hull Prison for absconding from their smacks. As Peter unfastened the chains, Nathan shouted at them, asking them who they had signed indentures with. All five of them were off Henry Mundol smacks.

'Then you come with us,' he grinned, wild with excitement, rushing up and down the carriage, his face completely haggard, his eyes blazing with drink and pleasure. There were bottles of aniseed whisky scattered about the floor of the carriage. The policemen had obviously sold the drink to the lads to get the last of their money out of them before they entered the blind doors of the prison. Nathan was drunk on whisky and laudanum. I couldn't imagine how he had managed to get hold of that. When they were all free, Hubert chained the policemen and we were finished.

'You still with us, Matthew?' Nathan asked gladly, grabbing my hand and shaking it so that the fingers felt as if they'd been crushed. He noticed the wound to my head. 'You want to watch your head,' he laughed, 'you might end up bruising your brains.' His strength was terrifying, manic and uncontrolled. He seemed to find my injuries hilarious. 'Is Lizzie here?'

'She's on the platform,' I gasped.

But Elizabeth was already coming down the carriage. She flung her arms round Nathan's neck and then hit him hard on the shoulder. 'You fool,' she told him, clinging to him again.

'You came to save me, Lizzie.'

'Only because we had to. You promised me you would never touch that gun again.'

'We ent got time for this, Elizabeth,' Hubert shouted urgently down the carriage.

Nathan shrugged indifferently, kissed Elizabeth on the cheek, and waved to the boys who had been sharing his prison chain with him. 'Come on then you boys,' he shouted. 'I promised you freedom, and here it is. Let's get moving.'

We clambered out of the carriage and back down to the platform. Isaac and Bannister had the driver and fireman tied up now, and locked in the waiting room. The mist was still dense around the isolated station, strange and eerie, drifting from the nearby river, but with pale pink sunlight filtering through the morning clouds. I could hear cows lowing in the fields, and a dog barking somewhere on one of the farms. A herd of cows suddenly appeared out of the mist, munching along the lane and nuzzling the boy trying to lead them. He turned and stared at us. Passengers in the other carriages were at the windows, watching what we were doing. Nathan bowed to them, and then followed Hubert across the tracks and up the bank into the field. The boy with the cows stood with his mouth wide open, his cows straying on to the tracks, the driver and fireman in the waiting room shouting at him to wake up and come and lend a hand. In the train, nobody offered to get out and help. The air was full of the sound of cows mooing.

Nathan and Elizabeth were walking arm in arm.

'Let me introduce you to somebody,' Nathan said

cheerfully as I came up beside them. A young lad was walking with him. 'This is David Croft,' Nathan went on. 'Shake Matthew's hand, David.'

The boy held out his hand, blushing and stumbling in the long grass.

'Who is he?' I asked Nathan, irritated by his games, my head throbbing from the wound and blood still trickling down my forehead.

'He signed indentures with Henry Mundol, then did a run. Only you didn't get very far, did you, David?'

'No, sir,' the boy admitted. He was fair-haired, not much older than thirteen or fourteen. He looked exhausted, hungry, and his clothes were filthy. He must have been travelling for days before Mundol's men caught up with him.

'Where did you get to, David?' Nathan went on loudly, ignoring my impatience.

'Butterwick Low, sir, down the Wash, that's where they caught me. But I wasn't doing what they said. They kept saying it was something to do with tobacco. I didn't know anything about tobacco. They locked me up in Boston and then sent me back to Grimsby, only I wouldn't agree to go back on the smack, I said I would rather go to the treadmill than do that.'

'You hear him, Matthew,' Nathan said with a grin. 'He'd rather go to the treadmill than take passage on one of Henry Mundol's smacks. The magistrates thought that was very funny.'

I couldn't take in what Nathan was saying. I saw Hubert listening, trying to concentrate on what we were saying and make sure we didn't get lost at the same time. You could smell the sea by now, and we kept heading towards the sound of herring gulls. Elizabeth turned and smiled at me, a secret, happy smile, her hair wet with fog, her eyes shining with relief.

'You reckon this is the boy we were meant to pick up?' I asked.

Nathan smiled at me triumphantly. 'I know it is,' he smiled.

'How can you be sure?'

'Duffy told me the lad's name,' he said, 'when we arranged the deal.'

'So you knew he would be there?'

Nathan laughed at this as though it was the greatest joke on earth. I had the strangest feeling he had known all along, that he never doubted the truth of Duffy's story or suspected me of being involved with Henry Mundol. But why should he disguise the fact, and when we were alone and there was nobody to make anything of the truth. It seemed pure madness.

But I couldn't think clearly now. We plunged on through the soaking grass and fog, swarming across the country like a nightmare plague towards the muddy waters where *Dancing Sally* waited to take us to freedom. The short journey seemed to take forever. My mind was full of cold and mist and violence. I could hear shrieks and calls for help, voices carrying across the waters. And then we were running across the flat marshes towards the river, the earth and the water merging together in a brown muddy flatness, the seabirds wheeling and screaming in the sultry air. As we ran, more boys dodged out of the hedges and ran with us. There seemed to be dozens of them, fleeing from the lanes and ditches. The news about the indentures must be spreading like a fire.

Then the fog was suddenly lifting. A white cloud lay across the countryside for miles around us but on the river I could see dozens of vessels, fishing smacks tacking towards the shore, men waving and shouting from their decks, more smacks turning into the river and making for *Dancing Sally*. It was a fleet of smacks, pouring out of

Grimsby, tacking down the river towards the mudflats. I tried to shout and point but no sound came from my throat. I was having difficulty breathing. Then we were plunging into the water, and the longboats were racing to collect us, and the fog was lifting on the empty river, and *Dancing Sally* was the only smack in sight, the rest a vision in my mind. As I reached the longboat, I fainted with the pain and loss of blood.

Thirty-five

I came to and Nathan was kneeling beside me. His eyes were white with delirium, his clothes stank of laudanum. Mundol's men must have dosed him overnight to keep him quiet, but the drugs drove him wild, gave him an energy that was out of control and terrifying. He watched me, his eyes darting across my face, his nose twitching as if he smelled my fear.

'What is it?' he whispered, his lips pulling back in a grimace.

'There are vessels,' I tried to say, my voice dry and cracking.

'Vessels?'

'On the river, hundreds of vessels.'

'You're seeing things, Matthew,' he said, his voice sneering and lethal.

'They're going to get us, Nathan.'

'Nobody's going to get me, friend. You're having your visions again.'

'Henry Mundol . . .'

I lifted myself and saw boys swarming on the deck of *Dancing Sally*. We were heading down the river, and the mainmast was alive with boys, the decks crowded and noisy, bustling like a market. I saw Isaac at the tiller, Hubert in the bows. *Dancing Sally* tacked down the river like a herring gull riding the tides, her bows lifting to meet the waves, white spray fuming over the bulwarks.

I collapsed back into Nathan's arms, and he brought a mug of water to my lips. The water was cold as ice. I shivered and then drank greedily. Elizabeth came up from the companion and joined us. We were in the stern, by the starboard bulwarks. I could see white water, and the deep muddy water of the river flashing by. The Lincolnshire coast shimmered far away, like a mirage trembling at the edge of my dreams. We seemed to be heading for the far shore, not tacking up the main channel, but I couldn't hold myself up long enough to see what we were doing.

'A children's crusade,' I said wearily.

I saw Nathan glance at Elizabeth. 'What's he talking about now?' he muttered.

'You've heard of the children's crusade,' I said and laughed. The water ran down my chest, and I shivered again. The blow to my head must have damaged my brain: I felt hot, and then frozen; a lump throbbed on my forehead. 'This is a children's crusade, Elizabeth,' I said with more laughter, the hysteria rising in my throat. 'This is a journey into death.'

'Try and rest, Matthew,' she whispered, leaning forward and bathing my forehead. 'I'll go and fetch some more water.'

At her side, Nathan was gazing at me with a blind hatred. 'You're very friendly where you shouldn't be, Matthew,' he said, his lips flecked with spittle. 'You want to mind yourself.'

'Listen, Nathan.'

'You want to remember who she is.'

I was gripping his arm, forcing myself to sit up. 'You know I was right about the indentures,' I told him.

'What?' he snapped, distracted, glaring at me in confusion. 'What the hell are you ranting about now?'

'I *saw* the burning indentures. I told you. I *saw* them.'

'You are mad. That's the only reason you act so friendly with my sister. You're mad.'

'I *saw* them, and I *saw* Mundol's vessels. They're going to come to Spurn. They're going to attack us there.'

'Keep your mouth shut, friend.'

'You know Mundol can't let this go. We've burned the indentures. He knows that by now. Isaac has been spreading the word all night. Mundol has to attack you. He has to do something. There must be thirty children on this smack running away from his fleets because of what they've heard and he can't stand that. He can't let you go free, Nathan.'

'Sunk Island,' Hubert suddenly cried from the bows of *Dancing Sally*. I sat up desperately, clinging to Nathan's arm.

'Sunk Island,' I gasped. 'What are we doing, Nathan?'

'Getting ashore,' he sneered, prizing my fingers free.

'We have to leave,' I shouted, my head pounding with agony, fresh blood running down my left cheek. 'We can't stay here.'

Nathan pushed me aside with a brutal anger and stood up. His lips were twitching and I could see blood on his teeth. I tried to hang on but he kicked me savagely in the ribs and I fell back. As he went for'ard to the bows, Elizabeth climbed the companion with a bowl of water. She saw what happened, and hesitated, the bowl in her hands. I saw her lips move, the confusion on her face, then she rushed to my side and knelt down.

'You've opened the cut again.'

'Tell him, Lizzie.'

'Don't call me that.'

'Tell him!'

'I don't like it. I told you.'

She was preoccupied, hurrying, bathing my forehead and then trying to force me to drink some of the water. *Dancing Sally* was already hove-to off Sunk Island, and Nathan was shouting orders. I managed to stand and then reeled as the deck lifted with the rough waters. We had never landed this side of the Spurn before, where the waters were so shallow and dangerous. The longboats were quickly over the side, and boys were clambering off the smack, laughing and shouting, falling into the river in panic. Hubert was busy getting the anchor over the side when Nathan stopped him, telling Isaac to keep *Dancing Sally* hove-to. We wouldn't be hove-to if we were staying on Spurn. I wondered if he had listened to my words. I saw Nathan whispering to Bannister and then Charlie Blow, then he talked to Isaac, glancing in my direction. Isaac nodded and came across.

'He says we're to get ashore,' he told Elizabeth.

'Right,' she nodded.

'I'm not going ashore,' I said. 'There's no need.'

'Matthew . . .'

'We're leaving, can't you see that? He's decided to leave.'

Isaac shrugged and nodded to Bannister and Charlie. 'You're going ashore, friend, one way or the other. Give him a hand, lads.'

I tried to fight, but with Elizabeth climbing after me, I daren't struggle in case I upset the longboat in the treacherous waters off the shore. Elizabeth sat in the bows and watched as the men rowed the longboat to Sunk Island, and there we waded into the muddy water and stood face to face with Nathan. He was watching the boys and men cross the narrow channel to the mainland. On Spurn, dozens of women were greeting the men, little children running around excitedly, dogs barking and yapping in wild excitement. I saw Sidney Lill go ashore and make straight for the largest fire, where food was being prepared.

I could smell bacon on the air and see the women handing mugs of tea to the men. The boys we had brought with us stood around in groups, dazed and confused, trying to make out what was happening. I stopped in front of Nathan.

'If we don't leave, Nathan, you'll be to blame.'

'Is that so,' he sneered.

'Come on, friend,' Isaac encouraged me, taking my arm.

I shook myself free. 'This is madness,' I said bleakly. 'We haven't a chance.'

'So you keep saying.'

'I said *move*,' Isaac snarled at my side.

'I'm coming,' I muttered.

'Now!'

I thought Isaac was going to start a fight, saw him glancing back to the longboat where Bannister and Charlie were watching, but Nathan suddenly interrupted. 'Let him be,' he said quickly.

Isaac spat and gave up. He plunged off the island and across the shallow channel to the Spurn. Charlie and Bannister still watched us from the longboat. I gazed beyond *Dancing Sally* across the river back towards the Lincolnshire shore. The river was more or less empty, one or two fishing smacks coming and going, a few barges. There was no sign of anything unusual. I shook my head wearily and met Nathan's eyes.

'You going now?' he asked.

'If you won't change your mind.'

'I won't.'

I turned and saw Elizabeth watching us from the Spurn, talking to Hubert Caldicott. 'Why did you fire the gun?' I asked curiously.

He was still driven by excitement, demonic, overpowering. He grinned at me as if he hadn't heard my words. 'I thought you were going?'

'The gun, Nathan!' I insisted. 'Why did you fire it?'

He flinched. His smile disappeared slowly in a frown of irritation. He looked up at the sky distractedly, taking a deep breath. He was sweating, and he seemed tired all of a sudden, as if exhaustion had finally drained his nerve and determination. He held his breath for a long time, then let it out very slowly, so that the sound was like the sigh of the dead, their souls leaking out of their coffins in some deserted graveyard.

'He dared to harm my sister,' he said in a voice I could hardly hear.

I watched his eyes all the time, trying to see into his mind. 'You're talking about Henry Mundol,' I said, seeing the venom in his eyes, the brutal hatred. 'You said it was Augustus Jackson in court.'

'Did I?'

'You know you did.'

He thought for a moment, then nodded almost to himself.

'Hubert told you,' he said, smiling sarcastically.

'Yes,' I agreed. 'But I don't believe you. It was Mundol you were after.'

'If you say so.'

'Then why didn't you shoot him?' I asked quietly. 'Why didn't you shoot Mundol?'

His smile gradually froze. A line of sweat broke out at his forehead and he was shivering, his face working convulsively. He looked as if he was going to have a fit. He glanced away from me towards *Dancing Sally*, a nervous, agitated look, his hands twitching restlessly at his sides. When he looked back into my face, his expression was hard and cruel, knowing.

'They overpowered me,' he lied.

We stared at each other for a long time, and then I turned and waded off Sunk Island. I thought he would follow me. I didn't look back. My head was aching again and I paused in the shallow water, splashing my face and trying to think.

I didn't know what was going on, but Nathan seemed to be blaming me for something. I felt dizzy, faint, unable to think clearly. I had no idea what he was doing, but I felt guilty, depressed with strange emotions and feelings I wasn't used to and didn't understand. My mind seemed to be blank with despair. I looked up, and saw Elizabeth waving, and then Hubert running across the sands towards me. Isaac had only just waded out of the water and was walking towards them. I heard Hubert shout and then realised Elizabeth was screaming.

I turned. The longboat had gone straight back to *Dancing Sally*, and Nathan was at the tiller, Edward and Charlie hauling the jib and staysail back round to the wind. The smack was no longer hove-to. As I started to run through the water for Sunk Island, I saw Nathan glance over his shoulder, and then *Dancing Sally* was tacking slowly away from the shallow waters and making for the estuary. With the tide running fast, it took them minutes to be well beyond our reach. They were in such a hurry, they left one of the longboats bobbing in their wake, then drifting drunkenly back towards the treacherous waters of Greedy Gut, the sandbank just down the spit from Sunk Island.

Dancing Sally was making for sea, but I was no longer watching *Dancing Sally*. Across the river, their sails red and ochre in the morning sunlight, half a dozen vessels were heading towards our side of the river. There was no chance that they were making for the estuary. They were sailing straight for Sunk Island. In a moment's panic, I looked around for somewhere to run, but I was trapped. There was nowhere to go.

Thirty-six

I plunged back into the shallow waters between Sunk Island and the Spurn and joined Hubert and Elizabeth. Isaac was running towards us, splashing through the water and waving his arm, cursing. 'Where the hell's Nathan going?' he shouted. *Dancing Sally* was already round the end of Spurn, disappearing in the morning heat haze. Isaac was white with fury.

I glanced at Elizabeth. She was bewildered, shocked, her face ashen with confusion and fear. 'He's going round to Old Hive,' she said quickly, trying to understand what had happened. 'He doesn't want *Dancing Sally* damaged.'

'I'll damage the bastard,' Isaac yelled frantically, glaring at us as if it was our fault. I had never seen him so upset, uncertain. He stared after the departing smack as if she were a dream floating out of his reach.

Hubert was watching the vessels approaching across the river. He took no notice of Isaac's rage. 'Six of them,' he said, counting carefully. 'Maybe thirty or forty men.'

'It's Nathan they're after,' Isaac said angrily.

'You think they'll stop to ask?' Hubert said sarcastically, putting his arm round Elizabeth's shoulder. 'You all right, Elizabeth?'

She was shaking. 'What shall we do, Hubert?'

'Your brother won't be here to answer, you can bet good money on that,' Isaac said viciously, glaring at her, still trying to grasp what was going on. 'He's left us to sort his mess out for him.'

'Leave it alone, Isaac,' I muttered.

He was round on me immediately, glad of a genuine target, his hands shaking, his eyes frantic with disappointment and fury. 'You brought this fortune, Jonah . . .'

That was when Hubert lost his temper. 'Shut up,' he shouted, his voice like a ton of gravel, his fists clenched in Isaac's face. 'We got things to do, Prusey, and dishing out blame won't help. Get the oars from the longboats.'

'You watch your mouth, Caldicott . . .'

Isaac was furious, crouching and weaving in front of Hubert, but Hubert simply turned his back on him and shouted to Sidney Lill and Edgar March. 'Get the longboat oars,' he called to them. 'Grappling hooks. And find some rocks. Anything you can throw.'

Sidney and Edgar ran for the longboats drawn up on the sea side of the Spurn, and Luke and Joel started searching for rocks. The lads who had been standing round in groups joined in, and soon everybody was scouring the dunes and foreshore, the rough grassy earth, coming back to Hubert with rocks and heavy wrack and anything they could find to throw. Edgar and Sidney collected a dozen oars.

Out in the river, the smacks were getting closer. We could see men in the bows watching us, talking and pointing. Lads were shouting down from the mainmasts of two of the vessels. In the bows of the first smack, I could see a black figure standing rigidly by the bowsprit. Augustus Jackson was watching everything we did through a brass telescope. Every smack in his small fleet had her bowsprit out.

'Spread out,' Hubert shouted his orders. 'Along the tide-line.'

We had a dozen men and twenty or thirty lads. The women from the camp went on searching for rocks, the youngest children helping them. Hubert took charge of everything. Elizabeth kept to his side, lifting rocks, dashing around to help the children, white-faced and agitated.

'Nathan will come straight back,' she said as I worked with her, trying to stop her lifting the heaviest rocks and stones. 'He'll berth *Dancing Sally* and come straight back from Old Hive.'

She could see as well as I could that *Dancing Sally* had not gone round the headland. There was no sign of her tacking up the coast to Old Hive. In the heat haze hanging over the estuary, it was hard to see far out to sea, but I thought I saw her beyond Spurn, drifting on the dazzling water, lost in light. I wondered if he was taking her back down the Lincolnshire coast, or far out to sea before heading north.

'Take it easy, Elizabeth.'

'You don't know my brother.'

'No, I don't.'

'He will come back.'

The first of the smacks was drawing close to the shallow waters now. We could see the figure in black watching us, shielding his eyes from the sun. They had the midday sun right in their eyes.

'That's Augustus Jackson,' Hubert said quietly.

'Yes, I saw him.'

'At least the sun will help us,' he mused, watching everything that was going on.

'You think Henry Mundol will be with them?' I asked.

'No, he leaves this kind of work to Jackson. Wouldn't you?'

Jackson was shouting orders, and his men were lowering the first of the longboats. As the longboats splashed into the water, the second smack hove-to and began lowering its longboats. Men were clambering over the bulwarks and down to the rocking boats. We could hear shouts and laughter, and some of the men on deck were waving codbangers in our faces, jeering and blowing kisses to the women who stood in our line.

'Get ready,' Hubert shouted.

Most of the men had oars, and their own codbangers through their belts. The lads stood with piles of rocks behind them, ready for throwing.

'You only get to throw them once,' Hubert was shouting. 'Make sure you hit somebody, or the longboats. Try and sink the longboats.'

Elizabeth pushed forward into the line and seized a rock. She was trembling, pushing her hair back out of her eyes.

'You can't do this, Elizabeth,' I said.

'Leave me alone.'

'You'll get hurt.'

'You think I'm not hurt already?' she flashed at me, her eyes filling with tears. 'You think I *care*?'

It was pointless arguing. She lifted the rock in her hand, weighing it carefully and gazing at the first longboat ploughing through the rough water towards us. They were making for Sunk Island. I noticed that her hands were filthy and covered with cuts and scratches, blood running down her wrist as she lifted the heavy flinty rock. She smiled at me, her blonde hair falling down across her forehead, her face still white with nervous agitation.

'Nathan will help us,' she said calmly. 'You can trust him.'

'I trust you,' I told her quietly.

Then Hubert was shouting again: 'They're coming,' and suddenly the first of the longboats was lifting and plunging into the surf in front of us and a dozen rocks hailed through the air, hitting two of the men at the oars and sending a third over the side into the water. As the man in the bows turned to help his friends, Hubert and Edgar ran forward with their oars, and started pushing the longboat away from the shore, heaving at it until the rocking motion tipped the boat to port and she lifted out of the water, sending five men over the side. As they floundered in the river, a dozen boys ran forward and hurled rocks and stones at them, yelling and cursing in their excitement. Isaac and Sidney Lill plunged into the water after them, hoisting their own oars and smashing them into the longboat, staving the sides and then turning on the men, lashing at them with the heavy oars. I saw two men go under the water, and the rest turn and begin swimming for the second longboat.

A great cheer went up from the line, and I could see Hubert rushing up and down, shouting at the boys to get ready with fresh stones and rocks, urging everybody to get back into the line. Out in the river, men were swimming desperately for the second longboat, and the two men who had gone down into the water were scrambling on to Sunk Island, collapsing at the low edge where the sheep grazed at the tough grass. They lay motionless as the men in the second longboat tried to haul their friends aboard.

'It won't be so easy next time,' Hubert said at my side. 'Look at the buggers.'

A third smack was hove-to now, and three more longboats were rowing towards us, bringing at least fifteen grown men with codbangers and oars ready. They wouldn't be in the mood for giving up after the rout they'd just seen. The two men on Sunk Island were sitting up now, gazing stunned out to sea, watching what was going on. The men in the second longboat were arguing, shouting at each other, waiting for their friends.

'Fire,' Hubert said under his breath, staring at the longboats.

'What's that, Hubert?'

'Get brushwood, wrack, anything that will burn.'

'What . . .?'

He turned suddenly and started shouting at the women. 'Get wrack, seaweed, old wood, anything that will burn. Pile it up behind the line. Right along the foreshore.'

The women rushed about immediately, fetching wood and dried wrack from the camp. They had been collecting for weeks, building up fuel for the camp fires, the cold autumn nights that would come with September. The children joined in with several of our boys on the line, keeping their eye on the longboats out in the river. Soon the heap of wood was spreading right down the foreshore behind our line of men and boys.

'Keep at it,' Hubert yelled. 'Whatever happens, keep at it.'

He turned back to the river. There were now four longboats making for the shore directly in front of us. There was nowhere else they could land between Sunk Island and Hawkins Point to our right. The mudflats and sandbanks were too treacherous for landing anywhere else.

I had my own codbanger ready now, and an oar in my hands. Elizabeth let out a gasp of fear and panic, but when I glanced at her she managed a tight, determined smile. The women and children behind us were still adding fuel to the fire, and other children were running up with rocks and stones. I could see several of our men had their gutting knives ready.

'Let them get close,' Hubert shouted. 'Stave the boats.'

In the bows of the nearest longboat, I could see Augustus Jackson, standing up, watching everything we were doing. He was blinded by the sun. In his arrogance, he carried no weapon.

'Ready,' Hubert yelled.

And suddenly the longboats were ploughing through the low shallow water again, and the air was thick with rocks

and stones, yells and shrieks from the falling men, the cries
of our own boys. Hubert led the charge into the water. I
heard a great shout from the line, and then I was wading
through muddy water, hoisting my own oar and bringing it
down savagely on the head of the first man out of the longboats. He fell with a sickening thud against the boat as the
oar landed across his shoulders, and then he was over the
side and face-down in the river, floundering for his life. I
hit him again and then went for the longboat with all my
strength. Two more men were clambering over the side. I
held the oar in front of me and charged straight at the hull,
ramming the oar as hard as I could through the thick wood.
The oar broke in half, splintering into the side of the longboat. I heaved myself into the longboat, and started
ramming the splintered oar through the bottom.

I could see a man climbing over the stern of the longboat
after me. I lifted the oar again and tried to ram it through
the bottom of the boat before he reached me, and then the
man was in front of me, lashing out with his codbanger,
cursing as I spun to face him.

It was Ben Lowther. His face was livid with drink and
fever, his eyes yellow and vicious. He didn't recognise me
at first. He swung his codbanger behind his shoulder,
lashed at me with a yell, and then crouched, getting his
balance, ready to attack again.

'You,' I said, hefting the broken oar between both hands.

In the pause, Lowther grinned, took his chance, and
then lashed out with his codbanger, the wooden stave hitting me hard on the left knee. I was down in the bottom of
the boat before I could react, the oar kicked out of my
hands and Lowther standing over me, his eyes closed as he
brought his codbanger down with all his force towards my
face.

'Bastard,' he was screaming in a high-pitched bellow.

I turned sideways as the blow crashed down and heard

the codbanger splintering the seat I was sprawled across. Carried forward by the weight of his blow, Lowther lurched into the bottom of the boat and I grabbed his arm, twisting it behind his back. My left leg was useless, numbed from the blow to the knee. I twisted myself round and as Lowther tried to get to his feet, butted him straight in the mouth. He went backwards, blood pouring out of his mouth. I hit him as hard as I could in the groin and as he went over managed to get to my feet. He was staring up at me, his mouth working desperately as he tried to breath through the gush of blood, his hands scrabbling in the bottom of the boat for the codbanger he had dropped. I grabbed the broken oar and hit him as hard as I could across the head, and he went down again, sprawling backwards with a sickening gurgle into the rowlocks.

Another of Mundol's men was clambering over the side now and I went for him with a blow from the oar before he could recover his balance. He fell backwards, and I lifted the splintered end of the oar and drove it straight into his stomach. The shriek made me feel sick, and then Isaac was climbing into the longboat, grabbing a free oar and smashing it into the bottom of the boat. As he worked frantically, another man struggled towards us through the water and tried to climb aboard. I lifted my broken oar and threw it with all the force I had into his face. He went down with a cry, falling backwards over the side into the river.

The longboat was sinking, and Isaac plunged out and started wading towards the other boats. Hubert was in one of the boats, grappling with two men. I could see Augustus Jackson in another boat. Peter Loft and Edward Trevitt were together, fighting three or four of Mundol's men, using their codbangers. There were bodies floating unconscious in the shallow water, two or three more men floundering away to Sunk Island. My ears cleared suddenly, and I heard screams and cries for help.

In the heat and confusion, I saw Michael Hart, running back to the foreshore, splashing through the water, crying and trying to cover his head with his arms. A big fisherman from one of the longboats caught up with him and sent him sprawling to the sands where he started to kick him, his boots thumping into Michael's back, his codbanger flailing at his head. There was nobody nearby to help the boy.

Then a blow caught me straight across the mouth, and I was down in the water. I saw the man with the codbanger, lifting it ready to hit again, and then Isaac was behind him, hitting him with a savage blow in the kidneys. The man's face seemed to collapse, his eyes turning upwards and his mouth gaping inwards before a gush of blood shot straight out and hit me in the face. I was drenched with blood. Isaac grabbed my arm and lifted me out of the water. I was drowning in blood.

'Run,' Isaac was yelling.

I saw the others running, floundering out of the water, struggling back to the beach. Luke Hobbins was being carried by Joseph Ablett and Peter Loft. Edward Trevitt was in one of the longboats, fighting four or five men, going down into the bottom of the boat as they kicked and beat him, two of them holding his arms behind his back while the others aimed blows repeatedly at his stomach and groin. He slumped forward in their arms but they went on with their vicious beating. I could hardly see for the blood on my face.

'Get back,' Hubert was yelling, and we struggled on to the muddy shore and scrambled behind the line of firewood. The women were already there, helping the wounded men, crying and yelling abuse at the longboats, rushing around with water and bandages. As I staggered on to the beach, I found Michael Hart's unconscious body, sprawled face-down on the sands. The man who had been kicking him was floating in the shallow water, the back of his head covered with blood. Using the last of my strength, I got hold of Michael's arms and dragged him away from the tideline, up the foreshore behind the line of firewood.

I was exhausted. I couldn't breathe. When we were clear of the firewood, I let go of Michael's arms and fell on my knees to the sand. I heard the air whistling through my lungs. I thought my chest was going to explode. One of the women gave me water, and I saw Elizabeth sitting on the beach a few yards away, her dress soaked, her hair hanging straight down her back. Hubert was giving her a drink, glancing behind him all the time to what was going on out in the river. I took another drink and tried to slow my breathing, get control of myself. I closed my eyes and held my head between my legs. When I could breathe, I got up and went across to Elizabeth and Hubert.

She was drenched with sweat and water, her legs splattered with black mud. She was shaking, her teeth chattering as if she had a fever.

'Is she all right?' I asked Hubert.

'She's fine,' he nodded. He glanced towards the smacks. All six of them were hove-to now and a dozen longboats were making for the shore. Men were sitting all over Sunk Island, nursing their wounds. I could see Augustus Jackson in one of the longboats, standing alone, watching us. 'We can't take any more,' Hubert said briefly.

Sidney Lill joined us, bringing cold meat and cheese. 'Haven't got time to brew tea,' he said with a laugh. He had a bandage round his forehead, and blood was running down his arm and fingers on to the plates. A woman followed him, carrying water in jars. I took some more water and shook my head at the food. My mouth was still full of blood, and I washed it out with the water and then drank gratefully.

A seventh smack was hove-to now, and three more long-boat were rowing towards us. Hubert seemed stunned, not knowing what to do. The longboats were ploughing through the rough water, men standing up ready to leap overboard. I tried to stand and felt dizzy. In the water, Augustus Jackson was wading towards us.

'Light the fires,' Hubert shouted.

As Jackson reached the muddy shallow waters, a dozen men swarming after him, several of the women from our camp rushed forward and set fire to the row of dried wood and seawrack. The flames took hold immediately, and a wall of fire blazed between us and the men in the sea. Black smoke billowed into our faces. Holding Elizabeth's arm, I stood up and stared at the raging flames, the shadows of men dancing beyond them in the water. The fire would burn for minutes, and then we would be left at their mercy.

Thirty-seven

The flames were burning our faces. The dried wood crackled and hissed and the seawrack sent blue light dancing into the sky. The sun was burning our backs, and our lungs were full of black acrid smoke.

'Be ready,' Hubert shouted, seizing a stave and brandishing it in front of him. Isaac and Joseph Ablett were gathering the rest of the men. The boys were going round, searching for rocks, grabbing staves to defend themselves. Edgar March and Luke Hobbins were sitting on the ground, their heads resting on their forearms. I could see blood on Luke's cheeks and clotting in his fair hair. His Bible lay on the ground beside him.

'Edward Trevitt didn't get back,' Hubert was saying at my side.

'No.'

'You see what happened?'

'They had him in one of the longboats, five of them.'

'Cowards.'

'Michael Hart is over there.'

I pointed to where Michael was lying, one of the women kneeling beside him trying to give him water. He was crying, resting his head back against her shoulder as she tried to help him.

'He's a child,' I muttered. 'He shouldn't be in this.'

Hubert nodded blindly, preoccupied, thoughtful. He kept glancing at the fire, checking the firewood. The flames were sinking all the time. We could see Mundol's men through the flames now, waiting at the tideline, standing in black muddy water, their staves and codbangers in their hands. Augustus Jackson was pacing up and down in front of them, waiting for the fire to burn itself out. They were resting while the fire burned. They had no need to hurry.

Edgar and Luke were struggling to their feet now. Isaac was still searching for rocks, scurrying round like an animal terrified by fire. I could see Sidney Lill and Joel Cross picking up staves and going wearily back to the line, Peter Loft and Joel Cross helping each other. Joseph Ablett was busy throwing more dried wood on to the fire in a desperate attempt to keep the blaze going, prevent Mundol's men coming through. Some of the boys and women were helping him, glad of anything to do.

But the fire was dying on us, and on the other side, I could see Augustus Jackson talking to his men. They were laughing, waving their weapons above their heads. Jackson turned and pointed through the thinning smoke, his voice scraping the air like a razor blade. 'I want the girl,' I heard him shout. 'The girl and her brother.'

Elizabeth was standing at my side, shivering. I put my arm round her shoulder and glanced desperately at Hubert. He avoided my eyes.

I saw Augustus Jackson searching through the smoke, looking directly to where we were standing. He was the tallest man I had ever seen, with thick heavy shoulders. His face was white as bone, but with a red burn down the left cheek. He was still wearing his black suit and black silk top hat, crazy-looking in the mud and pouring smoke at the edge of the river. He looked like some strange madman, preaching to the waiting crowd, shouting damnation to the women and children crouched behind the dying flames, waiting helplessly with their pathetic rocks and staves of wood, silent in the tight blazing heat of the summer afternoon.

The first men into the fire fell as a shower of rocks rained from the sky. I moved in front of Elizabeth and lifted my broken oar in my hands. I could see Jackson turning to his left, looking up the shore away from Sunk Island and towards Hawkins Point. There were shouts and loud cracks in the air, and I thought the cracks were the sound of guns being fired. Then more of Mundol's men lurched forward over the hot glowing embers of the fire and we were flailing at them with our codbangers, fighting hand to hand as more rocks fell from the sky. I had my first man down with a single blow from the oar, and then two more were coming straight at me, one of them swinging a frayed rope and the other lunging at me with a long oar. The oar hit my shoulder and I swung round, trying to avoid the rope, but it lashed me straight across my chest, sending me reeling backwards. I saw Elizabeth lift a rock and throw it directly at the man with the rope.

Then both of them were running. I staggered to my feet and grabbed hold of Elizabeth's arm: she was trying to run after them. There were yells coming from the tideline, and swarms of men seemed to be pouring down the foreshore from Hawkins Point, falling on Mundol's men and driving them into the river. Running forward, I hit one of my attackers on the back of the head with the broken oar, and he floundered on his knees into the river, sprawling in the black mud and then scrabbling for one of the longboats. I could see Jackson, working frantically at the oars of another longboat. There seemed to be dozens of men in the water, flailing at the retreating boats, yelling and shouting curses.

Then I recognised Duffy. He was wading out towards Sunk Island, a dozen men with him waving staves and scythes, their heavy sharp-edged excavating spades suddenly deadly weapons in the fray, the blades gleaming in the sunlight. I gave a yell, and waded out into the river. There were several of Mundol's men on Sunk Island, and Isaac was already there with Joseph Ablett and Peter Loft, hacking at them with codbangers.

'Let them go,' I heard somebody shout, but nobody was taking any notice. A longboat was beached on Sunk Island, trying to pick the men up, and more men waded into the narrow channel, hammering at each other, yelling and cursing. I stood up to my knees in muddy water, laughing out loud, drenched by the salt water, my hands black with mud. I couldn't stop laughing. I turned, and saw Elizabeth on the shore, her hands clenched in front of her, going down on to her knees.

In a kind of delirium, I waded back to Elizabeth and sank down in front of her, holding her arms with my filthy hands. She laughed at the thick mud. Her face was splattered with mud now, and there was seaweed caught in her dress. She was crying. 'Thank God,' she kept saying. 'Thank God.'

'Thank Duffy more like,' I laughed, glancing back at the raging fight still going on in the churned-up waters. 'He must have a hell of a grudge against Mundol to get involved in this fight.'

But the fight was more or less finished now. A dozen of Mundol's men were left unconscious on Sunk Island. The rest had scrambled into the longboats and gone back to the smacks. Augustus Jackson was in the last longboat to leave. We could see him, stiff and erect in his black suit, climbing aboard the nearest smack. To my amazement, he was still carrying his black top hat, and seemed to be talking to the men on the deck, watching the safe retreat of the last of his men.

But I couldn't think about Augustus Jackson. The fight had raged for no more than a couple of hours, but I felt as if it had been going on forever. I collapsed on to the sands beside Elizabeth, and closed my eyes. I went to sleep.

When I finally woke, Duffy was coming towards us from the tideline, satisfied that the longboats had all gone.

'That was a rare fight,' he grinned when he reached us.

Elizabeth was awake at my side. 'Bless you, Duffy,' she said, getting up and kissing him on the cheek.

'No need for that. I just wish Henry Mundol had been here himself.'

Over by the ashes of the fire, I saw Isaac talking to some of our own men and then coming to join us.

'Did you get a chance at Augustus Jackson?' Elizabeth laughed.

'Not the man for me,' Duffy said with a wink. 'I got more sense than that. Good to see you again, Matthew.'

'Why did you come?' I asked, watching the Irish stagger back up the shores, collapse on the sands and start to talk and share their flasks of drink. The women were already busy with fresh water and food, looking after the hurt and wounded, and I could hear several men groaning. Peter Loft had a nasty cut across his forehead, and two or three of our men were on the ground, unable to move. The young lads who had come with us from Ulceby were mostly stretched out flat on their backs, done for the day.

'Why *did* you come, Duffy?' Elizabeth urged him.

'Nathan's a good friend,' Duffy said cheerfully. 'And we don't hold with Henry Mundol and his kind. Never miss a chance for a bit of revenge. That's our way.'

Isaac was standing beside us now. He offered Duffy a drink from a flask. 'You seen what they're doing?' he asked, nodding towards the smacks out in the river. They were still there, the longboats tied alongside, the decks crowded with men.

'You don't think they're going to come back for more?' Duffy said with surprise.

'Looks like it.'

'The bastards.'

'Do you have enough men?'

'More than enough,' Duffy grinned. He got up and rubbed his hands together. 'Give us that flask, Isaac,' he said, and drained the flask at a single swallow. 'There, that's fine stuff. Better get ready then.'

He went off, shouting to his companions.

Isaac remained standing. 'You seen Hubert?' he asked quietly.

I glanced round the beach. Hubert was nowhere in sight. I stood up.

'He's gone,' Isaac said.

'What?'

'You heard. He's gone.'

'He might be hurt somewhere,' I said.

Elizabeth was staring round now, shading her eyes from the sun, looking for Hubert. 'Matthew's right. He must be hurt,' she said quickly. 'Hubert wouldn't leave us.'

'No more than Nathan,' Isaac said bitterly.

She turned on him, her eyes flashing with temper. 'You don't say that, Isaac.'

'He's not here, is he, your precious brother?'

'You still don't say it!'

'And why not!' he shouted back at her.

Elizabeth slapped him hard across the face, and lifted her hand to hit him again, but he gripped her wrist, bending it back.

'Take it easy, girl . . .'

I knocked his hand away, getting between them. 'Give over, Isaac. Let it rest, you fool. If Mundol's men . . .'

There was a shout from the foreshore, and we turned. Duffy was waving to us, pointing out to sea. On the smacks, men were climbing down to the longboats.

Isaac scoffed. 'No *if*, I reckon.'

Elizabeth was at my side, glaring at Isaac. 'You want to run away?' she sneered.

He stared at her blandly, his eyes full of malice. 'Not me that's running away, girl. Your brother Nathan took two of our best men. Now Caldicott's gone, and he's taken three . . .'

'What?' I gasped.

'Edgar March, Sidney Lill and Luke Hobbins. Not that a Bible pusher is going to be much help with this lot, but we could have used the other two. But I reckon they'd had enough. Like your brother, girl.'

Elizabeth lunged forward but I held her arm. 'Look,' I shouted.

The longboats were heading for the shore now. There were eight or nine longboats, with six or seven men in each boat. Duffy was down at the tideline, wading into the water. He seemed to have dozens of men with him. Our own people stood around in desultory groups, the women staring at the longboats in disbelief, the boys too exhausted to stand.

At my side, Elizabeth suddenly became very still. Her shoulders slumped. She was crying. Her hands hung limply at her sides.

Isaac and I both stared at her.

'This is a nightmare,' I said blankly, trying to think what to do.

Isaac stared levelly at me, his sneering smile hovering on his thin mouth, his eyes condescending and flat with lifeless malice. 'Yes,' he said with a kind of gleeful pleasure. 'You could say that.'

Down at the mudflats, there was a yell, and we saw that

the longboats were all making for Sunk Island. They were going to land on the island and make their main attack from there. With a shout, Duffy was leading his men across the muddy water to the strip of rough land. The sheep were scattering in confusion, plunging into the river, running in frantic circles in their panic. As Duffy made for the island, most of our men and women went with them. We were left alone on the Spurn, surrounded by the wounded and the children, the young boys we had brought from the railway station. Even they were beginning to get up and make their way down to the narrow channel and across to the island.

'Nathan's Kingdom,' I said softly under my breath.

'It could have been,' Isaac said bitterly. 'If you hadn't come and started all this frenzy.'

Before I could answer, Joel Cross staggered towards us and asked us what he was supposed to do. He was holding a jug of fresh water. His eyes were full of tears of terror. He was twelve years old.

Thirty-eight

Then Elizabeth was running. 'I must find Nathan,' she was shouting.

'No, Elizabeth!' I yelled, startled by her sudden departure.

'I must find Nathan,' she called again over her shoulder.

She was running down towards the shore. Isaac flinched, rattled, alarmed. I think he half expected her to run straight for Mundol's men.

Joel was still standing there, crying, staring after the fleeing girl. 'Come on,' I shouted, grabbing his arm and pulling him. He wouldn't move. He stared at me as if I was insane. 'I said come on,' I yelled, punching him hard on the shoulder. He came awake then, and started forward with a jerk, following me blindly.

Elizabeth was down at the water now. She did not run towards the narrow channel separating us from Sunk Island, but further up the shoreline toward Smeaton's Lighthouse and the end of the Spurn. She had seen a long-boat being carried towards the shore by the tide, unnoticed by the swarms of men already fighting on Sunk Island.

I caught up with her as she waded into the deeper and faster-running water this far along the shore. She was panting for breath, struggling to climb into the longboat. 'Elizabeth!' I cried.

'Leave me alone,' she shouted at me, glancing over her shoulder and fighting harder than ever to get aboard the swinging, lurching boat.

I could see the stern spinning round towards her. 'Let us help,' I yelled, ploughing through the water and pushing her aside. The stern of the longboat came round sharply and knocked me sideways, but I hung on and felt Joel beside me. The next minute, Isaac was in the water with us. We clung to the longboat as she righted and then I hoisted myself over the side. We were up to our waists in water now, colder and deeper here than at the shallow Sunk Island crossing.

'Grab hold,' I told Elizabeth, reaching out over the side of the longboat, and she seized my wrist, trying to climb over the stern as the longboat lurched away from the shore. Isaac clambered into the stern and got a good hold on her other arm. We managed to pull her over the side to safety as the longboat was taken further away from the shore by the fast-running tide. Joel was already shivering on the seat in the bows, a pool of water gathering at his feet. Another minute, and we would have been out in the river.

'What the devil are we doing?' Isaac asked, panting for breath and rubbing the water out of his eyes. We were all drenched. Joel was beginning to cry. 'This is madness,' Isaac said desperately, staring around at the fast-running river.

I grabbed the oars. 'Where to, Elizabeth?' I asked as we drifted even further away from the safety of the shores.

Elizabeth scrambled for the tiller and settled herself firmly in the stern, her mouth clenched in determination, her hands gripping the wooden tiller. 'Round the Spurn,' she said, gritting her teeth to stop her voice shaking.

'What!'

'Round the Spurn!' she shrieked, beside herself with impatience.

I started rowing, not bothering to think about what we were doing, and Isaac stumbled into the seat behind me. I could hear him gasping for breath, reaching for the second set of oars. Joel sat in the bows with his face buried in his hands.

'You know what you're doing?' Isaac managed to ask between gasps for breath.

'No, but she does.'

He laughed bitterly. 'She's off her head.'

'You want to go back?'

We could hear the fighting on Sunk Island. Men were shouting and crying out in pain. Wooden staves thumped into the boards of longboats. Women shrieked in terror. We were facing forward, rowing for the dark waters of the estuary, the raging turmoil where the sea and the tidal floods met with dangerous waves and murderous sandbanks. We had to get away from the waters close to the end of the Spurn, where the sandbanks Greedy Gut and Old Den were clearly visible through the clearer water: we wouldn't stand a chance if we got caught in the turbulent waters over those banks. We wouldn't be much safer further out, but at least we needn't think about that yet.

In the stern, Elizabeth was clinging on to the tiller, fighting the tide.

'Keep her out,' Isaac shouted his orders.

'I know.'

'You got sandbanks just along here.'

'I *know*!' Elizabeth shouted back. 'I'm not a child.'

There was a harsh yell from Sunk Island, and I wanted to turn in my seat and see what was happening to Duffy and his friends. The fighting seemed to be going on for a long time, the screams of the women getting worse. But I couldn't turn round: I would have tipped the longboat over, and in these waters the strongest swimmer wouldn't stand a chance.

We were past Smeaton's Light by now, and Joel was drying his eyes, staring around him in pure terror. 'Where are we?' he asked, as if he'd woken from some dreadful sleep of dread, some foul nightmare.

'Sit still, Joel,' I told him.

'We're at sea,' he gasped, making to stand up.

I leaned forward and hit his leg hard with my fist. 'I said sit still, boy, or you'll have us over.'

The force of the blow brought him to his senses. He gripped the sides of the longboat, gazing in terror at the water racing past us, then back to shore as we were passing Smeaton's Light. In the lighthouse, men were standing on the wooden balcony, watching the fight, waving to us as we made our slow clumsy progress. Then we steered sharply to starboard, and were out in the violent waters of the estuary, and I had no time to worry about Joel or anything else.

The waves lifted us and Joel stumbled head first into the bottom of the boat. Water flooded beneath the seats. I heard Elizabeth splashing between the seats, baling with the bucket kept underneath the stern seat. She shouted at us to keep our bows into the water, but we couldn't do that unless she was at the tiller.

'Get the tiller,' Isaac was shouting, half turning and yelling at Elizabeth.

'I can't.'

'Get the tiller,' he bellowed furiously. 'Pass the bucket down to us.'

I could hear her floundering between the seats, struggling to hand the bucket for'ard. I clung to my oar, which was being wrenched from my hands by the force of the tide. I hung on frantically. We were heading straight for the estuary, a line of white surf flying in the air where the tidal waters of the river met the inflowing waters of the sea. 'Get on with it, for Christ's sake,' I yelled. Then Isaac had the bucket and was leaning forward, passing it to Joel. Joel stared at him in blank terror. 'Clear the water, boy,' Isaac was yelling, but Joel didn't understand. I felt the boat right itself and head up into the waves as Elizabeth seized the tiller, but we were swamped with water beneath our seats, which was a good foot deep by now and getting deeper.

Isaac suddenly leaned forward and hit Joel hard across the face. I heard the crack of the blow. Joel fell backwards against the bows, and then stared at Isaac in horror, massaging his cheeks.

'If you don't bale,' Isaac yelled, 'we'll all drown.'

Joel seemed to stare at him with dumb terror for minutes, but then suddenly he was scrabbling forward, and baling for his life, and ours. He lifted bucket after bucket of water over the side. Sweat was pouring down his face, and his arms were red with bruises and blood. He worked like a maniac, down on his knees in the bottom of the longboat.

'Keep rowing,' Isaac shouted at me, and I grabbed the oars and bent my back into the force of the waves. All the time, the white turbulence of the estuary was getting closer. Elizabeth kept us headed straight into it, the Spurn to our left, the distant shores of Lincolnshire gleaming in the sun to our right. We saw smacks going past us up the river, the crews leaning over the bulwarks, waving and shouting their surprise. The longboat lifted and rose with the waves, and Joel went on madly baling, less and less water in the bottom of the boat now, his hands cut to shreds by the metal handle of the bucket, the rough sides of the boat as he hefted the water back into the river. And then we were riding up on a huge wave, and the sky was tilting backwards, sliding to our port side as the longboat rose and fell and took a plunging heave downwards into dark green water.

I heard Elizabeth scream in the stern, and almost let go of my oars, but Isaac was yelling in my ears, keeping us both at the oars, shouting at me not to let go for heaven's sake, not to let the longboat get out of control, and then we were choking in water, going straight through a green wave like a fish sliding in a watery grave, and I thought we were done for, drowned in the icy torrents of sea.

The longboat rode the wave like a cormorant, lifting out of the swell and suddenly sailing free in brilliant sunlight, rocking steadily out of the turbulence and slowing as we clung to the oars, unable to make any more effort. She was through, and I half turned, looking back at Elizabeth in the stern, sitting there like a blonde mermaid, water running out of her hair, seaweed hanging from her shoulders, her eyes tight shut as she spluttered and tried to cough the water out of her lungs. But we were through, free of the turbulence, we were drifting into calmer waters beyond the estuary. We were at sea.

'God bless you, Elizabeth,' Isaac shouted. 'You handled that tiller like a real fisherman. You were grand.'

Then he stopped laughing.

The longboat in front of us was empty. In the turbulence, Joel had gone over the side, lost in the green waves. He was gone.

We sat for several minutes, stunned by the force of the sea, all three of us crying as we searched the calm surface of the sea beyond the estuary for any sign of the boy. There was no sign. His heavy seaboots would have dragged him straight to the bottom in seconds. He wouldn't have stood a chance.

'If he hadn't kept baling, we would have drowned,' Isaac said bleakly, water running down his face, his eyes full of tears. 'If I'd done the baling myself . . .'

I put my hand on his arm. 'Stop it, Isaac.'

'He was twelve years old.'

'I know.'

'Twelve years old, did you know that?'

'I know, Isaac.'

'Do you!'

'He was a child.'

'Yes, like my child, like my Daniel. He was a child, and I hit him, and he shouldn't even have been with us at sea, he should have been at home with his family like any other child.'

We sat silent for a long time, the longboat rocking on the waves, herring gulls sweeping above our heads. We were beginning to drift to port, out beyond the Spurn, and that would take us into even more dangerous waters over Stony Binks.

I took a breath. 'He couldn't have managed the oars, Isaac. We would all have drowned if one of us had done the baling.'

He was silent for a moment, then nodded his head, wiping his eyes.

'That's two lads in a month,' he said bleakly.

'I know.'

'John Parnham and Joel Cross.'

'Yes.'

'We can't even give them a proper burial.'

In the stern, Elizabeth made a sound. I turned and watched her. She was unwinding some seaweed that was draped round one of the oars. Isaac looked up in the silence, and glanced over his shoulder to see what I was looking at.

'There's some seaweed,' she said simply.

Isaac watched her for a minute, and then nodded briefly.

'You say the words,' he said roughly, embarrassed suddenly.

'All right.'

She lifted the seaweed and it hung heavily in the hot

afternoon. It should by rights have been dried, but we had no time for that. She held it high and out over the water.

'For John Parnham,' she said quietly, dropping a strand of the weed into the sea. 'For Joel Cross,' she said again, dropping another strand after it. 'May they rest in peace.'

'May they rest in peace,' Isaac muttered.

'May they rest in peace,' I said.

'And light perpetual shine upon their souls.'

The seaweed was gone. We sat for several minutes in silence, letting the smack drift slowly towards Stony Binks, listening to the wash of the waves against the longboat, the mourning cry of gulls overhead. After a long time, Elizabeth sat up and took the tiller. We were both watching her, lost in our own thoughts, resting on the oars. She was staring over my shoulder, out to sea, then pointing, trying to shield her eyes from the glare off the water. Then she was standing up, rocking the longboat dangerously, waving her arms excitedly.

'It's *Dancing Sally*,' she screamed. 'It's Nathan come to help us.'

I turned quickly, hanging on to my oars, and saw the smack to our starboard, half a mile off Stony Binks. She was not tacking, but lay hove-to in the green water off the Spurn.

'It's *Dancing Sally*,' Elizabeth cried, and we started rowing wearily towards the smack, the noise of the fight on Sunk Island gradually fading in the stillness, the smoke from the camp fires drifting slowly across the cloudless sky. 'He hasn't betrayed us,' Elizabeth said triumphantly as we worked at the heavy oars, our hands covered with blisters, our backs burning in the sun.

I wasn't so sure.

Thirty-nine

Dancing Sally was a scarlet mirage: her sails were brilliant red, her mainmast and boom and gaff shone the same colour. Edward Bannister and Charlie Blow were in the longboat alongside, painting the hull with the same dazzling lurid paint. She was a nightmare, blazing against the grey-green of the deep water, like a shining phantom floating on the wild seas.

At the bulwarks, we could see Nathan shouting down to the two men. His voice was carried away in the stillness, and a swarm of black-backed gulls flocked over his head, drowning any sound with their raucous hunger. Edward and Charlie looked as if they were terrified, working like maniacs in the blistering heat.

'God help us,' Isaac whispered, leaning against the oars.

Nathan must have kept the spare set of sails hidden down below. I had certainly never seen them. There were smacks that had dull red sails, but not this wild nightmarish colour, the colour of the walls in the brothel in Satan's Hole, the deep red of corruption we had found in Henry Mundol's gloomy house.

'God help us,' Isaac muttered again.

'He won't if we just sit here,' I said, glancing at

Elizabeth. The longboat was drifting again, but she wasn't paying too much attention to the tiller. With the tide, we would be carried back to the estuary if we weren't careful. I saw Isaac turning and studying her face.

She was in a trance, her eyes closed, her mouth slightly open as she breathed. She might have been asleep. We looked at each other, and Isaac shrugged hopelessly. 'I don't know what to do,' he said quietly. He seemed to have given up, lost his driven fury, his sly crafty mind; all the calculating had gone from his eyes. He was like a defeated man.

I looked towards *Dancing Sally*. Nathan had seen us now, and was watching us with his eye-glasses. The sun caught the glass and dazzled me for a moment, then I saw him turn and shout something to Edward and Charlie. Both men turned and looked in our direction. They seemed to be arguing, and then for a second I thought I heard Nathan's voice, harsh in the dull afternoon stillness, scraping across my nerves. I wasn't sure I ever wanted to hear that voice again.

'Why red?' Isaac asked at my side, still gazing in amazement towards *Dancing Sally*.

'Hell?' I suggested wearily.

He looked at me, scared, thinking fast. He said nothing.

'Hell,' I muttered again to myself.

Then I remembered the story Elizabeth had told me at the Freedom Tree. The story about the model of a fishing vessel Nathan's father had spent hours making. I looked up. Elizabeth was watching me. She nodded faintly, knowing I had remembered, and then glanced at Isaac, telling him about the boat but keeping her eyes on me all the time.

'Nathan had a model when he was a child,' she said in a dull emotionless voice. 'My father gave it to him. When my father . . . died . . . Nathan set it adrift in the sea off

Yarmouth. We could see the fire burning for a long time. Drifting out to sea. It was a very still summer night. No wind. We watched the fire, until it sank into the sea.'

She paused, looking at me.

Isaac watched her nervously, waiting. 'So?' he said.

Elizabeth shook her head, biting the inside of her mouth. There were tears of hopelessness in her eyes. 'He painted the model with red paint and wax,' she said quietly. 'To make sure it burned. That's why it kept alight for such a long time. Like a red candle, floating out to sea.'

She was silent then, gazing at the vessel, holding the tiller lightly with her right arm. You might have thought she was in a dream, or on a comfortable boating lake with a girlfriend, lazing away the afternoon. But we were drifting further away from *Dancing Sally*, and all the time the tide was taking us back towards the estuary.

Isaac hardly seemed to have registered what she said. 'We got to do something, Elizabeth,' he suggested wearily.

She smiled at him. 'Do something?'

'Go to your brother. We've nowhere else to go. He might need your help.'

The last words seemed to bring some life back into her face. She glanced towards the smack, and noticed how far we had drifted. 'The tide,' she said urgently, glancing at the tiller and then at me.

'Yes,' I said.

She seized the tiller firmly then and smiled brightly at Isaac, like a child deciding to be brave. I felt my heart yearning when I saw that smile. I dreaded to think what we were going to find when we finally reached *Dancing Sally*. I took the oars again, my hands raw with blisters, my back aching as if I had just been flogged on *Happy Jack*.

It took us half an hour to row to the smack. All the time we were making our slow progress, Edward and Charlie went on with their painting. Nathan waved to us from the transom stern, pacing up and down, stopping every few minutes to shout at the working men. He was wearing his heavy cotton fearnoughts but nothing on top, his chest tanned by the sun, his arms tattooed with blue mermaids. His hair, bleached almost white by the sunlight, was long and curling down the back of his neck. He looked like a caged animal, pacing up and down the deck, shouting at the men and glaring at the bright sun.

'We're not going to get very far on a smack painted this colour,' I muttered to Isaac.

'No,' he agreed.

'Maybe that's the hell,' I said briefly.

'What you on about, Matthew?'

'No escape, no freedom.'

As we got closer, Nathan came to the bulwarks and shouted excitedly to Elizabeth. 'I knew you'd come.'

'Are you all right, Nathan?'

'I told them Henry Mundol wouldn't be able to keep you.'

'That's right,' she smiled, standing up, trying to sound cheerful.

We got alongside, and Charlie gave me a rueful smile, continuing with his gruesome work. He was covered with red paint, the same as Bannister, and both of them looked exhausted. We threw the painter up to Nathan, and he secured the longboat and then helped us climb aboard.

'You stay there,' he shouted down to Edward and Charlie. 'I want the starboard side finished before we set sail for Lerwick.'

He straightened then and held his arms out to Elizabeth. She was shivering, watching him like a nervous bird, wary and frightened. When he put his arms round her, she rested her head against his naked, sweating shoulders and started to cry. Nathan beamed at us over the top of her blonde hair, impervious to her tears, running his fingers through her hair and down her shoulders, caressing her like a lost child.

'I have to get *Dancing Sally* ready for the summer voyage,' he told us solemnly. 'Elizabeth always wanted to visit Iceland. We're a bit late, we should really have sailed in June, but I keep my promises. I told her, the Arctic summer is all red sunlight, but the winter is constant darkness. So, we need our own sunlight for such a voyage. What do you think? The new set of sails are fine, but the hull needed painting. I couldn't do that with Hubert hanging around. You know what he's like, Isaac: steady-as-she-goes-Caldicott. He wouldn't have approved of my favourite colour. He wouldn't have understood the poetry and the symbolism. That's one thing we Catholics know about, isn't it, Lizzie, poetry and symbolism?'

She nodded, breaking free of his arms and smiling at him. 'It is,' she said very quietly, her voice sad, resigned, as if she couldn't believe what was happening.

'It won't take long,' Nathan said cheerfully. 'A few more hours, then we'll be ready for cast-off. You want to take the tiller, Matthew? I'm sure Isaac won't mind.'

Isaac watched him carefully, keeping his distance, alert and watching the estuary for any sign of Henry Mundol's smacks. They might get word of the strange apparition beyond the estuary and come looking for us any minute. He seemed to have recovered his energy, his eyes sharp and bright, his mouth tight shut.

'Isn't that right, Isaac?' Nathan said again, a dangerous edge in his voice.

'What's that?'

'I said, you won't mind if Matthew takes the tiller.'

'She's your vessel.'

'That's right, *Dancing Sally* is my vessel. You didn't always think like that though, did you, Isaac? You didn't always think she was mine?'

Isaac stared at him directly now, facing round with his back to the mainmast, casually reaching his hand to the gutting knife in his belt, checking that it was there. 'I don't know what you're talking about,' he said steadily.

'You didn't trust me about Matthew did you, didn't think I was making the right decision?'

'So?' Isaac said warily.

'You didn't trust me when we went down to Butterwick Low.'

'The lad wasn't there.'

'Not by the time we arrived, but he was there, he was waiting for us. Just like Duffy said. You thought it was a trap.'

'So,' Isaac said angrily. 'I had my suspicions. I was wrong, it seems,' he added, glancing quickly at me. 'I got it wrong. But I had a right to speak. You want men round you who can't speak?'

Nathan put back his head and laughed brightly. 'That was never your fault, Isaac.'

'No, it wasn't, and never will be. I'm my own man.'

I didn't see Nathan take the knife from his back pocket. It was a pearl-handled knife with a long thin blade. One minute he was waving his hand in Isaac's direction, the next he had the knife held out in front of him. Isaac blinked and then reached for his own knife.

'Nathan,' I shouted, stepping forward, but his look stopped me in my tracks.

'You were right, Isaac,' he shouted suddenly, staring at me as if I were the devil who had climbed out of the sea on to his smack. 'You were right all the time.'

I saw Nathan lift his hand and the blade of the knife glint in the sunlight. Elizabeth screamed. Turning quickly, I saw Isaac moving towards me and Nathan coming at me from the other side. They both had their knives ready. For a brief second, I looked from Nathan to Isaac, and he was

getting ready to use his knife, snarling at me with all the
venom I had seen in the first days after the cockle beds, his
suspicions finally confirmed. I went for my own knife but I
knew it was too late.

And then Isaac was sprawling on his back on the deck.

Nathan's pearl-handled knife was protruding from his
left eye.

There was a silence, stretching unbearably through the
tight heat, and then Isaac twitched and let out a horrible
gurgling cry, the blood welling out of his eye and out of his
mouth at the same time. His body went on jerking on the
deck for several minutes, banging into the wooden planks,
jerking sideways as if trying to escape some terrible agony.
And then he lay still, and we were left standing alone on the
deck, the three of us staring down at Isaac's dead body, his
head surrounded by a pool of blood, his fingers raw and
bloody where he had tried to claw his way through the
deck.

Nathan was the first to speak. His voice was like a
monotone, tired, lifeless now that he had taken a life,
drained of human sound. 'You were wrong, Isaac,' he said
listlessly.

There was no movement from the corpse. At my side,
Elizabeth was breathing in great rasping gasps for air, like
an asthmatic in the worst kind of attack. I moved towards
her, but she flapped her hands desperately, holding herself
together, clenching her eyes and forcing herself to look at
Isaac's lifeless body. At the bulwarks, I saw Charlie peering
at us, his eyes wide with shock and fear.

Nathan stood transfixed on the deck.

And then he told us.

'It was me all along, Isaac,' he said with a half smile,
almost tender as he spoke the words, kicking Isaac gently
with his foot as if to wake him from a dream. 'It was me
working for Henry Mundol.'

Elizabeth let out a tight shriek, clasping her hand to her mouth.

I saw Charlie disappearing back down to the longboat, and heard him arguing with Bannister. There were raised voices, and then silence.

'It was me,' Nathan said at last, his shoulders suddenly slumping, his face going down on to his chest, so that he appeared to be staring at the deck, his hands hanging loosely at his sides. I noticed for the first time that sweat was pouring from his face.

I went to Elizabeth and took her arm. 'He's ill,' I said calmly.

Nathan didn't move.

Behind us, Charlie climbed over the bulwarks and came and stood at my side. 'You need a friend, Matthew,' he said quietly.

'I do, I reckon,' I said, glancing at him, glad to see him despite the splashes of red paint all over his chest and face. The skin on his back was burned as red as the paint and he looked more tired than a man can stand, his eyes bruised with weariness and fear, his skin tight with anguish and uncertainty. He was one of us now.

Then Nathan started shaking. His hands were clenched into fists and the knuckles were white bone through the thin skin. I stared, and to my horror saw that the skin was bursting, peeling back from the bone and bleeding. I stepped forward, but Nathan was hardly able to stand, his body jerking and dancing on the deck, the sweat weeping from his face and body like water. He opened his mouth and let out a shrill, piercing cry, and suddenly a thin stream of vomit started pouring out of his mouth, dribbling and vomiting down his chest and splashing on the deck.

Elizabeth screamed.

Forty

I caught Nathan as he collapsed. 'Get a blanket or something,' I shouted to Charlie, and he disappeared rapidly down the companion, coming back in minutes with three thick blankets and a pillow from one of the bunks. I was kneeling beside Nathan, holding him in my arms. Elizabeth was washing his face with water from *Dancing Sally*'s watertub, which had also been painted red.

We lifted Nathan on to the blanket and he sank back on the pillow, a dribble of vomit coming out of his mouth and down the side of his face. Elizabeth knelt forward, washing him with a cloth like a mother tenderly caring for a child. Nathan opened his eyes and smiled at her. When he opened his mouth to speak, more vomit poured out and he retched helplessly, banging back against the deck, his stomach jerking and retching so violently I thought he might break his spine.

Charlie scrambled hurriedly back down the companion and soon returned with more blankets. We knelt in silence, watching Nathan's awful writhing pain, the vomit spewing over his face and neck and down his body. A cluster of horrible boils seemed to sprout suddenly on his neck, and when his eyes flickered open, they were red with broken blood vessels. When he finally lay still, we cleaned him and washed his face and then lifted him gently on to fresh blankets and pillows. He sighed, groaning piteously as we lifted him, and then opened his anguished eyes, looking straight at me.

'Matthew, is that you?'

'Yes, I'm here, and Elizabeth.'

'Yes.'

'We're both here.'

'My legs ache so,' he whispered.

'It's all right, Nathan.'

'They ache so.'

He said nothing else, sinking into an abrupt sleep. I freed my arm from behind his back and stood up. Charlie was standing at my side, watching helplessly. Elizabeth remained kneeling on the deck, rocking backwards and forwards, her hands clenched together as if she were praying.

'It's cholera,' she said in a low whisper.

I nodded, not able to speak.

'He must have caught it in Satan's Hole,' Charlie said. 'When he was in prison waiting for the train.'

The festering streets and brothels of Satan's Hole were plagued by cholera, the disease returning every few years as the population grew and more and more foreign trading ships visited the port. He would have had no resistance to the disease, trapped in the overcrowded cells, weakened by his years in the deserts of opium.

Upset, alarmed, I got up and went to the weather bulwarks. I wanted to feel the sea breeze on my face, watch the clean restless movement of the seas. I saw Bannister, rowing as hard as he could away from *Dancing Sally*. I let out a small exclamation of surprise, and Charlie came and stood at my side. 'Bannister's gone,' I said bleakly.

'Good riddance,' Charlie laughed.

'How the hell are the two of us going to sail this smack?'

'We aren't,' Charlie said briefly. I glanced at him. He shrugged and looked back at Nathan. 'We got the other longboat,' he said. 'We'll have to leave Nathan and go for help.'

'Help?' I laughed ironically.

'There must be somebody left on Spurn.'

'For all we know they're all dead.'

'Not likely,' Charlie said cheerfully. 'Might be roughed up a bit, but Mundol won't want murder charges hanging over him. All he wanted was to break up the community, stop lads running away to Nathan. He's done that. He wouldn't have bothered at all if Nathan hadn't made such a fuss about helping the runaways.'

I still didn't fancy the thought of rowing all the way back to Spurn only to find Augustus Jackson and his men in charge and running riot. They might not kill anybody, but they would have some fun trying not to.

I heard Nathan groan, and looked at Elizabeth. She was washing his face, trying to cool the fever. We had plenty of water in the watertub, and clean blankets. I had no idea how long this was going to take, or whether we could do anything else to help. If the fever broke and he survived, he might live through the disease.

Charlie suddenly grabbed my arm. 'There's a smack,' he said urgently. I looked towards the estuary. A ketch was leaving the estuary and tacking straight towards us. She was a mile or so away, and moving rapidly through the rough waters, her bows lifting gaily, her sails taut in the wind. I strained my eyes and then looked round quickly for Nathan's eye-glasses. They were on the deck. I trained them on the smack and then gasped. 'It's *Waterwitch*,' I shouted, turning to tell Elizabeth.

She looked up, puzzled, busy with what she was doing for Nathan. '*Waterwitch*?' she frowned.

'It must be Hubert with the other men.'

I turned back to the smack and tried to see who was on deck. I could recognise Hubert's solid figure at the tiller, and three other men on deck: Sidney Lill, Luke Hobbins and Edgar March. They were checking the sheets, doing something with the staysail. I could see Hubert glancing up at the mainsail, shouting orders. *Waterwitch* was racing towards us through the green waters and I nearly shouted for joy, running along the bulwarks to get a better view in my excitement.

It took the smack half an hour to reach us. She must have passed Edward Bannister at some point but I had lost sight of his longboat and couldn't find it even with the eye-glasses. By the time *Waterwitch* reached us, I had forgotten all about him.

'You all right there?' Hubert shouted from the stern as Luke and Sidney heaved their longboat over the side and prepared to join us.

'Nathan's sick,' I shouted back, glancing quickly at Elizabeth. She didn't seem to hear me. I saw Hubert talking with Edgar, and then he left Edgar in charge of the smack and joined the other two men in the longboat. They rowed across to us, and all the time Hubert was watching our smack, keeping his eye on Charlie and me, straining to see Elizabeth.

I reached out my hand and helped Hubert climb aboard. Luke and Sidney followed. As soon as he was on deck, Hubert went and knelt down beside Nathan. He paled, glancing quickly at Elizabeth. She didn't respond to his greeting or his hand on her shoulder.

He stood up and came to me. 'Cholera.'

'Looks like it.'

'It is. I seen enough.'

He glanced around the smack, staring at the red sails and reddened masts, the blood-red decks. 'Nathan's been busy,' he said unhappily.

'He had Charlie and Edward doing it when we arrived. They didn't get a chance to finish.'

He grunted, and went back and felt Nathan's forehead. Luke shook my hand and Sidney Lill stared round in amazement at the red sails and masts, his hand massaging his mouth thoughtfully, his eyes wide open. He was still wearing the bandage round his forehead, the blood seeping through the wound making the cloth as red as *Dancing Sally*.

'Having a party were you?' Sidney said with a dry laugh.

'I'm glad to see you,' I said, shaking his hand.

'No more'n us, Matthew. We're a bit shorthanded on *Waterwitch*.'

Hubert stood up and went and examined Isaac's body. He shook his head, staring at the pearl-handled knife. He leaned forward, and removed the knife carefully, giving it a strange look before flinging it over the side. 'His father gave him that,' he said quietly.

'I never saw it before.'

Hubert shook his head. 'He kept it hidden,' he said wearily, as if unhappiness had taken all the life out of his voice.

'Why did he do it?' I asked hopelessly. 'Kill Isaac?'

Hubert shrugged. 'Because Isaac loved his son, always mourned him. He was a true father. Nathan could never stand that.'

I stared at Isaac's dead body, the clotted eye swollen and blackening in the sun, the stiffening limbs.

'We're going to have to bury him,' Hubert said.

'Over the side?'

'Be best.'

'Lost at sea,' Sidney said in a soft, almost caressing voice.

I saw Luke glancing to the heavens, muttering words to himself.

'Best do it now,' Hubert said in a whisper.

We buried Isaac over the side while Elizabeth stayed with Nathan. Charlie and Sidney lifted the body, and Hubert said a few words about the sea taking another fisherman, his soul going to the Lord. Luke had his eyes shut, and went on praying long after the body hit the water. I was too tired to feel much, drained of feeling, but I stared at the water for a long time after Isaac's lifeless body had sunk beneath the waves.

Hubert stood at the bulwarks, irresolute, staring sightlessly at Nathan. He seemed half-asleep, like the walking dead.

'How did you get down the river?' I asked him.

'Nobody bothered us.'

'They let you sail right past Sunk Island?' I asked in surprise.

'Too busy fighting. I think Duffy was getting the best of it. Mundol's men were trapped on Sunk Island, and Duffy's men seemed to be smashing the longboats up. They wouldn't have recognised us anyway, even if they'd been interested. They don't know *Waterwitch*. They've never seen her. We always worked the fleets from *Dancing Sally*. I reckon Duffy will be all right. His men know the Spurn and they know Holderness.'

'You reckon they'll get away?'

'We'll never know, will we,' he said with a brief shrug.

He went back to Elizabeth and knelt down beside her. 'You know we've got to leave, Elizabeth,' he said gently.

She looked up at him, her eyes vacant, her hands restlessly touching Nathan. He was groaning, writhing on the blankets and then lapsing into silence, sweat pouring down his face.

'Hubert?' she said vaguely.

'We've got to leave, Elizabeth. Take Nathan on board *Waterwitch*.'

'*Waterwitch*?'

'I've got her seaworthy now, Elizabeth. She'll do us proud. Take us all the way to Lerwick.'

Elizabeth nodded quickly, smiling and keeping her hands on Nathan. 'Nathan would want us to do that,' she said quickly.

'Course he would.'

'He always wanted to go to Lerwick.'

'I know, Elizabeth.'

She let us lift the body down to the waiting longboat, and then Sidney and Luke rowed back to *Waterwitch* with Elizabeth in the bows, cradling Nathan's head on her lap, Charlie in the stern at the tiller. They got him aboard the smack, and then Sidney rowed back for us.

'We'd best set fire to her,' Hubert said bleakly.

'Like Nathan's model?'

'She told you about that?' he said with interest.

'She does tell me some things,' I said sarcastically.

'Yes, well, it will come, with time. But you're right, we'd best do it. We don't want anybody finding evidence. Bodies travel a long way in these currents. Best if they think he drowned. The fish will soon do enough damage to disguise the wounds.'

We fetched oil from the galley, and went round *Dancing Sally*, splashing oil all over the decks and sails, the brightly painted masts. It seemed a sacrilege, after the way she had taken us across the seas to the fleets, but Hubert did the work quickly, finishing before Luke arrived back with the longboat. We went to the side, and I climbed down, leaving Hubert to strike a match. He glanced round once, then lit a taper and threw it towards the sails. With the oil and the coating of fresh paint, the flames went up like an explosion, the canvas sending sheets of white light into the sky, the timbers roaring and crackling within seconds.

'Look out below,' Hubert shouted, and dropped down

into the longboat, landing with a thud as the boat lurched away from *Dancing Sally* and Luke and I heaved at the oars. 'Let's get out of here,' Hubert shouted as the flames began to lick at the bulwarks above us.

We rowed hard for several minutes, and then sat back and rested. *Dancing Sally* was sending flames as high as heaven, and the roaring heat blasted the air in our faces. They would see the fire for miles, and that didn't give us much time to get away in *Waterwitch*.

But Hubert wanted to watch. 'That's a sad sight,' he said, gazing across the green water, dancing now with the flames of the fire.

'It is,' I agreed.

On *Waterwitch*, I could see Charlie and Sidney watching from the bulwarks, Edgar March standing at the tiller. I could not see Elizabeth. We watched until the hulk broke apart and *Dancing Sally* sank into the sea, her topmasts still burning and smoke rising from the water as if a dragon was trapped beneath the waves, struggling hard to breathe. We watched, even as the last ripples of water drifted away from the wreck, and herring gulls swooped low over the waves, searching for food in the wreckage.

Then Hubert turned and settled himself at the tiller.

'Right,' he said, 'let's get ourselves back to *Waterwitch*.'

Forty-one

We arranged Nathan as comfortably as we could on the deck, and then prepared the smack for sailing. Hubert checked the charts and talked about the handling with Edgar March, Luke Hobbins and Charlie Blow. Sidney was already down in the galley preparing our first meal. *Waterwitch* was a ketch, and with the mizzen sail would take more handling than a cutter like *Dancing Sally*, but if we all pulled together we would manage. Hubert wanted me to stay with Nathan and Elizabeth as much as possible.

'We've got a decent wind,' he said, watching while Edgar and Charlie secured the halyards and hoisted the mainsail out with the sheets. 'We should be fine most of the time, weather like this. You take care of him.'

I nodded, and watched the men working *Waterwitch*. As they secured the sheets, the great mainsail bellied into powerful curves, and the spars creaked as they settled into position. 'Lovely she goes,' Hubert said at my side. The mainmast bent a little under the strain, pulling the four windward shrouds iron-bar taut, and the heavy vessel, heeling a little, slipped forward through the steepening seas, dancing to the tiller, gaily as the sunlight on water, with no strain or sense of urgency.

As *Waterwitch* tacked slowly away from the silent waters where *Dancing Sally* had gone down, I took a long look back. I wanted to settle the place in my mind, even if the sea looked more or less the same wherever you went. I didn't think I would ever forget *Dancing Sally*'s resting place.

Then I went to the bows and watched as we sailed past Spurn. There was no sign of life now, the fires dead, the rough cottages empty. The smacks that had brought Henry Mundol's men had gone, presumably going back to Grimsby. We passed Old Hive, the creek where *Dancing Sally* had been kept hidden, and I saw the spire on Patrington church glinting in the late afternoon sun. I wondered if I would ever make the journey back down the coast from Lerwick and Shetland.

When we had left Spurn behind, I sat down on the deck beside Nathan, watching as Elizabeth bathed his face. He seemed to be in a deep sleep, but she went on soothing his forehead, singing a song very quietly.

'You make a good nurse,' I told her.

She smiled at me, the colour back in her cheeks, her eyes red with tiredness but without the anguish I had seen when Nathan had murdered Isaac. She poured more water on to a cloth and held it to Nathan's face.

'I used to do this when he was a boy,' she said.

'He should have been doing it for you.'

'Why?'

'He was older.'

She laughed softly. 'But I was the woman,' she pointed out.

We sailed on for two or three hours, and Sidney brought plates of hot food to the deck. It was a quiet calm evening, the sky cloudless, the sun sinking down in the west. I realised it was September now and the evenings were already cooler. The food tasted good after the long day, fried fish and roast potatoes, with treacle duff to follow and pots of scalding hot tea. I tried to get Elizabeth to eat, and she took some of the white fish but didn't want much else. She drank two mugs of tea, watching Nathan all the time.

At about nine, Nathan began to sweat again, the sweat pouring down his face and body, his back arching against the deck. In minutes, he was writhing in pain, fighting my arms as I held him down. Edgar came and helped me, and as we struggled, he let out a scream of pain, lifting his body off the deck. His eyes opened and stared wildly and sightlessly into our faces. As we lowered him to the blankets, he opened his mouth and a stream of vomit poured all over the blankets and deck. The vomit was colourless but the stench made me retch. He was still writhing, jerking against the hard deck. I hung on, waiting for him to stop, his body banging up and down against the planks, his neck arching and his eyes wide open as he choked. Another stream of vomit shot out over his stomach.

He calmed down after several minutes of retching. His body slumped back against the blankets, and Elizabeth hurriedly bathed his face while Sidney fetched some fresh blankets and pillows. He seemed to fall into sleep like a child. We could hardly hear him breathing.

'Sweet Jesus,' Hubert said quietly, standing up and staring at the night sky. 'Sweet Jesus.'

Nathan lay like that for an hour, Elizabeth bathing his face, Hubert taking his pulse every few minutes, the crew busy sailing the smack.

'He's calmed down,' Hubert whispered finally.

'Yes,' I nodded.

Elizabeth didn't speak.

When Nathan opened his eyes again, the sky was full of stars, and we were sailing an empty sea brilliant with moonlight. You could see for miles, and there was nothing on the sea apart from *Waterwitch*. The silence seemed to go on forever, stretching out to the distant horizons, the remote coldness of the stars. 'Lizzie,' he said in a hoarse whisper.

'Yes, Nathan.'

'You there?'

'You can feel my hand?'

'Yes.'

'I'm here.'

She held a cloth to his forehead, squeezing the cold water on to his face. He licked the side of his mouth and grimaced.

'I'm thirsty,' he whispered.

'Try and lift him,' she said, glancing at me.

I got him upright against my shoulder, and Elizabeth held a cup to his mouth. He swallowed hard, and seemed relieved. His stomach muscles worked hard in a sudden spasm, but then he relaxed.

'I think I should lie down,' he whispered.

Sinking into the blankets, he closed his eyes for several minutes and we thought he had gone back to sleep, but he moved suddenly, opening his eyes and looking round as if searching for somebody.

'Is Isaac there?' he shouted, his voice harsh and in a panic.

'He's asleep,' Elizabeth said immediately.

'Down below?'

'Yes, down below.'

Nathan seemed to believe her. He relaxed, then turned his head to the side and stared at me. The flicker of recognition crossed his eyes, and a brief sardonic smile. 'You still with us, Matthew?'

'I'm still with you.'

'I bet you wish you'd stayed with *Happy Jack*,' he said with a harsh laugh, and I glanced at Hubert, amazed that he should remember the smack I'd been on after everything that had happened.

He slumped to the blankets again, and rested for several minutes. The mainsail was taut in the wind, and the booms and gaffs creaked in the immense silence of the night. Far away, a cormorant sent its haunting cry over the waves, like a messenger ghosting the waters, hovering over our smack. Then the sound was gone and we were alone with the night silence.

Suddenly, Nathan was talking again. 'I was working for Henry Mundol all the time,' he whispered, staring at Elizabeth, hanging on to her hand. We had to lean forward to hear what he was saying. 'I went through Jackson, but I was working for him right back from when we first settled at Spurn,' he said, speaking only to Elizabeth, trying to make her understand.

'I know,' she whispered urgently. 'Don't worry.'

'You know?'

'Yes, I know.'

I could tell she was lying, trying to make him rest.

'It doesn't matter?'

'It doesn't matter, Nathan. You did what you thought was best.'

He shook his head again, and his eyes were full of tears, falling helplessly down his face. 'I did what was worst,' he said, gulping for air, swallowing his own tears. 'I didn't mean to. I wanted to get near to him, I wanted to make him pay. He said if I ran *Dancing Sally* to the fleets he would get me what I needed. He didn't care whether I did it or not. There were plenty of traders taking tobacco and alcohol. I was just another trader to him. But I thought if I could wreck the fleets like he wrecked my father it would be something to make amends. I thought, if I helped enough lads to run away, he wouldn't be able to keep his fleets working. I wanted to get close to him and hurt him like he hurt us. But he didn't even know my name. He didn't know who I was.'

He was distressed again, gasping for air, his breathing coming in short hard gasps. Elizabeth clung on to his hand. 'You must stop it, Nathan,' she begged, appealing to us for help, urging him to rest. 'You must get some sleep.'

We knelt beside him, but there was nothing we could do to calm his anguish. He didn't hear our words. He was far away in his own grief. He cried for several minutes, the tears wetting his face, his teeth clenched in an agony of despair. 'He didn't know my name,' he kept whispering.

When he finally got control of himself and stopped crying, he seemed calmer, more determined. He held tight to Elizabeth's hand, as if he was frightened she would run off if he let her go.

'In the end,' he said, 'I couldn't manage without the laudanum. He gave me the laudanum. I got so that I couldn't get from day to day, and he always had a supply, he always sent me gifts. I had to work for him to get the laudanum. I had to keep close to him for my own supplies. When he learned about the indentures, how we'd stolen the indentures, he said I would stay in prison forever and nobody would ease my nightmares.'

Elizabeth glanced at me in alarm, squeezing cold water on to Nathan's face and bathing his forehead. 'You must rest now, Nathan,' she whispered gently against his face.

'Not much more,' he said with a sigh. 'You have to let me speak, Lizzie. I've dreamed about the man for years. He's been living in my mind. He knew how much I needed laudanum. He gave me such sweet dreams to stop the nightmares. He knew about the nightmares too. He must have heard me raving. He was my friend in the end. I had to help him. I had to keep working for him. He was my only friend.'

He slipped into sleep as abruptly as he had woken, and

slept for almost an hour. When he woke, it was peaceful
this time: he was not sick again. He simply opened his eyes
and smiled at Elizabeth.

'I feel better now,' he told her.

'Do you, Nathan?'

'I don't feel so hot. You could fetch another blanket.'

'We could light the fire in the brazier,' Hubert suggested.

'Yes, please do that,' Nathan whispered.

Luke went and fetched a blanket. Charlie and Edgar got
the fire going in the brazier, and we wrapped the blanket
round Nathan's lower body. He couldn't stand anything
on his shoulders. He looked up at the stars as we busied
ourselves around him, and when I sat down again, he was
holding Elizabeth's hand.

'I did try to kill him,' he said quietly.

'Henry Mundol?'

'Yes. I tried to shoot him.'

'It doesn't matter now, Nathan.'

'I wanted to kill him. I saw him in the hall, coming down
those grand stairs, and I wanted to kill him. But it was no
use, Lizzie. No use. I only fired one shot. I missed him.
They had servants in the house and they grabbed the gun.
I couldn't kill him. I couldn't kill him, Lizzie. I could only
kill my father.'

He was crying weakly now, like a child, the tears falling
gently down his haggard face. 'I could only kill my father,'
he repeated, the words like a whisper of guilt in the vast
emptiness of the night.

He died peacefully, slipping away from us like a smack
ghosting the seas, a herring gull floating across the stars.
Elizabeth sat on one side, holding his hand, patient, silent.
I knelt on the other, watching the two of them together for
the last time. Hubert came and stood at Elizabeth's side,
waiting for her, staring at the face of the man he had followed up and down the coast for years. The rest of the

crew stood in the shadows, Luke Hobbins reading from his Bible by the light thrown from the brazier, the rest of them simply watching.

There didn't seem to be a moment when life left Nathan Anstey. For some time, I thought he was still breathing, but then I saw the way his mouth was moving, the slow collapse of his cheeks. Even as we watched, he seemed to be growing old: his immense physical strength drained out of his body with the tears and sickness; his beauty faded and disintegrated with the rotting of the drugs and disease. As we watched, he became an old man in front of our eyes.

We buried him off Wick on a fine September morning. Hubert read the prayers from Luke's Bible, the passage in St John about peace which begins with the lovely words, 'Let not your heart be troubled.' I thought there was a tremble in Hubert's voice as he said the words, and he had difficulty getting through them. Elizabeth wept quietly at my side, but stood on her own, refusing all help as she watched the body go over the side. We sang a hymn, but not all of us knew the words. Long after we had finished, Elizabeth remained at the stern, watching the waters where her brother had been buried, on watch as the sun rose bright and lovely in the sky.

I spent long hours every day with Elizabeth. We sailed on north, leaving Wick behind and heading for the Faroes. The days were fine and *Waterwitch* took the seas as gaily as a young stallion running free along miles of deserted shore. She was a fine smack, with a deep heel and plenty of ballast, and a long keel to give her an easy comfortable motion in a rough sea. Some fishing smacks have bows so fine that they drive through the waves and make the boat slushy to handle and wet to live in, and if the builder doesn't know his job, they can be too broad and buoyant, making the vessel pitch heavily and throw unnecessary strain on the rigging. The man who built *Waterwitch* knew all there was to know about distant waters.

As we passed Westray, I finally asked Elizabeth about her name, why she allowed no one but Nathan to call her Lizzie.

She smiled sadly. 'That was the name my father always called me,' she said quietly.

'Only your father?'

'That's right. From a little girl. My mother never used it. She didn't like people to shorten names. I was always Lizzie to my father. But I came to hate him in the end. The way he treated my mother. The way he behaved. I hated him. I hate that name.'

I stared at her, confused, wondering whether I should say what I was thinking. She glanced at me, reading my mind.

'I know,' she smiled. 'Why did Nathan go on using it?'

'Yes,' I said, puzzled. 'You don't have to say.'

'I don't know,' she shrugged. 'I never knew. He knew how much I hated it. I've never known why,' she said ruefully.

On the day before we reached Shetland, I was standing in the bows, leaning on the bowsprit. It had been an easy voyage, lovely weather and fine winds. I was enjoying the sun on my face, the excitement of approaching Lerwick. I hadn't been for a couple of years, and some of my finest memories were of the granite town perched on the edge of the green oceans. I didn't hear Elizabeth coming up behind me.

'I never told you about *Waterwitch*,' she said at my shoulder.

'No, you didn't,' I smiled, turning to welcome her.

She stood at my side, watching the spray thrown up by the bows, the gulls following us towards land. 'She was my father's first fishing smack,' she said sadly. 'She was called

Waterwitch because when my mother was a child, the old folk used to say she was a sprite, a mermaid escaped from the sea. She had beautiful long hair, very dark. Nathan and I had our colouring from our father. My mother's hair was almost black. She used to sit on the doorstep singing songs when we were children, and the old folk said she must have been a waterwitch in another life, singing the fishermen on to the rocks, she had such a beautiful voice. She always used to laugh at them. Said they were talking nonsense. But I think of her whenever I think of *Waterwitch*. She's a beautiful lady, like my mother. That's why.'

I turned, and took her in my arms. I wanted to hold her forever.

'I remember a girl who was dreadful to look at when I first met her,' I said gently.

'Do you?'

'Horrible scars of smallpox. You wouldn't believe the ugliness.'

'Wouldn't I?'

'She fair turned my stomach.'

'That's awful.'

'But she's improved greatly with getting to know.'

'I'm glad.'

'She's become a real beauty.'

'You mustn't exaggerate, Matthew.'

'I never exaggerate,' I told her.

She was silent for a moment, studying me with her thoughtful smile. 'And does she make you happy?' she asked at last.

'Yes, she does,' I said firmly.

She laughed briefly at that. 'No more visions then?'

I knew she was remembering Nathan's words, about visions being the gift of the unhappy. His ghost darkened briefly in her eyes.

'No more visions,' I promised.

She was restful then for a moment, watching the distant blue of the islands, the lift and roll of the horizon.

'And they were happy together,' she said aloud, like a mother talking to a child, finishing a favourite story. She looked up into my eyes. 'Is that enough for now?'

'For now?' I asked.

'For now.'

'Sounds fair enough to me,' I said, looking for a long time into her grey truthful eyes. 'Sounds a fine way to begin a lifetime together.'

'And to me,' she said simply.

THE LOST MARINER

William Bedford

In the summer of 1877, Samuel Vempley, mourning the loss of both his former skipper and his girlfriend, boards the *Rechabite*, a fishing smack bound for Iceland. He knows the boat will call at Grimsby, and it is there he hopes to discover news of Miriam, his lost love. But he hasn't anticipated the horrors of Satan's Hole, a debauched, brothel-ridden area of Grimsby, nor the cruelty of life at sea.

The *Rechabite* is guided by Charles Oliver Everitt, a self-righteous religious fanatic. On board, too, is Walmsley, the malicious and bullying third hand.

The aura of suppressed hostility has a dangerous edge, and as Samuel struggles with his own demons, he senses himself – and the boat– being pushed inexorably towards disaster.

Boldly evoking the harshness and beauty of life at sea in prose of great power, *The Lost Mariner* is a compelling and utterly credible story of redemption both chosen and forced.

'Bedford powerfully describes the horrid and dangerous conditions under which sailors toiled while simultaneously conveying a sense of the comradely atmosphere engendered by those very conditions'
Sunday Telegraph

'effective and persausive'
TLS

'thrilling stuff'
Sunday Telegraph

QUITE UGLY ONE MORNING

Christopher Brookmyre

Winner of the 1996 Critics' First Blood Award

Yeah, yeah, the usual. A crime. A corpse. A killer. Heard it. Except this stiff happens to be a Ponsonby, scion of a venerable Edinburgh medical clan, and the manner of his death speaks of unspeakable things. Why is the body displayed like a slice of beef? How come his hands are digitally challenged? And if it's not the corpse, what is that awful smell?

A post-Thatcherite nightmare of frightening plausibility, *Quite Ugly One Morning* is a wickedly entertaining and vivacious thriller, full of acerbic wit, cracking dialogue and villains both reputed and shell-suited.

'The dialogue is a joy throughout and the plot crackles along with confident gusto and intelligence . . . an assured debut by a talented writer'
The Times

'Very violent, very funny. A comedy with political edge, which you take gleefully in one gulp'
Literary Review

'A wicked satire . . . excellent plotting and a goodly amount of acidic one-liners'
The Scotsman

A sharp, funny novel, with strong characters and some smart dialogue'
TLS

Now you can order superb titles directly from Abacus

☐ The Lost Mariner	William Bedford	£6.99
☐ Country of the Blind	Christopher Brookmyre	£6.99
☐ Quite Ugly One Morning	Christopher Brookmyre	£6.99
☐ The Big Picture	Douglas Kennedy	£5.99
☐ The Crow Road	Iain Banks	£7.99

Please allow for postage and packing: **Free UK delivery.**
Europe; add 25% of retail price; Rest of World; 45% of retail price.

To order any of the above or any other Abacus titles, please call our credit card orderline or fill in this coupon and send/fax it to:

Abacus, 250 Western Avenue, London, W3 6XZ, UK.
Fax 0181 324 5678   Telephone 0181 324 5517

☐ I enclose a UK bank cheque made payable to Abacus for £ ....

☐ Please charge £.............. to my Access, Visa, Delta, Switch Card No.

☐☐☐☐☐☐☐☐☐☐☐☐☐☐☐☐☐☐☐

Expiry Date ☐☐☐☐   Switch Issue No. ☐☐

NAME (Block letters please) ....

ADDRESS ....

....

....

Postcode ....Telephone ....

Signature ....

Please allow 28 days for delivery within the UK. Offer subject to price and availability.

Please do not send any further mailings from companies carefully selected by Abacus ☐